INTERNAL CHAOS

A NOVEL

By M.W. Moore

Internal

Chaos

By M.W. Moore

M.W. Moore Publications
2008
Production by Axess Printing
www.axessprinting.com

Copyright © 2008 by M.W. Moore
All rights reserved. No part of this book may be reproduced without the publisher's consent.

M.W. Moore Publications
P.O. Box 61242
Houston, Texas 77002
www.mwmoore.com

Library of Congress Control Number:
2007904394

ISBN-10: 0-9776116-1-2
ISBN-13: 978-0-9776116-1-4

Printed in the United States of America

Cover Illustrator: Daymond E. Lavine
Cover Photography: Eric Blackshire

Although loosely based on some actual episodic events and geographical locations, this fact-based work chronicles embellished tales with fictionalized names as part of the author's creativity. There is no intent to disparage likenesses.

M.W. Moore Publications
1 2 3 4 5 6 7 8 9

Preface

I wrote this novel for those suffering from lost relationships resulting from addictions, prison and other unhealthy strongholds. My hope is that by acknowledging these issues, individuals can prepare to conquer them as well as overcome negative perceptions of themselves and others.

Most of the main characters are fictitious, but their situations are based on real-life occurrences. The individuals portrayed may be from dysfunctional families or, perhaps, just coping with identity crises.

And for some people, as in my case, it takes prison to discover talents and self-worth. However, not all offenders achieve this. Many still languish in ignorance due to denial, lack of ambition, low self-esteem and fragile egos that cause them to regress or become stagnant. Simply put, there does not appear to be a remedy for what ails them.

It is not my intent to offend readers with revelations about prison life. Nonetheless, when I was incarcerated, fellow offenders shared their stories with me. Other situations, oddly, were coincidental or stumbled upon accidentally. I've literally witnessed every possible situation in prison. I've also observed the brute behavior of many men, as well as submissive characteristics that would be considered taboo even in the free world. But being locked in "cages" can bring out all types of behaviors.

Most of the men I was incarcerated with were open about their feelings, desires and failures. I welcomed the many surreal stories from my fellow "throwaways," as labeled by society. Among these were gifted, intellectual and introspective brothers serving sentences of 40 to 70 years. And, for some, their talents were being held captive, too. As a result, their hopes faded – like a once-brilliant day overshadowed by rolling storm clouds.

I want people to be aware of these facts: Ten times as many Americans are in prison for drug offenses today than in 1980. There are 458,000 or so men and women now in prison in the United States for drug convictions. That's 100,000 more than the population of all prisons in all of the European Union.

And just as alarming is the fact that blacks are overwhelmingly more likely than whites to be imprisoned for drug offenses, according to a study by Human Rights Watch. Oddly, only 13 percent of regular drug users in this country are black, but 62.7 percent of drug offenders sentenced to prison are black.

So, with that said, brace yourself as I prepare to take you on an excursion into the reality of prison – and its chaos. Hopefully, my personal experience will help better illustrate and explain the realism and the reasons for some of the unscrupulous behavior of men behind bars. I will expose demons and address the shame of incarceration. I'll even tell you how I survived in such a wretched environment.

The journey starts now.

Be bold. Be brave. Be blessed.

Acknowledgments

I humbly thank those who helped make this second installment of my semi-autobiographical trilogy possible. I reserve my highest honor for God, who gave me the strength and endurance to boldly tell my story about tragedies and triumphs.

I especially thank my seasoned editor, L.A. Warren, who served as the anchor for this project. If I had all the money in the world, it still wouldn't be enough to pay you for your devotion and services.

And thanks to the people who were my last defense for making sure we fixed as many problems as we could before going to print: my proofreaders – Ray E. Baker, Alfred D. Davis, Reginald Gulley, Denita Jones, Nolan McClinton, William McGee and Cedric Voss.

Also, I'm grateful for technical and professional support from Eric Blackshire, Daymond E. Lavine and Ferrell Phelps.

As well, I thank my family for giving me the time to complete this work and allowing me to share part of our history with the world.

Disclaimers

The subjects in this fact-based novel are a rendering of the author's creativity. Similarities to actual lives are coincidental and unintentional. Plots and characterizations may have been embellished for dramatic continuity.

Many characters in this novel – straight, gay, drug addicts, HIV-AIDS sufferers – portray semi-fictional roles. However, prison – like the rest of society – would be incomplete without them.

In Loving Memory:

My father, Ardell Moore

Websites:
Internal Chaos: www.mwmoore.com
For What I Hate I Do: www.forwhatihateido.com

Chapters

1. Confession
2. Creeping Cancer
3. A Mother's Shock
4. Bam! Damn! Slam!
5. Property of the State
6. Frowns, Tattoos and Codes
7. Daddy Boy
8. The Transfer
9. The Overcomers
10. Cost of Violence
11. Fools and Folly
12. Daddy Girl
13. Rumor Has It
14. The Rumor Mill
15. Kill-Offs
16. Caught in the Trap
17. Make You Wanna Holla
18. Selfish Danger
19. Inner Demons
20. Low-Maintenance, High-Maintenance
21. STDs
22. Confrontations
23. Childhood Trauma
24. Double-Minded
25. Mayhem
26. Lost in Transition
27. Same Script, Different Cast
28. Parting Ways
29. Lost in Translation
30. Justifiable Cause
31. A Rebel's Nature
32. Blind Ambition
33. Personal Rediscovery

Chapter 1
Confession

Young man, do not resent it when God chastens and corrects you, for His punishment is proof of His love. Just as a father punishes a son that he delights in to make him better, so the Lord corrects you.

Proverbs 3:11-12

Only a day had passed since my last bank robbery. And the rising sun on this new day began to distribute its warmth throughout the more than 1,700 square miles of Harris County. It was a surprisingly dewless Saturday morning in Houston.

I was all aglow and gleeful on this 6th day of December in 1997 – full of expectations. I had my loot, my laugh and my life of luxury – at least so I thought.

For those following this saga, as well as those being introduced to it, let me recap a pivotal scene from my critically acclaimed first novel, For What I Hate I Do (www.forwhatihateido.com). My fact-based life story in that book explored the darkest sides of promiscuity and marriage infidelity, male prostitution, drug addictions and HIV/AIDS.

I had gone to a party at a local crack house to get my groove on with some dastardly characters from the city's Third Ward.

My road dog, Alex, and I went zooming down Interstate 45 to a house party all decked out in our finest – crewneck sweaters, Ralph Lauren corduroys, Adolfo crocodiles, black DK belts and leather jackets. We tooled around in one of many rental cars I'd used in a series of bank heists. He and I, if you remember, had been having a fling, hooking up for sex and drugs. Alex could have easily been a model, but he lived his life on the streets. At the time, he was a Texas Southern University football player – a rugged, attractive hustler with a major crack-cocaine addiction.

Well, we had ventured to an area notorious for its illegal drug culture. We were to connect with one of the biggest crack-cocaine dealers in this quadrant of Houston. His name was Oz, a slender but cut, tough-talking, gold-teeth playa with a shady past and his own dark secrets.

I had gone to the party to impress and flaunt my image as a brother who knew how to handle his business, even though I loved getting high. I wanted to be seen as a baller.

Oz had been warning me about "the strike of 12." I didn't quite understand what he meant. Actually, I was completely clueless – until I realized much later that a conspiracy was being concocted.

After realizing that Oz, too, was "getting down" – having sex with other dudes, and using drugs – I concluded that he wasn't the "businessman" I thought he was. As much as I was stunned to see him jeopardize his own "bank" by putting his mouth up to a "glass dick" to inhale a smoky crack pipe, I was equally shocked to see him naked in bed and locking lips with Alex.

To fast-forward a bit, I realized I was no better off as I got my ass into a very serious jam by dealing with both those dudes. I was practicing unsafe sex while boning Alex, who, at the same time, was giving Oz head as we all got high.

As the night stretched into the next day (12:06 a.m.), I had gone outside to move my car, only to be swarmed by a sea of blue lights and my head being crushed into the hood of my rental car by police and FBI agents while I was in handcuffs. The warning from Oz about the "strike of 12" had manifested. It would appear that he and Alex had scored the winning shot in a game of "playa-hating." Acting as unofficial informants, they collaborated by ratting me out to the police and feds. My string of bank robberies had finally come to an end.

This also appeared to mark the beginning of the end for my days as a free man. But I tried to remain positive. I reasoned that this could perhaps be the start of a new covenant with God. I wanted so desperately to be free from constantly doing the things I hated the most: lying, sexual promiscuity, infidelity, crack cocaine, manipulation. And finally, but most importantly, I wanted to end my temporary separation from God and realign myself with Him. So, I set out to readjust my attitude from "immorally doing what I hate" to "morally doing what I love."

Is it possible? Let's find out.

•••••

The authorities who arrested me had little regard for me, even as I was dressed to the nines. They informed me of my Miranda rights to remain silent and to have an attorney. I realized I had now joined the ranks of the common criminal. As I rode in the back of the squad car I felt as if this were all a dream. The reality didn't hit until we arrived at our destination, and I was yanked out of the car and escorted en masse by armed officers. I was fingerprinted, photographed and booked into a cramped damp cell.

I was detained in the Harris County jail. My body was weak and tired, allowing me to drift off into a deep sleep in spite of the foreign environment. I began to dream during the wee hours of the morning. But this dream was a bit different from previous ones. I began to levitate, floating high above an unrecognizable metropolis of high-tech freeways, glass structures and futuristic vehicles.

I had never seen an angel before, but an extraordinary cherubic figure accompanied me as she and I hovered above the city, trying in vain to locate an adequate place to land. I was terrified, not knowing what was keeping me afloat and believing I was going to fall to my death.

With all that's been going on, God knew I needed a place of refuge, but somehow I sensed the Creator allowed this celestial journey to terrorize me for my rebellion. But then I peered into the most magnificent and brightest atmosphere I'd ever experienced through disparate eyes, wondering why I was pulled into such a place so peaceful, pure and heavenly. It was as if I were caught up in the Rapture. But I felt out of place, unworthy. Don't mistake me; I longed for this tranquility.

As I relaxed more, I reached out to grab the smooth glowing ankles of the accompanying angel flying next to me. I figured she would continue to guide me to safety. Instead, she quickly turned away from my pleading eyes when I tried to grip her. I managed in that lickety-split moment of eye-to-eye contact to steal a look into her radiant face and the sadness in her wondrous eyes.

To my astonishment, features of the fleeing angel resembled Tish, my former wife who demanded a divorce after all the mess and misery I caused in our relationship – the drugs, infidelity, lies. Nevertheless, this image of her now was simply stunning. I wondered once again what all this meant. Why the visions? Why now? Why Tish's likeness? Odd, because most angels generally appear in the form of males, at least in the Bible.

The angel, noticing my confusion, reached for my hands, but we failed to connect as a sudden suction swept me away with a mighty and frightening force. Soon after, a mysterious white cloud appeared covering everything within view. But, ultimately, it dissipated to reveal a door that was slightly ajar. By now I was at ease, although still feeling unworthy of this glorious encounter. I moved in closer to the brightly lit entranceway. Once there, I was greeted by the same angel that led me on this venture. We reached out toward one another, finally clasping our hands. We floated for a moment together before a roaring thunder of earthquake proportion shattered our union, jarring loose our grip and sealing the brilliant passageway, dimming my glorious experience quicker than the speed of light and sending me crashing back to Earth, splattering like a meteor out of orbit.

Was this a sign that my earthly star had faded? Or even worse, that I was being suddenly rejected by God for all my misdeeds?

My eyes opened rapidly at 7 a.m.

I would discover that the thunderous disturbance and sudden fall from the heavens were brought on by the county's inconsiderate jail guards, yelling and rattling the bars of the cells with their nightsticks.

The sounds intensified.

"Chow time! Chow time! It's seven o'clock! Everybody, wake up now!" announced the female picket officer, a person who opens cell doors electronically by pressing a button on a control panel.

This time, my red, irritated eyes met a blinding fluorescent light above me in my 7-foot by 9-foot cold jail cell with its white ceiling.

There was no doubt now that my dream had ended.

"I said, `Everybody up, and get ready for chow!' " the guard demanded again after opening the electronically sliding metal doors from a secured booth outside the cell area.

Asking no questions, I sheepishly exited my top bunk into an open area filled with stainless steel seats and adjoining tables. Still a little groggy from the abbreviated sleep, I gingerly glided my body across the floor then sat on one of the hard cold benches that immediately stiffened by buttocks. After a minute of sitting uninterrupted, I suddenly realized I had been arrested for bank robbery. I was also aware that there might be irrefutable evidence that would prevent me from overcoming an impending charge.

I mumbled, "My God! My God! What have I done?" I held

my head down in despair in the sealed holding area that carried odd but competing scents punctuating my nostrils – urine, sweat and other body odors clashed with the distinct smell of pancakes and eggs.

I tried convincing myself I was dreaming. But my hunger defied that thought. There was no denying that I was starving for a meal after the previous night of bingeing on a crack pipe.

During the temporary moment of solitude, I began to think about Mom. I knew eventually I was going to have to call her. Shame descended upon me like the force of a 100-foot tidal wave that easily capsized my Third Ward neighborhood cockiness. Nothing prepared me for such embarrassment, which I was sure would bring dishonor to her and my family. How could I be so selfish and contrary? I needed more time to think about how to break the news, but for now I needed some type of nourishment. My body was feeling weak.

As a rumble of noise filtered through the pod, I scampered toward the prepared breakfast along with other alleged offenders, who likewise had a long day of processing and interrogations ahead. Raising the plastic fork to my dry mouth, I looked at my wrist. I remembered that when I was arrested I did not have my cherished Raymond Weil Allegro watch that I had purchased during the months of my crime rampage.

I was certain that that punk Oz was now the proud owner of my jewelry. "What a bastard," I thought, believing he'd probably never owned anything as elegant. It was probably the most expensive "bling" he'd ever worn.

I still was reeling from having possibly been snitched on to the police, letting my guard down and losing my valuables. I loathed the thought of Oz banging Alex.

The damage had already been done, but I should have never gone to that gig in the first place. I ignored all hints of a possible setup. And now I must endure the consequences of my actions. The ménage à trois with those dudes was the beginning of the end for me. I had surrendered to greed and the temptation to get my jimmy wet.

Now I was staring at the possibility of being put away for a huge chunk of my life.

"OK, guys. Listen up!" said the female officer, blurting out her next command. "Individuals with the following names need to line up on the right side of the holding tank door when I call them out."

Many grumbled because they hadn't even finished breakfast.

The name count began, and one person after another stood and moved toward the door. I examined the many faces of hostility as the line grew.

There were looks of shame, bitterness and indifference – perhaps from those who had been down this road before.

"Miguel Morris," the guard bellowed.

I took my position along with the others. I stood behind a frail, dingy man with poor hygiene. I looked away from him, holding my breath from the stench. I became more nauseated when someone nearby belched, smothering the air with a sour, putrid odor.

We all were rescued from the stench when the heavy door that separated us from security opened to another shielded area where we were guided. There, we were instructed by the female officer to sit on more concrete slabs to wait for the next phase of our ordeal.

I was on the brink of a mental meltdown as nearly an hour had passed before my name was called again. I wanted to be defiant but, instead, I followed protocol. This time I was led away from the chilly holding tank where I could not get out fast enough.

I was still wearing the black outfit I was busted in last evening: Ralph Lauren corduroy, crewneck sweater, Donna Karan belt and a black leather jacket. I knew they would be replaced with a hideous orange jailhouse jumper.

The guard, along with other armed officers, escorted a group of us to a predetermined location. We ambled down a long hollow underground corridor that led to an adjacent building. The obscure route – which was cold, quiet and eerie – was used as a public security precaution. The secret tunnel was like a dungeon but equipped with high-tech surveillance cameras and tear-gas systems that jutted from 10-foot-high cement ceilings.

I sensed the watchful eyes of security as we snaked our way through the end of the elongated shell that led to a building with colorful signs and arrows showing directions to courtrooms, waiting areas and FBI offices, where I would be taken.

I reluctantly followed the guards. My new destiny was unwelcome.

As I entered the secured glass sliding doors, a full-figured female officer swooped out, mildly acknowledging me. Plodding ahead of me with her holstered gun secured to her right hip and a metal nightstick to her left, she led me down another corridor. Her sparkling handcuffs – dangling from her belt and reflecting from the overhead lights – caught my attention. My escort then quickly veered left, and I followed – although lagging a bit in leg shackles. When I finally reached my destination I sat quietly, waiting to start the process that would dictate my future.

I had a moment to reflect.

The thoughts of my recent and past transgressions left me bitter. The many unfortunate events easily agitated me and reminded me of the frustrations I felt as a child getting into trouble. I was never a person known for much tolerance or patience. It was a trait I'd inherited from my father, I suppose – a behavior I wanted so badly to abandon.

I constantly ignored my many "thinking errors," or hangups, including the issues of appearance and identity. Even though I might have been handsome to some, I lived with the stigma of being dark-skinned, not to mention being sexually confused.

Despite my rich, dark-chocolate unblemished skin, I felt that brothers such as me were either loved or loathed. I hated my tone. Even so, my muscular 6-foot-2 stature demanded attention from females and males alike. There even seemed to have been times when I was envied or lusted by some people, but I still couldn't see what others saw in me beyond my physique.

I absolutely despised my complexion. That self-hatred resulted from the years of verbal abuse and hazing I received from my younger brother, Troy, when we were kids. His skin tone was fairly light brown. He had sandy red hair like our dad. But I took my tone from my mother, who never expressed having a problem with her skin color. She often told me "black is beautiful," but I wasn't trying to hear that then. I was, in fact, color-struck. I wanted light skin like some of my other siblings and resented being the "Tar Baby," or "spook," as often referred to by Troy.

Even with the name-calling, I could not blame Troy for my other situation – same-sex attractions. This was probably the one factor that had caused me so much turmoil because instead of embracing my emotions I vigilantly fought against them. Had I responded differently, life could have turned out better. As a result, I was medicine to some and poison to others.

Several long minutes passed after I had been escorted to the office of a federal lawman. While waiting to be interrogated, I took note of the many pictures of wanted criminals – several from the Houston area – on the walls. I sat across from a tall slim Anglo FBI agent. Meanwhile, I scoped the "wall of shame" more, observing the men and women suspects. A reward was posted under some of the alleged criminals. On further review, I gazed at the wall and noticed my very own image among the notorious roundup with a $20,000 reward for information leading to my capture. This indicated a serious offense on my part.

It was now after 8 a.m. Time for interrogation.

"OK, Mr. Morris. Do you know why you are here?" Agent Pat McClure asked, staring at me emotionless. Aside from the cold greeting, his pensive sinister blue eyes and black mustache intimidated me. He was quite dapper, though, representing the Hugo Boss brand with his snazzy black attire and fresh haircut to boot. A person could tell he was not from Houston. Up North, perhaps, or even the West Coast. But, surely, he was bred elsewhere, no native-born Texan.

"Yeah, I know why I'm here. Someone said I robbed a bank," I answered nonchalantly. I was still slightly drugged and operating on little sleep.

"Well, Mr. Morris, we have a series of photos showing you entering six area banks and retrieving money by threat."

We were soon joined by two other white agents, Jim Warren and Mark CarMichael, who sat on opposite sides of me and the paper-filled metal desk. They initially avoided my roaming eyes. The shorter of the two, Jim, wore a white button-down shirt with a pair of tight, blue jeans and eel-skin boots. He sat with his thin legs crossed while retrieving a collection of photos from the hands of Agent McClure, who studied my reactions to the printed images that showed my likeness.

But CarMichael seemed to be the designated scout – the person assigned to watch my every movement. His attire practically matched Warren's with exception to his top garment – a beige Texas-style goose-down sweater.

While these guys did their investigation, I remained as stiff as a rock but fear began to grip me. Agent CarMichael, who might have been the smartest of the three, paid strict attention to me. He was looking for excessive body twitching, including facial contortions and stuttering – possible signs of irritability and distress that could suggest guilt. I offered the best poker face I could by appearing to be unbothered, calm and relaxed. But I wondered if it would be enough to fool the experts.

"Mr. Morris claims he's not the guy in those photos, Agent Warren," said McClure, who then leaned back into his oversized leather-back chair doubting my claim.

"Is that so?" asked Agent Warren, passing the photos to Agent CarMichael, who took a pair of glasses from his thick sweater pocket. He placed them atop his pale nose to examine the images. "Hmmm," he mused.

While my silence may have hinted of guilt, I wasn't about to spill out my guts. Hell no!

"Mr. Morris, have you been read your rights, sir?" Agent CarMichael asked as he dropped the stack of photos he'd been studying onto a pile of folders on the desk.

"Mr. Morris' rights have been read, Agent, and he understands he has the right to an attorney."

Agent McClure, the first of the federal officers I met, then took over the conversation.

"Gentlemen, if you all don't mind, I would like to speak to Miguel in private, please."

The other two didn't object. They just casually got up and left as the office door squeaked behind them.

Now the real test was about to begin: me and Agent McClure in a battle of wits and wordplay. He got right down to business.

Agent McClure slowly stood behind his desk. He lifted the robbery photos, then kindly passed them on to my hands for viewing. I silently looked at the compelling evidence against me. There was little I could say at that moment. Truth is, I was busted. The images were of me parading around in different baseball caps while orchestrating a series of bank holdups – crimes I never thought in a million years I could commit.

There was a long period of silence on my end.

"OK, Morris, let's try this again. You're telling me that these images are not of you, sir?" asked Agent McClure, appearing to be impatient. He then walked from behind the desk toward me as if he were going to violently lay hands on me. Instead, he stood over me and stared deeply.

"That's what I'm saying," I responded, knowing I was lying. It seemed that I had become so accustomed to telling falsehoods. Even so, my denial didn't stop the agent from hovering over me and breathing down my neck.

The agent decided to play his trump card.

"What if I told you that fingerprints were left on every counter of each bank robbery, as well as on the threatening notes to the tellers, and that they matched yours in each case?" he asked, pausing. "Will you still deny your guilt after all this evidence against you?"

With a smirk on his face, he appeared to delight in the revelation as he studied me.

I needed a quick response to deflate his egoism. But I could only offer one, albeit a very weak one.

"These pictures are not of me!" I continued saying foolishly to hold my ground. I considered asking for a lawyer to end this charade because I was on the brink of throwing in the towel.

"Mr. Morris! You were caught robbing a bank on Highway 6 and Bellaire yesterday, sir! The teller followed you to your rental car and recorded the license plate. When we ran the number and consulted the rental company, it showed your VISA card was used for the transaction. Is that not true, sir?" McClure growled. He wasn't about to let up.

I knew I was being outwitted. There was too much evidence against me: the pictures of my likeness despite trying to conceal my face by wearing baseball caps, the fingerprints, and, most importantly, the inner guilt. I began to wonder if it was even prudent for me to continue this futile fight for my freedom. Should I just confess and hope for a fair deal?

"Look, Morris," said Agent McClure, sitting in a nearby

chair and then scooting next to me, "the best way to handle this situation is to come clean. If I have to go through all your bank accounts, holdings and credit receipts to check your spending habits and visit places you patronized during the time of these robberies, I will. But it will make things more difficult for you and your family if you're found guilty by a jury for these federal crimes. Does that make sense, sir?" Agent McClure asked.

Damn, this man was clever, I thought.

"Yeah, it does." I began to drop my hardball role and eased up on the stubbornness, particularly at the realization that I could face a jury of my "peers" that may not have anyone of my ethnicity on the panel. But even if there were others who looked like me deciding my fate, they still might not care to understand my plight or what led me down this destructive path. And, worse, I began to think about my mother. Did the agent say that I would cause my family to endure a difficult trial?

"Listen, Morris. All I want to do is help you, fella, because you don't look like the type of guy who commits crimes for a living. Matter of fact, we traced your last employment and were impressed. We could not understand why a technical coordinator who worked for a Fortune 1000 company would start robbing banks."

"It was the drugs," I said, admitting my shame and offering the first confession to the crimes. I then gave the photos back to the agent who noticed my embarrassment. His vigorous and clever attack began to abate.

"Well, Miguel, I suggest that you do the right thing – considering times are really harder in prison nowadays. You could be looking at 40-plus years in the federal penitentiary if you don't cooperate. Let alone repeat offenders, jurors are offering no pity to first-time offenders either."

Shaken by the reality of that possibility, I crumbled.

"Forty years? I can't do time like that. What about 10, nonaggravated?" Oops. What a stupid remark. I again unintentionally confessed to the crimes for which I was certain to be indicted. What the hell, I thought. I was in too deep to retract my confession now. The thought of prison sent shockwaves throughout my body. My eyes began to wander around the room as I squirmed for a way out of this mess. In reality, there was no escape.

Agent McClure pondered for a moment before speaking.

"Morris, are you a Christian? I mean, do you go to church and believe in the Lord Jesus?" he asked, smiling.

I couldn't figure if his smile was a ploy to get me to officially confess or a dirty trick of some sort? Perhaps, though, he was being genuine.

"Yes, sir. I am, but ..."

"Well, so am I, Miguel. And given your clean record prior to these incidents, I would like to try to make things as easy as possible for you with the fewest years of incarceration as allowed under sentencing guidelines. But I will tell you that the possibility of a maximum of 10 years behind bars or even probation is out of the question. But whatever short sentence you manage to get will depend on your cooperation in this investigation."

I listened to the agent, but I really wasn't trying to hear any talk about spending time in prison, no matter how short. But his offer did pique my curiosity.

"Like how short?" I asked as my face became awash in nervous sweat.

"Well ...," said the slim agent as he paused, "your crime carries a sentence of two to 10 years per offense. And you have six counts of robberies."

"Ten years?" I asked, horrified. My eyes froze, facial veins swelled, and breathing intensified.

"That's the max, Miguel. The least you can get is two years on each count. Multiply that by six, and you're looking at 12 years max. With good behavior, you could be out in five. Do the math. If you buck on this offer and try your chances in court, you could end up with a hard-ass, no-nonsense, intolerant judge."

This was a lot of information for me to process. But there is one thing I can say about Agent McClure: Ol' dude was as good as they come in law enforcement. He knew how to lay it on the line, straight no chaser.

Do you have money for a lawyer?" he asked.

"Well ..., " I said, dragging out my answer. I didn't want to admit having money from the bank robberies. I wasn't ready to offer an official confession, particularly since I didn't have any legal representation during this interrogation. I didn't want to admit to crimes only to find out later that the offer I received for confessing was bogus and undocumented. So, I denied having any funds. "No. I don't have money for a lawyer."

I certainly wasn't going to tell him about the money I had hidden in a kitchen light fixture inside my apartment.

"At any rate," the agent interjected, perhaps doubting my claim, "I'll try to work something out to help get you an early release – three to five years, depending on your attitude and if you stay clear of trouble while you're in there."

The agent appeared to be getting ahead of himself.

I still had doubts about his claims and his integrity. My belief in people, especially in men, was almost nonexistent. I'd been burned too many times in the past by false relationships and friendships. So my faith in others was at an all-time low.

I turned to the agent for his advice.

"What if I don't confess?" I asked. I wanted to weigh my options, but I knew I had to keep it real.

"Well, that's your right, son. You even have the right to have an attorney present if you wish. The ball's in your court. If you feel that's the right thing to do, then do it."

But, of course, he knew he had me by the balls. Pulling me out of my bunk in the wee hours of the morning was a sure bet that I would be tired and likely more susceptible to confessing. He was right by saying I wasn't a hardened criminal. So, why was I trying to present that image? This could be the break I was looking for because there was no way I could spend 40 years in federal prison.

"So, you're a Christian, huh?" I sincerely asked as I pondered the agent's actual motives.

"Yes, I am, Mr. Morris. So, as I said, let's make your time as easy as possible. Preferably, no federal time. I can turn your case over to state officials if they agree to take it. More than likely they will. I've got a hookup downtown with some legal muscle who owes me a couple favors. And you really don't want this case to end up in the hands of the federal government.

Chances are that it will go to the feds if you choose not to cooperate. On top of that, you're taking a greater chance of being shipped to another state, maybe New Mexico or even Nevada. And that's not good."

Agent McClure was now on the brink of closing his sale.

"It's cold up North, Morris."

He just had to go there. I was a native-born Texan from the hot, humid climate of Houston. I've dealt with sweltering conditions all my life. I was not in the least bit interested in freezing my butt off.

So, for a few more minutes I weighed all options, trying not to appear desperate. I could sense that the agent knew he had me just where he wanted me. My guilt showed in my eyes.

I thought about the possibility of federal prison in another state. Forty years and no visits from friends and family was a hard pill to swallow.

"OK," I said. "What do you need from me?" I couldn't believe these words were coming out of my mouth so quickly. Nevertheless, I felt some sense of relief from the drama of this entire ordeal. I still had my doubts. Could I trust Agent

McClure to keep his word? I knew I had to start somewhere with somebody.

"Well, first of all, you're doing the right thing, Miguel. Let me bring the other two agents back in and let them know you have decided to cooperate fully without counsel, OK?"

Agent McClure appeared relieved. His demeanor had taken a 180-degree turn as he prepared to call in his colleagues as witnesses.

Despite my feelings of uncertainty, I knew deep inside I had done the right thing by confessing. I saw this as just another time, like many, that God's grace had protected me from eternal doom. It was time for God's intervention.

As I waited for the agents' return, my mind shifted to my mother.

My, God! What was she going to think and how would she feel about me and my wrongdoing? Is it possible that she knew I was in jail for these bank robberies? This was, of course, a high-profile case. She must already know, I thought. And what was Lazlo thinking? He was the only one who really believed in me even when I didn't trust myself. He was the only person who truly loved me despite my faults. He kept giving even as I kept ripping out his kind heart, forsaking his trust and being unappreciative of his many efforts to rehab me during my constant battles with crack cocaine and sexual addictions. I didn't deserve him. I didn't deserve his love. I was only concerned about me and my selfish ambitions.

The few people in my life who really cared about me were soon going to learn that I finally hit rock bottom.

As I meditated and wallowed in sorrow, the office door squeaked open. The other agents re-entered.

"Well, gentlemen, Mr. Morris has decided to cooperate with a confession," said Agent McClure, beaming with pride and folded arms as he sat atop his desk. The other two agents stood behind me, each grinning with satisfaction.

"Good. Good, Miguel. You're doing the right thing, brother," Agent Jim Warren confirmed.

Agent Mark CarMichael nodded in agreement with his graying hair shimmering under a soft light and his hands planted tightly in the pockets of his boot-cut jeans.

"Mr. Morris, do you need to make a phone call before we proceed with the rest of the formalities?" Agent McClure asked.

I was still taken aback by his display of care and concern.

"Yes, sir," I answered. "But I need time to pull myself together." My weary body needed rest. I still was left numb by the entire interrogation. I was just ready to get this phase done.

As physically drained as I was, I still had major hurdles ahead. I didn't even have time to feel sorry for myself. The time was approaching for me to explain my troubles to my mom, siblings and Lazlo.

Chapter 2
Creeping Cancer

At such a time as this shouldn't your trust in God bring you confidence? Shouldn't you believe that God will care for those who are good?

Job 4:6

The first cold day of the official winter season had arrived on this Saturday morning in December 1997 as my mother, Mattie Morris, sat in her doctor's office for a rare weekend consultation. As she had done a few days ago, she sat in quiet contemplation. Although the chair was comfortable, her circumstances appeared somewhat less so as she waited for lab results to determine the source of pain near one of her breasts.

To relax her nerves, she lifted a magazine from the coffee table and began reading an article from the latest issue of Ladies Home Journal. She stumbled upon some statistical data from an article highlighting AIDS and HIV among women in America, especially African-American women.

It reported thousands of new AIDS cases among black females compared to much fewer for white females within a year.

The statistics were even grimmer when the alarming rate of infection in black and Hispanic men were compared to white men.

The numbers were brutally chilling for my stunned mother. She then reflected on the summer of 1990 when I revealed I was HIV-positive.

Then, astonished, she tearfully listened as I explained my

health issues, my plight and pain. She was always a good listener and a loving mother who would never abandon her own flesh and blood regardless of the circumstances.

But, even so, my carefree living was crazy, she thought. She had many questions:

How could he be HIV-positive? Who had he slept with other than wife Latisha before and after their marriage? Had Latisha contracted the virus? Did drug use infect him? She had so many questions.

But with each of her questions then, I couldn't or simply refused to respond. Instead, I merely accepted blame for my troubles.

Little did my mother know but bigger problems were on the horizon.

While casually reading her magazine and watching the news in the waiting room, she failed to recognize me in the media report about an offender in a series of bank robberies being apprehended. At the time, I was too thin for her to make the connection. Blame it on the drugs and my failure to eat regularly. As far as she was concerned, the image on the video could have been someone from another segment of Houston or a nearby city or even the suburbs. In her mind, the suspect could have even been someone in her neighborhood – but certainly not from her own address. Surely, she had reared her kids to be smarter than that even though a couple already had had brushes with the law.

It was only after she stared for a minute longer that she thought that the suspect pictured might have resembled a young man who lived two blocks away from our house – an individual she remembered me hanging out with on a few occasions, perhaps. She glanced even more at the young culprit who looked ill and drugged, thinking that if it were a friend of mine that I should have known better than to hang out with someone capable of robbing banks.

Turning away from the depressing television news report,

she paused to thank God for the health of her sons, daughters and herself.

Suddenly, a familiar voice summoned her, breaking her meditation.

"Mrs. Morris, the doctor will see you now," a smiling nurse said.

My mother rose from the sofa with a nervous smile that highlighted her brown eyes.

She was escorted to a small examining room where the smell of rubbing alcohol wafted throughout the area. She panned the room, noticing sterile bandages and needles. The thought of having an injection, or just merely being pricked, shot up her blood pressure. Afterwards, her vitals were taken and the doctor entered moments later.

As her anxiety got the best of her, goose bumps covered her body. She began shivering as she wondered about the doctor's diagnosis. She watched and listened in horror as he sighed and pulled on his chin while analyzing documents and X-rays from a recent lab report. He stood a few feet away with his bifocals tilting from his widened bronzed nose.

With her hands firmly clasped in her lap in the refrigerated room, she wondered what gave the doctor such a puzzled look. Her concern was tempered only by the lowered thermostat and a rush of cold air assaulting her neck and shoulders, forcing her to focus on staying warm.

After carefully pondering, the doctor spoke to my mother.

"Well, Mrs. Morris, one thing is for certain. You've been very diligent with self-examinations throughout the years. That's good because your observations helped to spotlight a concern that was discovered in your X-rays. We found a small malignant lump in your right breast, which is what caused your pain a few days ago."

The doctor glanced wearily into the eyes of my astonished mother. This time her normal aplomb was ripped apart by uncertainty as she avoided immediate eye-to-eye contact with her physician.

My mother then wanted answers to some important questions.

"How serious is it, Dr. Milburn?" she asked, cutting to the chase. "Is it life-threatening?" she continued while trying not to hyperventilate.

She normally kept her poise, but this situation wasn't normal.

"The discovery of cancer is always serious, Mrs. Morris. But I can truly say that it looks like we — you — caught it in its early growth stage. It's about the size of a miniature marble."

He approached her with the X-ray then raised it to a lighted board, showing the small tumor.

She pursed her soft red-painted lips and asked about medical options – this time trying to display composure amid a traumatic discovery.

"You have several," the doctor said with concern, while avoiding signs of pity. "Thanks to medical advancement the biopsy revealed the malignancy, indicating that radiation therapy is an option."

Upon hearing that, my mother shook her head in disapproval. Radiation was out of the question for her.

The doctor, taking note of her resistance, offered surgery as another option against this non-discriminating foe.

"A mastectomy would be somewhat painful after the removal of the breast, but with pharmaceutical drugs there's a greater chance of the cancer not recurring," he explained, folding his arms while standing next to her at the credenza and firmly gripping the X-ray. "Listen, Mattie," he lamented, using her first name for a more personal approach, "this is a complicated time for you. What I'm going to suggest is that you take advantage of the support groups provided by the National Cancer Society and then weigh your options carefully. Only you can make a decision on how you want to pursue this matter. In the meantime, I will prescribe a series of drugs to prepare you for treatment, whether it's surgical or radiation."

He placed his hand on her right shoulder to show his support. His cold touch reminded her of her own chilled hand just nights ago when she stood in her bathroom mirror for a self-exam.

She lapsed into a prolonged trance, reliving that fateful night.

On that night, the tiny lump wasn't noticeable until she raised her right arm. At first she doubted, then curiously frowned at the pea-size growth. Her next action was to sit somewhere before she fainted because she began to think the worst. She gently lowered the nearby toilet seat, where she meditated.

First came a slight tear down her caramel cheeks. Next came the "Almighty" interrogation: "Why me? Why now, Lord?" Then a warm flow of tears gushing from her dark eyes began to cascade down her aging face as her muffled cry morphed into a sob. Her conscience told her to be brave, but her alter ego tried to usurp control.

"To hell with being brave," she thought. "What if I lose my breast? What if I lose my hair if I choose chemo?" Terror engulfed her that late evening, gripping her like a huge fishing net ensnaring its prey. The panic attack crept upon her with unrelenting force that seemed to cement her to the toilet seat unable to budge. But this mother of strength was able to subdue the mother of all burdens by prying her body loose with every ounce of strength she could muster. She arose, standing boldly, yet nauseated and weakened in the knees.

She crept toward the small sink and vanity to splash cold water onto her face and neck to ward off the urge to vomit. For several minutes she repeatedly cupped her hands to draw water toward her face to calm the inner storm that frayed her nerves.

Truth is, she couldn't imagine living deformed after losing

a breast. Nor could she imagine living in pain. She reached for the soft white towel that hung next to the sink then dried her face. She realized she had choices.

"Mrs. Morris! Mrs. Morris!" the doctor's voice boomed. "Are you OK?"

My mom snapped out of her daze when Dr. Milburn summoned her abruptly.

Her initial thought after the doctor's remark was, "What a stupid question to ask at a time like this." Then, she queried him, giving eye contact. "Surgery will leave a flat spot, won't it?"

Sighing, the doctor – with his hands planted on my mother's right shoulder for assurance – responded.

"There are prostheses available. Damn good ones, too."

She almost wanted to laugh – not so much at the doctor, but from the craziness of this life-changing moment. As in the past, she tried to find a bright spot in coping with the diagnosis of breast cancer.

"Hell, I'm 65. Who needs cleavage at my age?"

She finally laughed at herself, determined not to let this cancer – that crept upon her like a late-night invader – conquer her. She was a fighter but, more so, destined to become a survivor.

•••••

Little did he know, but things were going to start heating up for my best friend Lazlo – in the form of Donna Dangerfield. She was an executive at the company where he worked, and she had her eyes on him.

Donna was in her office Saturday gathering her laptop and cell phone near the end of her workday when someone unexpectedly knocked on her door. She initially ignored the knock and continued logging off her desktop. But her superior, Franklin, bolted inside uninvited.

"Hey, Donna, I apologize for the intrusion."

He took a seat at her desk, crossing his legs.

Donna, caught off guard by his entrance, then stood and admired his professional dress for the second time that day.

"What's up?" she asked as she stuffed her leather tote with her personal belongings.

"I'm going to be very direct. The position in research and development needs to be filled immediately."

"That position is nine months out, Franklin!"

"I know that, Donna. But I'm proactively seeking the right person for the job, and I would prefer to hire within as you suggested."

"I have a person of interest in mind," said Donna, closing her bag and taking a seat behind her desk.

"May I ask who?"

"Lazlo Veasey. He's a pharmaceutical rep who's on top of his game."

"Is he aware of the new directive we've implemented for management personnel?"

"You mean the proposed directive."

Franklin, uneasy at being corrected, shifted in his seat but kept his poise.

"The fact remains that we are in a crisis as far as security is concerned. This new future directive is expected to be embraced by all levels of management. If Mr. Veasey has a problem with this security issue, he may not be the right candidate for the position."

"Isn't this premature? I haven't even approached him yet with an offer, Franklin. This topic is time-sensitive, and I trust Lazlo will fall in line with protocol when the directive is implemented."

"I sure hope you are right, Donna."

As Franklin stood to exit, he urged a hasty hiring decision.

"I trust that you will make this happen sooner than later."

"Trust me, Franklin. That position will be filled on time,

with or without Lazlo Veasey. But, it's my hope that he will bend."

"It's your call, not mine. Enjoy the remainder of your day," said Franklin, walking out but leaving Donna a bit baffled over the sudden urgency.

Chapter 3
A Mother's Shock

Oh, my people, haven't you had enough of punishment? Why will you force me to whip you again and again? Must you forever rebel? From head to foot you are sick and weak and faint, covered with bruises and welts and infected wounds, unannointed and unbound.

Isaiah 1:5, 6

Before calling mom a day later, I had imagined the smells of hickory bacon, coffee and Hungry Jack biscuits releasing their aroma throughout the house. With my ravenous appetite, I began to drool for her usual delectable breakfasts. Oh, how I missed her home cooking. Even as I daydreamed, she was probably sitting at the kitchen table sipping coffee and reading the morning paper.

Oh, no! Not the morning paper.

I was certain that, by now, the story of my arrest was plastered all over the print and broadcast media, particularly anchored somewhere in the City and State section of the Houston Chronicle. My only hope was that she or my siblings hadn't stumbled across the story yet. But who was I fooling? The whole neighborhood probably knew by now.

I was a popular guy in the 'hood because of my past athletic career. I wasn't quite a household name, but I was known by many in the Houston area who followed athletics or fashion.

But if my mother had now become aware of my arrest, I was certain the telephone was ringing off the hook — people asking tons of questions about me and wondering what made me snap.

My only hope, a fat chance, was that no one made the distinction since I did not fit the image of a criminal. Perhaps there could be dozens of people in the fourth-largest city in the nation with my same name. Even so, my face was well-hidden from surveillance cameras, obscured by the various baseball caps I had worn.

I began to take comfort in the fact that few folks in my surrounding community read the daily newspaper, particularly the younger ones who spent their time watching television shows and little news programs. My brothers, Troy and David, often worked late anyway and never got home in time to watch the local networks. Besides that, the three of us had all gone our separate ways. We had our own agendas and didn't talk much to each other.

But the reality was that this wasn't going to be a typical day for my mother.

Slowly exiting her cozy king-size bed, she carefully kneeled to the side of it for morning prayers. The stillness of the room allowed her to meditate on thoughts that flooded her mind with peaceful ruminations of daily blessings. As usual, she petitioned for the well-being of family, friends and even strangers. Instinctively, thoughts of me swam about her head, but there was a subtle piercing that gnawed on her like a splinter to a finger. It was much like a maternal epiphany – or, in other words, a mother's intuition that warns of impending trouble or alerts about a recent tragedy.

After her mind settled and calm was restored, divine assurance cuddled her spirit. She offered the highest praise of hallelujah.

And, then, "Amen," she said.

Now, standing in front of an oversized chest of drawers, my mother grabbed her light-blue nylon gown with matching robe. She then prepared for her mid-morning shower and grabbed other garments out of the oak-finished furniture.

Even as her mind never quite stopped thinking of me, the smell of the fresh cedar wood also triggered her memories of her own deceased mother, the woman each of the grandchildren affectionately referred to as Big Momma.

The cedar smell transported my mother to her childhood in south Texas because back in those days furniture was a bit more genuine and pure. Those days are long gone now, but the period helped her remember an era of innocence and gradual prosperity, unlike today's generation – rife with all sorts of modern calamities, crises and catastrophes. A dying generation of offspring. Whatever happened to the gains of the '50s, '60s and '70s, she thought. The wisdom, respect and purpose. Despite what would be seemingly a bleak future, she reasoned that faith would help her endure.

These were my mom's regular thoughts. But there were moments when unexpected events happened suddenly, without any hint or warning. That time was now when my mother's bedroom phone rang, interrupting her scheduled shower.

Putting up no fuss, she approached the nightstand between her bed and wooden rocking chair. She unconsciously touched her right breast, knowing she would have to eventually contemplate cancer treatment.

As she prepared to answer the phone, she noticed the time on the clock near the Living Bible on the nightstand. It was close to 11 a.m.

She sat, pressing down gently to relax onto the comfortable mattress. Positioning herself just right and exhaling gently, she said in her ever-so-inviting gracious tone, "Hello. This is Mrs. Morris."

The next sound she heard made her wince.

It was an automated call from City Jail, seeking permission to connect her to me.

As if stricken by a bolt of lightning, she was stunned but obliged the request.

My voice was shaky, and words garbled with evidence of fatigue.

"Hi, uh, Mom. This is, uh, Miguel." I really wasn't sure where to begin or how to even start my first sentence.

"Miguel?"
Her voice appeared strained.
"I'm in the city jail."
"Jail! For what, Miguel?" she demanded to know.
"I'm in trouble, Momma. Big trouble."
"Trouble? What kind of trouble?" Her concern seemed to turn to anger.
"I'm in jail for robbery, mom. I robbed a bank." I spit out the truth – or at least part of it. The whole truth would have been telling her that I robbed six banks. Instead, I just told her about one. For a long time now, it had been hard for me to tell the truth when I had deceived so many people so often in my life because of my fears and ignorance.
"You did what?" she said.
Her voice raised to the roof. I could almost see the veins popping from her temples.
"Please tell me you didn't say you robbed a bank? Did you rob a bank, Miguel?"
"Yes, ma'am. I did."
"For what, boy?" Her voice trembled.
She sounded more fearful than me. I felt so guilty sending her through more turmoil again.
"I had a relapse on drugs and ran out of money. I couldn't pay bills and ...,"
"Miguel, Miguel!" she quickly interjected, "What have you done, son?" She began to cry and scream. Any worries she might have had before this call were quickly forgotten. Her sobs grew stronger and stronger, her breathing more and more compromised, her head throbbing with greater and greater intensity. My irresponsible behavior might well be the death of her, I thought.
As her wails began to swell, so, too, did her eyes. Her outcry against my behavior was justified.
I told my mother I didn't know why I did it, that I just got caught up in the act as the craving for crack reached a critical

point.

There was really no excuse for my behavior. And as I listened helplessly to her emotional breakdown, I pondered uncertainty about my freedom and future.

After she composed herself enough to talk, her next response was perhaps predictable.

"Why didn't you come to me for money if you were in a financial bind, Miguel?"

I was certain that I would be hearing that question quite a lot from the few people to whom I was closest.

"Momma, it will work out," I said. "I've been meeting with the FBI to cut a deal. I might be able to avoid a trial." I futilely attempted to calm her with talk about a planned plea bargain, but she remained in a catatonic state.

She couldn't get beyond her initial shock. What's more is that my mother was so traumatized that she didn't bother to mention anything about the health problems that she recently learned about. This was clearly not the best time for her to bring up the topic.

Before we hung up, she affirmed her love. She then kneeled down in prayer. And sobbed.

I was miserable. Afraid. Lonely. The only thing I could do was to pause and pray. I felt that I was destroying my mother, who still expressed her love. I wept, pleading for mercy and forgiveness. I told myself I would rise above this by reflecting on a scripture in Deuteronomy: "Do not be afraid or discouraged."

Well, now that I had telephoned my mother about the situation, I'd planned to contact my best friend, Lazlo, later. But first I needed to talk to the federal agents to get a better idea about my fate.

•••••

Despite my troubles, life for my best friend, Lazlo the

pharmacist, seemed to be quite smooth. He spent this particular lazy Sunday stretched in his warm bed reflecting on his future and career. He didn't have much planned for today, other than just resting at his home.

His apartment was not lavish but modestly furnished. It included tasteful furnishings and art. There were a few crystal pieces positioned throughout, with designer rugs in the living area and beneath his king-size bed that served as a focal point.

As Lazlo rummaged through some files that hour, his honey-brown eyes locked onto the morning newspaper's headline about a bank robbery, with an accompanying picture that looked strikingly like someone he knew. More specifically, me.

He did a double-take and then proceeded to read the Houston newspaper article:

> "The assistant manager of a coffee shop confessed to five area bank robberies after being arrested outside a southwest Houston crack house early Saturday, according to law enforcement officials.
>
> Miguel Morris, 38, was charged with five counts of robbery by threat in connection with robberies at five banks in Harris County. He also is a suspect in a sixth robbery that occurred Friday night in Fort Bend County. ... "

Lazlo was mortified.

"This could not be true," he told himself. He instantly became disoriented, but once he regained his composure, he called my mother.

"Damn!" Lazlo wondered aloud, "How is Mrs. Morris handling this tragic news?"

He decided to call her.

After she answered the phone, he greeted her, then asked about the news story in the morning paper.

She confirmed the story, albeit still in disbelief. Through her tears, she told Lazlo that she had spoken with me briefly and that I had blamed the robberies on my drug relapse. She also mentioned that the story was being broadcast on local television stations, showing me at the teller window wearing a baseball cap to shield my identity.

Lazlo told her that he had no clue my addiction was so severe that I would resort to such a major crime. But he assured her he would try to get to the bottom of the issue. He again offered his support to my mother and told her how sorry he was about the shocking events.

After the phone call, Lazlo began to wonder about my sanity, reflecting on my past stint with drugs, habitual lies and vile sexual past that I secretly hid from everybody important in my life.

Lazlo, who once looked up to me, thought about the baseball cap he'd purchased for me months earlier as a peace offering after a harsh breakup. He wondered if I'd used it during the heists.

Before I got into this legal mess, he and I had been apart for some time. There were the occasional phone calls, but that was as close as he got to me for a few months.

But now I was in a jail cell, pondering my fate. Will I go to prison? I was sure that time behind bars was in my future. Lazlo assumed that as well.

When he did finally see pictures of me on the television news, he was aghast at my frail image. I had lost a considerable amount of weight due to my drug binge.

Aside from being known as a crackhead, I also wore the title of "Patient Bank Robber," a phrase coined to suggest my docile, non-hasty, friendly approach to tellers. Like other clients, I would await my turn to approach the window.

●●●●●

"You've got mail!" alerted the computer from across the room.

Lazlo calmly uncovered his half-bare body – wearing only the bottom of his green-and-white striped PJs. After tossing the blanket to the side, he hoisted himself from his bed. His handsome face was pleasantly smooth and clear. His bare chest, as smooth as a baby's bottom, was well-developed thanks to his regular exercise regimen. His iron-man athletic physique exuded that of a triathlete. Fitness was very important to him as he observed himself in the oblong mirror positioned near his chest of drawers.

Many people often said he resembled running back Emmitt Smith, who at the time played for the Dallas Cowboys. The self-confident Lazlo wasn't narcissistic or one who thrived on attention or adulation. So, he'd usually downplay compliments, preferring instead to remain low-key.

As he prepared to sit in front of his computer, still with heavy thoughts of me on his heart, the bedroom phone rang early afternoon. He glanced at the Caller ID, then back at the computer screen, reaching for the phone receiver.

"Well, well. Hello, my brother," Lazlo answered. He had noticed that the phone call and e-mail alert were both from his friend and colleague Roland.

"Did I catch you at a bad time?" asked Roland, a fraternity brother of Lazlo's who is a pharmaceutical sales representative specializing in marketing for a Washington, D.C., laboratory. He and Lazlo had become close over the years, and Roland knew just how important – and sometimes fragile – friendships were, especially among black men who secretly lived an alternative lifestyle in an industry with so few African-American males.

"Actually, I just got some disturbing news. Let me call you back. I have something pressing to deal with," said Lazlo, promising to return the call once things settled.

As Lazlo spent the better part of his afternoon trying to piece together my tragic criminal developments, I finally got the nerves to call him.

With the phone ringing, I took a few deep breaths trying to figure out how to start the conversation.

"Hello, Lazlo. I'm sure you've seen the newspaper or television," I said.

"Yeah, I have. I just want to know if any of this is true."

"Yes. It's true," I said.

"Why? How could you even dream of a plan like that? You do not fit the stereotype of a bank robber? What could possibly have led you to do such a crime?" Lazlo asked.

"I just got into a financial bind," I said.

He was completely floored by my admission.

"You could have come to me for money if you were that desperate," Lazlo claimed.

His response didn't surprise me. I knew that he would say that because he's always been the type of person who tried to rescue people from situations and sometimes even themselves.

"So, what happens next?" he asked.

"Well, I'm meeting with the feds to work out some details about my case. They want to continue interviewing me to see where my head is. For now, they don't understand why someone like me would resort to robbing banks. Even they are stunned because I don't match the profile of a criminal, and I don't have any priors," I said.

"Well, I know you can't talk long, but let me know what I can do to help. I am really disappointed and angry, but I promise not to abandon you. I don't understand fully why you chose this route, but now is not the time for me to jump down your throat. Right now we need to figure out a way out of this mess," Lazlo expressed.

"Yeah, I have to go. I will try to contact you later with more information. I don't know what's going to happen, but for now I'm being held in the Fort Bend County Jail in Richmond for interrogation. They have me in a private cell because of my high-profile crime. I'm sorry that I disappointed you. I just got caught up. And I know I'm in big trouble. I know all your friends have probably seen me in the news. Again, I'm sorry to disappoint you."

Lazlo hung up the phone. And prayed.

•••••

It was late evening before Lazlo returned Roland's phone call. Without going into details, he started out the conversation saying a personal matter had come up with Miguel.

Lazlo, attempting to sound upbeat, then said, "Long time no hear from. I needed this break."

He then quickly moved the conversation to his career.

"It's been a busy year for me with all the prescription clients and all. Even so I've been trying to keep up with the latest industry news," he said, "particularly the AIDS epidemic in Africa and elsewhere on this planet. The sad part is we got all the necessary meds, but just having difficulty dispersing them to the needy throughout the world."

"Yeah, tell me about it," Roland said. "Money is the rule, man. Anyway, congrats on your selection as vice president for the Houston chapter of black pharmacists. You deserve it."

Lazlo acknowledged recognition of the honor.

"Meanwhile, I hear Houston is having its share of problems with light-rail issues," Roland said, changing the subject after sensing uneasiness in Lazlo's voice.

Lazlo agreed but said immigration and crime were even larger issues for the city.

"Did you get my e-mail?" Roland asked.

"Looking at it right now," said Lazlo, reaching for the mouse.

"Well, read it thoroughly when you get a chance. I called earlier because I wanted to hear my ol' friend's voice," Roland said.

Thinking about Lazlo's earlier comment about a personal problem he was dealing with, Roland recalled that Lazlo had been getting quite a bit of grief and drama from me. But Roland was always reluctant to pry, so he decided to wait until an invitation presented itself.

"Your ol' friend is reading your message right now," Lazlo said to Roland.

"Don't sweat it. I was going through some old photos from the National Association of Pharmacy convention in Atlanta and saw you posing with a big smile next to Carol Carton. I scanned them and decided to electronically send you copies. Also I was wondering about your plans for this year's Phoenix convention? You are going, aren't you?" Roland asked.

"As usual, I'll be there – if God says the same. I'll be hawking products for a longtime client. She's a physician who formerly worked for the government. Now she's written a few books, one of which details the medical state of the union. In it she draws parallels between the cost of medicines and the pharmaceutical giants."

"Amen to that. What a way to put knowledge to use, huh. Maybe we'll finally get a straight answer from a true medical standpoint from a person of color. Good luck on that project. Anyway, who convinced organizers to pick a convention spot in the middle of the desert, in the dead of summer for this year's convention?" Roland asked sarcastically.

"Your guess is as good as mine. You're the marketing specialist. It certainly wasn't my idea, my brother."

"Well, I guess we'll just have to cope with snakes and spiders," joked Roland, who did not know that Lazlo was petrified of both.

"Spiders?" Lazlo shuddered.

"Relax, my brother. There haven't been any recent fatal bites reported." Roland had hoped to take Lazlo's mind off his problems.

The reality was that many of Lazlo's problems were directly linked to my "stinking thinking" and selfishness.

When the opportunity arrived for Lazlo to share his pain with Roland, he withdrew. Instead, he continued their superfluous conversation.

"Tragic bites? What do you mean?" inquired Lazlo, returning to the matter about spiders.

"Oh, just don't worry," Roland suggested.

Because Lazlo often played jokes on Roland, his fraternity brother decided to play into Lazlo's fears.

"Spiders usually bite when you're asleep under the covers. And, at first, you won't feel a thing. They like to keep warm when they creep through the night, you know. A person usually doesn't know he's been a target until a small blister develops. Eventually, it becomes infected with little eggs and may require antibiotics and, in some rare cases, surgery. They are some creepy little bastards."

Lazlo was freaking out over the talk about spiders. For the most part, he wasn't easily intimidated. His strong qualities were that of being a thoughtful, generous brother who could be sensitive at times. Generally, he would give people the benefit of the doubt and sometimes the shirt off his back.

But I had often warned him about being so trusting, particularly with my history of deceiving people and being deceived. I'd even cautioned him about the many nefarious people, gay and straight, who preyed on people they considered weak and gullible. Sometimes Lazlo was a bit too lax around others he didn't know too well, but, more often than not, he maintained control over most situations. He was a bit unorthodox because he was known to have the patience of the biblical icon Job, who withstood the tests of Satan in the

Old Testament. Lazlo was the epitome of a Prince Charming or Robin Hood – the one who rode the white horse to save the world from itself.

So, it's rare to see Lazlo intimidated. He did, however, begin to sense a bit of exaggeration from Roland, who's been known to embellish a bit.

"I was just trying to have some fun, man. Stay with me, my brother," said Roland, grinning, as he began to back off from his playfulness.

"Whatever!" Lazlo retorted. "Anyway, how many brothers and sisters will your company send to the convention?"

"Around 20. It will probably be the usual group: department heads, a few pharmacy reps. And what about the Houston group?"

"About the same number, I suppose. There's word from one of our fraternity brothers, who's active with the national association, that this year's convention will be stronger, especially with the increased support from southern regions that include Atlanta, Miami and New Orleans," Lazlo said.

"Make sure you add Houston to that list," Roland said.

"Hell, yeah! That's right," Lazlo said. "We have a lot of new faces leading research just here in the Houston area alone. Oh, by the way. Did you hear what happened here with Marlene?"

"Yeah. It was bold of that sistah to walk offstage in the middle of her lecture. She was one of the top corporate executives, too," said Roland, chuckling.

"It happened during the annual board meeting for shareholders. She slammed Med Tech, accusing it of unfair promotion practices and quotas. Some people close to the situation say she felt Med Tech had been biased against her, as well as with a few minority pharmacy managers and chemists within the firm."

"So they're claiming racial prejudice down there too, huh?"

"You better believe it," Lazlo said. "Marlene deserved better. I don't blame her. I would have gotten out of Dodge, too, although I would have been more tactful. Still, she deserved better than that sort of treatment."

"Don't we all, Lazlo? Don't we all?"

"You're absolutely right, Roland. But, hey, I'll get back with you on this matter later and with a few other delicate issues, too. As you can probably tell, I'm a little bit on edge. I will tell you more about those soon. But, anyway, thanks for the photos and the e-mail. They were definitely a cool reminder. It certainly brought a smile – something I greatly need right now," Lazlo concluded.

•••••

Time slowly passed as I sat days later at the cluttered FBI desk, in Agent McClure's office, giving my final confession about the robberies.

Agents Jim Warren and Mark CarMichael then informed me that they had secured a warrant to search my apartment for other evidence and money, which I had stuffed in the kitchen light fixture and still wasn't planning to give up. I did, however, store about $2,000 in an obscure box near the living room. That cash was to be used as insurance just in case I was surprised by a late-night jack move from one of the drug thugs who might try to follow me home. Anyway, I still had to try to figure out a way to get the rest of the $8,000 from the light fixture. Who could I trust at this point? Lazlo, perhaps. I would weigh my options as agents Warren and CarMichael headed out the door to my apartment.

Agent McClure then began to wrap up quickly by typing the last of my confession.

I was glad that this part was nearly complete because my attention was slowly fading as my body was overcome with weariness after they again had pulled me out of my cell early in the morning. I was so sleepy that I nodded off and my upper body suddenly collapsed onto the metal desk and startled Agent McClure. After realizing what happened, he merely laughed.

"Morris, are you OK?" he asked, still grinning but realizing I was plagued by fatigue.

"I'm fine," I said, lying. My dreary red eyes told the real story.

"I'm just about finished, Morris, so hang in there. I know you didn't get much sleep. I'll be done shortly."

McClure continued to type but at a more rapid pace now. The clacking of the keyboard, though not loud, held my attention in the quiet office.

"Yeah, I'll be OK," I said again. I then lazily glanced at the clock on the wall. It was 4:15 p.m. Minutes after that, Agent McClure turned to address me.

"There, I'm finished," he said after he sent the document to the ink-jet printer.

"Morris, I have one question."

"Sure. What is it?" I asked, sounding uninterested. My sleepy eyes were burning, my empty stomach growling. Only thing I wanted was for this horror to end.

"What made you relapse?" he asked.

I paused to think. Of course, there was no way I was going to tell him the turmoil began over my lust for a piece of ass.

"Just plain old stupidity," I answered, thinking back on my selfish actions. "It was just plain old ignorance and hunger for something I couldn't handle." The thoughts of drugging and exotic dancing came to mind. These were once things I couldn't ever imagine doing. But when I got deeply involved, I did so with ease as if it were second nature. I am now paying the consequences.

"Crack is a horrible drug to deal with, huh, Miguel? Most guys who rob banks have problems with drugs of some sort. They start stealing to support their habits and lifestyle. That's really unfortunate for people who get so caught up. They end up ruining their lives by robbing businesses, strangers and loved ones. And most of these actions result from anger, hurt and fear," McClure expressed. He glanced at the papers from the printer and then his eyes penetrated me as if to say, "What a terrible way to waste a promising life."

I didn't say a word, and I wasn't ready to be lectured after another a long day with the feds.

• • • • •

Agent McClure gave me a chance to rest while we waited for the other agents to return from their search of my apartment.

Before long, the office door opened. I snapped out of my daze. I was still tired and could barely hold my eyes open to focus on the activity swirling about me when agents Warren and CarMichael entered. They were toting a load of items in a black plastic trash bag, which was tied tight at the opening. Agent Warren placed the bagged evidence onto the floor next to an empty cubicle.

"Well, mission accomplished," Agent Warren uttered as he removed his London Fog overcoat, putting it on one of the empty chairs next to Agent McClure's desk. Obviously, from the way they were dressed, it was getting cold outside.

"Most of the evidence that we need to complete this investigation is here in this bag, except for the black sweater that was used in the second bank robbery," Agent Warren said.

"I threw it away," I said, giving a rushed answer. I had placed it in a trash bin near some condominiums. I was certain that by now it was well-buried underneath days-old trash in a landfill.

"Well it's not essential at this point, Jim," Agent McClure explained. "Mr. Morris has formally completed his confession, and we're just about finished here."

"That's good, because it's been a long day, and my family is waiting on me back at the ranch," said Agent CarMichael, viewing some of the printed pages of my confession.

"By the way guys, how much money did you recover?" Agent McClure asked, ready to record the lump sum in a ledger. "It needs to be documented."

"A few thousand dollars was found where Morris said it would be," Agent CarMichael responded, still observing the confession with his wire-framed glasses tilted on top of his nose.

I decided to give them a little bone to play with – the stash in the box and nightstand. I figured a few grand would satisfy them and partially get me out of the legal maelstrom.

"That's fine. I guess we can wrap it up, gentlemen. I would like to get home at a decent hour, too, so I can enjoy the rest of the evening with my family as well."

Hearing that from Agent McClure made me homesick. Oh, how I wish I could be at Mom's home now instead of here.

Agent McClure then shut down his computer's hard drive and terminal.

After the other agents disappeared, he asked me to hold tight for a few more minutes so he could tie up some minor loose ends. Eventually, though, those minutes accumulated into hours and darkness settled over the city before we finally left.

While shuttling me to my next destination, Agent McClure and I drove into the parking lot of a nearly empty Whataburger restaurant. With me locked inside the vehicle, he went into the building and ordered a couple chicken sandwiches and fries. When he returned, we began wolfing down the food. I was certainly appreciative of this random act of kindness, particularly from a stern law enforcement official.

With that, I was convinced the agent saw me as a non-threatening captive, not the typical offender he dealt with on a daily basis.

Earlier, when I sat in the back seat of his cruiser, he expressed that he felt I wasn't a bad person. Instead, he said, I was a good person who simply got caught up in bad things. So, for that reason, he chose to go out of his way for me. I recalled Agent McClure saying he was a Christian. I was now convinced.

"I don't routinely have an offender sitting in my squad car without handcuffs and later sharing a hot meal with me," he said. "But God has confirmed to me that you're OK," he explained.

I listened intently, confirming his acclamation with a nod, and then silently gave thanks to God.

He wanted to know one more thing before we finished our meals. So, I urged him to ask and that I would oblige with an answer. I figured that was the least I could do for his generosity.

"How did you know there were transmitters and dye packs hidden in all that money you stole from the banks?"

I almost wanted to laugh, but I didn't because I was too tired. So I told him the real deal.

"I used to be a teller years ago at a local bank. I knew how to spot marked money. Usually, in a robbery situation, a stack of currency disguised as $1,000 really only has a $20 bill on the top and bottom. The middle of the pack contains just $1 bills. I also knew to break the seals of the stacks to look for potential trouble spots. I never took sealed money, unless it was in fifties or one hundreds because they come in stacks of $1,000. And, besides, they're too thin to hide transmitters or dye packs.

I wasn't bragging, I just knew the policies and procedures of financial institutions in Texas. There were other intricate details, too, that I didn't bother to discuss. But I did discuss my getaway plans.

"I always picked times when I thought the traffic would slow the police. As well, I used the high-occupancy vehicle lanes for quicker escapes," I said.

Agent McClure was impressed.

He said, "I told agents Warren and CarMichael that you were one of the smart ones. You had too much patience and were too cool during your robberies. You were not spontaneous, but, instead, had a well-planned strategy. You even took your time at writing out your non-threatening notes, neatly. In fact, the writing surprised us because we were so used to sloppy planning and penmanship. On top of that, you even disguised your notes by using blank check stubs. That was smart because the tellers never knew they were messages announcing a bank robbery in progress until they turned them face up and read them."

After detailing my strategy to the agent, we left the restaurant parking lot in his unmarked vehicle.

"Do you know how many bank robberies fail in this city because of sloppiness?" Agent McClure asked.

"I never gave that question much thought," I answered.

"Maybe one in twelve only get away. And the smart ones get away because they think through their plans in much the same way as you did, Morris. Incredibly, you did six robberies in a month's time."

After our conversation, the squad car moved closer to its final destination.

I so desperately wanted to ask whether I was his trophy catch now that I had been apprehended. But I withdrew the thought, thinking that question would be inappropriate.

"Indeed, you were clever, Morris. That's why you earned the moniker the 'Patient Bank Robber.' "

"Well, not clever enough, though, because I eventually got caught just like the less-intelligent ones. I feel like a mouse trapped in the mouth of a stray cat," I said.

We continued our journey.

It had been such a long day. Eventually, our white squad car pulled into a police docking area for inmate booking. It was time for Agent McClure and me to separate. It was a bittersweet departure.

I was now about to be processed again into the Harris County Jail in downtown Houston. He escorted me inside, and I was forced to sit and wait patiently in a small holding area with the stench of urine. Not exactly the Hilton or Embassy Suites. This foul and filthy place reeked of various odors. And I was about to be tossed once more among other hardheads in unsanitary conditions. I noticed that some of those being held in the same areas were asleep on the concrete floor, and others rested on the concrete slabs that were mainly used for sitting. The repugnant sights and smells kept me alert through the remainder of the night as I was transferred from one cell to another.

My resistance to sleep lasted only so long as my body began to scream for rest. I succumbed and joined others in the crowd and looked for a place to lay my weary body. I had to reprogram my thoughts. I had to find a spot, any open spot, where I could nestle before the start of another unpredictable day.

•••••

Spraying with the intensity of pine needles, the hot shower was still a temporary respite from the surrounding filth. The force of the water from the shower head assaulted my skin with intermittent jabs. Indeed, quite an eye-opener. I was just simply elated to feel the water ripple from my body as I stood in a trance in what appeared to be a pool of water that seemed to take its time to drain.

"Oh, how refreshing," I thought, as I delighted in the pulsating pleasure of a shower. I thought of all the jailed men with troubled faces and broken spirits. And I was among them. I was lonely and beginning to lapse into deeper depression.

As my shower neared an end, guilt descended upon me

like dark clouds forming suddenly. It was like an immediate slap in the face. My humiliation magnified; shame engulfed me. I even felt embarrassed to utter to the people in jail with me how I ended up in a wretched place like this. Surely, I can't be and shouldn't be among the worst of us in here, I thought. I don't even look like these other cast of characters. For a moment, I wanted to believe I was better than they were. I also wanted to believe that over time I would be out of here because I've never been in this kind of trouble before. I wanted to justify everything that was wrong with my detainment. How is it that I'm locked up with these scofflaws and violent criminals? It was obvious I was not ready to accept my fate or the truth about my behavior.

While under the shower, a vision of my robbery escape popped into my mind: Rain was pouring as I speeded down Beltway 8 fleeing one of my crime scenes at 90-plus mph. It was a fantastic adrenaline rush as the freeway filled with water and the car began to hydroplane. My heart was pounding fast, revved up like the pistons of a performance vehicle. Whew! I'd gotten away with the crime. I slowed down only when I remembered that there might be a speed trap and that "smokey" might be laying in wait. I didn't want to draw attention to myself. I then eased off the accelerator, becoming more relaxed. The rush dissipated. And, yet, another clean getaway for me. Cocky? You can say that.

My eyes popped open after a loud command instructing us to prepare to exit the showers.

"Five minutes more!" a husky voice ordered.

I quickly abandoned my reckless recall and turned my attention to the officer posted in the area. Once the showers were turned off, he asked us to line up to prepare to gather our state-issued orange jumpers and thick plastic black sandals.

The sight of broken tile and mold and mildew was yet another reminder of where I was and would be for a while.

I gave my clothing size to an inmate who stood behind a wooden door with a cut-out window. He then handed me my necessities. He was tall and dark like me and had a fresh cut. He was rugged-looking, too. His gold teeth highlighted his handsome face and pronounced jaw. For a second, we stared into each other's eyes, but just for a short second, perhaps trying to remember if we knew one another from past scenes or events.

I began to experience a strange feeling that took me back to my days on the streets. It didn't help that I was standing in line butt-naked trying to control my hormones. Sinful, seductive thoughts threatened to creep up on me again.

When my orange jumper was tossed through the window from another inmate working in the back of the storage room it landed on the floor next to the right of another stranger standing near me with wandering eyes. I bent over to retrieve the item, then walked away.

As I began walking away, a voice thundered from behind. "Say, man! You wanna dry towel?"

I quickly turned my naked wet body around and walked back toward the cutout window to retrieve the towel from the handsome dude I had admired a moment ago. Again, our eyes met. But this time he looked at me in a lustful way, scanning me all the way down to my waist and later craning his neck to examine my buttocks.

Shit! This Negro was definitely violating me. While it was fine for me to examine him on the sly, his actions were making me uncomfortable. Besides, he was clothed. I then ignored his gawking and decided against revenge because it was already too early to be caught up in any kind of mess. But the thought of knocking the brother's teeth down his throat had entered my mind.

At this point, I just wanted to assimilate, try to fit in without any problems. I tried not to stand out among the crowd. Of course, there was one small problem. I was forced to wear a purple-and-white wristband, which indicated I was a high-profile inmate. This was a hard pill to swallow.

As a result of that distinction, I was immediately placed in a 6-foot, 9-foot concrete cell and isolated from the inmate population while waiting for my final hearing and sentencing later in the week.

Until then, I focused on trying to avoid suicidal thoughts. I never seriously entertained that idea, but I knew that anything was possible, given that I was in a place that restrained my movements and curtailed basic freedoms. I no longer had access to all the foods I loved nor the clothing I liked to wear. The orange jumper that had now become my daily uniform hung uncomfortably from my thin but still muscular body. I figured that I had lost about 15 pounds during my crack episodes. I could even feel my tailbone pressing against the 7-foot-long, 3-foot-wide bunk bed as I contemplated a phone call to my mom's house as I sat and watched an episode of the daytime talk show The View from a black-and-white television supplied by the City Jail. Giving up was easy to think about, but I decided to hold out a little longer.

Meanwhile, as days progressed to weeks, my coping skills improved a little.

It had now been three weeks since I entered this God-forsaken place, waiting on the snail's-pace legal system to pick up steam.

I took comfort in knowing that I still was getting support from the free world, a term inmates used to describe the non-incarcerated society. Mom, brother Troy and best friend Lazlo had often visited me during this difficult phase of my life. And because Troy and I had had a strained relationship over the years, I was particularly grateful for his support. Our past animosity toward each other had never actually been addressed. It was eating me up inside, the same kind of emotionally piercing pain akin to a stab in the heart.

So I set out to fix the problem. I put in a request with the social services division for inmate affairs to provide a portable phone so that I could place a call to my mother's home. After my request was honored, I dialed the number. The phone rang three times before I heard a voice. After the costly collect call was acknowledged and received, the automated system connected us.

Troy answered, but as customary I asked if mom was there. He said that she and my sister Adrea had gone shopping at the mall. It was just as well that Troy answered, even if his impatience was evident.

Nevertheless, I greeted him as I sat in the right corner of my cell next to the secured steel door with the receiver and cord snaking through the tiny door space used to insert food serving trays. Trying to maneuver the telephone through the tight opening restricted my movement.

Troy appeared to be occupied and ready to end the call. But before he could, I wished him a belated Merry Christmas. I was feeling quite lonely because it was the first time ever that I had missed the December holiday with my family.

After a few seconds of pausing, Troy acknowledged my greeting with his own yuletide offering. As I thanked him, my heart became heavy with emotion. I wanted to say more, but my pride consumed me. Somehow I mustered up the courage to remove my inhibitions.

"I've been thinking about something for a while that's been weighing heavily on me," I said.

"Thinking about what, man?" Troy asked hesitantly.

"Well, you remember all the times we used to fight when we were young?"

"Yeah. What about them?"

"I just wanted to address the past and my bullying, man. We would always tease each other, and sometimes you would get the best of me. I guess I just couldn't handle it, man. I wasn't mature enough to take it as a joke. I took a lot of things so personal back then, Troy, especially the teasing, man. All I knew to do was to lash out, fight and get even, man. You feel me?" There was a long moment of quietness, but I continued. "You know how sensitive I was about wetting the bed and the darkness of my skin. So when you teased me about those things it really hurt. And I wanted you to hurt, too. So I guess what I'm trying to say is that I'm sorry. Will you forgive me?" I asked, seeking atonement. I began to feel better.

Again, there was silence.

"Yeah, Miguel. I forgive you, man. I was wrong, too. I remember the fights and the scars and bruises. You would sometimes bite me, man! And that shit used to hurt. Made me mad as hell. I hated you for it," said Troy, laughing. "I forgive you, man. It's about time we end this rivalry and be the men we're supposed to be."

I could hear him chuckle as if he were relieved we'd finally had this conversation.

We both were at ease after all those years of avoiding each other. We both were proud, stubborn young men then.

Being incarcerated I realized that it is never too late to admit past mistakes. I was hoping that I was nearing a point in my life where I was disarming my ego and beginning to learn how to embrace truth.

I remembered those fighting days of ours as if it were yesterday. They weren't the types of fights young brothers would normally have: a little shove here, a little shove there, and then back to normal. Our fights, unfortunately, were similar to gang wars. We were blood brothers, but the drawing of blood often resulted because sometimes we used whatever weapons we could find to administer the worst kind of pain.

I remember a particular summer when Troy and I got very physical. I was 13, and he was 12. The heat was brutal in our Southpark neighborhood. We were playing a game of basketball outside with other neighborhood boys on the court. Troy and I were on opposing teams. When play action began I got the ball, dribbled and faked out a couple opponents. As I made it to the top of the free-throw line, I prepared my jump shot, only to be blocked from behind. My ego was shattered, especially since there was a small crowd viewing.

I was humiliated by the cheers after my two-point attempt was foiled.

Trying to take the edge off, I called a foul on the play, but the opponent denied me the ball and became verbally abusive.

Troy was perturbed by my call, especially since he was on the opposing team and the one who blocked my two points. He and I were about even in height and stature, but I was stronger and more aggressive. After he started arguing with me, our tempers flared. So, I gathered the ball and clamped it underneath my right arm and dared anyone to take it. I was sweating like a bull in the sweltering sun. Enraged, I acted out. We got into a serious fistfight and then I slammed the orange ball into my brother's chest, knocking him flat on his ass onto the cement court.

"Get up, punk!" I shouted.

At that point, Troy got up and walked away from the court. This time he was embarrassed.

"Don't come back, fool!" I ordered, bullying him even more.

Many on the crowded court were disgusted with my unsportsmanlike conduct, but I didn't give a damn. We then all prepared to resume playing ball despite the perplexed and angry emotions from everyone about how I treated my younger brother. Even so, no one was daring enough to approach me. The ball was then put back in motion, and my team was still behind by six points. As I stood at the free-throw line once again to try to collect my two points from my foul call, I suddenly felt as if my body had been crushed by a freight train. I became faint and toppled over.

Troy had returned and whacked me across the head with a 2-by-4 that he found at a nearby trash bin. The board landed across my skull, leaving me dazed and semi-conscious.

Never before had I experienced a blow quite like that before as I wobbled like a drunken fool amid echoes of derisive shouts and laughter.

Troy ran home to Mom for protection.

To this day, I can still feel the small lump atop the crown of my head.

But it was only now that I realized I actually loved my brother and that he genuinely loved me.

Our call ended on a note of pardon from both of us. We agreed to let bygones be bygones.

Chapter 4
Damn! Bam! Slam!

Wake up, you drunkards, and weep! Wail, all you drinkers of wine. Wail because of the new wine, for it has been snatched from your lips.
Joel 1:5

It was now Week 4 of my jailhouse incarceration, and my day in court had finally arrived. I nervously looked into the calm blue eyes of a thin, black-robed judge wearing specs as he was perched on his lofty bench contemplating a judgment against me. The tick-tock of the courtroom clock was the only sound that punctuated the deafening silence. The presiding judge looked at me, then the charges, then stared at me again. I had no way of knowing what he was thinking as his wire-framed eyeglasses tilted off the bridge of his thin nose.

After what seemed like hours, his mouth finally opened, spewing out seven important words to my court-appointed attorney.

"Counselor, does your client understand his rights?" asked the judge, laying the documents face-up on his bench.

"Yes, Your Honor. He does," my defense attorney answered.

I had no second thoughts about my planned plea. I felt it was the right thing to do.

So, the judge continued.

"District Attorney Daily, are you in full agreement with the terms and conditions of this order?"

"Yes, Your Honor. I am."

The DA looked toward me as I lowered my head and stood

like a lifeless tree. I was very shaky, but I was not about to tumble. I had to be strong. I'd been wrestling with the various possibilities about my fate. I was certain that I would be punished; I just wasn't sure how badly.

I was aware weeks before that District Attorney Daily and FBI agent McClure had agreed upon a plea bargain. I was not aware of any possible changes, but the deal seemed to be a fair trade. McClure agreed to put me under the care of the state of Texas for a lighter sentence. I was happy about the deal but preferred not having to serve any prison time. The agreement was for three years on each offense, which wasn't bad considering that I could have gotten a maximum of 10 years on each count of bank robbery.

The other blessing was a dropped charge for my last offense. This happened to have been in the county where agents Warren and CarMichael represented. This was reasonable considering that the charge of aggravated bank robbery could not be corroborated. That resulted because a bank teller said I had a gun, which wasn't true. The claim just didn't match my pattern. I passed notes, not bullets. Nor did I ever brandish a weapon, neither gun nor knife.

Nevertheless, it was to my advantage to let the state of Texas deal with my transgressions rather than the federal government.

With an upcoming local election, the deal offered was just as palatable to the district attorney. By nabbing me, "The Patient Bank Robber," he could brag on the campaign trail that he was tough on crime. Indeed, a badge of honor to behold for political gain.

As the stone-faced judge studied the documents, it was hard to determine his thoughts. Periodically, he would look up from his bench to examine my emotions. It was evident to him that I was quite nervous as the courtroom scene was horrifying, much like my early childhood memories of trembling during storms that produced furious lightning and thunder.

In those days, my siblings and I were often comforted by our grandmother, who instructed us to turn off all radios and televisions in the house so the Lord could do his work. But with my grandmother now gone, I relied on my faith alone. I stood firm believing that God would touch the heart of the judge who would have to sign off on my plea deal.

While waiting on a ruling, I wondered about the ultimate Judgment Day. Will God have mercy on me? Will my name appear in the Book of Life? Will I escape eternal damnation? Are there "close calls" in heaven, or is there no leeway at all?

In the courtroom, the waiting became more and more torturous. An orchestra of noise converged, including the staccato sounds from the tick-tock of the clock and the sudden fever-pitch shuffling of papers that seemed to lighten up only when the judge spoke out in his baritone voice to start the proceedings. It was just a matter of time now for him to render his judgment from his lofty perch.

"Great. Since everyone's ready, let's proceed," he said, again picking up the documents from his towering desk. "Mr. Morris, the state of Texas has found you guilty on felony charges of robbery against the peace and dignity of this state. Do you understand this charge, Mr. Morris?"

He stared deeply into my soul.

"Yes, sir, I do," I answered with trepidation.

"It is therefore ordered, adjudged and decreed by this court that the defendant, Miguel Morris, is guilty of robbery, as confessed in the said plea herein made, and that the punishment be fixed as assessed by this court, by confinement of 15 years in a Texas Department of Criminal Justice facility."

As the judge continued, my knees wobbled.

"The court further finds that there was a plea agreement between the state and the defendant and that the punishment being assessed does not exceed the punishment recommended. Does your client understand this agreement, counselor?" the judge asked, his piercing eyes focused intently on my lawyer.

"Yes, he does, Your Honor," my lawyer, feeling confident that I understood, answered with clutched hands.

"All findings, orders and notations will go into full force in this case, counselor. The clerk will have some final documents for Mr. Morris to sign before he's turned over to the Sheriff's Department, which will honor the directions of this sentencing."

Although there were no real surprises, the judicial declaration seemed to put an official stamp of approval on my sentencing that seemed to suggest that it could not be undone.

BAM!

The gavel sounded off as if it were a firearm.

"This court is adjourned," the judge said as he rapped the wooden gavel, which rang out in the courtroom and upstaged the monotonous sound of the wall clock that had been echoing in my head before and during the sentencing phase. As the black-robed judge exited to his chambers, I waited silently to begin the next step of my journey.

•••••

Damp cool air rushed through the cracks of the elevator doors. I was being escorted back to my cell, where I would wait to be shipped and warehoused like bewildered livestock to my next destination. I had no idea to which prison I would be assigned.

When I arrived to the fifth-floor holding area, reality hit me like a ton of bricks. I walked handcuffed down the well-lighted hallways, passing cells that packed men barking at each other like wild hungry dogs.

"Keep the noise down, inmates!" demanded the officer escorting me.

"Go to hell!" one prisoner yelled in response.

The war of words continued as the officer yelled, "Tell your momma to go, you coward bastard!"

A few moments later, I reached my private cell and was unshackled as the officer removed the handcuffs from my wrist and placed them back into his holster.

The clinking and turning of the large cell key to secure my lockdown caught my attention, as well as the background chatter about me by fellow inmates.

"That's that fool who was on TV for robbing those banks," said one, alerting the others.

After he was done, the guard left the wing, slamming tightly the steel windowed cell door of the long corridor. I immediately felt a migraine developing. I approached my cell bunk, sitting and meditating. Memories flashed at the speed of a meteor. I reminisced about Lazlo, who had stood by my side regardless of my thoughtless actions and wanton behavior. Then there was the thought of Patrick Porter, an accessory to my sexual and crack addictions that were used to manipulate male prostitutes.

In addition to that, Patrick was a misogynist; he absolutely despised women, particularly those who pushed up on his man. The thought of my past friendship with him haunted me, left me dismayed and is partially to blame for my current mess that has me incarcerated now. Our reckless behavior on the city's streets and in the clubs was criminal and reprehensible.

"Damn, damn, damn!! How could I have been so stupid," I shouted, expressing my mental anguish. I remorsefully planted my face into the thin mattress of my 7-foot by 3-foot bunk to muzzle my cries and hide my tears. The pity party was in full swing as I began to question how my life, which was once primed for prime time, faded to black. All of my accomplishments, including the numerous prestigious track-and-field honors, were overshadowed by my stupidity. These sorts of things happened to other people, not me.

There was no escaping my punishment as thoughts of my

past evil-doing swam in my head. The relentless mental torture was marked by the repetitious rap lyrics by 8 Ball sounding off in my head: "The devil made me do it. The devil made me do it. It was the hands of the devil." This went on until I screamed, "Shut up!"

I thought about Deuteronomy again: "Do not be afraid or discouraged."

I then arose from the bed with urgency and summoned the jail guard. I requested to use the telephone as my convictions had begun to absorb me.

While waiting on my request to be honored, I thought about the many drug counselors from my past who cautioned me about this day – haunting dreams and thoughts that were initiated by my past drug use.

Those warnings zoomed through my overloaded mind, sparking my tension headache.

"Drugs will make you do things you normally wouldn't do," they would say. "You have to surrender old habits, eliminate past failures, play by the rules. Drugs bring three consequences: hospitalization, prison or death."

The fortunate thing for me was that I only experienced two-thirds of those consequences. I had entered a drug rehab facility before and now was going through the incarceration phase. I would now try my best to just stay alive. Heck, I was only 38. I still had a lot to accomplish even though it seemed that my college education had been wasted. I realize now that I should have gotten my bachelor's degree since I was just a few hours shy. At the time, completing all my goals wasn't a major priority. I now hated myself for thinking like that. I considered myself to be highly intelligent, but was plagued by procrastination or, more accurately, a lack of focus. My priorities were not in line with the reality that someday I might be caught unprepared, destitute and lonely because of rotten choices.

I pondered all these issues while waiting on the phone so I

could place a collect call.

After several rings and no immediate answer, I wondered if I had missed my chance to hear a comforting voice that would mitigate my pain and bandage my wounds.

Just before hanging up, the other line opened with the sounds of a fumbling receiver and slightly audible panting by Lazlo, who obviously was rushing to the telephone.

After the normal protocol with the automated service, two old hearts were reconnected.

"Hello! Good morning," the voice intoned.

I was relieved that I didn't miss my opportunity after all. My nerves calmed, and I immediately squatted in a small corner near the iron door of my gloomy jail cell to catch up with my special longtime friend over the phone.

"Good morning, man. I thought I missed you. You're home late this morning," I said, resting my head in my left palm as I looked down at the cold cement floor.

"Yeah, I got a CPR class to go to around 11 a.m., so I decided to go in late today. I'm pretty much caught up with most of my work back at the pharmacy. Oh, no. I forgot! I'm supposed to be at Bible study for 11," he reminded himself, sifting through papers and pens to write out the rest of his day's agenda. "I guess I have to reschedule CPR for another day."

Unlike mine, his priorities were usually in order, although I yearned to be more organized.

"What about the later Bible class at 3 o'clock you once told me about?" I reminded him.

"You know, you're right. I totally forgot about the 3 p.m. session being held in the employee conference room on the fifth floor. Thanks, buddy."

My memory and senses, not as sharp as before, seemed to be returning slowly. During my "drugging" days, the only thing that mattered was getting high; everything else was secondary. And that included my mental health, work and relationships. Oddly, my sex drive, despite having engaged in the act often in the past, was sometimes foiled by the effects of cocaine and paranoia.

Now, with those things behind me for the moment, I might be able to contribute something worthwhile to others. With that in mind, Lazlo thanked me for reminding him of the second Bible study session and then asked about my day in court.

I could tell in Lazlo's voice that he felt empty without me, as he had once said.

That's understandable since we were lovers for years. And now we're separated again, and it's my fault. In reality, I missed him, too. For a while at least, I told him there would be no more Friday night movies in River Oaks. No more late-night strolls that we used to savor. No more shopping sprees. No more afternoon lunches that I would often bring to his office on a whim just before 11 a.m. I would sometimes take him an assortment of food from our favorite Chinese buffet in nearby River Oaks. It was only a few minutes from his office tower. The spring rolls were his favorite, along with the crispy hot chicken wings and miniature barbecue ribs. It amazed me how much Lazlo could put down. I often teased him about his appetite, telling him it was a miracle that he hadn't inflated like a helium balloon.

I reminded him that I truly missed those days.

Lazlo chuckled over those memories as I babbled on and on about the good things in our past. He then shifted the conversation to a more serious topic.

"So how did court turn out today? You know I've been waiting on this call all morning."

"I took it."

"You took it?" He paused. "You took the offer? The 15?" asked Lazlo, who slumped into his chair after realizing that an integral part of his life was about to be taken away for many years. He became depressed then a little perturbed, because he couldn't understand how or why this situation came to this point. He was at a loss about how I could just give up my freedom by committing a crime. He blamed all of this mess on crack, but I knew that drugs were only part of the problem.

"Yeah, Lazlo, I took the offer. It was the right thing to do." Tantamount to a drug rush that takes the mind to a level of paranoia and excitement, my throat tightened and my heart rate increased. I knew I had let him down.

A conversation by me about going to prison was so odd, let alone saying I had accepted a 15-year term that could mean at least five years of incarceration before parole eligibility. This nightmare was so out of my character. I still had to deal with the fact of living with other offenders who had committed murder, rape and other violent assaults. Not to mention prison gangs.

What I had once achieved in the past would matter little now as I prepared to enter prison. I would be stigmatized forever. Voting privileges revoked. And, perhaps, unemployable.

I was once among the most productive people and never gave much thought about incarceration or inmates. For that matter, I couldn't care less about what criminals thought or how they survived in the prison hellhole.

There were many times on the freeway that I would pass by a white prison bus full of inmates headed to Huntsville. I would drive by that caged vehicle never feeling their pain or any sympathy for them.

It was humiliating to know that other motorists now might have those feelings about me when the day arrives for me to board one of those "jail on wheels" headed to a faraway prison for intake before subsequently being shipped to a more permanent location.

Questions hounded me: Would I be bunking with a rapist? A murderer? Or even a hot-tempered psychopath waiting to explode? Chills rushed through my body, but I didn't want

Lazlo to detect my fear.

I tried to justify the plea bargain.

"A 15-year prison sentence was the best I was gonna get. It could have been worse, man. I could have been required to serve 40-plus years in a federal prison. I would have been an old man by that time. Man, God is good." I couldn't help but to praise Him after all I had been through and still managed to survive.

"All the time, Miguel. God is good all the time. He saved you, man. You know that?"

As I paused for an extended period, Lazlo became silent as he waited for my next response. He was always patient and humble, qualities acquired during his small-town upbringing in Michigan.

"I'm aware of that now, Lazlo, since my judgments have returned," I finally remarked. "I'm also aware of how much you care for me, man. It's funny how it took this to happen to me for my eyes to open," I said, lifting my head and wiping my teary eyes.

Lazlo reminded me that I could have died – not just of a physical death but spiritually, too.

"A lot of people didn't get a second chance like you, Miguel. Now it's time to correct yourself and start putting this mess behind you, man. You hear me?"

I absorbed every word from Lazlo, knowing he was right. I then told him I would work to leave the past behind.

"Before I forget, Miguel, I moved everything out of your old apartment and into storage. I also got the money you had stashed away."

"Why didn't you take my things to Momma's house?" I responded abruptly. "There's a spare room there. Did you put the eight grand into CDs for a five-year term as planned?"

My quick response, suggesting that I was still in charge, left me thinking that I still had a lot of work to do to fix my commanding nature.

Even so, I knew I could count on Lazlo, who seemed to be somewhat co-dependent. However, I don't blame him inasmuch as I take responsibility for influencing his behavior.

I also thought about the risk Lazlo took to secure my spoil.

"Listen, Miguel," an obviously perturbed Lazlo responded, "I was trying to get things done as fast as I could without being obvious. The feds aren't stupid you know. And your mom lives way across town on the south end of the city. That's 24 miles away from my place. And a public storage facility was just a mile away from your old place. So, I weighed my options. Besides, the storage rental is only for six months. It's not as if you can't afford it. When the contract expires, I'll move them to your mom's house. Deal?"

He was quite insistent but still sensitive about my concerns.

"You're right, man, I'm just trippin'. Worried about nothin."

I then adjusted my legs for a more comfortable position on the cold jailhouse floor. Moments later, hunger pangs caused my stomach to growl. Oh, how I hated that feeling, which was a reminder of the times when I would sacrifice meals for crack.

Unaware of my need for nourishment, Lazlo continued to spout words of encouragement.

"Just remember one thing. I'm not going to abandon you, man. You hear me, man? I'm gonna stay the course."

I heard him loud and clear. And I knew Lazlo meant every word.

"Yes," I responded. "I really appreciate your support. No other friend has reached out to me but you."

Lazlo further assured me of his loyalty by avoiding any reference to my faults or my corrupt associations with Patrick, Oz and Alex.

Patrick, my "partner in crime," did not influence my bank

robberies, but I blame him for something even worse: our late-night prowls through the streets of Houston picking up male crack addicts for our personal indulgences and pleasures. At best our behavior with our targets was consensual, but at worse it amounted to criminal sexual assault against individuals who were chemically impaired and being exploited.

I thought about those awful days, right before my call with Lazlo was interrupted by a beep and an automatic recording.

"You have three minutes," it warned.

I told Lazlo that I knew that he and my family were behind me and somehow I was going to make it right again this time, even in the face of having screwed up often.

"We'll be waiting on you to get out of there. Prison isn't your home. Your home is out here with us – your family and me. So, stop worrying," he said quickly, anticipating the call to soon end abruptly.

His optimism further helped to build my appetite. Indeed, this was a good sign.

Beep!

Lazlo's final words were perfectly timed as our conversation expired.

Chapter 5
Property of the State

For I know the plans I have for you, says the Lord. They are plans for good and not for evil, to give you a future and a hope.

Jeremiah 29:11

Harris County jail was now history for me as I was now being transported from Houston to a faraway prison in southeast Texas. During the early morning trip of March 31, 1998, I observed Texas bluebonnets that dotted a long stretch of Interstate 10 West. It appeared as if we were heading through desolate farmland of El Paso. Later, we turned south to another area devoid of inhabitants but saturated with cactuses and tumbleweed. Our bus traveled for miles on an asphalt highway leading to a remote prison site.

Fellow inmates and I stared silently out of the windows of the caged bus. As my mind flashed back to Tish and our failed marriage, one of the prisoners behind me posed a question about our destination, but no one answered. Of course, no one other than the guards knew where we were headed. All I knew was that we sat uncomfortably cuffed and shackled by our ankles and wrists. We sat in twos with knees crammed against the hard backs of the brown vinyl-covered seats that offered no mercy on our backs, legs and thighs.

The bus was unusually quiet, except for the wind howling through the open windows. That sound and the euphoric smell of Texas wildflowers were our only delights.

We were well into our trip before anyone uttered another word. At first I was too dazed to focus on the conversation. I stared hopelessly into the open fields and the sky.

The conversation on the bus reached epic volume when the subject of drugs came up. Some offenders became passionate about their opinions, with many even yelling about how much money and how many women they used to have and who the big-time drug dealers were on the streets of their towns. Multiple conversations spread like wildfire. And relief came only when the gracious corrections officer who was driving turned on the radio to defuse the trash-talking.

Another guard, a husky brown man, then also broke his silence.

"Say, fellas!" he yelled, "This'll be the last time y'all probably hear some funky sounds for a while. So I suggest you shut up and enjoy it."

The driver then pumped up the volume even louder, with speakers booming like mad crazy to the smooth sounds of R&B.

Most offenders took heed to the suggestion by the guard, whose armed white partner – who didn't appear amused – kept a watchful eye on us. Perhaps he preferred country music over the urban sounds from the distant San Antonio radio station.

As Monica crooned her hit Before You Walk Out of My Life, I had a moment to reflect on the time when my ex-lover Lazlo and I took a much-needed getaway from the hustle and bustle of Houston to South Padre Island. Although the prison bus was headed in that direction, one thing for certain was that the two trips were incomparable. Then, Lazlo and I were planning a fun-filled trip that included water skiing, parasailing and volleyball.

In contrast, the current trip will consist of uncertainty and a high fear factor.

This trip also left me as rigid as a board. My body stiffened even more when the offender next to me fell asleep and brushed his leg against mine. Eventually, his warm left thigh rested upon my right one. There was no immediate insecurity. Instead, it was just a harsh reality that wherever the hell we were headed, space was going to be next to none. So, it was best that I quickly get used to being in cramped quarters.

Some eight hours later, and several stops in between to other prison facilities, I was startled out of my sleep when my seatmate's right hand fell from his lap onto my left hand. It happened as our bus slowed abruptly to make a sharp right turn, approaching a row of secured buildings. Razor-sharp wire fences protected the vast fortress. This place would become my temporary home while I prepared for a maximum 15-year term, not factoring in possible parole. My presence in Beeville, Texas, validated my new identity as a marked criminal. I became gripped by fear of never seeing freedom for a long, long time.

Garza West was a transfer facility, infamously known for male offenders' sometimes violent behavior and their harsh treatment from guards, who struggled to control prison miscreants. The unit is about 60-plus miles from Corpus Christi, 30 miles from the resort island of South Padre and nearly 200 miles from Houston.

Once our bus entered the facility and parked, the driver gave orders to remain quiet.

Upon our exit, my chained fellow offenders and I couldn't help but notice a profound message on a large sign above us: "Attention: Profanity is a Public Statement of Stupidity."

Before any among our group of 50 could offer an opinion about this facility, a thunderous voice with a strong southeast Texas accent demanded that we drop our white storage bags. After that, several officers began to unshackle our hands and feet.

"Attention, inmates!" an imposing figure shouted. "Welcome to Garza West, gen-tle-men!" said the burly, cocky, sarcastic sergeant with the Texas Department of Criminal Justice (TDCJ). "There will be no talking, spitting, questions of any kind until this process is complete. You are now the property of the state of Texas! And you will do as you are told. Is that clear, inmates?" He yelled louder each time in an obvious attempt to intimidate us.

"I ain't the property of no damn body," one offender stated with equal tenor, suggesting he would not submit to any authority nor was he anybody's sissy.

"What was that, inmate?" asked the guard, who addressed the bald, golden-brown convict in a nose-to-nose encounter. Just an inch closer, they would have been touching lips. "Oh, I see. You wanna stud-up now, huh, boy? I'll knock that smirk off your face, you damn faggot!" he yelled.

Another officer then joined in to berate the outspoken inmate.

"He's a ho', Sarg. Don't bother with that one."

The corrections officers decided to have fun with the loose-lipped inmate as the intimidation continued.

"Yeah, just as I figured. A wannabe badass. You gonna be somebody's boytoy soon, boy. Matter of fact, all of y'all strip out of those damn jumpers and drawers and spread eagle!" the sergeant ordered.

The outspoken brown-skin offender who had challenged the sergeant earlier clammed up and was the first among us to disrobe. His tough act ended quickly, and he caved in just as the no-nonsense sergeant predicted.

I thought, "What a coward." I then observed as everyone, including me, began to strip. Our orange Harris County Jail jumpers that made us look like sanitation workers would be traded for white TDCJ overalls.

The redneck sergeant, resembling former bodybuilder Arnold Schwarzenegger, observed our every move. He was a Hercules of a man, a brute standing about 6-feet, 4-inches or more. His short blond crew-cut hair complimented his deep Texas tan and chiseled face. With such strong features, this guy was not one to toy with. His massive biceps and triceps suggested that he might at one time have been a competitive bodybuilder.

His hands and knuckles were as huge as I've ever seen. As he walked back and forth, his thundering thighs seemed to scream for release from the Confederate gray pants that clang to every curve of his tree-trunk quadriceps and massive calves. His body was intimidation at its best. And I had no intention of creating any waves with this dude.

With clenched fists, he continued to plod his way down the warm cement path, staring coldy into pessimistic faces and barely clothed bodies, testing wit and experience against dubious and fearful inmates. By itself, his stone-faced image — a deep-dark tightened face — could squash egos and subdue any would-be badass.

After the last of our handcuffs and shackles were stripped from us, I focused strongly on the message I'd noticed earlier that informed us that profanity is a public statement of stupidity. The sun glared on the sign, making it impossible to overlook its bright-red letters. Zooming in on those meaningless words in this prison environment was my attempt to forget about my humiliation.

It was clear that the message wasn't meant for the prison staff because the sergeant and his goons were spitting out all kinds of cuss words. As a matter of fact, words of respect were conspicuously absent and easy to count because they were so few.

"OK, inmates!" the sergeant continued to dictate, "Strip 'em down to your bare asses, and fast!"

We all dropped our white boxers. And I sensed that officers delighted in dehumanizing us. Breaking down egos and bad attitudes seemed to be their goal, but their approach was brutal. Their torment irritated the hell out of me, but this is prison.

Along with me, several other offenders, as ordered, began to cross a nearby yellow line that was used as a traffic-control barrier. It was there where we stood naked with the sun beating down on our dry skin, no less a result of the lye soap we used for showering back in Houston.

When some people lingered behind the yellow line a little longer than expected, another officer verbally blasted the violators, sounding off in a gruff tone, while also displaying a sinister smirk. I realized this was just another intimidation tactic, but his hollering and screaming pissed off everybody.

The bastard was literally laughing at us with his damn mind games.

"Get your ass back across that damn yellow line, inmate!" an officer demanded when a smiling dark-chocolate brother waddled behind. The offender was an effeminate dude who was about to become an assault target.

"Oh, you think that's funny, huh, inmate?" said the officer, popping the inmate on his tail with a towel that seemed to strike with the intensity of a tiny jolt of electricity. "If you think that hurts, that ass may eventually feel much more than that later," said the officer, teasing as the inmate rolled his eyes as if to say bring it on.

He then intimidated another inmate by encroaching on his space when he stood eye to eye with him, seemingly molesting him as the top of the officer's uniform repeatedly brushed up against the inmate's naked body every time the officer's chest thrust forward as he exhaled violently while spouting foul language. The guard also instinctively spewed nasty spit in the offender's face at a rapid pace.

The inmate, in rapt attention and with closed eyes, stood as stiff and rigid as steel beams. He refused to breathe, fearing that any little natural body movement could trigger more fury if the offender's facial hair even accidentally grazed the skin of the officer, who was absolutely standing too close for comfort anyway.

After a few more moments of that encounter, the guard issued another demand.

"Listen up, gentlemen! You gonna stand your naked asses out here until you learn to stay put as instructed. If you don't know shit about prison life, you better start now noticing lines, signs and following authority. Is that clear?" he asked with a funky attitude.

Of course we heard him loud and clear.

"Yes, sir!" we replied like Army cadets in basic training.

"Now turn around and face that fence and spread those butt cheeks. I mean now, dammit!"

I was becoming more and more distraught, but I, like the others, followed orders and faced the fence butt-naked, standing on the sun-baked cement slab that toasted my tender feet.

The verbal attack continued, however.

"Bend over and spread your butt-cheeks, inmates, and keep them open!"

I then observed as the first sergeant zeroed in on a golden-brown offender, watching the humiliation as officers scanned his private areas.

They were probing for weapons, drugs and a host of other contraband. But they seemed to delight in this invasive examination.

When my turn rolled around the guards seemed to troll the cavity of my ass a little longer than average. They then took note of my physical characteristics, including my tightened glutes. Their actions bordered on perversion and voyeurism.

•••••

Suds from the aqua-blue lye soap rolled down my body and that of my fellow offenders as we assembled in a community shower to clean up after sweating in the bruising sun during our processing. As we showered, there was a collective sigh of relief after we were forced to endure a brutal first day in the penitentiary.

While under the water, I noticed from the corner of my eye that same dark-skinned effeminate inmate who was harassed earlier by the prison guards stealing a glimpse of my water-drenched body.

"What the hell are you looking at?" I asked sharply.

He appeared to be embarrassed and totally surprised that I noticed his wandering eyes. He then turned away.

Oddly, I began to notice other offenders satisfying their curiosities, too. They randomly checked out each other's private parts, comparing anatomy or perhaps sizing up each other to separate the strong from the weak, at least from a physical standpoint. This just might be the start of the prison mental game for survival of the fittest, I reasoned.

Whatever the case, the covert actions of most of these men kept the notion alive that black men, in particular, felt that expressions of interests and admiration for another brother were taboo, thus perpetuating homophobia.

After I exited the shower and the peep show, I was housed in a building filled with a mass of metal bunk beds and stainless steel tables. When I entered I observed veteran offenders playing dominoes, chess and Scrabble. Their eyes zeroed in on the newcomers as we unpacked our belongings and placed them underneath our assigned bunks with matching steel lockers.

Hours after an intense intake that frayed everyone's nerves upon our arrival, the day dragged on.

It was now around 4 p.m., and I was still on edge. The entire experience left me drained. Much of that was due to the repulsive behavior of the prison officers from Planet Hell.

As I sat on my metal bunk, I stared blankly because my future seemingly appeared caught in a black hole with loud, boastful men yelling at each other and at whatever was showing on television.

I watched all of this unfold from a distance and was determined to somehow miraculously block out the drama. It was a bit tough because of the competitive board games going on simultaneously and the blaring television monitors mounted high above our heads. The herd of men was gathered in the cell area that resembled a huge warehouse, with bunk beds totaling around 70 lined against each of the four walls.

From the looks of the design of the dayroom, the unit was part of a new innovation. The center of the large housing area was filled with metal tables and benches for games, chow and seating. It was definitely a "new wave unit." I heard that term from imposing, or "ear hustling," on a conversation earlier on the bus from fellow inmates.

Then a moment arose when I was finally able to settle my nerves. But it didn't last long. I was quickly rattled by a noisy commotion when a rambunctious inmate fired off his mouth at someone sitting at a table with him.

"That's bullshit, fool! You cheating!" a towering offender accused as he stood over another with his fist balled, ready to punch out his lights.

I affixed my eyes on these two clowns, both refusing to back down over a dispute about a chess game.

"Hey, G? You got me confused, fool. I ain't cheating," the small light-skinned brother said in his defense. He stood his ground, too, raising himself from his seat to challenge the threat.

As they stared each other down, the dayroom became as quiet as a mausoleum as all attention shifted to the two angry black inmates exchanging boastful words, reminiscent of out-of-control boxer Mike Tyson, and preparing to inflict harmful blows.

Then it started.

Pop! Bam! Whack!

The sounds and images of fists connecting to flesh were startling. Blunt jabs connected to jaws and chests in a mad scramble to declare superiority and scuttle the opponent's ego.

The fight turned even more brutal as another explosive blow rapped the jaw of the large dark-skinned aggressor. It was so powerful that it snapped his head backward, causing him to tumble onto a nearby table and then to the concrete floor, blood spewing from his nose and head.

Wow! Talk about an undisputed knockout of "David and Goliath" proportion.

By the time the alarm rang out, it was over.

"Fight! Fight!" a guard yelled from the other side of a secured enclosure.

Several guards responded, grabbing metal nightsticks from a nearby room equipped with riot gear. The guards, donning body armor and outfitted with tear gas, burst in once the secured metal door was unlocked. They were ready to act indiscriminately.

"Everybody, get on the wall!" a guard, running into the room, ordered.

He exerted his authority yet appeared frightened for his own safety. Who could blame him since he was clearly outnumbered in a roomful of heartless murderers, rapists, robbers and child molesters, to name a few?

As some guards tried to restore calm, their colleagues closely monitored the movements of the victor and other mean-looking offenders, who were spectators.

"Hurry, up! Get on the damn wall!" yelled a guard, standing in the middle of the dayroom. He then ordered the victorious fighter to kneel on the floor with his hands behind his back.

Somewhat reluctant, the brother complied. He undoubtedly was swayed by the show of lethal force.

"Lock him up!" the once-frightened guard ordered. The corrections officer mustered a bit more courage after shackles were placed on the inmate, who was certain to get 30 days in isolation for the altercation. That meant all privileges would be denied, including games, recreation and most reading material – with the exception of the Bible or Koran. Also, there would be no weekend contact visits.

After several officers paraded out of the dayroom area with the violator, only two remained to guard the unconscious inmate – stretched out on the cold concrete floor – as they awaited the medical staff.

The entire commotion left me a little frazzled. It was at this moment that I decided to keep a daily diary of my personal experiences and the surrounding chaos.

For this is my new home – all because of my wayward behavior and the sentence handed down after I confessed to six bank robberies.

Chapter 6
Frowns, Tats and Codes

A man never knows when he is going to run into bad luck. He is like a fish caught in a net or a bird caught in a snare.
Ecclesiastes 9:12

"I'm sorry for the delay in writing you, but quite a lot has been going on. But understand that it's always a pleasure to hear from you. You must still be wondering why I've been delayed? Well, for one, I have been snowed under since recently being elected vice president of the Houston Association of Black Pharmacists."

I smiled, proud of Lazlo and his accomplishments. If anyone deserved to be honored, it was he. I continued reading his letter.

"I've also been trying to get my health checked. Do you remember the times I visited you in county jail and was experiencing abdominal problems? Well, the problem seemed to have persisted for much too long. I was afraid that something serious might have been wrong because of the constant diarrhea. My doctor referred me to a specialist, a gastroenterologist. I had some lab work done and discovered I was mildly anemic. Results did not reveal any other problems with the blood, which also was screened for HIV."

The letter continued as I began to sit upright on my metal bunk bed, thanking God that Lazlo was not HIV-positive. He was one of the blessed men in this lifestyle with a clean blood panel.

"I will learn more about the X-rays during my next appointment. Preparing for my colonoscopy was somewhat unpleasant because I had to ingest a gallon of laxative solution in 1½-hours, restrict my diet and fast for the evening. It was quite uncomfortable.

"Nevertheless, bro, I want you to know that I have not abandoned you like your so-called friend Patrick. I never will. Anyway, stay encouraged. Let me know when I can visit you and how I am listed on the visitation roster. I believe this is the month that you can make revisions, right? Keep in mind that I will be your support system for as long as I can. I love you," the letter ended.

The inspiring message triggered a series of lumps in my throat and tears in the corners of my eyes. I swallowed my pride after reading the letter. But as soon as I rested the letter next to me on my bunk, I noticed a handsome, husky inmate staring my way. Shirtless, his caramel complexion looked irresistibly tasty; his thunder thighs seemed to almost rip through his white prison pants. He could have been the spitting image of former Heisman Trophy winner and NFL standout Hershel Walker. His body was artwork at its best, masterfully chiseled. Anyone standing next to him would easily feel inadequate and threatened because of the frown on his rounded face. It seemed to have killer instinct written all over it. A pit bull of a hunk.

"Say, dude. You got an envelope I can use so I can write my momma?" he asked, standing proudly with his chest swollen like a plump cock.

"Yeah, man," I answered in a deep masculine tone with exaggerated bass that was clearly out of my regular pitch. I then carefully retrieved a stamped envelope from my secured locker-box beneath my metal bunk. I had purchased it several days ago from the commissary.

My kind gesture prompted a change in his attitude and expression.

"Thanks, dude," the titan expressed as a broad smile

swept across his face. "By the way," he paused, "my name is Chrome."

He smiled again. This time he extended his right hand for a firm shake, probably to size me up and test my masculinity. I had learned quickly through observation that this was typical behavior. It was clear that in order to survive in this environment a man must stand his ground – be matter-of-fact, dogmatic and even at times hardcore to repel the human roaches that preyed on the meek.

Without any challenge, the rugged and handsome intruder was satisfied. And so was I. He was hardly an unwelcome intruder. Quite the contrary. Though nervous at first, it was a pure delight to meet someone of his caliber – a mortal man of steel who fit the description of a superhero. Besides me, he, too, appeared satisfied. Indeed, this was a boost to my confidence.

After our meeting, he then bounced, galloping regally throughout the unit and giving others a peek at his proud physical perfection.

Hmmm. Did he just "pull game" on me? Whatever it was, I was almost left breathless by his sheer presence.

But not everyone on the unit appeared to be as amused as I was.

"Say, Chrome! Take off that mask! You ain't nobody. Who you think you foolin'?" a fellow inmate besmirched and shouted across the dayroom, then shot Chrome the bird.

My suspicions were confirmed when Chrome didn't challenge the comments. He just smiled and plodded along his way.

I had just been schooled again on the head games that many inmates play to swindle goods and services from newcomers such as me. No one had ever prepared me for this kind of behavior. I realized I had a lot to learn.

So, I was bamboozled. Luckily, since it was just for a stamped envelope I didn't sweat it. Shortly thereafter, I strolled down to the chow hall for a bite to eat and stood in the controlled serving line. To my surprise, the brown husky inmate Chrome, who hustled me for the envelope, was ahead of me creeping along and displaying his muscles. He profiled from side to side in his bulging shirt in what seemed to be a deliberate effort to show off his extraordinary triceps and biceps. With an up-close look, it became clearer why this fool's alias was Chrome. He sported a tattoo on each arm of his triceps that illustrated massive veined hands with trigger fingers powerfully gripping automatic firearms. This was Chrome's code: Shoot to kill.

Few, if any, words were spoken as we all stood waiting for chow. While it may have been as quiet as a monastery, the tattoos spoke loudly, indicating an association with criminal behavior and the warped attitudes of each offender who came in prison sporting one or acquired during his incarceration. Some of the designs even seemed to suggest which types of people to avoid.

While standing in line, I relished the temporary tranquility. The sign hanging above our heads reminded us that silence was an enforced rule. And most folks complied.

"Attention!" it read. "No talking during chow or you may become the next meal." As we shuffled to our designated seats, our movements were strictly monitored by frustrated prison guards.

With the crowd moving to and fro, I began taking notice of inmates of every racial makeup and their painted body art to better understand their motivation and the motto of the images.

Never before had I seen so many tattooed bodies boasting with pride and code. These dudes were like walking billboards advertising a product. Perhaps, indeed, they had something to sell. Misleading gestures were typical and quite visible anyway. Despite stern looks, prancing and dancing in front of each other were common signs of sexual aggression. These exaggerated body movements were suggestive and often consumed the unit daily. But no one could tell these inmates they were less than real men. They tried to pair their vanity and cavalier attitude with toughness in a bid to convince other inmates and guards they were the "baddest and meanest." For inmates, it was a badge of honor to be feared. The reality is that they were more narcissistic than women. They cared about how they looked and were perceived by others. Some even could be classified as prima donnas.

After getting my food, I watched Chrome as he sat with his fellow militant-type Muslim brothers. They sat left of me praying over their food. Word on the unit was that they were ex-gang members using their faith, Islam, as a cover-up for protection. I also noticed that the guards granted all religious groups the freedom to pray and assemble under the protection of the First Amendment of the Constitution. The tolerance extended to every religious sect, regardless of whether inmates resembled tattooed gang members.

•••••

"Who da hell are you – the welcoming committee?"

To my surprise, this question was posed by that same dark-skinned effeminate inmate who had scoped me out during my shower days ago when we were being processed into the system. But this time he wasn't talking to me.

The target of his verbal attack, just minutes after chow in the recreation yard, was a lighter-complexion dude milling around chatting with various folks and then acting as if he were repulsed by homosexuality.

He picked the wrong target because although the dark-skinned dude was overtly gay, he didn't hold back his tongue either. The quite attractive 6-footer was black as tar and a rambunctious femme. He didn't seem to care much that others knew he liked dick.

His excessive hand and eye movements seemed odd for someone with strong masculine physical features. So, it was even stranger to see him rest his hands on each side of his sturdy hips. His open tight-fitting white prison shirt was lifted a little beyond the waist, resembling a woman's halter. This fool even had a mad six-pack that was quite the envy of the yard. He was really working it.

The lighter-toned inmate stood eye to eye with his interrogator.

"Nah, I'm not the welcoming committee, but I'm everything you ever wanted, sweetcakes."

Oh, I could see where this conversation with these two hardheads was about to go.

"What I really want is for you to get the hell outta my face, Miss Thang!" the gay dude responded. Several other femmes stood close by as if they were part of a posse.

"Leave all those hos alone, fool!" another inmate spectator named Block warned from across the yard.

"School him, Block, cause he gonna step in some shit he can't handle," one from the posse advised. With hips locked and arms tightly folded, he was ready to defend his "sistah."

"For real though," piped another, snapping his fingers and swiftly jerking his head from side to side in a "hey-girl" manner.

The handsome Block intervened to try to keep his fellow fair-skinned "fraternity" brother from getting into deeper trouble with the gay group. He knew the group was not one to back down easily. Block was a very handsome fella, and rumors had it that he was gang banging, among other things, regardless of the consequences. He was part of an avowed ex-gay group called the "Overcomers," known for afflicting harm onto those who disobeyed its protocol. I wasn't sure of the group's purpose.

Block then escorted his big-mouth frat to another side of the recreation yard far from harm's way.

I was in disbelief as I watched the events unfold. For a moment there, the war paint had thickened on the faces of the prison femmes. And speaking of image, their arched eyebrows were as perfect as that of supermodel Naomi Campbell. And their makeup was flawless. Not even the female prison guards could compare.

It was clear that these men by far wielded power and influence. It appeared they had strong connections in order to parade around looking like Valley dolls on testosterone. They seemed to rebel against change despite being confined to this male-dominated environment that prided itself on masculinity. This group was placed in a controlled area that allowed them to carry on in a free-spirited manner.

One thing was certain: Sex is a powerful tool behind prison walls, and the administration knew it. Many men in here had strong sexual desires and some couldn't care less if a person was effeminate.

At the Garza West Transfer facility, like many others, it's understood that "queens" were as much a part of daily life in prison as rival gangs. And they both could be influential.

•••••

Shortly before darkness, the population was ushered back inside the building. It was also mail call, one of the most cherished and anticipated moments for every inmate. The reason was because it was our only way to personally connect with the outside world that included family and friends. Because of the constant rattling of paper, each occasion sounded like Christmas Day, a time when anxious children fiercely and rapidly tear the wrappings off gifts. But in here, the loud tearing meant the opening of envelopes and sifting through pages of letters that created enormous excitement.

It was a delight to watch many sit on their private bunks gleefully reading correspondences from their kids, mothers, friends and significant others. This was the rare moment when noise from the television monitors and running water from showers seemed unobtrusive. The most important and loudest sounds were from papers that talked about momma's and daddy's health, children's grades, sister's marriage, siblings' newborns, neighborhood updates, family sickness and death and expressions of love and future-release reunions. Then there's the extra joy of reading requests by loved ones to send extra money slips so that family and friends can put money on the books for inmates to buy commissary.

Amid the loudness, I sat empty-handed. It was protocol to sit on the bunks while mail was being distributed. When we were free to move, I, along with others who did not receive mail, decided to prepare for a hot shower and shave. After gathering my underwear and other items, I had a sneaking suspicion I was being watched. Looking to my right, I noticed my neighbor staring intently at me. I ignored him and continued toward the wet area with a stone-cold look so hard that I gave myself a headache. The walk to the showers was like a strut down the Soul Train line with bold and secret stares from brothers checking out me and my non-tattooed body, which was rare in prison and placed me in the minority. I stood out like a sore thumb.

After arriving, there were other offenders waiting in corners to shower and near stainless steel sinks shaving.

After a few moments, a voice called out to me.

"Say, man, don't I know you from somewhere?" the light-skinned inmate asked.

"No, I don't think so, dude." I answered harshly to repel his interest.

"You from Houston," he insisted.

"Yeah! I'm from Houston. Why?" I asked with a mild frown.

"So, you don't remember me, huh?" he said, staring with his light-brown eyes. "I met you in the "Trey" (Third Ward) last year at Oz's crib. Do you remember now?" he asked, smiling devilishly and caressing his firm, defined hairless belly that was marked with a Thug Life tattoo in a rainbow formation.

I was hit with a rush of anxiety after now remembering the tattooed inmate. He was the one I referred to as a witch doctor, brewing tainted herbs on a stove from the small kitchen of a crack house in Third Ward last year. During that time I was heavily into crack cocaine and unhealthy sex. And, of course, the bank robberies, too.

"Yeah, I remember you now. What the hell are you doing in here? I thought you had your shit together, man."

I immediately began undergoing a small mental relapse. My stomach churned, and I became light-headed and nervous.

"Got caught selling 'cheese,' man," he said, referring to crack. "Shit happens. But I'll be outta here in 18 months. My lawyer got me a hook-up and then after that I'll be back on the streets slangin' that cheese," he expressed, lowering his white boxer briefs below his knees and exposing his thin firm build. "You gonna shower?" he asked, pointing to an unused spigot.

I wondered if this fool was tempting me with the invitation to shower next to him.

"Yeah!" I blurted out. My heart skipped a few beats as I tried to ignore the youngster's handsome body. After I disappeared into my stall, I told him that we would talk later.

This encounter proved to me that I had to get myself under control. My sexual urges were becoming full-blown again. I was beginning to have a tough time resisting my physical desires. It seemed that no matter how hard I tried my past continued to surface. Reminders of sexual strongholds, misconduct, life on the unforgiving streets and the drug culture and its people pressed me from all angles, even though I was in prison. During my crises in the free world, I had no discipline or victories due to my drifting attitude.

And now evil lurked behind these prison walls in the language, the people, the environment and the lures. This place was consumed with the concept of the "thug life." It seemed to swallow the jailed population. Prisoners, and guards alike, were engulfed by its grip, false glamour and ruthlessness. I was not unaware that those who lived by its code could suffer bitterly for embracing a corrupt culture.

•••••

Since I realized I was going to have plenty of time to waste or write, I decided to start a collection of my thoughts and experiences about being incarcerated. I pulled out my journal and gave it a title. Here's my first entry:

Whuzzup, Diary?

It's my first month in the TDCJ system and never would I have imagined that I would run into anyone in this place I'd associated with on the streets. Nonetheless today proved me wrong. Of all the people to run into, I ran into that little jerk I had met at one of Oz's crack houses. Yeah, Oz – the dark skin drug dealer who likes to sleep with men on the cool. The down-low thang. I should have known he was drilling my fling, Alex, because of his jealous rages toward me whenever the name Alex was mentioned in his presence. Anyway, this little pest from today's shower scene is now suffering the same fate as me. Oddly, I never realized he was so physically defined. It was perhaps due to the baggy pants and athletic shirt he wore when I met him. I shouldn't be too surprised to learn he's on the DL, too, since he was one of the "boys" who worked for Oz – a young and soft-looking drug runner. It's sort of funny how the truth surfaces, huh!
 Later, he approached me after we had showered. We talked for a little while. The dude's eyes were as penetrating as a dog in

heat. He sat across from me at one of the stainless steel tables. All he could talk about was drugs and Oz. That was his world. What an annoying little dude he was. In a way I felt sorry for him. Perhaps because it was obvious that he would soon be someone's little playmate if he didn't toughen up his prison act.

Sometimes revenge is refreshing, especially when it doesn't come from your own hands. I hope I'm not sounding vengeful. Maybe I am. He did, after all, contribute to me getting high.

In the end, it really doesn't matter, because I'm in the same sinking boat as this little guy and the rest of my "prisonmates." We all were sick at some point. And some of us remain that way. After all, this is why we ended up here – not by admission but by omission. I lacked discipline and refused to remove impediments. In short, I never saw victory because of immaturity and childlike behavior.

Nonetheless prison isn't totally what I expected it to be. It's still dark, lonely and hot. While it's definitely not a Club Med, I'm certainly grateful it isn't what it used to be in generations past. I remember the institution in the shadows of corruption during the '60s, '70s, '80s and early '90s. The people in the system ran amuck. It was a time when prison officials routinely covered up brutal murders, rapes and tortures administered by both inmates and guards alike. Medical care was more like "don't care." I remember stories of untrained and unlicensed inmates in Texas performing botched surgeries, setting broken bones and prescribing and dispensing medications. And it took a federal court decision to right those wrongs and vanquish the ghosts of Texas' past.

One final observation: As I sit atop my metal bunk recording this first entry in my prison diary, I can't help but notice the sad eyes of three black offenders. I'm told they're the youngest at ages 20, 19 and 18.

The latter is here for manslaughter of his 9-year-old sister by imitating a killing on the Internet from a site called the "Faces of Death." Apparently, he was influenced to lift his little sister over his head and slam her to the floor. Then he stood on the sofa and crashed down on top of her, crushing her esophagus and cracking her small skull and causing her to hemorrhage.

It was a horrific incident, and the courts ruled that the kid was a threat to society and was beyond counseling. And now he's locked up with conniving and murderous men and does not appear to be getting any psychological therapy to explore his deeper problems.

This makes me question whether prison is the only answer for deterring bad behavior in people with low IQs. For some maybe, but not for all. (End: 9:47 p.m. Day 29)

Chapter 7
Daddy Boy

My son, if sinners entice you, do not give in to them.
Proverbs 1:10

It was April Fool's Day 1998 when each of us inmates was well into our journey to another assigned prison unit. But we were met with a delay that would mean a weekend layover at a neighboring facility, which was at least 20 miles away from our final destination.

The Darrington Unit was a dinosaur of a prison, having been constructed sometime in the early- to mid-1900s. It was roughly 40 miles south of Houston.

I was being transferred closer to my native home because of inadequate health care in the south Texas region. Better-equipped medical units for treating HIV were mostly in progressive areas such as Houston or Dallas. Besides not having a choice in the matter, I welcomed the transfer because I needed my meds in order to stay healthy.

After exiting the white Blue Bird prison bus, we entered the aged building, readying ourselves for another lengthy intake process that would include assigned housing and a temporary cellmate.

Hours later, we crowded inside a small dayroom that normally was used to segregate aggressive inmates. It was originally designed to accommodate 50 men, not the 75 who were now about to be processed. Once complete, we would be free to eat and shower before rack time.

From a far corner, I noticed the dark-skinned Taye Diggs-looking femme staring through my soul, as if he knew what I was thinking and feeling. One thing for sure, he didn't know that I really wanted to beat his sissy ass for the unwelcome gaze. Since I wasn't about to get in trouble, I knew that would be inappropriate behavior. I abandoned the thought. As he stood several feet from me, I noticed how easily it was for him to strike up conversations with others and how the other offenders appeared quite comfortable with him, despite knowing he was a "prison punk." Unlike me, they weren't the least bit paranoid during the friendly chats.

How could this be, I wondered? This effeminate type of guy, despite his muscular physique and sexiness, was my most dreaded nightmare.

I then quickly broke eye contact. I still couldn't understand how anyone could embrace a female impersonator-type in this joint?

As those questions roiled me, a Darrington guard arrived to announce our housing assignments and "cellie," short for cellmate, with whom we would be locked up for the next three days.

"John Thompson and Billy Wittner!" the TDCJ guard yelled.

They were first on the list to be paired together.

I had a few preferences for a cellmate but knew that this was not going to be a democratic process. If given a choice, I wanted someone who was clean, quiet and respectful. Being handsome would be a plus, too.

One thing for sure, I didn't want to be in a cell with anyone who was obviously gay and effeminate. My stomach turned at the thought of that as a possibility. As the pairings continued, I became more and more adamant about the type of roommate I wanted as I looked with disdain at the dark-skinned femme whose name hadn't been called yet either. I was becoming so enraged that I felt I was giving this dude too much power over my thoughts.

I tried pulling myself together and took slow breaths to calm down. After doing this, I realized how discriminating my thinking had become. I had allowed my paranoia to expand wider and sink deeper than ever before toward feminine males.

Reflecting on my past insecurities and fears, I made a strong effort to avoid their company. Like many masculine bisexual men, the girly gestures and body movements were a turnoff to us. I adopted the biased thinking of many roughneck brothers: "If I wanted to be with a woman, I would choose a real one, not a femme!"

With this attitude, my outreach and networking in the gay community was significantly limited, except for a few occasions when I came in contact with a few drag queens in some clubs during my days of exotic dancing.

I was the type of bisexual male who lived as a heterosexual but behind closed doors fancied the gay lifestyle. I knew how difficult it was for a black man to come out of the closet in an intolerant world where black gay men were abused and alienated in their own communities. Some were exiled from families. So, with that said, the last thing I needed was for someone to discover my sexual preference – especially these men in prison. This was not the place for masculine men to have a gay reputation.

Because of this widespread attitude, prison was full of hidden secrets. And it was best to leave it that way. If there were questions about sexuality, you'd be better off being known as a "stud." In prison, this was a bisexual man who played the role of a heterosexual male, but indulged in homosexuality behind closed doors. The distinction would be that the "stud" assumed the aggressive masculine role, with his flamboyant partner as the more submissive type normally associated with females.

Although warped, this thinking seemed to be accepted by

most offenders.

Despite that, I still wanted a roommate I would jibe with pretty well.

Waiting was like being a contestant on the former long-running game show Let's Make a Deal that started airing in the early 1960s in which contestants would gamble for prizes by picking one of three curtains. The right choice could mean a spanking new car. On the other hand, a wrong pick could reveal a dud, such as a live farm animal. It was the element of surprise and risk involved that captured the interests of contestants and viewers.

While I didn't get to choose between a trio of options, the odds still seemed to be in my favor as there were quite a few decent-looking brothers left standing. The suspense was building, my anxiety indescribable.

So, it was after the 20th name was called when I learned who my cellie would be.

I only knew a few people. And that was by their prison aliases only. Real names were not commonly used. So, when the name Barry Williams was called, I didn't have a clue who he was or what he might look like. As feet moved and people shuffled about to make room for the shorter inmate, I began to get my answer.

My entire body locked up and went into shock: paralysis in my legs, a gradual sinking spirit, a seemingly ruptured heart, a breath-stealing revelation. My head dropped into my chest.

"Ohmigod! It's him," I said, stunned.

Barry Williams: dark-skinned, handsome, muscular and ... the femme!

My dreadful thoughts had come to haunt me. I felt that my reputation would become tarnished.

As far as I was concerned, this deal was indeed a dud.

When I got the nerve to look at him again, Barry appeared to be elated. But I was in total despair.

Oddly, this event is reminiscent of a nightmare I had a year ago involving a female impersonator. I was sitting in a strange room engaging in a controversial conversation about the differences between gay men. Being vocal and adamant about my views, I caused a stir with some in the room who were participating in the debate when I said that most femmes are boisterous and clowns and that they would do anything for the attention of a man and a hard dick.

I dug myself a deeper hole when I added they were too extreme and always caused havoc, similar to an unrepentant sinner who continues a behavior even after repeated warnings.

As I railed on and on, one such femme suddenly stormed out of a back room and pointed a pistol to my head.

Without even a greeting, he pulled the weapon's trigger and the sound rippled throughout the room.

POW!

I tilted like an unstable ship listing on its side before crashing onto the floor. I lay sideways, spewing blood with the intensity of a fire hydrant struck by a wayward driver.

I couldn't move as my body had become lifeless. As I lay dying, I began falling into an abyss. That's when I awoke from the nightmare.

Ever since then, I have been terrified of most female impersonators and femmes alike.

I couldn't rationalize in my mind why God would put me in this situation with Barry. I didn't want this. I didn't ask for it. Could there be a reason?

"Sure, God, I have biases, low tolerance and little patience for certain types of people, but this is a bit extreme, don't you think?" I asked.

From what I can tell, there was no response from the Almighty.

And if this was somebody's attempt at a sick joke, I was not finding it quite funny.

In the end, since I couldn't change the outcome, I tucked

my tail and went along. Perhaps, just maybe, a lesson would come of this. I wasn't optimistic, though.

Even so, I do have to remember that I, too, am one of these "throwaways" as deemed by the public. Crimes committed by my fellow inmates may be different from mine, but many of us shared other experiences such as drug addictions.

My late grandmother, affectionately known as Big Momma," admonished us about "the pot calling the kettle black," a hypocritical stance of someone with a fault insulting someone else with a flaw.

Remembering this, I sought to calm myself even if I were still miffed at discovering I would have an effeminate roommate.

Knowing that it was a done deal, my cellmate and I glanced at each other and left together to our assigned housing area without mumbling a word.

The next three days would be the beginning of another first for me.

•••••

Days after my meds were delivered, I still had not spoken a word to my cellie, who was asleep on the top bunk. Although my stomach was growling, my mind shifted to the 6-foot, 9-foot cell, which reeked of urine. I lie on the bottom bunk still thinking of ways to avoid speaking to my unwanted cellmate, wishing instead that I could have been teamed with a more desirable "young buck" who might be easily influenced into having sex. I knew this was sick thinking, but I still wrestled with unresolved issues by using sex to cope with loneliness.

Just as I thought about how quiet it had been, a voice echoed through the dusty three-level prison wing unit.

"Chow time, everybody. Get ready for chow!" a prison guard yelled, entering the wing and dangling large metal keys for entry into the main area that controlled the cell doors.

Accompanying the guard was a Darrington social services inmate, or SSI, pushing from floor to floor a large stainless steel warmer filled with noontime chow.

Being a light sleeper, my cellie acknowledged the call and rolled over from his sleep, yawning and squealing like the sissy he was.

"Uh! Faggot!" I uttered quietly.

"Was that chowwww?" he purred, giving dramatic emphasis on the word. As he sat up, his feet dangled toward my head below.

One thing for sure, the fool had pretty feet for a man. Thank goodness they didn't smell.

Reluctantly, I spoke for the first time, but dryly.

"Yeah, that was the chow call." I then rose from my bunk, grabbing my toothpaste and face towel, and headed to the sink that was a couple feet away to wash my face and hands with the harsh blue state-issued soap with an awful chemical odor.

"Damn! That toilet stinks. Don't it?" asked my cellie, attempting to start a conversation.

When I didn't respond immediately, he moved to the head of his bunk with his pretty, but dry feet still hanging from the side of the bunk. Oddly, I was a bit envious at how well-groomed they were.

"Yeah, it stinks," I said in a reserved tone.

"Well, I know how to solve that problem. I'll just work that SSI who's feeding chow when he gets up here. He'll get me some cleanser and shit. Watch me work him, baby," said Barry, with a snap-snap of his thin fingers. The sound reverberated throughout the wing.

Taking some interest, I acknowledged him again but not as pointedly or harshly as before.

"Oh, yeah? How you gonna get anything out of him with that guard escorting and watching him?"

"Take notes, baby. Just watch me work my jelly."

He leaped from the top bunk and prepared his quest.

After I flushed the toilet and finished washing my face and brushing my teeth, I moved to my original position on my bottom bunk without making eye contact with Barry.

Someone on the unit familiar with Barry's voice must have realized that he wasn't asleep anymore.

"Say, Kiki!" a strange voice blurted out from the cellblock among the other offenders' voices. Seemed everyone had gotten wind of the news that chow was being served. You could hear the wagon squeal its way throughout the block.

"Yeah!" responded Barry, who I just learned goes by the name Kiki. His high-pitched voice was undeniably irritating. After he washed his face and brushed his teeth, he pranced forward toward the cell bars for a better ear reception from the caller.

"Girl! You finally got up?" the other caller asked in an equally annoying tone that's not generally heard from a man's larynx.

Talk about "real." These two squeamish dudes take the cake.

"Girl, yeah! I'm trying to get cleaned up, child!" Kiki yelled.

"Sistah girl, what's goin' on with that big beautiful black Cadillac? Is it running yet?"

"Girl, I don't even know. I tried to get it started, but I think the motor is messed up," responded Kiki, moving back toward the sink and slyly glancing in my direction.

I caught on quickly, realizing that Kiki and his friend were referring to me – with my body being the black Cadillac and my narrow mind being the motor.

I began to wonder why all the femmes in prison adopted names such as Kiki, Pinky and Fluffy. I remember my first gay bar experience where my old, now long-lost, friend Patrick had taken me a year or so ago. The emcee there was named Kiki, too. But these two were like day and night.

Anyway, my cellie and his friend continued to talk in code.

"Girl, keep trying. It may crank!" he said, laughing loudly.

"I suppose! But I wouldn't hold my breath on it!" Kiki yelled.

I was amused by their intelligently coded conversation. Quite clever, I thought. I was definitely being schooled.

"Chow! Second row!" The guard yelled from the floor beneath us. He would soon be making his round to our level, where inmates snickered and chortled like hyenas at the coded conversation between Kiki and his friend. All the other offenders were hip to this language, too, and got a kick out of it. They were slapping high-fives and everything. Some were literally rolling on the floor.

"Say, Nikki!" Kiki called out to his friend, giving a name to the other voice.

"Yeah, girl!"

"Did you see that red Firebird earlier being cleaned at the car wash?" asked Kiki, laughing silly.

"Girl, yes! That's the kind I like, minus those ugly ass tires!"

"Girrrrrrrrrl. Wasn't those tires bad?" asked Kiki, referring to the feet of a light- skinned black inmate they had noticed in the shower shortly after intake.

"Girl, yes! And those chrome rims were rusty and had corroded – unlike what you'd expect of quality Vogues and Spinners. Those bad tires messed up the whole body of the car," explained Nikki, casting derision on the inmate for having ugly toenails from fungus buildup. "What a turnoff."

"Girl, you a mess. What you expect on a used car? Certainly not Pirellies," laughed Kiki, referring to the high-end tires outfitted for expensive performance vehicles.

"Hell, yeah!" an eavesdropping inmate offered.

"Sistah, who was that?" asked Kiki, sounding a bit annoyed by the intruder.

"Who do you want it to be?" said the strange inmate, teasing and laughing.

"Someone you can't be!" Kiki shouted. Then he snapped his thin fingers once again just as loudly as before.

"Well, all rightttttt!" said Nikki, laughing as chow approached.

"Chow! Third row!" the guard announced as he plodded behind the SSI issuing plastic cups and eating utensils to each cell. The SSI moved slowly with the chow cart that carried hot food on warmed blue plastic trays.

After getting my permission, Kiki sat on my bottom bunk for a quick moment so he could make his move. He crossed his thin legs before the chow cart approached.

I sat near the smelly toilet figuring out what my cellie and his accomplice, Nikki, were up to. I chuckled in amazement as Kiki prepared to "work" the SSI.

"What?" Kiki asked me rhetorically, knowing that I was on to his game.

"Y'all are damn fools," I said, laughing at their ridiculous behavior before the approaching handsome SSI would appear at our cell bars to issue two plates of chow.

Wearing only white boxers, Kiki grabbed his tray, which is kept inside the cell, and returned to his top bunk, crossing his hairy legs as the SSI got nearer. He laid his plastic plate to his right and told me to get on my bunk so the guard wouldn't harass me for being out of place. He explained the logistical reason behind the request, saying that once the guard passes by a cell ahead of the SSI, he does an ID check and head count. For that reason, it was best to be on your own bed.

Kiki then asked me if I had a pseudonym, or aka. He wanted to know what other name I used beside my last name.

I told him Moe, short for Morris.

As the SSI arrived, Kiki got in "work" mode.

"Psst! I got a deal for ya later, OK?" said Kiki, winking at the SSI, who had thick-dark lips. It was also evident that the SSI was a smoker. While watching the guard's every move, the SSI secretly nodded in agreement. He then continued his journey down the third row distributing chow and juice to each cell.

"A `daddy boy' " uttered Kiki, referring to the SSI, who was not within earshot of the insult.

I wasn't sure what a "daddy boy" was, but I aimed to find out later. I still wasn't totally comfortable talking to my cellie just yet.

As I prepared to eat on my bottom bunk, I kept hearing crumbling sounds coming from Kiki's bed. I couldn't quite figure it out, but my curiosity was getting the best of me. So, I got up from the bed and pretended to need some paper, specifically toilet paper, to wipe my mouth after breakfast since there were no paper towels. As I glanced toward Kiki, I noticed that he was removing Cheetos from their bags and then cleverly replacing them with rolled cigarettes.

One bag, in particular, held at least 20 smokes that were concealed inside before being resealed. This was the bounty that Kiki had promised the SSI who delivered the food earlier and would do just about anything for a cigarette.

I had just been schooled on the power of illegal contraband and the influence one can have over others, especially if the item was in high demand.

As I sat back on my bunk to finish eating my prison chow, I queried my cellie.

"So, that's how you do it, huh?" I asked, amazed at the witty Kiki.

"Yes, child. This is how it's done. Keep your eyes open, baby, for that guard. You'll learn a lot from ol' Kiki." After he finished stuffing and resealing the chip bags, he began to eat his meal. We then waited patiently for the right moment to seal the deal with the SSI, who seemed to know all too well how the prison game operated.

INTERNAL CHAOS

•••••

Oooh! Phew! Oooh! Phew!

Loud sounds rippled through our cell as Kiki maneuvered inside struggling, panting and pressing against the metal bars on this third and final day at the dreadful Darrington Unit. It was hot and sticky on this late afternoon with our bodies cramped in the small 6-foot, 9-foot cell. Despite the stifling conditions, the cell was clean — thanks to Kiki and his survival, or seductive, skills.

"Come on, Kiki. Harder!" I ordered.

"Oooh, Oooh! I'm trying, Moe!" said Kiki, using my nickname.

"Come on, man. You're almost finished. Hit it harder. Harder!" I shouted while grinning at his feminine ass trying to show his grit.

"Oooh! Oooh! I can't, Moe!" continued Kiki, through pain and anguish.

With Kiki squealing louder and louder, our nosy neighbor Nikki broke his silence.

"Heeeeeey! It sounds like love to me, sistah girl! What's goin' on down there?" asked Nikki, yelling and teasing from his cell.

"Oooh, child! This man is killing me, sistah! I can't take it anymore."

"Girl you need help!" asked Nikki, laughing.

"Girl, no! I'm almost finished with these dreadful leg squats. Oooh! This man is brutal."

Kiki then finished with a long sigh of relief — releasing his grip from the cell bar, which was used to support his lower body as he squatted in position.

With all the commotion, Nikki was puzzled.

"Squats! When did you start working out, girl?" he asked.

"Today, baby," said Nikki, snapping his fingers that sent a familiar echo through the unit.

I was about tired of that finger-snapping crap. It was really getting old.

"Well, all riiiiiiight!" roared Nikki.

I sat on my bunk laughing at the silliness of these two girly companions whose behaviors seemed to mimic clowns in a circus act. They were funny, and it was good to actually laugh again.

•••••

As I waited for recreation time, I settled onto my bed while listening to many of the conversations swirling around the cellblock from boisterous inmates. Most subjects were on the topic of drug selling and the manipulation of women, who were influenced to join their many schemes. For some guys, that meant having one "honey," or girlfriend, on the northside of town carrying their babies and living in Section 8 housing and other "hos," as they called them, slinging dope and managing drug houses on the southside and westside of Houston. All of this was for a measly payout of occasional sex and a little cash for trips to local malls to buy imitation designer wear and handbags.

The boastful inmates couldn't care less that some folks who were forced to listen were irritated by the bragging, much of which could not be validated anyway.

I wondered why these men seemed so bent on devaluing women. They seemed to objectify them. In some cases, they acted as if they were misogynists, hating everything about them. I wondered if they viewed their own mothers and sisters the same. How would they react if the women in their families were degraded and sexually assaulted? What about strange men belittling their daughters?

I couldn't forget about the sons of these men, either. Will they continue the vicious cycle of disrespecting women and ultimately end up in prison like their fathers? Unfortunately, the odds were not in their favor as many now were being raised in single-family households with mothers serving dual roles.

It was only when I heard Kiki's high-pitched voice that I was able to snap out of my doldrums. I knew that I was going to have to quickly learn to block annoying shouts and yells from surrounding cells. Otherwise, these idiots were going to stir up anger inside me like a swarm of bees ready to attack for tampering with their hive.

"Moe-eee," said Kiki, stretching out my name.

"Yeah," I responded.

"You got children? A son or daughter?" asked Kiki.

It seemed Kiki might have been listening to the chaotic talk about women and drugs, too. I realized that there was a great divide between us that needed to be bridged. I was carrying around a heavy burden of hatred, too. My thoughts about female impersonators and femmes had been weighing me down and tormenting me. At one point, I thought nothing could be more painful until I remembered how ancient Romans punished killers. Back then, the murderer would be conjoined with the dead victim, attached feet to feet, hand to hand and face to face until the body rotted.

It was a constant reminder of the horror of sin and death and how they both eat at you and infect the body. I knew I had to change my views about people, especially individuals such as Kiki and Nikki. Who in the hell was I to judge anybody?

For all practical purposes, Kiki and I were conjoined as temporary cellmates. So, it was best that we got along.

With that, I suddenly had an intelligent thought that maybe there was a divine reason for this temporary lodging with Kiki. Perhaps, it was an opportunity to teach me a lesson about tolerance and get a crash course on prison life.

After a pause, I finally answered Kiki's question.

"Nah, I don't have any kids. You?"

Kiki, also pausing for several seconds, gave an answer I

didn't expect.

"Unfortunately yes," he said sadly.

"Why did you say it like that? You love your kids, don't you?" I asked. He really piqued my curiosity now.

"A kid. I only have one."

"My bad." I apologize. "Boy or girl?"

"Boy. And, of course, I love him. But I'm incarcerated. I'm sick at heart that I can't be out there with him. He needs me in his life. I'm the one who's the screw-up and the deadbeat dad," he said.

Kiki's gloom seemed to cast a dark cloud over the once-bubbly aura of the cell. But once he said he had a son, one of my first thoughts was whether the kid even knew his daddy was gay and unabashedly effeminate. And if he knew, how did he cope with it. I wasn't sure how far to probe, so I decided to play it cool.

"When was the last time you saw him?" I asked.

"Ohmigod! It was three years ago. His mother decided it was best because of my condition," said Kiki, with his hands resting across his body and his voice hardening for a change.

This was odd because Kiki's mannerism and voice often matched his girly persona, but this time the two actions offered a rare incongruent moment of a man who appeared damaged and vulnerable.

"What do you mean when you say 'because of your condition,' " I asked.

"Look at me, Moe! I'm a femme, child! The boy is 10 now, but during the time he was younger he didn't know what a 'punk' looked like. Of course, I didn't look like this then, either. I was into the woman thing and all. I dated them. But some women can be so possessive. My girlfriend was 17 then, and I was a year older. I remember asking her if I could put her on layaway," said Kiki.

He laughed, and so did I.

"I was strictly about the females then, even though I was

fighting feelings for the same sex. I wanted to be with her, Moe. Still, though, I can't let my son see me like this. No way, no how."

"Why not?" I asked.

"Because! Because I'm not comfortable with it, and I'm still not sure I'm comfortable with him seeing me this way."

"So why can't you change? I mean you haven't always been ... I mean acted like this?" I said. I was a bit hesitant because I wanted to choose my words carefully and to understand Kiki's situation.

"I was turned out in prison. But I always knew that I liked men on the cool, but I wouldn't let it show out there in the world. Most guys loved to be around me and I around them. We would act butch and do our little dirty things in secret and move on until the next time. You know it hurts to be in hiding and to know that you are an embarrassment to your own child and your family. But I had to come out," Kiki exclaimed as his sullen voice echoed from his top bunk. "It really hurts, baby, but I refuse to be sad and lonely. I realized that I had to look at myself in-depth if I ever wanted to be happy. I knew I had feelings for the same sex but suppressed them."

"Do you love him, man?" I asked.

"What kind of question is that? Hell, yes, I love him! I just hate that I can't do anything for him like a normal father would do for a son. Teach him phonics, respect and all and let him know that he possesses intellectual capital."

Though I was not face to face with Kiki as he talked, I sensed that he was a serious intellectual himself. Over the years, I had run into many brilliant gay men and more than my share of stupid straight men.

"Intellectual capital, huh?" I said as I leaned on the back wall desperately trying to understand Kiki's dilemma.

"Hell, yeah! Most of these guys in here aren't aware of their intellectual assets. Many are lonely and hurt, have not been taught how to respect life and people and are wasting their talents. When I get out of here I'm going fishing. Oh, how I would love to take him fishing one day," said Kiki.

He grabbed his rec cloths, sensing that the time was near for outdoor activities.

"I made a promise years ago to myself that I would mold my boy to be a respectable man, a God-fearing man unlike some of these nut-heads in here."

"Yeah, I know what you mean, man. Still, how do you know your boy would be embarrassed by you?"

"I know because of the environment he lives in. He and his momma live in Section 8 apartments where there are a lot of kids and stupid-ass uneducated folk. Mostly our people, Moe. And many have no tolerance for gay people, let alone a femme like me," said Kiki, his voice becoming somewhat faint. "Moe, the last thing I want is for my boy to end up in a place like this with people like those out there," he said, pointing to the steel bars and referring to nearby inmates hollering throughout the unit.

"What makes you think there is even a possibility he could end up here?"

"For one, he lives in a ghetto community. You already know what's up with some of those places. Most are filled with welfare recipients, not to mention engaging in fraudulent activities. My boy don't need to be around that kind of madness, neither the drugs or the bullshit that come with it."

As I digressed a bit, I began to think that if Kiki had taken care of his business like a responsible man, maybe his family wouldn't be in the situation they're in now. So, I wondered, who really was at fault? It was probably inappropriate for me to think like this, but I felt that Kiki shared part of the blame.

Anyway, I decided to ask him about the family structure.

"Is she a good mother? I mean does she take time out with the boy and teach him the difference between right and wrong? The difference between good men and bad?" I asked.

"She's struggling to stay in college right now. But she tells me she ain't gonna give up on him, no matter what happened in the past with me. She says I'm still the boy's daddy."

"So she accepts your gayness?" I asked, thinking it to be an ignorant question.

"As sure as I am black, child!" he said, trying to make light of the situation. "My main concern is to make sure my boy gets an education and stay out of trouble. I pray every night he don't drop out of school later down the road, or join some damn gang. You know what I mean, Moe?"

"I feel ya, Kiki, but it's all up to you and how you present yourself to him."

Kiki also expressed that he didn't want the kid to be without the things he needed in life and that he knew he had to make a compromise for the boy's sake – perhaps a lifestyle change. He wanted to make sure that the boy didn't experience some of the same shit Kiki went through when he was a boy.

"What happened with you when you were smaller?" I asked, puzzled but sensing the worst.

"Day after day when I was a kid the only things that filled our fridge was a jug of water, a jar of mustard, mayonnaise and a lot of molded bread. Do you know what's it like to eat a mayo sandwich on a piece of funky molded bread for a week?"

As I listened to Kiki, I realized that I couldn't even comprehend the idea because as a child I wanted for nothing. My mom and dad were there for my four siblings and me. Even though at times we didn't have everything we wished for, we were always fed well and properly clothed.

"I can't imagine," I told Kiki.

"You're not alone. A lot of people can't. You see, there's a problem. And the problem is growing up poor. A lot of our young people are in poverty because of prejudice from the elite that cause many black kids to commit crimes and drop out of school because they can't see hope in their future.

They're feeble-minded, easily led astray and become angry at their condition and society for failing them."

"Was that you – that angry young male?"

"Yeah, that was me. I took my anger out on those who ignored me and my poverty. Hell, in the ghetto most kids can't help but be angry, loud, tough-acting and hard. It was a way to survive. Do you know how hard it was for me not to kill somebody, or even hurt somebody out there – or even in here – throughout the years?"

"Nah, man. I don't. I couldn't even imagine the thought of killing someone," I replied.

"Well, that's good. You should count your blessings, because a lot of these guys in this prison can. It was hard waking up every damn morning knowing that you didn't have clean clothes to wear to school, money to buy a hot school lunch or even a lunch to take to school. That shit was hard on a kid, Moe. I was that kid. I watched my welfare momma turn tricks and then spend the damn money on alcohol and dope," an emotional Kiki said. "That shit messed me up. So I ran away and stayed with my cousin. And it was no better there. They were dirt po', too – no food, no clothes, no hope. So I went back to my momma, who had no man there to guide us. Sometimes, I even wished I had a dad who would just beat my ass."

It seemed Kiki hated those who failed the poor, but there seemed to have been a hint of self-hatred, too.

I began to wonder if he ever knew his real father. It didn't seem that he had a dad who ever took him fishing or camping. It was apparent that he never experienced watching his dad make homemade ice cream like my father used to do and then allow me to have a "tease taste" just before it was ready. I remembered how my younger brother, Troy, and I would watch our dad use a wooden ice cream maker with a crank that would slowly turn the milky contents into sweet cream. Even now the sounds of the rock salt echoes in my ear. I regretted that Kiki never experienced such things.

His talk about growing up in the ghetto left me flabbergasted. I knew the ghetto was hard. Hell, I was even raised there the first 10 years of my life, but I had never experienced what Kiki and many of today's prisoners experienced. My childhood was mostly civil and happy at times. Of course, there were occasions when I thought my dad and mom didn't love me. But most kids go through that phase of life when they think parents are too strict. But never had my dad abandoned the family or my mom. He didn't cheat or drink around his children or even gamble.

The revelations by Kiki momentarily left me speechless. I then pressed him further.

"Do you blame your mom or dad for your incarceration?" I asked hesitantly.

"Moe, I can't blame nobody but me. I did have choices, even though I did live in poverty. I survived, didn't I? And, yeah, I did finally finish school, so I have no right to fault or blame my momma. She was abandoned, too. She was left with two kids, a drug habit and no hope."

"So, where does that leave your little boy?" I asked.

"He'll be led in the right direction, Moe. I know he will. His momma don't do drugs, smoke or cuss. She's struggling, but she is a survivor. A damn good survivor."

"So, she's not paranoid?" I asked.

"Paranoid? Paranoid about what?"

"Paranoid that if your son sees you this way he may catch what you have. Ain't that's how a lot of straight people think? They think that "we" have — whatever that is — a contagious disease."

"We? Did you say we?" barked Kiki, who nearly fell from his top bunk. "Child, you family?" he asked excitedly after my unintentional slip of the tongue. He then leaned from his bunk and stared into my brown eyes, asking, "You in the game?"

After my gaffe, I almost wanted to rip out my tongue and sew my lips together. Of course, I was only halfway serious.

"Yeah, Kiki. I'm bisexual," I said, feeling strange admitting it. But I knew confession was good for the soul. "Say, Kiki. Let's keep this between us, OK?" I requested as I eased forward and looked up at Kiki. I knew that I could learn a lot from him. But am I really willing?

"Child, yo' secret is safe with me," he giggled slightly. "So, the motor in that black Cadillac is good after all?"

Silently, we laughed, still absorbing all the yells and jeers from other inmates about sex, money, hos and drug-dealings.

With my sexuality now exposed, I probed my cellie for an answer to an earlier statement.

"Kiki, I have one question."

"What's that?"

"What in the hell is a `daddy boy' "?

Kiki laughed before answering.

"It's a boy who doesn't mind being a "top" or "bottom" during sex. In other words, a "flipper," answered Kiki, gesturing with a flip of the right wrist. "Don't confuse it with a prison hustler who would do just about anything to make ends meet."

"Yeah, I understand now. Hustling is more of a reaction to life," I said.

When I was on the streets I learned the mind-set of the hustler. And now I have been educated about "daddy boys." The expression has even more relevance to me now because I guess I would be considered a "flipper" by these guys' standards.

It would seem that prison jargon was just the tip of the iceberg in my indoctrination into prison life.

•••••

With Easter just days away, the dayroom rec area was all abuzz and festive. It provided an ideal backdrop for the ever-vivacious Kiki and Nikki, who both were delighted to mock the approaching Christian observance with their own brand of humor.

After they exited their cells, they made a grand entrance as if they were making a special ballroom appearance. At first glance, Nikki was not at all what I expected. Matter of fact, he was more like eye candy. He was 5-feet, 9-inches tall with alluring gray eyes and an attractive masculine build that easily won him attention. His clean-cut boyish looks made him even more intriguing and mysterious. If his entrance was designed to stimulate, he more than succeeded as all eyes were affixed on him. And you could tell that he loved every bit of it. He was, indeed, the center of attention.

"Ummm, Kiki. Look at all the Easter baskets in here, girl," Nikki joked.

I stood nearby looking for the treats Nikki seemed to gloat over. As I followed his eyes, I quickly caught on to the joke. After laughing at him, I began to chuckle to myself for being such a dimwit.

The reference to Easter baskets was a clever way of describing the abundance of attractive men gathered in the first-level dayroom participating in games and reminiscing about their past.

The play on words seemed to be common among prison offenders, especially those who thought they had game. Coded conversations shielded their secrets.

Daisy and Duke, well actually Kiki and Nikki, continued their strut through the dayroom.

"Yeah, child. There's that red Firebird over there you were salivating over earlier. You gonna work it, sistah?" Kiki asked.

"Watch me play man with him, child," said Nikki, laughing. "I'll hit him with the girl act afterward to let him know that

I'm up for grabs."

Nikki slowly walked toward the handsome youngster to explore his intelligence and sexuality.

I smiled broadly as I watched how the game was played against the so-called roughnecks by the so-called weak and submissive prison punks.

Nikki slowly inspected the young lad then approached him tactfully. Nikki was a "daddy girl," the opposite of a daddy boy. He liked being handled roughly. He didn't use his tool, only his saddle. And, man, was his saddle plump. Even with that, he wasn't my type. No way, no how. He was way too feminine and too damn pink for my flavor.

As Kiki stood by with folded arms and taking note of Nikki's approach, I approached Kiki with an offer.

"Yeah, what's up, Moe?" asked Kiki, who never took his eyes off Nikki.

"Wanna be my partner in a game of dominoes on the next up?" I asked with ease. I actually surprised myself even though I was a little paranoid of what some may think of my association with him. But I convinced myself that most in here were probably entertaining another man for their own fulfillment anyway. I was certain that many had hidden agendas and were sleeping with men, too.

With that in mind, I was emboldened to become more assertive and hard-core to gain respect. I knew I couldn't show any fear or hesitation after watching Nikki's successful bait to land his catch.

"Me? Your partner? Sure!" said Kiki, with wide-open eyes. After proudly accepting my invitation, he quickly transferred his attention to me now. He then moved even closer toward me as I observed the strategy of four dominoes-playing inmates slamming, scoring, boasting and placing their ivory rectangular pieces on the table.

The game of dominoes is a prisoner's favorite pastime to help offset boredom. But the game being cooked up by Nikki and Kiki had even more serious implications, not to mention the risks involved.

The two were quite successful, though, in drumming up interest from their targets, the red "Firebird" and the SSI. How they were going to pull off having sex in prison was a mystery – at least to me.

Chapter 8
The Transfer

Of what value is an idol, since a man has carved it?
Or an image that teaches lies.
    Habakkuk 2:18

My stint at the Darrington Unit had ended, and I had now arrived at the Ramsey Two prison facility, about 45 miles south of Houston. Once inside, I immediately felt the heat. The sun beamed through the opened barred windows when I arrived in the dayroom at 10 a.m. On a clear day like today, it was evident that the mercury was going to rise even more.

As I waited for my next orders, I wandered into the hazy, dusty dayroom, daydreaming about my ex-wife, Tish. Fine streams of dust floating through the spring air were noticeable when the particles mated with the sun.

It took a while but I successfully completed the newest orientation process, which was more like intimidation and interrogation.

I had to sit across from the assistant warden and a lunatic lieutenant who had the gall to question me about my six bank robberies.

"So, you like robbing banks, huh?" he asked, arrogantly sucking his teeth from across the table. The assistant warden just looked on and noted my reaction.

I answered "no" to Lieutenant RideOut, a handsome dark-skinned man about 40 years old, who reportedly wore tight pants all the time. But he did have one physical flaw, a bad case of razor rash on the nape of his neck.

I sensed that this dude was going to be a force to reckon with in the months ahead.

His cavalier attitude continued until I was given permission to leave.

I had been assigned housing and a job. I was placed in a category called Three Hoe. Even though it was a medical squad, it still involved agricultural labor using a garden hoe known as an "Aggie." I was told that the tool would be used to chop, cultivate and dig areas for crops under the command of an armed guard atop his horse.

My mind then drifted to the madness within this containment facility. It was marked by turbulent sounds from inmates near and far.

I had learned that this unit, about six months earlier, had a 65 percent homosexual population. It was filled with feminine men like Kiki, my former cellmate from the Darrington transfer facility.

While sitting inside the Ramsey dayroom, I sat next to an inmate who invited himself into a conversation with me, griping about how his cellie was taking advantage of him and his kindness by using up his commissary of junk food and personal hygiene products.

It was apparent to me that this inmate was one of the few gay men left behind from the exodus, perhaps because of his good conduct record and not-so-obvious effeminate ways. At least that was his claim. He suggested that he could easily assimilate into the heterosexual environment but still "cross over" to the gay side when necessary.

I'm told that the former majority gay population had refused to work on the farm even when ordered to labor just two days a week. Although non-compensated work was part of the punishment in Texas prisons, the gay majority was not having any part of it. It's rumored that they literally ran the facility and did things their way or no way at all.

Urban legend or not, the word is that during the gay-rule days, anyone – including guards or straight inmates – who got out of line by hurling insults or starting physical altercations became targets of violence by vengeful homosexuals.

One past incident seemed to have landed in the infamous hall of fame. Apparently, one summer there was a particular white male guard who confiscated a cache of cosmetics from a prison drag queen he didn't like. Shortly thereafter, a power struggle ensued because of the prison diva's popularity. Oddly, guards, inmates and the warden's civilian staff all liked him.

As hard as I tried, I couldn't imagine a person wearing the title of Miss Gay Congeniality in prison and, furthermore, outranking a guard, who would eventually find himself on the defense one hot summer. Well, this particular femme wielded great power.

The tale is that it started out quiet on the C-block wing, where I now reside, as nightfall consumed the small town of Rosharon. Later at 11 p.m., many of the inmates were sound asleep on their iron bunks amid the sweltering mid-80s heat and humidity. I imagined sweat pouring down their faces, much like now. I'm told not all were sleeping during that hour.

It appeared some of them were waiting for a particular guard to return from his scheduled break. He eventually returned to C-14 cellblock sipping a hot cup of instant coffee, even with the night temperature well above average. As he entered the officer's closet near the entry gate, he placed his steamy beverage on one of the closet shelves while he checked his roster and slowly plodded down the first floor of C-14 for his routine inmate headcount.

Midway through his journey, a loud sound of breaking glass overhead jolted him. Before it crashed to the floor, he leaped out of harm's way with his back turned to a series of barred cells. As he caught his breath, he turned and noticed that the broken glass had fallen from a second-level window in the middle of the long walkway. His nose then caught a whiff of something strange, but he couldn't quite figure out the odd smell.

It would seem this was just the beginning of his troubles as chaos instantly filled the unit. Laughter and profanity eventually woke up other inmates.

"You trailer-park trash!" one inmate screamed angrily to the guard.

"Get outta here, ho'!" another yelled.

Amid the barrage of insults came a deafening cry from the guard.

"Aarghhhh! Aarghhhh! Help me! I'm burning! Aarghhhh! I'm burning," he pleaded. He ran down the first floor toward the barred gate seeking help, screaming and gasping.

The Ramsey guard was covered with a boiling homemade cocktail of human feces, Blue Magic hair grease and urine. When the mixture splashed onto the guard's head, arms, legs and clothes, it stuck like tar and feathers.

Amid the cry of anguish and agony by the guard was a cry of laughter from the inmates.

"That'll teach you, bitch! Haha! You'll learn to keep your hands off other people's property!" one prisoner said about the cosmetics.

"Aha! You see!" another said, "We play for keeps down here! You gonna learn how to submit, white boy!"

The stifling air was fouled by the yucky blend of human waste and grease.

Surprisingly, there were other guards on duty but none willing to assist their comrade. It's believed that the tight-pants wearing Lieutenant RideOut was working during that shift. After the incident, there was no retaliation from prison authority.

That attack apparently sent a strong message to other guards and any of the straight inmates who dared to challenge the gay majority.

After sharing that story, the annoying inmate sitting next to me was determined not to leave me alone.

"Say, Moe! You still listening?" he asked.

"Yeah, man. I was just thinking about something," I said as I gazed out the window and noticed a large cat believed to have been adopted by the unit offenders.

"Yeah, about what?" he inquired, intentionally staring into my eyes.

"About how this place used to be," I said, without making reference to it being a former farm for punks. I didn't want to speak too openly, realizing that that very language could get me into some form of altercation. I knew I had to choose my words wisely around certain offenders.

My fellow inmate must have known what I was referring to because he took the ball and ran with it.

"Yep, the punks had it goin' on. Everybody was afraid of them, even the punk-ass warden. But not Lieutenant RideOut. He had this power over most of them. It could be because he wore his pants so damn tight. I don't know. He knew how to play his cards right. But I'm tellin' ya, watch your back. RideOut ain't no good," he warned. "There are still a few of us around, though, thanks to him, if that makes any sense," he hinted.

I didn't know what he was hinting, but I figured over time that I would find out. I then broke eye contact with him and changed the subject.

"Is it always this loud and hot in here?"

"Everyday, dude. You'll get used to it. You'll see. This is nothing. Just wait until football season rolls around when all these fools pile up in here. The heat in hell wouldn't even be able to compare."

Eventually, he got up and walked toward the refrigerated water fountain for a drink of cool water.

Thank God. He's gone, I whispered to myself, slightly rolling my eyes in relief from the unwanted attention. The last thing I wanted was to be linked to that known homosexual. I held on to the idea that if I pretended to be straight, people would accept me with non-discriminating eyes – even though I was fast learning that a growing number in prison didn't care if you were gay, bi or straight. It seemed that all that mattered was finding a way to manipulate and control those who were weak.

As I surveyed myself, I realized I, too, was vulnerable because of my attraction to thugs. And these dudes were the same bunch manipulating and causing all the chaos in this joint. Even so, I couldn't shake my lust. Many claimed to be studs, but I knew differently. I knew they were adventurous and sexual freaks.

From my observations so far, many were actually misguided little boys eager for attention and affection. Give them a little commissary here and there and they would hand the world to you on a silver platter. In this sense, that meant their bodies.

I quickly learned that alcohol, drugs and other "free-world" items were flowing steadily and secretly throughout prison facilities and were used to leverage power over those with addictions. A few inmates were fortunate to have dollars on their books to pursue such contraband that could be used to entice eager inmates, indigents and otherwise. And I had plenty of dollars on my books, but there was no desire for drugs or alcohol – just a hunger for the very thing I didn't need. That very thing was a hot sexy encounter with some no-good thug, who was usually irresponsible, unaccountable and unproductive. But, unfortunately, it also usually meant someone who was hot-tempered.

Even with that, it was clear to me that I could not flirt with the drug culture ever again. Not here, not ever. I didn't want to touch it, taste it, look at it or be tempted in any way with the shit that had caused me so much pain and grief. I had been down that road too many times before. I knew that even a tiny whiff of the drug could be disastrous. There would be no turning around for me.

As far as I was concerned, crack cocaine was a definite has-been. I needed to clear my head from sleeping with men, too. But I wasn't sure if that was ever really possible.

As I contemplated that, a loud whistle rang out, summoning spectators to the window.

Then an inmate abruptly shouted from within the large dayroom.

"It's goin' down, y'all! It's goin' down!"

Several offenders, howling like caged dogs, ran toward the barred windows on the south side of the building.

"I got two dollars on Roscoe," said an inmate, placing a bet.

"I got that bet!" another challenged.

I stood at a distance to scope out the hoopla: a mere cat-fight!

Roscoe was the prison unit's longtime feline. But not a felon, I'm told.

Apparently, it was a stray who was unofficially adopted by the facility. He was quite old, according to those around. The animal was about the size of a Boxer dog with thick fur that was light dirty-brown and patchy in spots – perhaps from the many fights throughout the years. I watched as Roscoe prepared to attack by marking his territory, kicking grass and dirt with his hind legs.

Bugsby, his challenger, was Roscoe's offspring. He was one of six from the second litter of kittens two years ago. Bugsby was brown and white, with the white highlighting his face, chest, tail and paws and upper back area in a swirling pattern. He bowed close to the ground in attack mode, anticipating the brawl.

The prize was Electra, and it was mating season. She sat quietly yards away grooming her silky striped-and-white coat and fanning her tail from left to right. She, too, was an offspring of Roscoe – from the first litter. And the rights to mate with her would be costly in this father-son matchup.

Loud roars echoed from the dayroom like Greek spectators cheering for Roman gladiators during Olympic Games in the famed Athens stadium.

A true fulfillment would be to actually see some of my muscular fellow inmates go toe-to-toe in a battle of brawn while wearing regalia from that age-old era, when many of those competitive athletes were scantily clad.

But, here we are. A mere catfight.

"Yeah! Whup that ho', Roscoe! Whup that ho', man!" a voice yelled out as if the cat were human.

Inmates cheered as Roscoe launched his attack against Bugsby. They were locked in a ferocious battle, screaming like young babies throwing a tantrum. They scratched, clawed, rumbled and hissed during their brawl on a grassy knoll.

Roscoe used his size and strength to pin down his opponent by chomping with his needled teeth into Bugsby's neck and jabbing his hind and front claws deep into the back and chest of his wayward offspring. Bugsby struggled to break free from daddy, but couldn't. But Roscoe, showing that you can never underestimate the power of the elder, released him for Round 2.

Throughout the battle, Electra didn't move a muscle. She posed gracefully like a Greek goddess waiting to be swept away and romanced, her coat gleaming in the brilliant sunlight.

It then looked like Round 2 was about to commence as the two lowered their bodies, clutched to the ground, and stared face to face with tails wagging. No growling this time. Just a tense moment.

The foolishness and bidding in the dayroom grew wilder.

"Bugsby ain't no punk. I got three on Bugsby," an inmate claimed.

His bet was quickly taken.

"What a fool," I thought silently. Anyone could see that

Roscoe was much too smart and big for the younger Bugsby. The fight resumed.

I moved closer to the barred windows, this time a bit more intrigued.

They scratched, clawed and tumbled a time or two but, again, Roscoe pinned Bugsby to the grassy arena. It was like watching a pit bull obliterate a Chihuahua.

In the end, their furry coats were disheveled. Blood seeped from ears, legs, backs and stomachs. But the second round was all but easy for Roscoe as he released Bugsby again. Their breathing was intense. They stood their ground once again, for a minute anyway. This time Bugsby peeled off to his left, surrendering and finding refuge next to the chain-link fence where he rested and licked his battle wounds. Roscoe swaggered toward the right near Electra.

The verdict was in: Son was no match for big daddy Roscoe.

After the match, bets were fulfilled, one of which included six, 33-cent government postage stamps.

Watching this transaction, I shook my head in disbelief and sadness for those individuals who obviously lacked enough victories in their personal lives that they now have to resort to encouraging animal cruelty.

•••••

I woke up to a bright Sunday morning glistening as fine as African gold for the start of the last week of April. I felt the marvelous presence of God as I assembled with other offenders in the prison chapel, absorbing the Word from an anointed minister from Houston who delivered dynamic sermons.

His message imploring us to avoid judging others seemed to have been tailor-made for me, considering I was the one with the figurative plank in my eye yet didn't have a problem trying to remove a speck from another sinner's eyes.

"Isn't it God's place to judge those who refuse to obey his law?" he preached, referring to the words of the great apostle Paul in the book of Corinthians.

"So, men, we must stop using a 6-inch ruler to measure others when we, in secret, use a 12-inch one on ourselves to give us a wider margin for errors and character flaws. Remember not one of us," he said, pointing into the crowd, "is better than the other whether they be thieves or saints!"

His voice rose as the applauses, amens and hallelujahs increased.

"We then have to acknowledge our faults and confess to our Creator all our wrongs. That means admit with your heart and spirit and repent!" He concluded with a reference to Romans: "For at whatever point you judge the other, you are condemning yourself, because you who pass judgment do the same things."

I heard the message and, based on the applause, others did, too. But it was common knowledge that many of those who sat in the back pews were committing sexual acts in the house of the Lord rather than listening to the Word. Church service was a rare opportunity for some to meet up with lovers who had been separated when they were moved to other wings. It was also an opportunity for them to indulge in sacrilegious acts. To make matters worse, guards on duty didn't bother to enforce proper behavior – apparently believing many were headed for destruction anyway.

The Word was enough for me to at least review my life. I knew of the scriptures written by Paul the apostle. I reflected on my sordid past. I had been guilty of passing judgment on others. Yet, I was performing deviant acts. My struggle was trying to hide my secret.

Before I could approach the minister to thank him for the sermon, a female guard entered the room.

"Jose Vasquez, C-15, and Miguel Morris, C-14!" she yelled. "Y'all have visitors!"

At that moment, applause rang out from fellow inmates acknowledging our visits.

Upon hearing my name, I raised my index finger and quietly stood to exit along with Jose, an attractive muscular Hispanic, whose physique I had made a mental note of him earlier before we left our individual wings that were close to each other, but not near enough to be next-door neighbors.

The "visitor applause" was just as much a custom in church prison as lifting a small finger to excuse oneself. I headed out of the chapel with my finger raised, an act that reminded me of my younger days when attending church as a child. The gesture seemed to hold significance in prison, too, because I noticed others would often use the same sign to excuse themselves.

After leaving the chapel, I entered one of many checkpoints to the visiting area. First, I collected my visitor printout from the officer at the visitation area. Then I entered a long corridor leading to the visitation room, south of the prison. It is there where I would be searched and stripped butt-naked, ensuring that I was not trafficking weapons, paper correspondence or other contraband.

After clearance, a small-frame male led me through a strong metal door to the secured visitation area.

I was escorted into a roomful of visitors and inmates. The area was lined with Formica tables and padded chairs, a welcome respite from the metal I was used to sitting on here. Sounds of laughter rippled throughout the area, along with the crinkling of candy wrappers, potato chip bags and fizzling of soda cans being popped open. The noise was overwhelming at first because it was much different than the boisterous madness of the inmate dayroom. But I figured these sounds were still far better than the daily superficial and silly yakking in the prison dayroom.

Scanning the room, I looked for a familiar face among the smiles and hugs. When my eyes zeroed in on a corner, I saw

my smiling mother wearing her usual colorful attire and patiently waiting to embrace me, her overzealous son.
She saw me coming.
"Miguel!" she exclaimed, standing with gleaming eyes, reaching out for my white-clothed body.
I held tightly to her warm body and asked how she was doing.
"Baby, I'm fine. How are you?" she asked, finally releasing her grip and standing to survey me. "You look wonderful, baby. Looks like you've gained a little weight, too."
I smiled.
"I have. Maybe about 20 pounds or more," I boasted, displaying my biceps.
"Oh, boy! You're a mess," she said, laughing and then sitting.
As I joined her at the table, I realized I had not seen my mother since last year after getting myself into this mess.
It was good to be close to her and to again see her steel-gray hair, styled flawlessly.
"So I see you're still using a rinse to highlight your gray, huh!" I asked, smiling.
"No, baby. This is natural," she said, patting her curls of gray. "I stopped using that stuff almost a year now." She glowed like her hair and seemed quite happy to see me.
I leaned back in my chair with folded arms and a smile.
"Baby, you won't believe it," she said, laughing, "but don't you know after I had called here to find out what the dress code was I still left the house with open-toe shoes. I didn't realize it until I got to the security gate, and a guard informed me that I couldn't wear them on the premises." My mother laughed at herself again. "Thank God Troy drove me here. He couldn't come in because he gave me his tennis shoes to wear so I could see you."
She looked down at her feet to reveal the Nike basketball footwear, which looked awkward with her attire.

We both laughed at the odd appearance and her forgetfulness.

"Well, Momma, what are we gonna have to do? Tie a string around your finger so you can start remembering things?" I asked, grinning. Surprisingly, she displayed a small white string already tied around her left index finger.

"Troy beat you to it," she said, breaking out in laughter.

"And they say I'm the one that's a mess, huh?" I asked rhetorically while smiling and reaching for her soft hands.

I began to remember how forgetful she was at times. After all, she was aging and like many elderly parents her memory wasn't as keen as it once was.

Her memory lapse reminded me of a long-ago incident when mother and I, on a cool spring day, had planned to go to a nearby mall minutes away from our home. Our trip was delayed because of her frenzied search for her car keys. She looked everywhere for them: under the sofa cushions, pillows and chairs. We then looked in the locked car in the garage, where our pursuit was still unsuccessful. When we entered the house for the third time to retrace her earlier steps, I searched the window panel above the double sinks and the bar area, then near the oven. Still, no luck.

I then detoured to the fridge for a drink of water. It is there that I noticed a shining object that appeared to be the missing keys. And sure enough, that's where they were – on the cold top shelf next to a plastic jug of Welch's grape juice.

So, having my mother visiting me was such a special moment because it brought back some funny memories.

"So, tell me. Are they treating you OK here? Are you taking your meds?" she asked.

"Yeah. I mean, yes, ma'am. I can't complain about much. And, yes, I'm taking my meds. My viral load is still undetectable and my T-cell count is up again. Above 500."

I was elated to be healthy again instead of out on the streets bingeing on drugs, not eating and losing weight.

"Mom, I did this to myself, you know. Maybe this is God's way of correcting me, huh?"

"Yes, we all have to learn from our mistakes, Miguel. Sometimes I still can't believe you're here. It's like a bad dream in a way, but I know that time will heal," she said as her eyes watered a bit.

"I wish it was a dream, but it's not," I said, releasing my grip of her hands and again leaning back into my padded chair. I knew I deserved this punishment. "So, enough about me, Momma. What's going on with you and everybody?"

She sighed.

"Well, I haven't been feeling well lately, and I had to put your sister, Dee, in a nursing home because I'm not able to handle her anymore by myself, baby. Multiple sclerosis is taking a toll on her body. And the doctor discovered a lump in my breast," she bravely revealed.

My body tensed.

"What did you say?" I asked, becoming nervous.

"Yes, honey, a small lump. I discovered it while showering. So I'm going to have surgery next week, but don't worry yourself much because we caught it in time," she smiled confidently. "I decided not to have chemotherapy because I don't want to go through the part of losing my hair and feeling sick all the time."

Again, I reached for her hand.

"So you're gonna get a mastectomy, Momma?" I asked, peering into her eyes.

"It's likely, honey. I'm old, baby. If I were younger, then I probably would have chosen chemo. I don't have a problem with losing a breast at my age. Besides, who am I gonna impress with these old things anyway?" she said humorously.

As laughter surrounded us from neighboring tables, I held even tighter to my mother's hands, fearing for her health yet admiring her bravery.

"Miguel, it's gonna be OK, baby. I'll be just fine, so don't worry yourself about me. Just concentrate on getting yourself out of here, OK? And stay healthy," she ordered. She then reached into a small purse full of coins, as paper currency was not allowed.

"Do you want something to drink, because I'm thirsty?" she said, changing the conversation.

I accepted her offer and my eyes followed her as she walked to the vending machines. I marveled at her courage and faith and vowed to be like her.

Chapter 9
The Overcomers

Be very careful never to forget what you have seen God doing for you. May his miracles have a deep and permanent effect upon your lives. Tell your children and your grandchildren about the glorious miracles he did.
Deuteronomy 4:9

At times, I wonder if God is still molding me into what he intended when I was born. Surely I was meant to be doing something better than what I'm doing now. I know one thing: I can't continue on this same course. I knew I needed time to regroup, so I resorted to writing:

"Whuzzup, Diary?"

God has shown me my wrongs when he allowed me to confront one of my greatest fears: drag queens. I was temporarily confined in a small 6-by-9 cell with Kiki and discovered he was cool. But I still had my doubts about his intentions. Kiki amazes me when he "reads" a person. I learned a lot from him, with his jet black behind and his physically striking similarity to actor Taye Diggs. He coached me on how to let go and relax and not to fear things just because of other people and their warped views. I'm still working on that.

The pastor was right last Sunday. I've been judging others for much too long, and the truth of the matter is I never knew guys like Kiki could be such fun to talk to or be around. Maybe I forgot that they are men, too. The paranoia I had about effeminate men began to subside. I was actually enjoying Kiki's company. He didn't tease me even when I inadvertently *expressed my hidden sexual interests in men. I wondered if I would have done the same if the tables were turned. Would I have honored his request for confidentiality?*

Kiki intrigued me with the story of how he was raped, or "turned out," in prison. He said it happened one evening while reading a book by Maya Angelo. He was facing the back wall of his cell when the doors automatically opened on the hour, as usual, to allow inmates to enter and exit their cells for a short break. He stayed inside and didn't bother to turn around immediately but felt a presence in the cell. As soon as he turned, a sheet was placed over his face and mouth. Voices – he wasn't sure how many – warned him to keep quiet. He was certain that two or more inmates were present when he heard the cell doors close. He then felt large warm hands gripping his ankles, arms and stripping his lean body. He was held down and brutally molested, leaving both physical and emotional scars.

Ever since, he's been known as a prison "turn out." Back then he was forced to wear makeup and arch his eyebrows by his prison "stud" master.

And for my final blow, my precious mother – the one who introduced me to church, God and His love – is dealing with breast cancer. But I know she'll be just fine, because she's a firm spiritual believer. But this didn't stop me from being bitter at myself. Here I am in prison, and my mother is at home preparing to undergo major surgery. I feel so helpless. And scared. I do not want to lose her. I am so nervous, but I have to remember Deuteronomy: "Do not be afraid or discouraged." (End: Sunday 12:09 p.m. Day 50)

•••••

Lazlo had tried convincing himself that living alone wasn't so bad. But his friend, Roland, felt that he needed to get away from work and enjoy himself more. He had suggested that Lazlo move on with his life and forget about me. He didn't suggest that Lazlo abandon me but that he move forward and stop trying to please everybody.

From past experiences with me, Lazlo knew that being an enabler had to cease and that now was as good a time as any to stop the behavior. So, he picked up the phone again to make a call to East St. Louis as recommended by Roland and called his friend Nathan, a person who had expressed interest in Lazlo awhile back.

•••••

It was another noisy day at the "camp" as fellow offenders and I sat around watching the television comedy Martin. Attempts to enjoy the program in the boisterous room proved futile. Inmate James Millner and I looked at each other in disgust over the loud babel. The dayroom was almost unbearable with voices constantly blaring, but I was determined to cope.

But Millner soon joined the raucous crowd when he spontaneously remarked that all women were nothing but whores and prostitutes.

I wasn't sure how that conversation popped up, but I gave him a blank stare.

"Why do our black people always have to show their ass?" he asked, clearly agitated.

I wanted to ignore him, but I didn't because I was curious to know what got him so ticked off.

Millner was a curly-haired brown-skinned African-American male who had served two years on his remaining 40 for a series of crimes. At 6-foot, 3-inches, he was 230 pounds of human fat with an oversized belly. Most female guards found him attractive. Yeah, he was a decent-looking dude, but just too damn weird for my taste.

He never fully explained his irritation, though.

But, he has an interesting background. He explained to me how he ended up in prison and how his crimes branded him the "Panty Bandit."

Here's his flashback, as told in story form:

In June 1996, Millner attempted to flee to Europe en route to Switzerland to elude U.S. authorities after he was accused in a string of alleged assaults and sexual crimes. While on the lam, Millner engaged authorities in a 72-hour cat-and-mouse chase. The former Marine, once stationed in France, thought that by successfully fleeing he could avoid being extradited on the charges. Unfortunately his plans were foiled by his sloppiness. He left a paper trail of credit card receipts and handwritten notes that he thought he'd destroyed in a fireplace of his abandoned warehouse bungalow in Houston.

His escape ended when authorities snagged him at an intercontinental airport an ocean away. Soon thereafter, he was placed on an Air France Airbus for a date with destiny in Houston's court system. Two well-built men escorted the handcuffed Millner, whose reddened skin and clean-cut face began to perspire due to the unsettling turbulence and the uncomfortable position caused by his handcuffs.

One week before Millner's arrest, a white female with fine straight hair dashed inside the double-glass doors of a Stop 'n' Go convenience store frantically screaming, "Rape! Help me. I've been raped!"

The stunned storekeeper stared at the wet, scuffed-up, half-naked body of the battered victim, who ran inside from the thunderstorm. He took off his shirt and covered her bloody body.

"He raped me!" she cried. "He raped me!" Her fragile body fell to the floor. She was in shock and in tears after running through the wet, steamy streets of west Houston.

Meanwhile, thunder shook the well-kept bungalow near downtown Houston where Millner resided. He stood in his darkened bedroom closet shining a flashlight on his prized collectibles, an array of colorful panties from many encounters with women that decorated the front wall of his walk-in closet. His wet woolly hair and damp hands dripped water onto the flashlight and the closet floor as he admired the undergarments.

"Ummm, ummm. Yes!" he mumbled erotically with his eyes closed while touching and smelling the newly hung pair of pink panties he'd stolen only a few minutes earlier. He developed an erection as he traced his left index finger on the crotch of the pink undergarment. He then placed his fingers under his nose, jerking back his head in ecstasy from the scent.

"Ahhh," he said breathlessly in the mostly darkened closet with images of his latest victim swimming in his mind. He was at full throttle and about to ejaculate.

But now, all that came to an end because he was being transported on a long journey back to Houston.

Millner, who had been silent throughout the duration of the flight, finally broke his silence.

"I didn't mean to hurt them. I just wanted to talk. That's all. But they would always look down on me like I was crazy or something," he exclaimed.

His short confession was recorded. And ultimately he was convicted.

It seemed that Millner was one sick puppy.

After that flashback, I took pleasure in the fact that Millner, who was still in the dayroom, had finished ranting mercilessly about women. I was hopeful now for a little peace.

Well, apparently, that wasn't going to happen. As soon as I looked over my shoulder I heard a whacking sound and saw fists flying in what appeared to be more typical chaos. A nearby inmate landed a blow to the jaw of another in a lovers' quarrel, which, in reality, was more of an attack. The pale victim was knocked silly and dazed as his face, neck and arms suffered berry-red bruises.

The incident finally brought stillness to the room as all talking ceased, at least briefly. The violence involved an aggressive black offender overpowering his white lover, whom he knocked to the floor. In an unparalleled match, the brown brute with bulky fists firmly stood over his submissive mate apparently daring him to move.

The brotha had hands of a prize fighter that were noticeably scarred, perhaps from more competitive brawls than this one that was clearly an unequal contest. Without a challenge, the dismayed injured lover, holding his jaw, simply kept his position on the floor.

"What you hit me for, J.T.?" he asked nervously. He even hesitated before wiping away the small amount of blood that dripped from his shivering mouth.

"Bitch! I told ya I wanted $20 in commissary, not $19, ho'! Not $19.50, not $19.99. I said $20!" He cocked his fist again for another brutal blow to the face but withdrew. "You gonna learn to mind, bitch, and follow instructions!"

His shouts drew unwanted attention but quickly the dayroom spectators, including me, just turned away and looked off as the dayroom hubbub continued. The sad part is that even the guards walked off and ignored the incident.

It was just another "normal" day in prison.

•••••

The flight for Lazlo wasn't due to land in East St. Louis for another 45 minutes. He was somewhat anxious. But he knew he needed this trip. His friend and fraternity brother, Roland, convinced him to do something special for a change since he was always helping others. He needed a break from it all: the job and Donna, the loneliness and the dilemma with me. Lazlo tried to put our past behind him as he soared 30,000 feet in the air.

The nine-day spontaneous vacation was an idea of his Midwestern friend, Nathan. When I wasn't there for Lazlo, he would travel often. And there were many times when Lazlo needed to get out of town. Nathan was always supportive by offering a sympathetic ear despite the 850 miles that separated them.

Well into the flight, he summoned the flight attendant. He was thirsty and hungry again for a hot lunch. The Continental Airlines attendant obliged his request since he was flying first-class, but cautioned that they would be landing shortly so he would have to finish his meal quickly. He didn't object since it was a late request and the attendants had to prepare the cabin for arrival.

Within minutes he had gorged his grilled chicken breast and pasta fettuccini but didn't touch the steamed broccoli, which didn't appear fresh. Lazlo hated mushy vegetables, especially broccoli, because they looked like processed baby food.

After alerting the attendant that he was finished with the meal, the captain informed passengers that arrival was near.

"This is your captain speaking. We'll be landing momentarily," he announced. "It's clear and mild in the East St. Louis metropolitan area, a pleasant 75 degrees."

Lazlo became anxious because it had been nearly two years since he and Nathan had seen each other. Until now, they had been relying on telephones and computers to communicate.

His jitters abated as the Boeing 737 jet got closer to the gate. It was now time for him to meet up with his new soul mate.

And he knew Nathan, who had never let him down before, would be waiting.

• • • • •

Clear and sunny days while locked up in prison were always hard for me. They seemed to be a constant reminder of what I had given up: my freedom.

The firecracker heat of summer had ended, and September

brought expectations of a new atmosphere at Ramsey Two.

For the moment, I was fortunate not to have a cellmate for an extended period. It wasn't an uncommon occurrence, yet many saw the opportunity of living alone for a while a blessing. But I knew differently.

My living alone was because of being HIV-positive, and TDCJ made a point of housing inmates who were medically compatible. I knew the reason, but I wasn't sure if anyone else was aware of my predicament. But then, who am I fooling? One thing I quickly became aware of is that people talk, even health care professionals within the criminal justice institution. My status couldn't be that much of a secret because every morning and evening I routinely stood in the pill line where offenders collected their medications. Rumoring inmates were known to buzz like a swarm of wasps about people's health. And HIV, also known as "That Lick," was always the conclusion.

Aside from that, drastic changes were on the horizon for the Ramsey unit, which had a large number of sexual assault offenders housed here — approximately 175. They were scheduled to be shipped to another facility miles away that would better meet their needs and help them cope with their illnesses.

As many of us gathered in the recreation yard lifting weights that midday, the shipping of human cargo by the dozens began in earnest. Many offenders yelled goodbye or used other gestures as they slowly loaded onto three Blue Bird iron-caged buses. But after they left, an army of yakking youngsters arrived hours later. We noticed them from afar based on the style of their attire: sagging white pants and tan Rhino boots. It was a prison fashion statement. The recreation yard was quiet with interest when the new arrivals plodded into the secured intake area after unloading, with Lieutenant RideOut trailing close behind like a street whore on a mission, swaying his huge ass in those skin-tight grey pants.

"Oooh weee! This motha is gonna get pumped up now!" one offender predicted, clapping his fist together as if he'd just hit the lottery.

"You ain't never lied, BamBam. Did you see the fat ass on that red fool up front?" said a buff gay offender, lifting weights and observing the newcomers bouncing in with hip-hop abandon.

His comment alone was proof that many in prison wore their sexuality like a flamboyant pair of lime green bell-bottom pants.

"There you go with that punk shit again, fool. How can you see how fat that fool's butt is with him being so far off? Stop trippin' and thinking about ass all the time, man! You need to get some help, man. Stop chasing guts and start chasing these weights on this bench, you booty bandit. Get to lifting!" ordered the straight inmate, laughing.

"What else is there, fool? Ain't no shame in my game. I ain't trying to hear that 'overcoming' bull y'all talking about. Boy booty is always going to be in my face and future, fool. I got a 50-piece (years) to serve." I ain't trying to overcome my sexual habits. And you the one to talk," he continued. "I know you been jacking-off on ol' girl on third shift, huh? So you need to stop beatin' that meat and pointing fingers."

Once again the gay weightlifter interrupted his workout as his eyes penetrated with lust at a light-skinned inmate entering the intake area.

The two rec buddies made sex the butt of jokes, it seemed.

But listening to the two buff inmates, I found the conversation rather funny because I had already heard about the weightlifter's frequent masturbation. While he accused his buddy of being a booty bandit, it was common knowledge that he was hiding in corners like a roach "killing off," or jacking off, whenever female guards were nearby.

Unlike me, both these dudes openly discussed their sexual

interests. I was a bit too timid to ask them about the term "Overcomers," fearing my inquiry would spark questions about my personal life, although I had gradually begun to learn a little history about the cult.

Hours after recreation, a different scene was taking shape as youngsters began arriving for assigned housing on each quadrant of the C-wing, and many began displaying their rebellion by using foul language.

Those in the dayroom who watched them enter wondered if they would become cellmates with any of these hoodlums, with their mean, rough attitudes. Quite a few were just in their late teens and early 20s, sacrificing their social growth for prisons. Drugs, gang violence and sexual crimes ensnared many of these fearless, disrespectful youngsters, who were poised to become some of the most violent and aggressive offenders here. The only thing that seemed to matter to them was self.

The gates of C-14 squeaked as they opened when guards began escorting a number of them to their housing areas.

I wasn't back on my unit yet, but other inmates and I could partially see where the new inmates were being assigned.

The constant turmoil and imbalance of life in this joint were constant reminders that prison and hell are first cousins.

"Hey, fool. Don't be mad when you find out who's going to your house," one nosy inmate informed as a newcomer was being admitted.

As I braced myself for another change, a long-leggy inmate entered my area, C-14-1-3, with a hint of confidence and sporting a low-cut fade. At first glance from a distance, the eyebrows of this dark-skinned brotha appeared to be arched. He had strong, pronounced facial features. He sat on the top bottom bunk and stared through the cell bars at inmates sizing him up.

A few short minutes later, panty bandit Millner greeted me with a huge grin as I strained to see who in the hell was in my cell. After a long day of working out – running and weightlifting, I was exhausted and ready to embrace change. When I peered closer toward my cell, my eyes sunk in disbelief.

"A punk, Moe! You got a punk for a cellie. Aaaah! Hahaha!" said Millner, teasing me like a little child.

I thought to myself, "Not again."

"Whatcha gonna do? Make him yo wife, Moe?" an Islamic inmate mouthed.

That offender nudged Millner in his right side as they both tormented me with laughter.

"Hell no, fool! That's y'all's style, isn't it?"

"You fucking wrong, man!" said the Islamic inmate, who said his sect abides by religious laws. Of course, he lied because a month ago I spotted him giving approval to an inmate who was engaging in a sexual act with another male inmate — doggy style. And the Islamic inmate was supposed to have been part of the Overcomers' movement, whose intent, I learned, was to influence Muslim inmates from sleeping with other incarcerated men.

Apparently, they wanted out of the game. And in some instances, a few had overcome these sexual urges. But not this knucklehead. I knew for sure because I once caught him in the act. I never said anything about it. I knew my place, not out of fear but respect.

I knew if his boys found out that he had dipped his jimmy in some male's ass he would have been beaten like a piece of tough meat being tenderized.

I then moved to the front of the loud dayroom and pondered if I should submit a move request. But before making such a premature decision, I decided to investigate.

I would come to learn that this "new" roommate wasn't exactly new to me after all.

Kiki was back!

And this time our living arrangement was certain to be longer than the three days we spent together at the Darrington Unit.

Chapter 10
Cost of Violence

I have come to stop you because you are headed for destruction.
Numbers 22:32

Having been in prison only a short time of my 15-year sentence, I knew an early release was virtually impossible. But, nonetheless, I waited anxiously for my first parole hearing next month. This was also during the time when other inmates and I were transfixed on an east Texas crime that had gripped the world.

It was June 1998, when the ripped-apart body of James Byrd Jr., 49, was found near one of Jasper's oldest black cemeteries. The victim's head and arms were severed. Byrd was apparently still alive when he was chained to a pickup truck and dragged three miles, during which his body was mangled beyond recognition.

Days after as other offenders and I were picking cotton in the fields, we began discussing possible punishment for the three white men accused of dragging Byrd. As I quietly reflected on the Byrd family, other inmates weighed in on the heinous act.

"Frankly I think those muthas should get the death penalty," a white young offender uttered as he filled his wool sack.

James Millner, other inmates and I were surprised by the tan-skinned offender's response as we – looking like migrant workers – trudged down the dusty cotton field.

"Oh yeah?" said a young Hispanic inmate, questioning the

white guy's sincerity.

"Fuck yeah, SA!" he answered, using the abbreviation given to Latino prisoners from the city of San Antonio – a high Hispanic population area.

This white inmate, who labored tediously with us, was named Druppy and hailed from upper west Texas. And since many people viewed that area as racist, I was particularly interested in learning about him because his views seemed to run counter to the presumed prejudices of that region. As a result, I was particularly curious about the crime that landed him in prison; he told me it resulted from an assault with a firearm on a hot, humid day four years ago.

The sweat-drenched cowboy explained that he had been working with his aging father on an open farm field, gathering hay as the west Texas sun beamed mercilessly on his shirtless back and hairless chest.

He offered this flashback of his past – told in story form:

Druppy was a fair-skinned young man from Mule Shoe, Texas, who often found himself in barroom brawls, usually after dark, at a small-town brewery.

On this night, his sandy blond hair brushed his broad shoulders, which were draped with boxing gloves used for one of his favorite sports. His deep green cat eyes enhanced his rugged smile that showcased a gold tooth, an oddity for a white boy. Even so, Druppy (Shawn Grimes) was the envy of the town among some men and the object of affection among many young women, who admired his athletic presence and stamina.

With the breezy air blowing from the west, he and his father, Todd Grimes, were ending a workday on the family farm by loading the last of the hay for the market when suddenly they began arguing about one of the other sons, whom Druppy accused of being a slouch.

"Dang, Poppa, I don't see why you always let Neil get away with ..."

"Boy! I don't wanna hear that stuff from ya now, OK! Let Neil worry 'bout Neil and Druppy worry 'bout Druppy!" demanded Mr. Grimes, wiping the rolling sweat from his left brow with his right wrist and securing the last of the cash crop.

Neil was Druppy's older brother, who always rebelled against field work. Druppy promised himself that he would not be a permanent farmhand and remain stuck in a small town that offered no future.

"My question for you, boy, is about that gal. What in the world is you gonna do 'bout her and that youngin' she's pregnant with?" Mr. Grimes asked as he entered the two-ton Ford truck and trailer.

"I don't know, Papa, but I can't stay here. Maybe we will leave and go to Amarillo or Dallas. I just don't know," Druppy answered as he buckled up in the vehicle. They then drove off toward the farmhouse.

"Son, you betta know 'cause that gal is underage, and her parents, the Wilsons, are pissed, boy! Don't you know they are talking about criminal charges, boy?" His dad shook his head in disgust.

"Papa, she'll be 18 next month, and ..."

"Damn, boy! Don't you hear me! The gal's parents are talkin' charges! Charges!" he said, angrily. Druppy just stared into space during the ride home.

After settling down, he decided to go out on the town to a place called Kallerhans, a country-western music joint known for having young girls and lots of drinking. On a summer night in July 1994, Druppy and his underage girlfriend, who was three months pregnant, went there for a night of two-stepping and buffalo wings.

Shouts of "yip-pee" and "ya-hoo" rang out as they made their way past a mechanical bull, where two long-haired female thrill-seeking blondes seductively rode atop waving one hand high above their heads while tightly gripping the rope securing them to the leather buckskin saddles. As Achy Breaky Heart by Billy Ray Cyrus pumped through the speakers, Druppy and his girlfriend found a country-styled table with a red-and-white checkered covering.

"Hey, Druppy!" said a cowgirl server, tossing her dark long hair from her shoulders as she walked by. She smiled and winked as her teeth gripped a small Confederate flag on a stick protruding from her mouth.

Druppy's jealous girlfriend was not amused by the flirtation as she slapped him on the right arm.

"Whatcha hit me fur?" he asked, pretending to be puzzled.

"You know why, Druppy! You betta respect me, boy!" she demanded loudly as many eyes were now affixed on them.

Druppy simply sat next to his young companion and stared back at the crowd. When the waitress approached, he was all smiles again, displaying his golden tooth.

"Hi, Druppy! Hey, Tina! So, whatcha havin' tonight y'all?" she asked, carrying a 15-inch round serving tray toward her breasts that fit snuggly in her costumed uniform.

"Oh, the usual: spicy wings and a pitcher of draft, girl," he said, winking.

Whack!

Tina again slapped his right shoulder.

"I told ya to respect me, Druppy. I ain't playin', boy!" she said with a frown, folding her arms in anger.

"Tina, stop trippin', gal," Druppy said after the waitress walked away.

"I ain't trippin'; you trippin', boy. Anyway, what are we gonna do about our baby, Druppy? You know my momma and papa is blazin' mad. They talkin' 'bout some kinda rape charge."

"Girl, I ain't commit no statutory rape, and you know that! You told me you was 18, remember?" claimed Druppy, leaning onto the table with both elbows.

"I will be soon," she said, rolling her eyes and leaning back into the chair with her arms folded.

Druppy was already bitter because Tina had lied to him about her age.

Shortly after the voluptuous waitress returned with a full pitcher of beer and the steaming hot wings, Tina's brother trotted toward their table with eyes as wide as a vicious grizzly. A confrontation appeared to be brewing.

"You thug-ass white trash! What you doin' with my sista out here?" asked the 6-foot, 3-inch cowboy as he towered over Druppy with balled fists.

As he swung, Druppy dodged the punch with a swift turn that caused his falling wooden chair to scrape the hardwood floor. It was a move he learned from boxing.

"Bubba Ray, go home!" Tina nervously screamed to her brother. "Leave me and Druppy alone! You know I'm not drinkin' nothin'. Go home!"

"Yeah, Bubba Ray," the waitress begged, "don't start in here tonight. Please, baby."

"Step your ass outside! I'm gonna shred you to pieces, Druppy!" Bubba Ray warned.

"Fuck you, Bubba! I ain't takin' yo' shit again tonight. You hear, boy! Let's go outside, you bastard. This time I ain't takin' no ass whoopin'!" said Druppy, pointing his fingers as he walked backward, watching Bubba Ray's every move.

They headed toward the front door with the fight-hungry crowd following close behind.

"Stop, Druppy! Don't y'all start this shit!" a tearful Tina demanded.

Bubba Ray positioned himself in the dust-filled parking lot, challenging Druppy to an all-out fist fight. Spectators cheered and jeered.

"Kick his ass, Bubba Ray!" one said.

"Y'all stop, Bubba Ray! Right now you hear!" Tina continued as other women held her back.

Whack!

The hit to Bubba Ray's face echoed, stunning him. After recovering, Bubba Ray lunged forward into Druppy's chest with a huge right fist, dropping Druppy. He then dived atop Druppy, attacking him from a kneeled position. A bloodied Druppy suffered blows and lacerations to the mouth, brow and nose.

"Ohmigod, Bubba! You killing him!" a panicked Tina said.

"Kick his ass again, Bubba!" a voice from the crowed encouraged.

A severely injured Druppy kicked and squirmed from Bubba Ray's grip and then ran toward his unlocked truck. His heart was beating as fast as a racehorse. When he approached his pickup, he noticed gobs of blood on his shirt that ran down his arms and scraped hands.

"Come back here you fuckin' coward!" Bubba Ray shouted, approaching Druppy.

As Druppy watched in horror with Bubba Ray charging forward like a raging bull, he didn't know what to do. With his body in pain and heart racing, he glanced at his loaded high-powered rifle.

He spontaneously pulled out the weapon and pointed it at Bubba Ray.

"No, Druppy!" Tina screamed in terror as she broke free from the women's grip.

Pow!

The blast sent the crowd scampering away as Bubba Ray just stood still.

Tina, who had freed herself from those protecting her, managed to push the gun away just in time to throw it off course, barely missing Bubba Ray.

She held Druppy's shivering and bruised body as Bubba Ray fell to his knees, thankful that his life was spared.

It wasn't long before police arrived on the scene, ordering Druppy to drop the weapon.

INTERNAL CHAOS

Because of this incident, Druppy was serving time for attempted murder.

That event happened awhile ago. But getting to know Druppy helped to dispel my beliefs and bury stereotypes about most West Texans.

•••••

"Northside Locos," read the heavy tattoo on the upper shoulder blade of the tanned back of Alberto Gomez, aka Big Gee – looking every bit like Cuban singer Jon Secada. He was a father of eight children. Not only was he Druppy's best friend, but they were also cellmates. Despite his many opportunities to advance educationally, Big Gee channeled his energy into a local gang known for corruption. A week before Christmas 1992, he and a comrade had robbed numerous shopping mall patrons of gifts and toys, crimes that led him here.

As we all worked the cotton fields, Big Gee seemed to be in another world.

"Earth to Big Gee, Earth to Big Gee," teased Druppy as he tried to get his cellmate to return to reality. "What's up, fool? Where did you go?" Druppy playfully asked.

It was quite common to see them together all the time. They were definitely homies, for real.

Big Gee appeared to have a lot on his mind, but later commented, saying, "Oh, dude, I'm here with y'all. I was daydreaming and just trippin', vato," he said, using the Latin term for "guy."

"Hey! Get to work, inmates!" ordered an officer interrupting us and slowly approaching with his gun in his holster and canteen on his hip. Mounted on his saddled horse wearing a straw cowboy hat, he put me in mind of slave masters of years past, minus the whip.

This was the kind of attitude we experienced almost daily.

Moments later another youngster intervened to offer

his comments about the treatment of inmates.

"Man, these fools ain't nothing but modern-day slave drivers," Cajun Red said.

I had noticed "Red" and his Cajun moon eyes earlier, but his expression caught my attention. There was rumor that he, too, was part of the Overcomers movement. However, his eyes told a different story because they were dreamy and much too probing.

"Welcome to Ramsey Two, youngster," Millner, grinning as we made a U-turn back toward our original point, said to Cajun Red. We dragged our heavy bags of cotton alongside us, wishing for the day to end and the sun to be snuffed out like a candle in the wind.

Chapter 11
Fools and Folly

Resentment kills a fool, and envy slays the simple.
Job 5:2

Monday night football was at its finest as the Denver Broncos on this cool November day were well on their way to annihilating their opponents. The C-14 dayroom echoed like a casino or a sports bar with noise rising to a deafening decibel. This was prison, nonetheless, but the cavernous room was punctuated by cheers and jeers with bets being placed with makeshift lottery tickets; dominoes and wooden Scrabble chips shuffling; and a finger-snapping game of dice rolling out of control in a far-off corner.

Several feet way, the 27-inch television monitor blared as it hovered above the boisterous crowded room with the aura of a miniature stadium.

"Yeaaaaah!" screaming voices belted after Denver scored another touchdown that featured the fancy footwork of the mighty Terrell Davis.

But it was the moves of a different force that brought the "house" to a standstill.

Boom! Boom! Boom!

No, it was not the percussion sounds of the half-time band on television, but rather the heavy knuckles of a frowning Lieutenant RideOut banging on the dayroom window ordering us to keep down the noise.

Once satisfied, RideOut – his pants once again as tight as

a pair of grip pliers on a stubborn pipe – galloped toward another wing to perhaps do the same.

Usually, dayroom chaos was at its worst during these long hours. Gambling, including placing bets for junk food, was in full swing. But this time there was no unusual disorder. Typically, this type of behavior was banned, but oftentimes many of the guards and ranking officers overlooked the activity.

Even Kiki took part in the mania. And while we had been cellmates for a while now, I wanted so badly to teach him how to be more butch. But that wasn't my place. Anyway, I thought, who was I to attempt to offer a "cure" to someone, especially with my own inhibitions and problems? Despite Kiki's femininity, he landed a handsome friend on C-wing. A partner. A prison lover.

As for me, I was still solo – tormented by my own thoughts and denials. Sometimes, I even wanted my desire for male companionship to disappear at the snap of a finger. Of course, it doesn't work that easily.

"Say, Moe, you want some cookies?" asked Kiki, approaching me with the goodies and a note.

Without hesitation I grabbed a handful, thanked him for the offer and concealed the note. I smiled with a raised eyebrow, wondering what he was up to. He reciprocated with a smile then returned to the arms of his brown-eyed lover.

They sat on a corner bench next to one of two giant barred windows facing the south end of the prison. It was odd that Kiki's lover would connect with my flamboyant cellmate, considering Lil' D's bad-boy background and past temper and resistance toward gays.

Lil' D's troubles began years before he entered the Texas prison system.

In story form, here's how his background was recounted to me in a poignant flashback:

During his early period of growing up, Lil' D was in a race for his pride, life and identify as he trotted down a reckless path. Growing up in a dysfunctional family led him to fall prey to outside influences, which led to his involvement with gangs.

He had been agonizing over his mother's mental illness and the indifference shown by his brothers. All of this took a toll on him as he watched her deteriorate. For many months, she sat swaying in a rocking chair with folded arms in a catatonic state.

She resided in a small padded room in one of Boston's state hospitals for the psychologically disturbed. Apparently, Mrs. Bishop suffered a nervous breakdown after her divorce and over the illegal activities of her eight sons, who were involved with the Crips.

Lil' D, aka Arthur Bishop, was the youngest at age 17. His nickname derived from his explosive temper and is short for Lil' Dynamite. He spent countless days watching his mother from a two-way window. Overwhelmed with emotion, his brown eyes would swell with tears that slowly fell to his yellow cheeks and tender red lips. His seven older brothers, pessimistic about her recovery, would visit sporadically.

One day, Lil' D contemplated running away from his family and never returning. As he scampered down the white-painted halls of the psychiatric hospital, he collided into the towering frame of his eldest brother, who was on his way to visit their mother.

"Hey, hey! Slow down, Lil' D!" the stern voice of the eldest brother ordered. "What's wrong?" Ray asked, grabbing the shoulders of Arthur, whose eyes were drenched in tears.

"Nothing!" he replied, wiping his eyes and face with his right hand.

"Stop lying. There something wrong, Lil' D. What is it?" he demanded as he released his grip on Lil' D's shoulders.

"I told you nothing, Ray!" stated Arthur, still sobbing. "You goin' to see Momma?"

"Yeah, how is she?" Ray asked.

"She's goin' crazy, fool! What do you mean how is she?" a peeved Arthur yelled. "Go see for yourself," he instructed while pointing in her direction.

"What's your problem, Lil' D? Why are you trippin', nigga?"

"I ain't no nigga. And y'all is my problem, fool. The gang, your ass, your sorry ass father! All of us are killing her, Ray. So the hell with all of y'all," he said tersely.

Lil' D then jetted out of sight, leaving his brother stunned.

Despite the imbalance in his life, Lil' D was an "A" and "B" student in school. Now, he was a runaway, settling in the Alamo City of San Antonio, Texas. While there, he was taken under the wings of other Crips – some of them family members. His education, at the 11th-grade level at the time, was in jeopardy because of misguidance and gang involvement.

During a late afternoon gathering near Plex Park on the eastside of town, he and fellow gang members whiled away the time after school taunting fellow classmates as they walked passed them. One of the bullying accomplices was Lil' D's cousin, Ricky, who recognized one of four preppie teen males being harassed as one of his classmates.

Ricky, a handsome caramel-tone brother, yelled out to get the attention of the preppie teens by raising his San Antonio Spurs jersey to flaunt a tattoo with the words "Thug Life" printed over his navel.

He knew exactly what he was doing when he raised his shirt. His intent was to entice his fellow classmate. Ricky was not new to the game.

In the past, Ricky served multiple months in juvenile detention and was exposed to all manner of behavior from sexually depraved males. He, like many in detention, yielded to desires and explored his sexuality. He was one of the many young men who had never given up sleeping with men, yet he still considered himself heterosexual.

As far as he was concerned, he just wanted to satisfy his

same-sex urges every once in awhile. There was never any emotional connection between him and his male partners.

"Say!" Ricky called out. "Yeah, you," he pointed as he smiled and leaned on the hood of his black Honda Accord. "Yeah, you, Derek! Come here, man," he waved and smiled mischievously.

Lil' D couldn't quite figure out what was going on and remained silent. He watched in astonishment as his cousin chatted with so-called outcasts such as Derek, a slightly feminine student. Punks, he called them. Because they typically bashed gays, Lil' D moved to the opposite side of the Honda. He entered the vehicle to avoid being seen near Derek. He shook his head, wondering what his cousin was up to.

Derek was the most masculine of the four, perhaps because of his athleticism. He was a member of the high school varsity tennis team. Even so, Lil' D still gave the intruder a stone-cold look. Derek, at 5-feet, 10-inches with medium-brown complexion, was muscular and attractive and very secure about his sexuality.

"Say, Derek, y'all coming to the party tonight at Club 402?" asked Ricky, grabbing his crotch as he spoke while leaning on his car.

"Yeah, if your cousin gonna be there," answered Derek, boldy peeping into the black-tinted windows of the Accord for another glance at Lil' D. Derek made it quite known that he was interested in Ricky's cousin.

To create a distraction and drown out the conversation, Lil' D cranked up the Alpine stereo that rocked the vehicle.

Boom! Boom! Boom! The thundering bass was paired with the Beatsie Boys rapping Check your Head!

"Yeah, man, he'll be there. Matter of fact, we all gonna be there and make things happen," assured Ricky, bouncing his head to the funky beat and watching Derek's three friends nearby grooving to the sounds like grand divas.

"Your friends are throwed, Derek," Ricky said. He then

knocked on the window to get Lil' D's attention.

"What's up, fool?" Lil' D asked as he leaped from the front passenger side with his hands flailing in the air to suggest his patience was thinning.

"Come here, man!" Ricky ordered playfully, smiling at his cousin.

As Lil' D made his way toward Ricky, he cringed as he noticed the brown eyes of Derek scanning his body.

"What's up, man?" asked Lil' D, pretending to ignore Derek while also trying to give the impression he was extremely agitated.

"Say, Cuz, we gonna go to Club 402 tonight, huh?" asked Ricky, winking.

"Why?" asked Lil' D, slightly noticing Derek's calves. Taking a cue from his cousin, Lil' D then raised his Dallas Cowboy jersey, which revealed his smooth skin and light-colored tone. He showed off his abdominal tattoo that read "Arthur the Great." He unabashedly rubbed his muscled six-pack, suggesting he, too, was just as built as his cousin and Derek.

"Well, my buddy, Derek, wanted to know, man, if you were going to show up at the club. He'll be meeting us there, you know. You down?" Ricky asked as he continued to sway to the sounds of the rap.

"Down for what, fool?" asked Lil' D, frowning and fuming. His homophobia was now taking center stage.

"For whatever, Cuz. They cool. You ain't trippin', huh?" asked Ricky, nudging Derek on his left arm.

"Yeah, Lil' D, I'm cool, man. We all one in the same," said Derek, breaking his silence.

"Says who, fool? I don't hang out with fags, man."

Derek's eyes widened and deeply focused on Lil' D.

"Say, Cuz, lighten up, man! He's not like those over there. He's cool. You know what I mean?"

"Cuz, a fag is a fag," Arthur replied. "Cuz, I know you ain't getting down with this shit," Lil' D remarked.

By now Derek's friends were becoming impatient.

"Say, Derek, let's go!" one of the preppie teens shouted from afar.

"Go ahead! I'll catch up with y'all," Derek instructed. He waved them off. He then turned to Lil' D to suggest that they hang out sometimes.

"Look, fool," said Lil' D, "I ain't doin' shit with yo' faggot ass. Maybe I oughta shoot your ass, huh? Right here in front of everybody." Lil' D then pointed his finger in the shape of a pistol.

"Damn, Cuz, chill out!" Ricky suggested. "They don't bite."

By now Derek had had enough of the hatred. He began to walk away in a dignified manner despite Lil' D's temperament.

Before Derek walked away, Ricky assured him that he and Lil' D would be at the club.

"Cuz just trippin'; that's all! We'll see you at the club, OK!" Ricky said.

Without looking back, Derek gave a thumbs-up.

That's when Ricky thought he'd have even more fun.

"Damn, Lil' D! Look at that fool's fat ass!" Ricky joked.

Lil' D shook his head at his cousin's comment. He was shocked by Ricky's behavior. But, silently and slyly with a little glance, Lil' D noticed that Derek's butt was big, even though he refused to verbally admit it.

A week after that encounter, Lil' D was making his usual nightly rounds. Like so many other late evenings, the July air was thick and humid.

It was also ripe for chaos.

Tat! Tat! Tat!

Shots rang out in the low-income eastside neighborhood near Plex Park.

Lil' D fearfully raced down a dark street after he and a rival gang member of the Bloods crossed paths. A confrontation ensued after bitter words were lodged against each other. It seemed the rival called Lil' D a "crab," which the Crips considered foul and vulgar. In retaliation, Lil' D insulted the enemy by calling him a "slob," which is equally offensive. Neither teen knew why there was so much animosity between the groups. Crips, briefly known as Community Revolution in Progress, was the forerunner of the two rivalries.

Nevertheless, on this night, the two warring teens pulled weapons on each other. Lil' D proved to be a fast and furious marksman by drawing fire first, striking the lone Bloods member several times.

The glaring streetlights revealed Lil' D's shock and horror as he watched the bloody bullet-riddled body crash onto the ground. He broke into a spirited run without fully knowing the fate of the injured teen.

He first sprinted toward his cousin's house several blocks over but turned away to avoid attracting attention by the adults standing outside nearby milling about. He surmised that they probably heard the gunfire.

With that, he galloped past several more streets seeking refuge.

Pop! Pop! Pop!

He ducked and dodged intuitively after hearing sounds that he mistook for a pistol. In reality, they were fireworks marking the Independence Day celebration. Several small kids frolicking on the adjacent street had ignited their small party explosives amid screams and shouts of laughter.

Still nervous from the bloody shootout, Lil' D remembered that he still was carrying his weapon. He knew he needed to make a quick decision about concealing it. His first inclination was to throw away the rusty revolver in a nearby street sewer.

After hearing another crackling pop from the fireworks that rattled him once more, he quickly ditched the pistol in a thicket near several houses nestled together, with one of these homes of particular interest because it had been pointed out to him previously by his cousin Ricky.

With little hesitation, Lil' D galloped into the driveway that led to the front door of a well-kept structure, an oddity because nearby there were many unkempt structures in this eastside neighborhood.

After several knocks to the solid-red wooden door, it swung open, revealing the self-assured tennis varsity athlete Derek, who was wearing only baggy blue jeans shorts that rested low on his hips. His shirtless body gave notice to his defined pecs and abs. There was even a hint of pubic hair, made noticeable by his shorts that drooped well below his navel and accented his "bubbalicious" basketball-size buttocks.

"What's up, Derek? You busy, man?" Lil' D asked as he glanced at Derek's body while waiting to be invited inside.

"Nah, Lil' D. What's up, man?" a smiling Derek asked as faint sounds of sirens could be heard in the background.

"Can I come in, man, if that's OK?"

"Yeah, sure. Why not?"

"Your parents home?" Lil' D asked as he quickly stepped inside the doorway as the sirens grew stronger.

"Nah, man, my mom's out with her boyfriend. They're celebrating the Fourth."

"Oh, yeah!" said Lil' D, a little uncomfortable but satisfied to know that they were alone.

"Come on in and take a seat, man. You look tired or something. You wanna beer or some water?" asked Derek, moving toward the kitchen.

"You got beer? I'll take one," said Lil' D. He then plopped down onto the sofa.

As Derek slowly walked to the kitchen, Arthur stared at his host's light-brown skin that showed a faint trail of thin hair that extended down his back and toward the crevice of his buttocks. It would appear that Derek's massive calves kept him anchored to the ground because his gargantuan glutes seemed to be filled with a hefty supply of helium that easily could have sent his ass floating aimlessly throughout the house. Moreover, his amazingly swollen rump could probably cushion him in a 10-story fall or, at the very least, be used as a life-preserver to keep him afloat on the high seas. In other words, the butt was big – and attractive.

Derek wasn't pleased with his last encounter with Lil' D, but he was curious to know what led to the turnaround in his attitude.

"So what brings you by here tonight, Lil' D?" shouted Derek from the kitchen.

There was a moment of silence, then the hissing sound of the beer can being opened.

"Just out for a stroll, man, and you crossed my mind," said Lil' D, telling a lie as he sat on the sofa playing with the television remote. He tried to pretend all was well by acting as normal as possible under the circumstances.

"Oh, yeah?" responded Derek, with a hint of sarcasm. It was clear that he doubted Lil' D's explanation.

"Yeah!"

Derek began to think that there was no way this fool would travel all this way just for a stroll in the 'hood. Besides, Derek had already been dissed by this so-called gay basher at a party a week ago. So, what really was up, Derek wondered.

"Here's your cold beer to settle those nerves," offered Derek, carrying the can in one hand and a glass of water in the other. As he tilted forward, he intentionally but slyly wasted his water on Lil' D's shirt and Khaki shorts.

Lil' D leaped from the sofa, clearly agitated and inflamed.

"Damn, Derek. What you doing, man?" asked Arthur, wiping the water deeper into his clothing.

"Ohhh, man! I'm sorry Lil' D! I'm truly sorry, man, for real!" said Derek, laughing on the inside. "Let me get you a towel, man!" said Derek, running to the back room. Now he was really grinning with excitement.

"Now I gotta go home wet and shit?" said Arthur, boiling

with anger. Frowning, he placed his canned beer onto the coffee table.

"I can fix that, man. I got your back," suggested Derek, fetching a towel and shorts. He left for a moment but returned quickly. "Here, wear these. I'll wash and dry your clothes. Try them on, Lil' D."

Lil' D tempered his anger, realizing that he needed a place of refuge after his earlier confrontation with a rival gang member.

He decided to take Derek's suggestion by accepting the clothes, even forgetting about Derek's sexuality for a moment. He began to disrobe, exposing his tattoo and sexy body. Derek then tossed a fragrant towel toward Lil' D.

"Thanks, man," acknowledged Lil' D, slowly releasing his belt that held up his oversized pants. He then unbuttoned and unzipped his pants, which slowly fell to the hardwood floor.

Lil' D's ease and comfort at undressing shocked Derek and elicited heart-throbbing excitement as Derek stood paralyzed watching Lil' D's naked body, with the towel draped on his neck.

"Wow, no underwear," said Derek silently as he observed his guest.

Once Lil' D regained his focus, he peered at Derek. His own curiosity and inquisitiveness began to unfold. He realized he was now standing before someone he had previously insulted.

As Lil' D paused, Derek remained frozen, unsure of his next move.

He got his answer after Lil' D boldly grabbed his own semi-erect sex, suggesting an invitation and a willingness to explore the "other side" that some of his tough homeboys had bragged about. These were the sort of secrets that took place in dark alleys and street corners.

Lil' D's actions confirmed that he was attracted to Derek. And it showed because Lil' D's body was on fire and his penis now throbbing. He felt different all of a sudden. This attraction wasn't similar to that for a woman. In some ways, it was more intense, more provocative. Although this was his first experience, Lil' D was ready to explore further.

He reasoned that if the act was good enough for his fellow gang members, then it was good enough for him, too.

"What the hell!" he thought to himself, believing this one-time encounter would be between only him and Derek.

They both smiled, agreeing on the next move. The night became a turning point for Lil' D, who realized he had now been initiated into a world he once saw as deviant. His attitude toward gays finally softened as he lowered his guard.

•••••

Seventy-two hours after the senseless shooting, Lil' D was staring into space from a hardwood chair. He began recounting the chaotic episode of that bloody Fourth of July night.

The dimly lit room where he gave his confession was intimidating at first. All he could think about at that moment was his mom in Boston struggling with mental illness and depression.

"Only if I'd stayed there this wouldn't have happened," he mumbled.

"What was that, son? Are you OK?" asked a detective, with arms folded and standing next to Lil' D.

"Nothing. I'm fine!" said Lil' D, lying. He knew that his life was about to take a serious turn.

Arthur Bishop, the real name used by officers interrogating him, was facing assault charges and an attempted murder charge. He listened to comments about his impending fate. Lil' D was informed that he could be sentenced to juvenile detention by the Texas Youth Commission until he turned 18. Thereafter, he would be shipped to the state penitentiary for 10 years to complete his sentence.

He stared hopelessly into space, his face listless, his mind distraught about his future and prison. This is when he began questioning his decision to join a gang in the first place. The thrill of walking on the wild side now seemed overrated.

Like so many others in prison, Lil' D's story, as told to me by my cellie, Kiki, touched me because of Arthur's fractured family life. I felt sorry for him because I never knew what life was like growing up without the influence of parents. I was fortunate to have my mother and father throughout my adolescence.

After thinking about Lil' D's situation, I turned my focus to the kite, or note, that Kiki left behind for me to read.

The note stated: "Say, Moe! You have power and don't even know it, and it's in your locker box. You're never gonna be happy until you look at yourself deeply and stop trippin' and get with the program. I know this `trade' who wants to get to know you. He's a flipper. A daddy girl, too. He's fine, clean and high yellow, just like you like them. He'll do anything you want. I mean anything. Feel my drift? He needs help with a few things, though, and I know your books are loaded. Just chunk him some commissary here and there every once in a while. He aims to please. Anyway, my son is coming to visit me soon, hopefully this weekend. Wish me luck. Kiki."

After I finished reading the note, I looked over in Kiki's direction. He winked at me, as did Lil' D.

Hmmm, I wondered. Are they in cahoots?

This was truly laughable. I shook my head in amazement at Kiki's proposal. Immediately, I felt that this wasn't the right path for me as red flags were raised in my mind. I knew if I embraced this act, it could potentially desensitize me and cause me to regress.

But it wasn't long before my imagination roamed as the desire to yield to my lust grew stronger.

My conscience kept telling me that a prison hookup with some high-yellow hustler who was only interested in some damn commissary in exchange for some sex was a dangerous game in the penitentiary.

Chapter 12
Daddy Girl

Of what use is money in the hands of a fool, since he has no desire to get wisdom?

Proverbs 17:16

After several weeks had passed, I began thinking about the so-called power in my locker box. I decided to use that power to purchase condoms and lubrication from an inmate on another wing. I hid the contraband in my cell for a week. Some days later, I discussed the offer presented to me by my cellie.

I was ready to find out more about Sheldon, the light-complexioned inmate from New Orleans who had lips as luscious as hip-hop sensation LL Cool J.

Sheldon, who did not have a cellmate, was one of those naturally muscular narcissistic pretty boys idolized by many. He clearly knew he was a commodity. Even knowing that, I still solicited him just like I did those thugs on the streets of Houston. I had something they wanted. They had something I wanted. I figured we'd both benefit. But I did not discount the fact that this was still prostitution and solicitation. The hook had been baited and my predatory instincts once again were on the rise. Carelessly, I didn't bother to question my behavior. I was more interested in fulfilling my desires.

Sheldon, the irresistible "eye-candy," had a dynamic smile, white teeth and clear, clean skin. I welcomed his seduction and respected his survivalist mentality, even if he were a hustler at heart.

Along with this agreement from my cellie came a clause that was not originally discussed. And I should have known there was going to be a catch involved. My cellie informed me about a consulting fee conjured up by him and his lover, Lil' D. I would be required to fork over three cans of Jack Mackerels, four Honey Buns and a Coca-Cola six-pack for the initial hookup with Sheldon. Lil' D also described him as a "daddy girl." It didn't mean he was the femme type. Instead, it referred to him as being a total bottom, which was fine by me. Even though I was versatile, I was not going to argue.

Although their proposal appeared to suggest hustling and pimping, my cellie and his beau were merely following long-held practices learned in prison. Rather, this gig was commonly referred to as Ph.D's, or a "prison hookup dating service."

I studied their proposal again and decided to compromise, concluding that their request was within my budget, not to mention that rumor had it that Sheldon was a star in the sack.

We didn't mess around immediately, but I would soon come to discover that Sheldon was that and then some. After a few escapades he and I came up with a strategy that afforded us the opportunity to freely move around from floor to floor without incident. We formed positive relationships with many of the guards who worked the evening shift. We both avoided trouble and maintained our discretion, which allowed me to further fine-tune a system of getting around from floor to floor without getting caught in Sheldon's cell, an act that would be considered a major offense.

For some reason that remained unclear, I felt that Lieutenant RideOut had his eyes on Sheldon and me. I had to be very cautious because there were plenty of haters and snitches who constantly served as watchmen for those in authority. These informants sought special privileges in return for their efforts. For example, they could obtain ice and wristwatches that were not sold in commissary.

All and all, it was quite simple outwitting guards, who weren't completely tuned in to every prison ploy. As for me, I just studied the officers' behavior and befriended those who were cool. I would shuck and jive with them to guarantee my safety in case a prison riot broke out, for example, and I got stuck unintentionally in Sheldon's cell.

With the guards primed and seasoned, I hoped that Sheldon and I would be like Lil' D and Kiki, enjoying each other's company in a setting other than a 6-foot, 9-foot cell.

And as time passed, Sheldon and I were officially a couple, by prison standards.

I was cool with it, but, still, feeling a little remorseful for what I was doing. What in the hell was going on with me by embracing a relationship all of a sudden? There was still an element of unhappiness and discomfort. Fact is, I was still battling my sexual habit.

Nonetheless, I felt rotten for what I was doing. And it was not so much about my guilt over Sheldon the hustler, inasmuch as it was toward me for engaging in same-sex practices. I was my own nemesis because I had been prancing around for weeks with little thought about my behavior until now.

•••••

Two days later, panic broke out as green, gaseous fumes filled our lungs as we lie on the cold, filthy floor in the prison chow hall. The "mad gas," which is how prisoners referred to it, attacked our eyes and skin with an irritating and arresting burning sensation.

This latest rout by the prison guards resulted from a football game and an overdue gambling debt that got out of hand when rowdy inmates began fighting. The result was a tactical maneuver by guards to tame the disorder. The officers' response sent men scampering, screaming, crouching, crawling and vomiting all over the place.

It wasn't a secret that bad gambling debts were a way of life in the penitentiary. In this current confrontation, a delinquent indigent offender was playing with fire by taking his chances at hitting it big on a make-shift board game that many prisoners concoct to make an extra "buck," which was actually just commissary items. Usually the items bid on are collected beforehand and kept by the game organizer. However, an exception was made in this case because each person knew one another well, or so they thought, and simply relied on trust.

This was a deviation from a basic tenet among prison inmates because it's common knowledge that Rule One is to never trust an offender who's indigent. Rule Two is never loan goods. And Rule Three is to watch your back at all times, even if it's a homeboy.

This gambling fight produced a rare sequence of events because it happened so quickly. No one saw it coming.

An event happening so abruptly like this is called stillin. It's when the aggressor goes for a surprise knockout against his unsuspecting opponent and slugs him in the mouth or administers a powerful uppercut to settle the score. The payoff for the aggressor is fierce bragging rights, superiority and fright.

The chaos continued with a symphony of yells from guards and anguish from terrified inmates. It was a tense moment for everyone except Lieutenant RideOut. This was the perfect storm for this tyrant. He marched in like a Rambo action figure with a teargas gun and only wore a protective vest and mask as he demanded that calm be restored.

"Get down, inmates, or I'll blast ya!" he yelled.

I imagined him laughing at us behind that mask. At one point, I could have sworn I saw him smirk.

With the gas oozing throughout the area, the lieutenant hopscotched between us looking for the culprits as each of us shielded our faces with our shirts from the irritating green gas.

With the help of snitches, it didn't take long for him to apprehend his target. The lieutenant grabbed the violator by the collar, lifted him from the floor and shoved him forward.

After subduing the inmates, the gas began to clear gradually and the wails lessened. Shortly after, we were ordered to strip down to our boxers and herded off to showers like cattle doomed for the slaughterhouse. The pulsating, cleansing water was like an antidote for the burning and stinging.

After the drama was completely over, I hoped I would never become a target of violence brought on by mistrust.

The fact is that I hated being thrown in the mix with fools who cared less about inciting a riot but more about hoarding canned goods and postage stamps for gambling.

•••••

After the chow hall riot and lockdown in November 1988, the unit was back in operation in less than a week.

Although it appeared we were on our way to a reasonable lull in violence after days of calm, most of us didn't get too complacent because we knew a volcano could erupt at any given moment.

And, unfortunately, for us that occurred only 72 hours after the most recent disorder that restricted our movements.

Apparently some fool named Martin Gurule, who was on death row, managed to evade guards at the Ellis prison facility, some miles away. The state of Texas was forced to conduct one of its largest manhunts in history.

It was the first time in 64 years that a condemned inmate had managed to slip away undetected from that highly secured facility. En route to an amazing escape, he eluded guards, who had extraordinary firepower and technology, by scaling a 12-foot barrier, using cardboard and magazines for protection from the razor wire at the apex of the fence. He even bypassed high-tech motion sensors and skipped past heartbeat detectors.

Because of this escape, we were again placed on lockdown.

These new developments changed my plans with Sheldon, with whom I had expected to hook up later. For that to occur, the last thing Sheldon and I needed was for the unit to go into a tight standstill once again so soon.

Our containment, fortunately, was short-lived because word filtered down hours later that Gurule was found dead in a nearby creek by two fishing buddies. The circumstances surrounding his death remained unclear.

Some people said his magnificent escape was reminiscent of one orchestrated by legendary outlaws Bonnie and Clyde in 1934, when they sprang accomplices from a Huntsville prison. They, too, eluded authorities cleverly.

With so much mayhem going on in November, Thanksgiving was almost an afterthought.

Weeks would pass before all privileges would be fully restored. I could hardly wait. I yearned to return to the rec yard and get away from the madness indoors.

And before we knew it, Christmas was upon us.

There wasn't a lot of merry celebration on Dec. 25, although I did enjoy hearing from my family and friend Lazlo.

Among the most memorable events was the holiday meal: turkey, ham, dressing, candied yams and various desserts. The usual holiday fare. There was plenty for our huge appetites.

And with the year coming to a close, my anticipation was great. I ripped December 1998 from my wall calendar and set out to establish benchmarks for 1999 that included AA classes and ways to improve my chances at any upcoming parole hearings.

Despite my incarceration, I decided to try to focus on happiness and not be so hard on myself. Not all my prison experiences were bad. There were pleasant carryovers from 1998 that I relished: Kiki and I remained cellmates, and Sheldon was still my "pig in a blanket." He put new meaning into the saying "a bag of chips and all that." Hell, Sheldon was the entire potato farm, hull and all.

And speaking of parole, I was up for a hearing within a few weeks of this new year. While it would be a tense moment for me, it was also horrifying period for the nation. More specifically, it was a political "hot potato" for President Clinton, who was facing an impeachment trial.

It seemed it was going to be a period of uncertainty, and not just for me but for those in high positions as well.

Meanwhile, I aimed to do all I could to avoid a chilly reception during my upcoming meeting with the Texas Board of Pardons and Paroles.

But, for now, my more immediate concern was the cold weather outside. I was awaiting word on whether I would have to go out in the fields to work. It took awhile for us to get a decision, but the field crew learned later that morning that we would be given the day off. I was happy. Whenever it's 40 degrees or lower, we are allowed to stay inside. On this day, it was 36 and dry.

Kiki and I had purposely missed 6 a.m. showers to get more rest just in case we had to work elsewhere inside the unit. We were allowed the extra time because, at least for the moment, he and I had won the favor of Lieutenant RideOut, notoriously known as Lieutenant "Hideout" because of his propensity to sneak up on people when they least expect. He was known for snooping indiscriminately, so it was often hard to predict his comings and goings. It was common knowledge that he would walk behind cells peeping through cracks looking for violations.

It was also believed that he would often visit the unit's wastewater plant after a raid just to look for illegal contraband such as cannabis, tobacco and even condoms that had been flushed so that he could resale them to inmates who had so-called money to purchase them.

The rumor that stood out most to me was that he's been trying to catch me and Sheldon having sex. Since he didn't have any proof, the clueless lieutenant was left to only assume.

It was now early morning, and I dismissed all thoughts about Lieutenant RideOut. I leaped out of bed onto the cold floor, ignoring my cellmate's snoring. I wobbled over to the sink to wash my face. The water was icy cold. Wanting to warm up my body quickly, I imagined a toasty cup of coffee, actually a fresh cup of French vanilla cappuccino would have been perfect about now for a thermal turbo charge.

Twenty minutes after I was cleaned and freshened, I was ready to skedaddle but had to wait patiently for the doors to roll open. My movements didn't arouse Kiki one bit as he lie asleep, motionless, while still snoring peacefully.

I was hoping to meet Sheldon in the dayroom for small talk and perhaps even a hookup later. I imagined sitting next to him licking his red sensual lips.

Sheldon's lustful eyes pierced me so deeply at times. My growing fascination with him had gotten stronger by the day. I just hoped that I was not setting up myself for future disappointment. Truth is, I was so dizzily wrapped up in romance that I didn't seriously concern myself about that. My raging hormones left me vulnerable as I didn't try to inoculate myself from potential hurt and pain. I thought of nothing else except being with him.

I was familiar with being trapped by these types of emotions from previous experiences. Yet somehow I was lulled into a false sense of security, even as my soul was suspended between two worlds – straight and gay. Oddly, I didn't feel that I belonged to either one.

•••••

INTERNAL CHAOS

Opinions about the impeachment of President Clinton ruled the airwaves and the crowded dayroom during the boisterous hour after lunch.

Comments by the so-called prison wit writers, or unofficial "prison paralegals" – often known for their acerbic, sarcastic and cynical remarks – dug deeply into the transgressions of the Clinton administration, from sexual favors from Monica Lewinsky to the Clintons' failed Whitewater land deal.

As some sat glued to the tube to quench their thirst for tabloid news, there was a noticeable absence in discussions about issues that personally affected us in prison, such as violence, greed, envy and the stunning incarceration rates.

I observed behaviors and listened to the conversations being bandied about as Sheldon and I sat next to each other – just as I had envisioned earlier. We sat on the last row of the hard metal benches while keeping our masculinity in check and our hands from one another. We tried not to draw any unwanted attention unlike some fools who didn't give a damn about their reputations. But Sheldon and I were an exception.

As for the wit writers, one such individual – an elder offender called "Pops" – was one of the biggest and oldest fools I had ever met. His real name was Ernest Green, a Vietnam vet in his 60s. He respected the "punk game" but had never slept with another man, in spite of his long incarceration. He claimed that he loved his wife, and it was obvious that she loved him because of her many visits on weekends.

Aside from that, he could be a bit radical.

"That bastard needs to be impeached!" blared Pop, venting over the Clinton affair.

"Man, that's crazy!" another inmate said. "A piece of ass doesn't warrant impeachment, fool!"

"I disagree," interjected Millner, the "panty bandit."

"Considering your rape case, you would," said Pops, unleashing words from his razor-sharp tongue. It seemed that everybody in prison knew a little something about their fellow inmates and their offenses.

"Watch yourself, ol' man. I'll still put these hands on your ass," warned Millner, displaying his large fists.

When everything else failed, it always seemed that a threat was the next best thing among offenders.

Of course Pops ignored him, mumbling that he could have avoided prison altogether had he just kept his parole appointment.

Millner heard Pops and ridiculed him, saying, "You violated! Regardless of how small you consider the offense, you violated," he repeated.

"And so did Clinton when he stuck that meat in that girl's mouth," Pops responded as the entire dayroom roared in laughter.

At this point, I had had just about enough of this foolishness from these brothers.

This led me to wonder about the internal chaos that brews inside inmates, including myself because of my own flaws. I was not exempt from strife.

As for Sheldon and me, I still felt I didn't know enough about him even though we'd been spending a considerable amount of time together. I didn't know enough about his agony. I often wondered about his relationships with other men that didn't involve sex. Who was his father? Was his dad present during his youth? Did he have a good relationship with his mother and other siblings? How many broken promises had he experienced? I had so many questions but few answers because Sheldon didn't talk much.

But at this moment, I just wanted to break away from all the madness in the dayroom. So, I counted down the time for indoor recreation, which was 10 minutes away. When the doors sprung open, I asked Sheldon to join me in the gym.

After he obliged, we headed to a different scene and away from the insults being hurled among inmates.

INTERNAL CHAOS

•••••

After several days on a late Saturday morning, Sheldon and I had hooked up again. I was still feeling guilty about exploiting him for my sexual pleasures, despite it being consensual. As usual Kiki warned me to stop trippin' and just enjoy the ride. The problem, however, was that I was beginning to dislike the ride. At least I tried to convince myself of that.

Could I ignore the G-force sexual rush and the explosive passion I shared with Sheldon? The idea of refusing booty and sleeping with men were tough choices, given my past addictions.

Even with my feelings riding high, I still sensed that Sheldon was sleeping around. I had no proof, but I also felt someone else was tapping the loins of my prison thug. I dismissed my concerns because I was really feeling the dude. His lack of tattoos and unblemished skin and light Cajun tone stimulated my interest beyond measure. Other than being a sex object, he was known to have a hustle or two going on. For example, he constructed "peep mirrors" for mischievous inmates who wanted to keep the guards under surveillance while offenders were busy conniving. This included boning and masturbating in their cells – just all manner of misbehavior. The glass was cut into three-inch squares from a larger recycled mirror and sold for the equivalent of a dollar in commissary goods.

Later that afternoon I had a surprised competitor during a pickup game of basketball on the outside courts of the recreation yard. A youngblood, Cajun Red, kept sweating me as he challenged my offensive court moves. He was very deliberate and bold, brushing his hands across my buttocks as he defended my moves toward the basket. Throughout much of the game, he maintained the same hand movements, an athletic behavior I was quite familiar with. It was a come-on that was poorly disguised as a genuine defensive strategy.

Because of his persistence, I showed that I had the gall to

play the same game when it was my turn to defend him. I became so enthralled that I grabbed a piece of his beefcakes on the cool. Surprisingly, he approved of the rough play, but the punk outsmarted me and scored on my horny ass because I had lost focus of the game.

He knew what he had done and smiled. After he had made his "points," literally and figuratively, his "game," again literally and figuratively, was over. He walked off leaving me in a daze. And I sensed there would be a forthcoming rematch.

I left the recreation area and proceeded inside the unit to freshen up after I was told I had an outside guest. When I got to my cell, I noticed that Kiki was not there. I figured that he must have been hanging out with his beau, Lil' D.

I then headed to the visitation area.

I was happy to see Lazlo, even though the visit was non-contact, meaning we had to speak through a partition rather than have hand-to-hand contact. That privilege was reserved for those I had listed as family.

As I pulled up a chair to begin my visit with Lazlo, my eyes cut to the left and I was stunned at what I saw. I did a double-take after I noticed Kiki chatting in starched white prison clothes and displaying a demeanor I had never seen before. He was acting "straight" and "hard."

It hit me upon further review that on the opposite side of the window, his young son, bright-eyed and smiling, had come to visit along with his mother. She was just as beautiful as my ex-wife, Tish. Her eyes were light, and lips full and luscious. She definitely had that collegiate look about her as described previously by Kiki.

I simply couldn't believe how he had "butched up." Kiki was now as masculine as any offender in the room. I realized at that moment just how skilled this fool really was.

As I continued my visit with Lazlo, my eyes kept scanning in Kiki's direction. I eventually had to ignore him to focus on my visit.

"Man, you look good," I told Lazlo. I was so excited to see him that my eyes sparkled with joy.

He returned the compliment, saying I, too, looked well. He smiled as he discreetly touched the wired cage that separated us with his right index finger. It was an obvious gesture to indicate the painful separation he was experiencing because of my incarceration.

We talked a bit and then Lazlo got up to go to the vending machines for various snacks. As he did that, my eyes again wandered toward Kiki, who had just really thrown me for a loop with his new attitude and behavior.

After Lazlo returned we dined on goodies. He had chips and soda; I had a pastry and a fruit juice. I told him that I had missed him very much and that I wished he really knew how much. But I avoided further emotional comments because I didn't want to stir up any old feelings that might affect us both. From time to time, I still wondered why he left his wife so abruptly. Was it really just to get involved in a same-sex relationship with me or was it for some other reason? I knew I had a particular magnetism that attracted him. It was a quality that my friend, pro football player Butch Webber, had identified about me.

Once I learned that I possessed that trait, I had to understand how to use it productively and not so much seductively. Oftentimes, however, it was the latter.

I then told Lazlo how crazy it was in prison, at times, but that I could cope.

"How," he asked.

"Trust me," I said. "I can write a book on the behaviors that I have witnessed so far in here."

Instead of telling Lazlo about my little prison fling with Sheldon, I decided to express to him how I had been using my time to draw and illustrate in my paintings the madness surrounding me. There was a lot of pain in here, I told him.

As time and small talk passed, Lazlo stared strangely into

my eyes as if he wanted to reveal something. I figured his thoughts concerned my upcoming parole hearing.

But his expression seemed to suggest something other than my parole. I sensed a little guilt in his face. But why, I wondered.

Gently, he began to share his thoughts.

Did I ever tell you that I have a roommate now?" asked Lazlo. He knew he had to start the conversation somewhere.

I maintained an appropriate expression.

"I don't believe you have. Male or female?" I asked, hoping for the latter, but knowing the odds against that wish.

He paused slightly before he answered.

"Male."

It seemed hard for him to say.

With a little envy, I asked, "Do I know him?"

"I don't believe so," said Lazlo, leaning back into his chair, sensing the start of an interrogation.

"Is he Greek?" I probed.

"Yeah, he is."

"Kappa? What?"

"No. Sigma."

His answer surprised me because I once recalled expressing to Lazlo when we first met that I had dropped line with Sigma in undergrad. And that was one of the first times that I had ever quit anything.

"Is he a co-worker?" I asked.

"Actually, he's still in the hunt for work right now. He just relocated to the city from East St. Louis."

"East St. Louis? In Illinois?" I asked as my heart fluttered, giving the impression I had ill feelings about the city. "Don't get me wrong," I quickly interjected, "there are some good people in East St. Louis," I said while knowing at the time the city was plagued with corruption and crime. But, then, so were many other areas.

Lazlo said his roommate was from the area near Missouri

and was also scheduled to enroll at the University of Houston for the upcoming semester to continue his studies in audio/video production.

"So he's media affiliated?" I continued, realizing I was being a jerk. Hell, I had no reason to be jealous, given my behavior behind bars that Lazlo had no clue about.

Lazlo smiled a bit at my questions.

"I guess you can relate it to the media. He's an actor and, like you, a former athlete, too," Lazlo said.

The conversation was really getting the best of me now as I sensed Lazlo was pushing his luck by comparing me to his roommate.

"Well, does he have a name?" I asked.

"Nathan."

"Has he found an agent yet?"

"Not yet. I was hoping you could help us with that."

Us? Could these two roommates possibly be a couple? I wondered.

"Considering you used to model, and may I add you were one of the finest, I was hoping that you could give me a few names of legitimate talent agencies in the city."

Page Parkes Center of Modeling in Uptown came to mind. I told him that she was the best in the city who didn't accept mediocrity, neither do her clients. I then asked Lazlo about Nathan's skills.

Lazlo said he'd never seen him act, but gave him high marks as a model after witnessing him on the runway a few times.

It seemed that Nathan and I had many similarities. I wondered if he was dark like me, tall like me, good looking. Was he Lazlo's new lover?

"He's rather good onstage. I'll send you one of his composites and let you be the judge on his looks," said Lazlo, who appeared to be bragging a bit.

My first thought was jealously but then I corrected my attitude and told him I would be happy to critique Nathan's photos. I was actually excited for Lazlo. I knew that it would be unreasonable for me to hold on to him for selfish ambitions. Hell, he deserved to be happy even if I wasn't.

Though I was kicking it with Sheldon, I was still a lonely soul in this crowded prison. I needed a real friend, not just some booty buddy.

Lazlo assured me he was not abandoning me. For me, that was his confirmation that he was dating this Nathan dude without me even asking the question. I really didn't have to hear him admit it because I had already formed my answer.

For the remainder of the visit, questions swirled inside my head about Nathan. I even wondered about his age since he was preparing to attend college. I couldn't bear to ask, but I just assumed that Nathan was younger and perhaps better-looking than me.

Despite Lazlo's vow of continued support, I began to feel sick and abandoned, perhaps fearful that this person would take up all of Lazlo's time and that he would forget about me and let me rot in this hellhole.

Chapter 13
The Rumor Mill

Oh, remember the bitterness and suffering you have dealt to me.
Lamentations 3:19

A few weeks had passed since Lazlo's visit. He sent the composites of Nathan to some of the places I had suggested, as well as to me. But he was now uneasy about that decision – not because he was concerned about my approval, but apparently there was a storm brewing between Nathan and him.

Recently, the two were invited to a get-together at the home of Lazlo's colleague, Donna, who lived in the high-end Uptown area. She was a top executive – running the quality control department – at a downtown Med Tech pharmaceutical laboratory, and he suspected she had a crush on him from the way she caressed his biceps and frequently placed her hand on his shoulders. She kept within close proximity to Lazlo to allow the fragrance of her intoxicating Fendi perfume to work like a love potion on him.

Donna Dangerfield was very attractive and very much single. Yet, she was a tad bit bossy. But Lazlo, known for his patience, knew how to deal with her demanding nature.

Being a top manager explained her dogmatic and matter-of-fact behavior. She looked every bit of a highly regarded professional – always impeccably dressed and everything she wore seemed to perfectly compliment her almond brown skin.

Her business attire seemed to leap from the pages of Vogue and various boutique fashion outlets that included designs from Prada and Donna Karan, to name a few. She was a fitness advocate who, during the week, spent countless hours at the gym. And it showed in the sexy curvatures of her business pantsuits that particularly highlighted her show-stopping glutes. Whenever she wore her knee-length Gucci dresses and size-7 stiletto-heeled Manolos, her pronounced calves would magically whip out like Pop Tarts as her muscles contracted with each waddling step.

Donna absolutely loved sports of various kinds, but she especially had an affinity for baseball and two of its sluggers, Derek Jeter and Barry Bonds.

Even with those flawless features, Lazlo brushed her off, partly because she was a manager at their company. But beyond that Lazlo was in a relationship with a man. And he was certain that Donna would never understand how a man like him could indulge in a same-sex union. But Lazlo seemed willing to keep his options open as he searched for love that was devoid of the stresses he had become so familiar with in the past – which included people with addictive behaviors.

As the night crept forward, a commotion in another room attracted the attention of some guests. There appeared to be a dispute, so Lazlo moved toward the disturbance to investigate. It was good that he checked because he discovered that an intoxicated Nathan had gotten a little too "happy," or buzzed.

Lazlo began to panic because he did not know what Nathan was capable of doing under the influence of alcohol. The louder Nathan got, the more negative attention he drew. Nathan wasn't speaking to anyone in particular but grousing at random as he wobbled through the crowd. That's when the hostess, Donna, began moving in to quell the disorder. But Lazlo intervened, telling her he could handle the situation.

She obliged.

Lazlo took a deep breath and approached Nathan, hoping to avoid further escalation. His friend stood in the middle of the room with a drink in his hand while berating other guests.

Lazlo immediately grabbed Nathan by the left arm and practically dragged him out of the front door as curious eyes followed them both. He had seen his friend drink on countless occasions but had never witnessed such uncharacteristic behavior before.

One thing was certain: Nathan had a drinking problem.

"Damn!" Lazlo screamed. He began to replay the agony he endured when I was in his life battling my own personal demons. Lazlo then wondered to himself: "Am I going to have to go around this mountain again with another man hiding from himself and his terrors?"

He abruptly left the party with Nathan without even saying goodnight to Donna. He angrily barreled down the freeway toward home. After arriving, he undressed Nathan and placed him in the shower. Lazlo decided this was not the night to discuss the embarrassment. He would wait for a more appropriate time.

•••••

My mother, Mattie, sat calmly at her kitchen table on this last weekend of February sipping a hot cup of Italian blend roast coffee. She thought deeply about the successful outcome of her mastectomy, agreeing that life now for her isn't bitter, but blessed.

The breast surgery left her weak, but she gained confidence in her recovery and dismissed any doubt about her decision after picking up a women's magazine nearby that stated one in two women diagnosed with breast cancer eventually choose to have a mastectomy because the procedure carried less risks than a lumpectomy, which treated the cancer with radiation but produced nasty side effects.

As she drank her coffee, she took a moment to praise God. She was so caught up in her worship that she realized something was missing in her hot brew. Aah, the creamer, she thought. As she normally does, she laughed at her absent-mindedness. She set aside the magazine and placed the cup next to its saucer to add the Coffee Mate.

The delightful aroma from the sizzling cup was like a sedative, with the taste that provided the tonic she needed to sustain her energy. She then added more cream for that perfectly desired taste. Returning the spoon to the saucer, she cupped the warm java with both hands, lifting it toward her pursed lips to savor every drop. It was indeed a moment for her to reflect on a trying period that turned triumphant.

Even as she faced months of recovery after her surgery, doctors insisted that she continue her treatment and therapy. She maintained a sense of humor about her breast removal, still joking that even if her body was as normal as before that no one would pay attention anyway to the sagging breasts of a 60-plus-year-old woman.

She reasoned that her impending prosthetic would cover up any imperfection left from the surgery.

•••••

On a cold Monday morning at 6:45, the sun had barely made itself known when I noticed the time on the clock radio. Kiki was still sleep, but he would soon be awakened by field guards screaming, "Work Time!"

Before that call, I started the morning as usual. I began with prayer and a hot cup of French vanilla cappuccino to knock the chill from my body. Having an invigorating cup of coffee was among the few perks, but prayer was my safeguard. I needed that spiritual covering because of the unpredictable daily events from inmates and guards. There were always bouts of anger and confusion over mundane events and battles involving fragile egos. The behavior was typical of inmates, but even the guards had their moments. Some officers wanted to project themselves as tyrannical rulers. And many of them were just as, or more so, close-minded than a lot of offenders. It was simply another day at the "farm."

With cabbage season in full swing, we were kept quite busy. And there was plenty in the fields to pick – too much as far as I was concerned. Many times I wanted to rebel because I was so tired of feeling like a migrant worker. But on this day, I quickly abandoned the thought and waited for the cell doors to fly open. I then peered at Kiki, who also worked in the field, as he slumbered peacefully and carefree in his bed. I was still amazed about the visit he had a week ago with his son and baby's momma. I was more taken, though, by Kiki's masculinity. I still couldn't figure out how he pulled that off. It made me question what was really going on with him.

As I stared at him resting, I was jolted by a reminder that Kiki had the day off. I remembered him saying that he had an appointment at the infirmary with the prison nurse for the Center for Infectious Diseases.

I didn't get into Kiki's business, but based on my personal experience I knew that a visit with the CID generally meant a serious health threat. There was already rumor that Kiki was HIV-positive, too, just like myself. I didn't assume the worst but tried to allay my concerns by suggesting he could be going there simply for a flu shot, given the season and the rise in the number of cases so far. I had hoped this was the reason, but even my casual suspicions suggested I wasn't completely optimistic.

Screeeeech!!

The barred doors began to open.

"Work time, ladies!" Get up! It's work time!" a field guard shouted.

Oh, how I hated this moment. It was so demeaning to

watch us being rustled out of our sleep and herded like cattle. Again, I thought about boycotting my work detail. Besides, I felt I had nothing to lose. My parole was denied. I got that notice days ago Saturday, when I also had received the composites of Lazlo's friend. And as I stared at the images again, I had to admit that Nathan was, indeed, a handsome fellow. I then filed away the composites and quickly brushed my teeth and combed my hair before exiting the cell to wait in a line of work squads that had formed in the hallway. Everything in prison was about control. That included talking and walking in the hallways.

"Keep the noise down, inmates!" Lieutenant RideOut belted. Hearing that warning, all of us knew that at least one person was happy on this particular morning. RideOut was definitely in his element. He seemed to relish every minute of his time at work.

Once in the fields, we worked tediously – bending, picking and dragging sacks for hours. Once the laborious backbreaking shift crept to a close, every inmate kept watch of every minute so that we didn't have to work a second longer. More than 200 of us were out in the field, and I'm guessing that more than 50 percent of us prayed daily for snow, rain, ice, thunderstorms – or even a tornado – to end the suffering that we compared to Hebrew slaves, minus the punishing floggings.

With no inclement weather, we knew we had a quota to fulfill: 20,000 heads of cabbage. That would equate roughly to 100 heads per offender. Once our jobs were complete, distributing the product was next. About 1,000 cabbages would be donated to charity, including 500 to a local food bank. The remaining would go to the market for profit, although prison officials denied this was the case. We all were hip to the real story.

Prisons in Texas were all about money with little regard for rehabilitation. Since inmates had no ambassador to represent us, we were powerless to reap any rewards from our labor, not a single penny. We were wards of the state, and the public couldn't care less about how we were treated. As far as they were concerned, we were criminals and should be punished. There should be no benefits or perks. And, heaven forbid, plush or cozy accommodations.

Many people would be surprised at all the recycled products made by prisoners, including linen, boots and clothes. Even human waste has been used as compost for fertilization because some horticulturists claim it's far superior to animal manure for enriching the soil. Now ain't that a bunch of crap?

"Hat time," somebody yelled.

The term was often used by a field officer on horseback who would raise his or her hat to indicate the end of the workday. All other officers would then organize their squads for a head count, which occurred at least six times a day.

We all were excited but confused for a moment because the four-hour shift was not over yet.

Then came the truth. It seemed that a nearby offender, playing a joke, gave the order.

After realizing it was bogus, a Hispanic officer galloped toward us on his tan horse demanding, "Get back to work, you damn inmates! Nobody told y'all asses to stop working!" he blasted.

About that same time, Cajun Red crept upon me suddenly.

"What's up, Moe?"

His eyes were seductive yet serious. His attire was no longer white and stainless, but his sex appeal glistened.

After the horseman trotted away, I secretly replied, because talking was prohibited.

"I didn't realize that you had caught up with me so fast," I said. "Anyway, the only thing up is this damn work."

I continued to pick my quota, as there were clowns on the

left of me and practical jokers to my right. With Cajun Red sweating me, I knew this could fuel gossip because I was really vibing the dude.

All it took was his scent, the smell of his sweat-drenched masculine body activating my hormones and sending them into overdrive. I tried to ignore his secret advances, but Cajun Red continued with reckless abandon.

I cautioned him to be wary of the guards. He then kept one eye on the officer and the other on me.

"You know, I don't know much about friendships, Moe. But there is one thing I like about you."

After he said that, I couldn't help but give him my attention.

"What's that?" I said, standing to stretch my back.

"You know how to keep your mouth shut. And that's a good thing in here. You feel me?"

Truth is, I felt him in more ways than I wanted to admit. I struggled to maintain control every time our eyes met. It was tough finding a way out of this lustful craze for him, and for Sheldon, too. I knew that the moment our lips met that I would be down for anything with Cajun Red. Just when I tried to snap out of it, he hit me with a question that left me speechless.

"So when are you gonna drop that zero and come kick it with a real G?"

I could not believe my ears. Was this fool finally coming around by telling me what he really wanted? I was already awestruck by his presence. But now his words took me totally by surprise and left me temporarily paralyzed. I stuttered incomprehensibly trying to figure out how to respond. Although I was pleased with his forward approach, I tried to mask my interest.

"You know I can't disrespect the game like that, Red," I said as I got back to work, avoiding his Cajun-moon eyes.

"What game, Moe? Sheldon ain't nothing to you."

"We kickin' it, man!"
"Don't be naive, Moe. Cut your losses, dude."
I knew Red was feeling me and at the same time spitting some real vibe. The reality was that he and Sheldon both were just for the moment. Too bad he hadn't realized it yet.
"Hat time! It's hat time!"
The official end of the workday was finally announced.

• • • • •

When you're in prison, it seemed that many Texas winters could be especially harsh, much like the attitudes of some of my fellow offenders. Heartless and cruel were even better descriptions. The hearts of these men could be just as cold as the falling mercury during winter.

After work and commissary, I headed up to Sheldon's place to drop off some items he wanted. Lucky for me there was a guard on duty who didn't give a hoot about inmates visiting cells just as long as we covered our behinds. I was happy that Lieutenant RideOut was off duty.

As I eased my way closer to Sheldon's cell, I heard an odd but familiar noise. It wasn't until I reached my destination that I realized the source of the whooshing sound.

I crept upon Sheldon, who, to my shock, was being poked by one of the Crips I had seen around prison. My heart was crushed as I stared for a moment. Sheldon didn't see me, but the fella he was with winked at me with a cavalier attitude. At that moment I wanted to kick both of their asses. Instead, I just bitterly turned away. I knew that any action from me could start a domino effect and bring unnecessary repercussions. Besides, why should I fight over some ho' like Sheldon anyway? He wasn't worth the trouble, I thought.

So, I scampered down toward the dayroom to ease my frustration. It seemed news had already spread about Sheldon and his fling. This further convinced me that men such as Sheldon, who are willing to give up the "goods" to a gang member or anyone else, were a dime a dozen in prison. I knew then that he wasn't mine anymore. It was finally time to let go.

Cajun Red was right when he suggested that I needed to cut my losses.

Chapter 14
Box, Bounce or Roll

Why should any living man complain when punished for his sin?
Lamentations 3:39

Kiki and I organized a meeting to talk about some of the rumors swirling around prison. After we returned to our lockup area, we stored our commissary and then began our cellmate-to-cellmate chat. We started out discussing the contamination of the soil in the work fields, apparently from a buildup of toxins from the past. It appeared that DDT, lead, iron, zinc and ammonia hydroxide at one time had been used to treat the soil. It's believed that officials used the banned substances and then tried to skirt federal punishment from the Environmental Protection Agency in an alleged cover-up of the violations.

The revelations could explain why many inmates who worked in the fields were diagnosed with boils and parasites under their skin. The blatant disregard for inmates' health and prison officials' self-governance and lax state oversight were examples of a system run amok. Kiki and I were pissed, knowing that we had been placed in harm's way. I particularly was angry because the exposure threatened my already compromised immune system. We could only hope that there would be immediate intervention for our civil rights, which really weren't guaranteed once we got thrown in the slammer.

After venting over those issues with several cups of cappuccino, we prepared to steer the conversation to the heart of the matter, or more specifically, matters of my heart: Sheldon.

I stood against the cool white wall adjacent to our bunks as Kiki sat on his top bunk. With jazz playing in the background from his Realistic radio, he placed thick white socks on his feet while waiting on me to start the conversation.

"So, what are you gonna do, Moe, just eyeball me for the next hour or are we gonna talk about you-know-who?" asked Kiki, with a rather cool demeanor.

Of course I just stared him straight in the eye, blaming him for my heartache. For it was he who introduced me to Sheldon's bitch ass. I realized, too, that I bore some of the responsibility because I chose to bite the rotten fruit because I could not better control my sexual appetite.

"Well, Kiki," I said, "now that I've been dumped I guess that I'm nothing more than a footnote in his life, huh?" I had to admit that this whole mess served me right for allowing sex to consume me.

But Kiki was more straightforward about my actions. He didn't waste his time with euphemisms to sugarcoat his words.

"You knew the water was troubled before you dipped your feet into it, Moe. Men like Sheldon are hustlers. They go for the hottest thing going for the moment. It's about survival in here, and it doesn't matter how pretty and fine these boys are. When you're indigent, you have to use your best commodity and oftentimes that is your body," Kiki said.

"So, the hell with respecting the game, huh?" I asked, knowing Kiki was right.

Kiki, crossing his legs, said, "The game is very much alive, but sometimes a fool comes along and disrespects it. And it ain't Sheldon's fault."

"Then whose fault is it?" I asked.

"There's a time when everything will be revealed, Moe. So, your best bet is to chill out and let nature take its course."

I wasn't sure what Kiki meant by that statement until he offered a hint.

"Violators in here are always punished. Mark my word," he continued.

I learned that the violator's name was Clear, the Crips member I caught all up in Sheldon's guts.

Now I was trying to figure out if it was my duty to avenge the disrespect by Clear, or wait to see if something was already in the works.

One reason I was pissed off was that I had provided the indigent Sheldon with so many personal items. But besides commissary, I gave him the most important of all: my compassion.

"Did I not provide for this dude enough that he had to sleep with that damn gang member?" I asked.

"Sometimes we sacrifice our bodies simply for pleasure, Moe. And there are many fools in here who think prison is about entertainment and gratification. The booty is a powerful tool when incarcerated, but that same tool can cost you your life if you step wrong," he warned.

"What are you saying, cellie?" I became even more attentive now as I sat on the toilet facing him, wondering what he meant.

"A lot of guys in here want to mess around but don't due to fear. They don't want to get caught up in some love triangle or death wish for sleeping with somebody else's piece. So they stay neutral. But every now and then there's a knucklehead who thinks he's invincible because he's part of some clique. He'll strut around all cocky and bold as if the code is irrelevant."

"You mean Clear?"

"Clear is the one."

"So, what's next? Where do I fit in to all of this? I don't want no beef with Clear and his boys. But, know this, if I have to box with those fools I will."

"There won't be any of that, Moe. Just bounce. Lil' D assured me that things will be taken care of. You just hold your peace, and family will take care of family. Get my drift?" Kiki asked.

I told him that I sort of understood but that I still hadn't resolved the issue with Sheldon. In my mind, I wanted to brutally bang him one last time. It would be my way of saying farewell for his damn betrayal.

After mail call and my last French vanilla cappuccino, I gathered the nerves to go back into the dayroom that night. And as usual, the entire wing was there. Cajun Red was at a nearby table playing chess. Millner and Pops were on the front bench with their faces buried in the television watching New York Undercover; Druppy and his crony, Big Gee, were on a back bench eating. And Kiki and Lil' D were in their usual position, hugged up near the window by the hall conversing while keeping a watchful eye out for Lieutenant RideOut.

As I moved closer into the room, a heavy hand landed on my right shoulder. Because I was already a little uneasy in this environment, I reacted coldly with an unfriendly expression. Given the current circumstances, I could have easily snapped and a fight ensued. But then I adjusted my attitude a little when I discovered it was not Sheldon. Thank God it wasn't because I wasn't ready for him just yet.

It was Jose Vasquez, aka Angel, the tall, dark and muscular Hispanic inmate I met during Sunday church services months ago when we were both alerted that we had outside visitors.

At first I was confused as to why he was on my wing of the prison but then assumed he must have been given a relocation order, or move slip.

"What's up, vato?" he said. It was a Latin term for "guy." Angel's eyes said more than I expected.

I simply told him not much but that I didn't feel like talking with him at the moment.

He obliged but walked off in a way that suggested he was a

little miffed at me for being terse.

Shortly after that a guard walked up shouting through the roomful of noise asking for Pops and Lil' D.

He called them by their real names: "Ernest Green (Pops) and Arthur Bishop (Lil' D)."

The two approached the bars.

"Pack your bags!" the officer ordered. "Y'all being transferred."

"Transferred? To where?" a frowning Lil' D asked.

The guard stared at the travel slip in his right hand and said Huntsville.

"Huntsville? For what?" said Lil' D, expressing his objection.

"Looks like y'all are going home, inmates. You wanna go home, don't ya?"

Suddenly, Pops released the loudest scream I'd ever heard from a man. The dayroom grew morbidly quiet as the two soon-to-be-released inmates basked in their impending freedom.

Kiki was stunned and in total disbelief. He realized then that he was about to lose his lover. It was a bitter pill to swallow.

I hurt for Kiki because I reasoned that Lil' D had been keeping secret the possibility of his release. But the reality was that this is the way things rolled in prison.

All of the madness that many of us endured was just for the moment, including same-gender relationships, the cliques, the tough act and make-believe friendships. Each of those things evaporates like standing water in desert-like conditions.

Generally when parole has been approved, even lovers are kept in the dark to avoid the prospect of some vindictive person dooming their chances at the last minute, causing them to pick up a case and longer incarceration.

The fact is that everyone knows sooner or later his name

may be called for release. And the best way to guarantee freedom is to keep your big mouth shut about upcoming pardons and paroles, especially if sex is involved between offenders.

"Whuzzup, Diary?"

It's been a long time since I've been back to the chapel or contributed to this journal. Truth is that I've been carrying on like some out-of-control demonic freak who's been consumed by sex, participating in lewd acts almost without fail. I feel like the Apostle Paul who raised the all-important question many centuries ago: "Who will rescue me from this body of death?"

I've always known I had been acting out of my nature, just as I've known that I have abandoned God in so many ways. Still a loner and feeling so different than other guys around me, I have tried to fit in by boasting about my masculinity just to appease the folks around me. That has made matters only worse for me because other men viewed me as cocky, at best. I really don't know how to cope with many of these men in here, so I have stayed to myself much of the time and draw visions of hope on my canvas. As I look back, I realize that all of my past relationships were based on sex only, not actual friendships. It was always so simple that way, I thought, because then there would be no emotional ties. I learned that this was not altogether true. I had hoped there would be no real connection or conditions between me and my partners. I discovered that I was sickened by loneliness. It was a hurt so deep that it felt like flesh was being ripped from my bones.

There were times I would sit back and watch Kiki and Lil' D (who has now traded this place for a taste of freedom) carry on like dogs in heat. I don't, however, think I could ever be that comfortable with a man in an environment like this, though. Even though Lazlo and I shared a lot of information and he was the first man I'd been honest with, I still could not embrace the same-sex marriage thing. I truly didn't know how to love until I met Tish, my ex-wife. I shared everything about my life with her except the fact that I was bisexual. But then I would come to realize why she actually stayed with me, even with my fears and secrets. It was because she needed the marriage to gain citizenship.

As for my current situation, I've been thrown into this prison pit and have lost the privilege to vote, sit on a jury, run for public office or even travel out of the state or country without prior permission. I wouldn't wish this on my worst enemy.

Still, I recalled what Kiki had said to me earlier in the day: "There's a time for everything and a reason behind it."

I sincerely believe that divine intervention allowed me to be here to weigh the error of my ways. I believe I am powerless to control my lust on my own, as I am lured by Sheldon's scent, his touch, his masculinity. This desire for Sheldon rivals that of Cajun Red. Granted, however, each time his buttocks touch mine on that basketball court, he sends chills down my spine. I'm sure I'm taunting him in the same manner. Fact of the matter is, we both are acting out our lust. We've come to accept that the "booty" is so powerful it can't be resisted.

This wicked mentality and submission are partially the reasons I'm here in the first place. I fell to the influence and deception of Curtis, the Houston Baptist University tennis player who introduced me to crack cocaine. I wanted that Negro so badly that I overlooked his vices. I simply closed my eyes, shielding them from everything except his killer smile and his drug habits. All I wanted to do was to test-drive his buns, but it placed me on a collision course that cost me my freedom. He played me like a funky piano. There's definitely a lesson in all of this drama. Even so, there are still many unanswered questions I have to confront. I haven't quite found the answer yet, but I sense there's still hope for me. (End Monday, 10:45 p.m.; Day 240)

•••••

In the last week of February, we were blessed with another cold day, this time in the 30s. And for us, that meant no work in the field.

Yahoo!

I decided to hit the showers as my cellie, Kiki, opted to stay bundled up under the heavy wool blanket. I sensed he was missing Lil' D. It showed in his demeanor as he lie there curled in a fetal position on his top bunk, clinging tightly to his pillow.

And they're off!

The doors rolled open, and the rat race was on.

With shower shoes, soap and shampoo, grown men scuffled and shuffled like wildebeests down rows and stairs and plodded past metal gates through a corridor to the wet area.

Once there, we were greeted by none other than Lieutenant RideOut.

Damn, does this guy ever have a day off?

"Slow your roll, inmates. Slow your roll," he said.

His voice was unusually calm, his eyes pensive, his back erect.

As I wondered what was up with him, I began scanning the area for Sheldon. But there were no signs of him. Apparently, he decided – as my cellie did likewise – to forgo the morning shower. I very much wanted to touch his booty one last time, but it appeared this was not meant to be today. Instead, I undressed, tossing my white boxers to the side. Oddly, even with the incredible noise, the lieutenant remained tranquil. He simply stood at the entrance of the shower, guarding it like a tamed, domestic dog. Not to be confused, he still was calling the shots and ushering us through, but ... calmly. It was almost scary.

As I was about to get in line for shower necessities, someone called out my name.

"Moe!" said a voice too hoarse to distinguish at first.

As I turned, it was Cajun Red. He summoned me to join him and about 10 other people already in the line. I couldn't figure out what he was up to, so I hesitated for a bit. I then moved forward toward his direction. To do that, I had to skip. Typically, that would have netted a fight instantly. But since I traded my place with an offender in front of Red, no harm was done.

Now, I was just where Red wanted me to be: in front of him butt-naked. Damn, how convenient was that? I could feel him breathing on my neck, and I sensed that he was getting aroused from staring at my chocolate buttocks that he'd often fondled on the basketball court. I wasn't tripping though. I loved the attention.

Once again, the noise level rose. I continued keeping a watchful eye on the "Lieut" as well as on inmates in case they were checking out the behavior between Red and me. We had to be careful because erections were considered offensive in the shower area.

"You better put that magnum back in its holster before you misfire," I teased, taking deep breaths to keep my own jimmy from swelling.

"Don't worry; it won't misfire. My bullets are too precise and much too valuable," he responded, slyly brushing against my firm buttocks with his jimmy.

His bold act stopped me cold, and I turned and looked at him with a little fire in my eyes.

"What's wrong?" he asked.

"I don't pop it like that, Red. I ain't no shower ho," I whispered.

"Come again," he responded.

I chuckled tersely at his silly-ass antics, but he heard me and understood. That's when he backed off.

We were now the fifth and sixth person from the necessities window.

"When are you going to let me get that?" a persistent Red asked.

Since I realized this Negro wasn't going to let up, I decided to flip the script.

"As soon as we get a few things straight," I answered.

"Things like what, Moe?"

"I don't play roles, Red. You feel me? I like what I like and when I like it. Can you handle the truth about what I'm about to spit at you?"

"I like a challenge," he said, teasingly.

"This ain't no basketball game, fool. I'm for real. We need to talk about some things before we get into the meat and potatoes of things."

"I like both, if that's what you're wondering," he offered, letting me know he was versatile and down for whatever. His voice, though hoarse, was hard and sexy. "I ain't trippin' either. You feel me?" he continued.

"Next!" screamed the worker handing out necessities. I moved forward to give him my sizes. Afterward, I headed toward a nearby bench and waited on Cajun Red, wondering how a guy as good-looking and masculine as him got involved with sleeping with men. I knew looks had nothing to do with sexual preferences, because from time to time that question had often been asked of me.

As Cajun Red was approaching, our eyes were locked onto each other like heat-seeking missiles with our lust supercharged as we peered at each other's naked bodies. Our muscular, sleek physique was similar. Some would call us "fine." I simply say "defined."

I then stepped ahead to move toward the water in one of the three separated stalls, but Cajun Red's heavy hand grabbed my left arm.

"Not that way, Moe. This way," he instructed.

I followed, heading toward showers that were designed during the '50s. Each had separate stalls. Through the years, prison administrators never bothered to update the facility with hardware such as adjustable shower heads or spigots.

Normally a guard would be patrolling the shower area from atop a catwalk 7 feet above our heads, but not on this day. This was quite odd. Even more weird was how an unusually subdued Lieutenant RideOut remained glued to the doorway, still.

OK. What's really going on? I pondered.

I was more curious about Red now as I soaped up and admired his fat, muscular buttocks. As I took a glimpse, I monitored other inmates. I didn't want them to see me peeping at Red's body.

"Hey, Moe," Red yelled out, "Do you remember what I had said to you this week?" he asked as he teased, lathered and washed his body.

"Can't recall," I said.

"I said that I liked you because you knew how to mind your own business. Remember?"

As Red spoke, he didn't bother to look me in the eye. He kept washing his hairless body.

Just at that moment I knew something was going down because of the noise coming from the stall adjacent to us. It was a muffled wail, yet quite audible. Then there were heavier grunts and moans followed by violent sounds of flesh attacking flesh. Even with the mostly indistinguishable sounds, everything else appeared to be normal as everyone continued to mind his own business.

By the end of the day, I found out what really had gone down in the shower near me.

Clear, the Crip who dipped his jimmy inside my boy, Sheldon, was being disciplined by his "family" because he violated territory. As a result, he became a target of the "Man in Gray" – the wrath of the lieutenant. Oddly, I discovered that it was RideOut who had convinced Clear to sleep with Sheldon just to see how I would respond.

He wanted to see if I would bounce, box or roll with a gang member and ultimately jeopardize my privileges, or, more importantly, my life.

Well, I proved that the lieutenant had me confused with someone else because there was no way I was going to fight over some damn boy's booty like others have done.

In the end, Clear learned a valuable lesson. He now knows to stay clear of another man's territory. His wounds and emotional scars would be longtime reminders.

Even with this, it was revealed later within the week, from the lips of Kiki, that "Lieut" still had it out for me.

But why? In this sea of men, what had I done to cause such disfavor?

Nevertheless, Kiki – the resident color analyst – told me how the brutal shower mess went down. He also told me that Clear was sent to lockup for 30 days by Lieutenant RideOut. Apparently, before his departure, Lil' D shared this information with his beau, Kiki.

It seemed that the lieutenant wanted to teach me a lesson because he had heard about Sheldon and me but was never able to catch us in the act. He was furious that I outsmarted him at his own game by covering up holes in Sheldon's cell walls that he often peeked through.

Chapter 15
Kill-offs

"Woe to me!" I cried "I am ruined! For I am a man of unclean lips, and I live among a people of unclean lips."
Isaiah 6:5

March's vibrant moon glowed from the east as Lazlo sat on a park bench sorting through options over Nathan's excessive drinking and the attraction Donna had for him.

The situation with Nathan had gotten worse. In the beginning, it was a glass of wine here and there. But, now, it was the heavy stuff such as vodka on the rocks.

Nathan was unwilling to share some of his hidden secrets with Lazlo. He didn't want to undergo the same humiliation he experienced with his sister back in East St. Louis. So to drown his sorrows, he resorted to drinking. Since the problem developed at such a glacial pace, Nathan's habit didn't seem so severe.

But over the course of time, his drinking began affecting their relationship as friends, let alone as lovers.

As for Lazlo, he didn't drink but he didn't condemn those who did imbibe moderately.

Depressing nights such as these often led Lazlo to seek refuge at a serene place such as the manmade waterfall in the Uptown Galleria area. The C-shaped structure resembled an ancient Roman outdoor theater. This brilliantly illuminated phenomenon sent clear fresh water cascading from its inner concave. The rolling gush was pleasantly mesmerizing and peaceful to the ears and soul.

As he used the time to reflect, Lazlo concluded that he would eventually have to address Nathan's intoxication and his pathetic personality borne out of the heavy bingeing. But he wanted the timing to be right and to avoid an accusatory tone for the eventual conversation. Instead, he wanted to pursue an avenue that focused on recovery, therapy and support.

Aside from his thoughts about Nathan, there was the issue of Donna Dangerfield, who was becoming more explicit with her body language. He knew he had to approach the matter of dating delicately or risk turning Miss Dangerfield into Miss "angerfield," without the "D." The last thing he needed was to trigger her wrath. As the expression goes: Hell hath no fury like a woman scorned.

Even so, there was no uncertainty about her goals. And it was clear that she had greater plans up her sleeve than Lazlo could imagine.

Not since his divorce had Lazlo had a woman in his life. He'd often talk about missing the gentle touch and warm caress of a woman's hands, walking side by side on the streets, in the parks, in the malls and even in church. He missed the freedom and normalcy of public displays of affection in heterosexual relationships. Although he sometimes missed the mental matchup of wits with the fairer sex, he learned that Donna, on the other hand, was a woman of a different breed. She was a company woman, highly aggressive, deeply dogmatic, and uncharacteristically assertive at times. But then, too, she was a senior executive at her Med Tech company, and it expected her to be an authoritative leader. With her position came a tremendous amount of power. And that dominance sometimes resulted in "power tripping."

Knowing that, he did not want to cross her. He knew that dragging her into his mess with Nathan could trigger a meltdown of nuclear proportion and derail his career.

A very tough decision awaited Lazlo. He still possessed

natural admiration and affection for women and was highly regarded for his chivalry. He also felt that his sanity would remain intact by developing a positive relationship with a female.

With this he pondered whether to stay the course with Nathan. To some degree, he felt like a deserter for even thinking about abandoning a special friend because of his alcohol dependency. He wanted to believe it could be conquered. But then Lazlo remembered what it was like dealing with me and my cocaine issues. Again, he had to wonder what he was getting himself into if he chose to stay in the fight.

He told himself over and over again that he was not going to become a "crisis junkie," one who gravitates toward people needing help so that it validates his existence.

After convincing himself of that, he knew what he had to do: confront Nathan once and for all if there were going to be any kind of normalcy in their lives and within their circle of friends.

•••••

Singer Jennifer Holiday would probably roll on the floor in laughter if she witnessed the scene from my cellie as he attempted to lip sync her Tony Award-winning song "And I'm Telling You I'm Not Going" from her Broadway hit Dreamgirls.

With Lil' D now gone, Kiki appeared to be finally coming out of his funk, contrary to what the song's lyrics suggested. In fact, it seemed he was ready to reclaim his glory days. Still, I always wondered why some guys would even attempt to sing ol' girl's song in falsetto, knowing full well that whenever they tried to hit a high-C at Jennifer's extraordinary range that those notes seemed to only strike back with a vengeance.

But I continued to laugh as Kiki added such dramatic flair to his performance. Actually, I liked it when he was himself.

His silly antics put me at ease and freed my mind of my own ills and past behaviors. But now that I have seen two sides of Kiki, I began to wonder if his feminine act was just that – an act.

After his moment on "Broadway" on this late Thursday evening, Kiki suddenly reverted to his masculine persona, more akin to a stuntman, as he leaped superman-style onto his bed. His voice got deeper and his demeanor even sterner. He became that person I remembered seeing months ago during visitation with his son and the woman with whom he birthed their child. Barry Williams, aka Kiki, had returned, looking rather appealing like a younger masculine Taye Diggs. Despite that I had no intention of redefining my relationship with my cellmate. Kiki and me together? Nah! There was no way I was going to go there with him.

Sometimes, it's easy for so-called or wannabe straight men to forget that feminine guys such as Kiki may also be fathers.

As another gay inmate once quipped, "You can dip me in chocolate and put me in high heels and call me Patty, but I'll always be a man."

Later during the hour, Kiki and I began talking as usual. I told him I was thinking about hooking up with Sheldon one last time.

His reaction?

"You must be desperate or out of your damn mind," Kiki said.

Maybe I was both. Still I wanted to test drive that Negro one last time.

We then moved the conversation to Lil' D.

This was one time Kiki was not in the mood to talk, but he did assure me that he was just fine without him in his life. He was "just for the moment," Kiki said.

Going from one conversation to another, we then shifted into third gear, steering it toward Cajun Red. I, of course, didn't have a problem talking about him at all. Besides, Kiki was kind enough to clue me in to the Sheldon/Clear mess and the big payback. That violent shower scene was a period of revelation, unlike what I thought my bathroom experience was going to be like on that day. I had a little freak brewing inside me while watching Cajun Red shower. But instead, on that day, I learned about the consequences of dishonor.

Once Kiki got a hint of my interest in Cajun Red, he asked what was up between the Crescent City native and me.

I replied coyly, "What do you mean?"

He didn't fall for my "blonde response." He knew very well that I understood his question.

Kiki's voice and demeanor were far from soft.

"If you intend on kickin' it with Red, Sheldon needs to become a has-been," he lectured. "As pretty as Red is, he's definitely not a Sheldon. He hustles but not with his body."

I was curious as to how he acquired all this knowledge about Red but then realized, again, that everyone knew something about someone in prison and word usually got out. I even tried to keep my relationship with Sheldon low-key, but many folks I had never communicated with were well aware that I was banging Sheldon. News of all kind was constantly dispensed and recycled in prison.

Still, there was no way of deceiving Kiki. He knew something was cooking between Cajun Red and me. I was just reluctant to spill the beans. Even though Kiki and I had become pseudo confidantes, especially about prison dirt, I preferred to keep some things secrets, at least for as long as I could before folks eventually found out.

I did, however, admit to Kiki that I was on to Red and his tactics. But I still tried to paint a picture that the two of us were mostly just basketball buddies.

That answer simply didn't seem to fly with Kiki. He laughed at me.

"You know the man's been asking about you. You know that, huh? And it ain't got nothing to do with no basketball game and the way y'all carry on during game time, grabbing each others' asses on the sly. Yeah, I peeped at your game, too, Moe."

My eyes widened at those words.

"Well then what about the questions concerning me? What was the nature of them?"

"You know, questions like, do you take pipe. Crap like that," said Kiki, laughing again.

"Anyway the man's nuts are on fire, Moe."

"What else have you heard?" I ignored the "taking pipe" comment.

"What makes you think there is anything else?"

"There always is. So, what is it?" I was getting a bit hot under the collar as Kiki hesitated. I wanted him to be brutally honest with me.

"Rumor has it that you're HIV," Kiki said.

I then stood for a moment because Kiki was spitting some real serious shit at me now. With that comment, the time had come for me to remove the veil and be honest with Kiki.

"Yeah, 1990 was a devastating year for me, cellie."

"How so?"

"That was the year I learned I had contracted the virus." Hmmm, I thought, I just revealed my health status to someone in prison for the very first time. I continued, saying, "The news was numbing at first and eventually I had to accept the consequences for my out-of-control behavior. First, I told my mom. Later, I told my ex-lover. He was mad at first, but over time he forgave me and loved me for me. The problem was, however, I couldn't love me just as I was because I had refused to identify with the fact that I was HIV-positive. My denial was because I was so full of vanity then. I felt as if I were invincible. Most athletes feel that way. And before we know it, we crash, falling miserably on our asses."

"Been there, done that, homie."

Did he just refer to me as homie? What was going on with

Kiki all of a sudden? He's acting hard and now using urban, ghetto-type vernacular that was far from being typical for him.

"Are you OK, Kiki?" I just had to ask. I wondered if he was suffering from a mild case of separation anxiety due to Lil' D's absence.

"Just fine, man. Just fine," he said. "They refer to us as Kill-offs."

"Huh?" I responded

"The men in the Texas penitentiaries call men like us Kill-offs. Just because we carry the virus they think we are dead men walking."

My eyes widened once more. Wow! Kiki just admitted for the first time that he, too, is HIV-positive.

"I'm not a killer, cellie. And neither are you," I remarked.

"They think differently," he said.

"Did Lil' D think that way?" I asked, guessing he didn't since they were together as a couple.

"Well, Moe, he was among our flock, too. Lil' D had a lot of issues, and I was there for him to help try to resolve some of them. Sometimes things don't look as they may appear. There are a lot of people wearing camouflage in this place. And sometimes we will assume various roles for the sake of saving face and our lives or simply to please the crowd."

"Well, Kiki, does Cajun Red think like that? Does he fear me because of the HIV rumor? Because if he does, he makes it so hard to tell."

"Cajun Red is clean."

"Clean. How do you know?"

"Trust me, Moe. He's clean. He's HIV-negative."

"How do you know that, cellie?"

"You'll know sooner than later. Red is a real dude, and he ain't about to compromise his health for the sake of the booty or the jimmy. He cuts for you, Moe, but show-and-tell time is in the making. So buckle yourself tight, homie, and deal with whatever the cards present you. And by the way, after this night my name is no longer Kiki. It's B.W., aka Barry Williams."

His sudden name change stunned me. But that was minor compared to what happened next. Barry, as he wants to be known, presented me with his parole notice. He revealed to me that he had made parole.

Now I was really curious. Was his entire feminine act all these years just a front to survive prison. I had to wonder if Lil' D had been flipping, too, by pretending to be something he really wasn't.

Barry more or less answered my question.

"There won't be any more fronting, Moe, for these fools. I'm going home soon, and I have a son to raise. That femme act is over for me. It was fun while it lasted. The softer sexier side of me wasn't as bad as I once thought. Even if I was "turned out" in here, it doesn't mean I have to stay that way. I love being a man more than a subservient. It was something new for me. And now I know how not to treat my partner and who not to partner with. Guys like Lil' D are fun to be around, but they are way too complicated for me," Barry said.

Wow!

Prison is full of surprises. There never seems to be a dull moment.

• • • • •

Two days had passed since the shocking news from Barry.

While I was surprised to learn about Lil' D and his "daddy girl" ways (giving up the booty) — after all his hard talk about being a Crip — I was stunned that Barry was anxious to restore his masculinity.

And I became further aware that just because some men act feminine, it doesn't mean that they like to be on the bottom during sex all the time. Some do, in fact, desire to tap the loins of their aggressive lovers.

The changes for Kiki meant no more arched eyebrows, no more lipstick, gloss, colorful nails or parading around like a fool in a prison theater pandering to the whims of lowlife inmates looking for a good lay.

I reflected once again on Barry's revelations about his health, even while I imagined being with Cajun Red despite my being HIV-positive. I also thought about Sheldon's firm rump, while hoping that we would "romp" again in bed one last time.

The opportunity for the latter came true when I submitted to my fleshly desires and went downstairs to Sheldon's place. Before my pre-planned arrival, Sheldon had arranged a night to remember with candlelight, soft jazz and chocolate to serve as a stimulator, sort of like foreplay. He smelled extremely fresh and fragrant. I knew the scent. It was Hugo Boss. Yep, even cologne was available in prison if the right deal was made.

My yo-yo behavior was reminiscent of a feral dog that goes back to its vomit when all else seemed to fail. I had to go back to that which I thought gave me pleasure. And Sheldon was hotter than usual on the inside, yet softer, too. This gave me an indication that someone else was still dipping into this high-yellow brother. But I couldn't blame the individual. After all, he still had that LL Cool J persona.

I just decided to enjoy the moment, lying fully nude on the cool floor and blanket with one of the "peep mirrors" he constructed. It was posted on the bars to allow us to keep watch for guards and any other movement.

Suddenly, though, while in deep thought, the prison doors began to roll open. It was odd because it was not the scheduled time for that to occur.

"Roll the doors! Roll the doors."

I became nervous after I heard the familiar voice call out the order

"Oh, shit!!!" I exclaimed.

Panicking, Sheldon and I both jumped up and scrambled to get dressed.

The plodding of feet grew nearer and louder as the sweat on my brow fell faster and faster.

"Damn!" I said. "That's the voice of Lieutenant RideOut!"

"Ahem! It's too late now, Morris," RideOut said, mocking me. "I finally caught your ass."

I was busted, standing in Sheldon's cell with no shirt on. My boots were nowhere in sight, and I was looking disheveled. I saw the elation in the lieutenant's sinister smile. For him, this was checkmate.

He had finally nailed his elusive, prized bust.

To further humiliate me, I was handcuffed and dragged out of Sheldon's cell.

Chapter 16
Caught in the Trap

"Skin for skin!" Satan replied. "A man will give all he has for his life. But stretch your hand and strike his flesh and bone, and he will surely curse you to your face."

Job 2:4-5

Lecturing me wasn't what I wanted to hear at that moment. But I had no choice but to listen because I was shackled while seated before Lieutenant RideOut after being busted for my embarrassing escapade with Sheldon. I struggled to listen to RideOut, who was gloating as if he had subdued a champion steer in a bull-fighting contest.

He studied me angrily while trying to decide how to write up my infraction. I wasn't sure what would be his next move. But one thing was certain, he made it known through his actions he was out to hang me.

"Morris," said the lieutenant, laughing, "I was wrong about you. You are just like the others in here. So damn stupid! Your ass deserves everything I put down for your case. But, you know what. It's your first time. I'm gonna be light on you."

He talked as if he were doing me a favor.

"How stupid can you get, boy, and jeopardize your parole like this? I watched your ass through my own surveillance device. I watched you hump that man like there was no tomorrow."

I frowned as he lectured, and he didn't like that a bit.

"Don't look at me like that," he demanded. "You're the one whose ass got caught. I see everything in this place, Morris."

I ignored his last statement and finally spoke up.

"So now you're Mr. Kind-hearted now, huh?" I asked sarcastically, with noticeable agitation.

"Don't get cocky, fool," he said, lifting his eyes from the pages of his incomplete report. "I can nail your butt with a sexual assault case, but I'm feeling generous this evening. Don't get me wrong, you will have a major infraction hanging over your head for the next year, but it'll be an 'out of place' case 'cause you know your ass shouldn't have been there to begin with. Now, ain't that special?"

Once again, he stared into my eyes waiting for a response, but there wasn't any. All I could think about at that moment was the case that would be haunting me for the next year or so and perhaps prolonging my chances for parole.

"I sure hope your ass was wearing a raincoat. And by the way, you can kiss C-wing goodbye. And Sheldon, too. I just don't know what to say. Y'all fools always getting caught up with these yellow-ass boys in here. Now here you are with a case chasing your ass, and Sheldon is still in his cell block enjoying himself. But not you, fool. You are headed to ISP (Investigative Segregation Process)."

He tried to ridicule me further.

"So, did you wear a condom?" he demanded to know.

Why was he so concerned about me wearing a condom? Looking into his eyes, I wondered what business was it of his anyway.

"Yeah," I answered bitterly. My response seemed to bring him some relief.

Lieutenant RideOut then pushed the paper aside and leaned far back into his chair and folded his buff arms.

"How long you and that young man been getting it on like that, Morris?"

"Damn lieutenant, do we have to talk about this? You know the deal in here."

Bam!

He slammed his right fist to the desktop, causing me to

shudder.

"What I do know is that you better stop putting your meat in these boys in here if you want to go home, Morris. You knew I was working tonight. So, why did you do it? Why did you risk your custody?"

"My custody?"

"Yeah, Morris. Your custody. This is a major case, and it will stick like stink on crap. If you haven't noticed by now, I run this prison. Not the warden, not the major and definitely not that sorry-ass captain. I am the head Negro in charge here."

To add emphasis, he pounded his chest with his fist.

After sitting there awhile, the handcuffs were eating into my flesh, and my nerves eating me up. If my custody level was about to change, it meant that I would either be transferred to medium or close custody. Both were places I did not want to be. Medium custody was a classification mandating that I be locked up 20 hours a day in a cell, with only four hours for dayroom and recreation. And close custody was even worse. It would mean a mandatory 22 hours a day in the cell and only two hours for recreation.

As if that wasn't enough, Lieutenant RideOut wasn't through with giving his spiel.

"Apparently you ignored the little fiasco in the shower the other week, huh? When I say stay clear of my boys in here, it's as good as written in stone, Morris!"

RideOut then stood. He called out to another officer.

"Sergeant!" RideOut yelled.

A black officer entered the small office with folded arms.

"Get this Negro out of here and ISP (segregate) him for 30 days. See you in court, Morris. Now, get out of my damn face."

I walked away pissed. But I still wondered if he was referring to Sheldon as one of his boys. I couldn't quite figure that out. Among inmates, however, the use of that term often had one connotation: the person is spoken for or is someone's intimate partner and is off-limits.

•••••

Med Tech Pharmaceutical had thrown many of its employees for a loop.

A new directive was being issued for most top-level managers to be screened and given an option to consider a security monitoring device.

Even though Lazlo had not accepted the promotion offer from Donna, he was not keen on this new initiative. He absolutely wanted no part of this cutting-edge technology that appeared to be too invasive.

The directive was optional but highly recommended. An aggressive push was expected to get all senior managers to comply.

Med Tech wanted to protect its investment and its longtime research in the development of a drug to eliminate cravings associated with addictions, particularly chemical dependencies involving cocaine and nicotine. The company was among others scrambling to build on initial research done by a lab in England and suggesting that a new epilepsy drug called gamma vinyl-GABA (GVG) showed tremendous potential for curbing drug addictions. It would be a major breakthrough. A pharmaceutical company in Great Britain rushed to be the first to reap the benefits of the potential groundbreaking therapy.

While Med Tech was well on its way to getting in on the action, a competing biotechnology company in Massachusetts chose to sell its rights to the British pharmaceutical company because there were too many attempts to kill the drug's development in the U.S. over fear it would impede profits. The reason was that addictions spell M-O-N-E-Y. Med Tech, however, refused to cave in to the pressure by outsiders who tried to offer the company cash to end its research.

Instead, Med Tech decided to press forward but keep closer tabs on its research. Only high-level managers would be allowed to access data about its efforts to pursue the drug's full potential. For clearance to the secured area, specially designated employees were being asked to undergo a minor operation for an implant that would grant them authorization and information on the development of what could become a multi-billion-dollar bonanza.

Its top-secret work left it no choice but to go on high alert. So, surveillance was a top priority. The future of this corporate giant could possibly ride on this single drug.

The memo read, in part: "It is imperative that the interest of the company and its stockholders be secured. As a result, a "simple" procedure is being administered to secure secrets and formulas. ..."

Lazlo sat at his desk staring at the memo, repulsed by it. As far as he was concerned, not even Nathan's drinking problem could top this issue, which was on his schedule later in the evening. Lazlo had already pre-written a letter of resignation just in case it came down to it. But he didn't want to be premature and rush to judgment.

He thought of Roland's encouragement, reminding him that everything would blow over in time. He hoped Roland was correct and that he would avoid management's new initiative. Looking at his right hand, he concluded there was no way he was going to agree to an electrical implant anywhere on his body. He then ripped the memo into small pieces, stood and stared out the window, thinking about how the approaching start of a new century was supposed to be a period of uncertainty as Y2K theories abounded.

And with this new era, biometrics, such as the digital scans of the iris or hands, was being touted. Critics such as Lazlo thought this to be too invasive and taboo. On the other hand, many of his white male colleagues seemed enthralled and embraced the idea.

After a moment of meditation, Lazlo prepared to buzz Donna for a late lunch, but instead decided to call Nathan on his cell, given that he felt Donna was toeing the line by heavily pushing the company's policy.

"Nathan," Lazlo sighed heavily during the phone call, "we need to talk. Tonight."

•••••

Day nine of my investigative segregation slowly crept to an end. I wasn't sure of the exact time, but I knew that night had now smothered the light once my shadow had completely faded.

As Lieutenant RideOut had predicted, I was officially found guilty of being "out of place" and sentenced to 30 days in the "crapper."

Not even a third of the way into completion, confinement was threatening to get the best of me. But now I was more determined than ever to avoid the same mental meltdown that other inmates suffered while in isolation.

I was angry at the prison system and fellow inmates. I even was at war with myself. The internal chaos left me bitter and vengeful as I damned everyone while confined in the dungeon where I'd been sentenced. But, once again, I tried calming myself. So, I recited Deuteronomy: "Do not be afraid or discouraged."

After chanting that a few times, I gradually began to regroup.

To further improve my condition, I developed a daily ritual of exercise three hours after dinner. I did sit-ups, push-ups and leg squats. My only reading material was the Bible. Aside from that, the other only approved book was the Koran. Newspapers and magazines were strictly prohibited, but writing paper was permissible. Mail was issued as deemed necessary.

The restrictions were designed to force a period of reflection on my behavior and the violation that landed me in this hell hole. The scriptures accomplished that for me. I learned even more how my living had been contrary to its principles and the church covenant.

On this day, I weighed whether to write in my journal since I had a lot on my mind. Instead, I chose to pick through some scriptures before settling in to bed.

The book of Job came to mind.

I went through the first chapter rather quickly. It was the second chapter that got my attention as it revealed how Job was being tested by Satan, who was allowed to afflict God's servant but not kill him. Job persevered and prospered, despite suffering extraordinary losses.

As I lie on my bed, I decided that I would work to rise above my circumstances. I could not blame God for my misery. And the Enemy would not be victorious.

At some point, I knew I had to deal with my feeling toward Lieutenant RideOut. I wanted to hate everything about him, even though I knew I was in error and dealing with an internal war. Because of this, I banished my harsh feelings for RideOut.

I eventually gravitated to Romans. I had already been introduced to Paul the Apostle by Butch Webber, a friend from my college days and former pro football standout who taught me that a person could overcome pain and misery much like he did after he got married and abandoned his same-sex interests. Butch, though, said it was a daily struggle but that he was committed to leaving that old life behind.

Well, it was through my personal "thorns" and stories of Paul's persecution that I gained confidence to restore my own life. I learned that it was sufficient to suffer for God's sake. And I had suffered through my own humiliation by trying to outsmart authority, while also satisfying my lust.

My life needed to take a new direction, and even though I knew the answer, I prayed asking God, "What shall I do?"

It seemed that He was telling me to stick with the Word, and all needs would be met according to His glorious riches.

But He also revealed to me through scripture that "there will be trouble and distress for every human being who does evil."

•••••

On Day 23, a Saturday, of my punitive isolation, I received a letter from Mom.

She wrote to say the family was doing well and that they would visit soon. Her prosthesis was a "perfect fit," she stated.

I was happy for her, but I'd been glad that she nor Lazlo had come to visit me while I've been in segregation.

After reading her letter, I began meditating. But my thoughts were interrupted when I heard the sounds of rattling keys.

It was Lieutenant RideOut.

He stood in front of my cell, filling out a card without initially making eye contact. After he finished, he began to taunt me by snickering.

He then ordered me to get dressed.

I asked why.

"You got a visit," he said dryly.

"Damn!" I grumbled. "How am I going to explain to my visitor the reason I'm being escorted in by several officers to the visitation area in handcuffs?"

I couldn't believe this was happening after I'd just expressed a wish that no one come to see me during this embarrassing time.

Anyway, I washed my face, brushed my teeth and hair and got dressed.

Chapter 17
Make You Wanna Holla

The man of integrity walks securely, but he who takes crooked paths will be found out.

Proverbs 10:9

The look in Lazlo's eyes displayed shock as I was led, with my hands cuffed behind my back, into a small private cage as if I were a wild animal. He watched in dismay as the male guard ordered me to turn around and face Lazlo. He then locked me inside the cage and ordered me to move backward and place my handcuffed hands into the small cutout window of the cage so he could remove the shackles. I then released my disgust over the embarrassment.

When I peered into Lazlo's watery eyes, I could see his hurt and confusion. Without knowing anything, he was on the brink of tears. He knew something was totally wrong with this picture. I was sure that he thought I'd been in a fight or a verbal confrontation with the administration or guards.

Whatever the case, it seemed he wanted to scream, "Why?"

Under heavy security, my publicly watched entrance by family members and friends of other guests was enough to warrant such a question.

It was humiliation at its worst.

Like Lazlo, I, too, wanted to shout to the top of my lungs.

"Abba! Father, help me!" were the words that entered my mind.

But I contained my emotions. It was enough that my visitor was already clearly distraught, even without us having yet uttered a word to one other.

Lazlo's first words were not unexpected.

"You screwed up, didn't you?" Lazlo said, shaking his head in disgust.

His watery eyes were now dry, much like the tone in his voice. His pain did not obscure his handsome face. His body was fit and tone, and his quarter-size caramel brown eyes were as attractive as always.

Telling Lazlo the truth was going to be very hard for me, but I knew that if I wanted him to be a continuous presence in my life I had to spill the beans.

I acknowledged him first and then took a deep breath. His body language suggested he wasn't feeling my greeting as he shifted from side to side. He pushed back in his chair waiting for an answer, an honest one.

I cleared the knot in my throat.

"I got caught in someone's cell," I said, getting right to the matter.

He questioned me harshly.

"What in the hell were you doing in another man's cell, Miguel?"

I sensed he already knew the answer. He then smirked and sighed sarcastically to confirm that he at least appreciated my honesty.

Once I thought he'd settled his nerves, I was a bit more emboldened.

"It's kinda obvious, though, isn't it?" I answered, giving a cavalier response. I really wasn't trying to sound arrogant, just frank.

Lazlo ignored my sarcasm and went on about his business to assess our friendship. I could tell that he was still attempting to rescue me from my own errors. That's why I loved him so — enough that I would never intentionally try to hurt or mislead him.

"What's obvious to me is your care-free attitude toward this whole matter. Sex in prison is so damn dangerous, Miguel. ..."

I cut him off.

"What makes you convinced I was having sex in his cell?" I asked, staging a smile and knowing all along my question was ridiculous.

"Were you?" asked Lazlo, who was unamused by my obvious avoidance of a straight answer.

I was now really on the spot. My integrity was on the line.

"We were hooking up every once and awhile, thinking we were outwitting the guards," I said, whispering as I leaned toward the wire partition. "I was introduced to him by my cellmate. We had connected in many ways. So, we decided to kick it while we were here – being that we were locked up. That's all." I was trying to justify my reasons.

"Without condoms, Miguel?" asked Lazlo, with brows tightened and furious concern. "What about STDs and ... "

"We protected ourselves, man!" I said boastfully, cutting his comment short, yet knowing my behavior was getting out of control.

"How? With what?" he asked as his rising voice now switched from his previous whisper.

"Anything and everything is available in here, Lazlo, even condoms and lubrication. Problem was I got too damn comfortable with this dude and got caught slipping in my game."

"So prison is a game now, huh, Miguel?"

"Just a figure of speech," I said, trying to assure him.

"How is your action going to affect your parole chances now? It's obvious you're in some sort of trouble considering the way you were escorted in here."

"I did receive a major case behind my action, but I'll be just fine, man. I'll get it right from this point on. Trust me on that."

"You better, because there are a lot of people out there in

the "free world" who care about you and want you out of here ASAP, particularly me and your family. Just promise me one thing," requested Lazlo, leaning in closer. "Leave these men alone in this prison. Does that sound familiar to you?"

Actually, his message did and it socked me in my gut. I had shared that revelation with Lazlo many months ago. That's when that same message was delivered to me by God, who had appeared to me while I was in the Harris County Jail awaiting my court date. Now, Lazlo was using that same warning to remind me that I was here to redeem myself, not to give in to the desires of my flesh.

We talked in-depth about the changes in my custody status for an additional 20 minutes over snacks and drinks that Lazlo had retrieved from the vending machines.

He surprised me when he said, "Medium custody is probably best for you until you get a hold of yourself. You need to be tamed."

He was right. My denial and hurt were causing me to go stir crazy. He assured me that while he understood that hormones can rage out of control, even in prison, I still needed to comply as best as possible with regulations.

Afterward, we moved to other irons in the fire.

Not surprisingly, Lazlo next brought up the subject of Nathan, which might have explained why he didn't seem to show signs of jealousy over my prison fling. He had his own personal, intimate issues.

He began by going on a tirade about how Nathan's drinking had become critical, even embarrassing.

Lazlo shared that he recently had told Nathan about our continued friendship and that Nathan wasn't too thrilled with the idea that his lover was still keeping it real with me, not to mention paying me visits such as this one. Nathan, dealing with his own addiction, had the gall to tell Lazlo that he was glad that he didn't have to deal with a person such as me.

And since this wasn't the first time I had heard that statement, I didn't let it faze me.

Lazlo thought it necessary to remind me that our continued bond would be based on trust. And for the most part, there was nothing he didn't already know about my past. This included my solicitation of male prostitutes, HIV, drug binges, lying and cheating, stealing from former employers and even trying to make deals with God that had no chance of being manifested.

As for Nathan, Lazlo said he felt there was something puzzling about him.

"You feel that he's misleading you to some degree?" I asked, taking a swig of my fruit beverage as I watched Lazlo's twitching eyes and shifting body — signs of disturbance.

"I know for sure that he is hiding something," Lazlo submitted as he exhaled heavily. "One day I came home from work early due to the fact that I was feeling a little crappy. When I entered the bedroom I noticed that he had left his briefcase behind. It was resting on the bed. I was tired that day, so I wanted to rest and lie down for a power nap. When I removed the briefcase from the bed, some contents fell out."

Lazlo then paused. I had wanted to ask if he actually rifled through the bag looking for anything suspicious, but I recoiled from that remark.

"What happened next?" I asked, knowing there must have been more to the story.

"Everything spilled out onto the carpet, Miguel."

Lazlo's eyes then shifted to each side.

Not answering immediately or directly, he said, "Nathan usually keeps that thing locked."

I wanted to ask how he knew that but passed on the opportunity.

"Did you find something incriminating?" I asked, remembering how investigative Lazlo was during our time together.

I tried to remain rational since I, too, once as a former young professional kept a business tote with all sorts of things, including a day planner, phone book, cell phone and private keepsakes.

But given Lazlo's recent situation with Nathan, I told him not to feel guilty about the incident. There were many red alerts that suggested depression, particularly the steady alcohol consumption. It's a natural thing for lovers to become concerned about their partners, I told him. And sometimes probing might avoid future crises.

"Well," Lazlo said, "after all his papers and belongings fell to the carpet, I gathered them up. One item had rolled underneath the bed. I kneeled to retrieve it. That's when I saw them."

"Saw what?" I asked, moving in closer to the window so I wouldn't miss a syllable.

"I remembered hearing something rattle when the bag flew open and spilled."

"What, Lazlo?" By now my patience was running thin.

"Two bottles of pills," continued Lazlo, noticing a guard entering the visitation area and standing near us as if probing.

"So, Nathan's popping pills and drinking?" I asked.

"It's much deeper than that. The pills are anti-retroviral," remarked Lazlo, slamming his closed fist in a fit of frustration. The guard nearby quickly turned toward us wondering what was going on. But, he said nothing.

"Damn!" I said. It was the only response I could offer.

Lazlo's anger was understandable and heartfelt. In his two relationships, it was the second time he'd had to deal with this issue. And both times he found out only after he was far into the relationships. Nathan and I were not courageous or honorable enough to let Lazlo know upfront about our HIV status.

And as I've since learned, it likely would not have mattered to Lazlo because he was only interested in real love. He was never one to judge.

INTERNAL CHAOS

•••••

I was finally released and placed in medium custody 30 day after being in the "crapper," a term synonymous with "shit hole" and used to describe the infamous segregation cell. I then was relocated to a new area, the A-wing, with stricter curfews and a longer daily lockdown of 20 hours. The only good thing about it was that I was living alone, at least for the moment. I was told that I would be getting a new job assignment. I still wasn't aware of the details or position, however. My exact prison status remained unclassified because of my new ISP background.

It was approaching 6 o'clock, when we would have dayroom and recreation privileges. Dinner was over, but more importantly the lengthy lockdown was about to expire. I was looking forward to the four hours of social time before our 10 p.m. curfew. I hated lockdowns, particularly when they lasted through the weekends. Still my problems seemed light compared to Lazlo and Nathan's. I'd learned long ago that holding vital information from someone could be lethal. I wondered what was going on in Nathan's mind as I sat on my bunk waiting for the clock to strike the hour.

As for my new prison status and location, everything was so different. Barry Williams, formerly known as Kiki, had made parole and was out the door much like his ex-beau, Lil' D.

Cajun Red was still on C-wing, and rumor had it that he and Angel, the handsome Latino inmate that caught my eye awhile back, were kicking it real tough now. Well, I guess Red officially abandoned the Overcomers movement he'd been rumored to be part of.

And speaking of rumors, I'd heard that Angel was a cutter – a person who carves into his skin for attention. I couldn't figure out why Cajun Red would get involved with someone like this. I figured he would have greater standards than that.

We're talking about a guy who carelessly exposed his blood, as well as open wounds that could become infected with any type of virus creeping through the prison.

I kept my distance from Angel because I sensed there was something uniquely odd about him, almost sinister, when he approached me in the dayroom months ago and tried to hold a conversation. His eyes and overall presence bothered me.

And as for panty bandit Millner, I'm told he was now heavily medicated after suffering a mental setback. He reportedly had been having visions of his deceased mother and referring to her as a whore, blaming her for his condition.

He was prone to going around chanting unceasingly, "I saw everything; I saw everything." Many say he was completely off his rocker. The facility should have sent him to a psychiatric ward. Instead, the unit's doctor just kept him sedated, fearing Millner was a threat to himself and others because he constantly talked about raping and stalking female guards. A peep mirror that he had purchased from Sheldon had become his best friend.

And speaking of Sheldon, I got word that he was still up to his old tricks: hustling male inmates on C-wing for gain and pleasure. I wondered if that included Lieutenant RideOut, who seemingly was overprotective of Sheldon. I had no clear proof, but RideOut's action toward me suggested he may have been boning some of the boys. And, interestingly enough, he seemed to give special attention to light-complexioned fellas – just like me. Well, that was my speculation. But whatever the case, I wasn't going to lose any sleep over it.

I would soon learn that I had now become the gossip of the A-unit. An unidentified source shared that I was the infamous "booty bandit" who got caught dipping my jimmy in Sheldon's "cream of the crop" and that scared a lot of guys here, especially those who may have once considered kickin' it with me. It was likely that they now would avoid any type of association with me because no one wanted to give the impression to their homeboys that they were "flippin' " with me. To avoid guilty by association, folks basically steered clear. It wasn't popular to be sexually versatile in prison.

My new nesting area on the A-wing was in stark contrast to my previous C-wing location. The men here were younger, but they appeared initially to be obedient – a quality I believed to be more effective if instilled during infancy and subsequent years of maturity. Just maybe, I surmised, fewer men would be locked up today had they been disciplined. I was well aware, however, that there were many men such as myself, who, despite our upbringing in a controlled environment, were greatly influenced by our peers' bad choices. Thus, some of us ended up engaging in the same repugnant practices and violent behaviors.

My focus now was to move on from the wounds of my past. I could still hear the warning resonating in my head: "If you wanna go home, you better leave these men alone in this prison."

When those words even came from Lieutenant RideOut's mouth, I knew then that even he was being used as a vessel to carry a divine message that I knew I should be adhering to.

Accompanying those thoughts was a cryptic reminder that I was flirting with death as a painful jab to my chest developed as I lie on my bottom bunk. I panicked, believing it to be signs of cardiac arrest, although I told myself it could only be an anxiety attack. Nonetheless, pressure built in my head and my heart pounded rapidly.

Ohmigod! Was I dying? The pain intensified over a few minutes before it abated. I then took a few deep breaths to calm down.

Fear gripped me. And fortunately I wasn't dying. I couldn't figure out what was going on. But I took it as a message that life was short and that I needed to work on getting my life in order. I'd learned long ago that feelings buried alive never die.

As I lie still for a half-hour more, I pulled up from the bed after being hit by a foul odor from a flushed toilet nearby.

When the cell doors opened shortly after, I escaped the nauseous smell and dashed to the dayroom anticipating a new change in scenery.

Chapter 18
Selfish Danger

The hand of the Lord was upon me, and He brought me out by the Spirit of the Lord and set me in the middle of a valley of dry bones.

Ezekiel 37:1

Midweek, I was still without a new cellmate or job assignment. So after lunch and Bible study, I took advantage of the solitude and pulled out my colored pencils, paintbrushes, poster boards and erasers. I was reading the Bible more often now and attending Sunday chapel services regularly. I had finally accepted that God had a plan for me. Looking back over my life, I realized I had been living how I wanted and simply expected God to just sign off on it without question. But He showed me He was not having any part of that.

Sexual identity is a real issue with a host of prisoners. Even if the issue isn't sex, we are sometimes unwilling to admit that we have made mistakes or behaved irresponsibly.

I was determined to overcome self-destructive anger that could lead to high blood pressure, depression, frustration and loneliness. But at the same time, I was experiencing an internal war that threatened to compromise my moral compass.

The battle is fierce, with the flesh having won often. But I've had many personal victories before. And I knew I needed another win. And this time, I had no intention of abandoning my core beliefs. I aimed to embrace the truth about myself. If not, I was destined for the road to ruin.

•••••

It was around three o'clock when the cell doors opened without

"Stand clear!" a female guard warned authoritatively.

As usual, we dropped what we were doing to see what the commotion was about.

As some of us stepped outside, she ordered us back into our cells. Again, we complied with her demands, but we stuck our heads out just to see what was going on. After we heard a rustling stampede of feet approaching, we then saw a band of new arrivals climbing up the stairs onto our third floor. I was at the very back of the row, cell 22. There seemed to be about six new offenders headed our direction for housing assignment. I was hoping that I didn't get a cellmate just yet.

I liked living alone.

My hopes were quickly fading when one made his way toward my direction, passing cells 18, 19, 20 and 21. He had nowhere to go now but 22, my cell.

He faced the cell and dropped his two large white travel bags outside. I stepped back and began removing my belongings from the top bunk, mostly artwork. My heart flickered.

Once I regained my composure, I quickly asked if he needed help with his bags.

"Yeah," he said.

So I reached out into the walkway area and retrieved two of his bags.

For someone who didn't want a roommate, I was eager to help this young lad. With my quick offer of help, I had to catch myself. But I knew the reason for my spontaneous response.

The dude was fine as hell.

Get a grip, Miguel, I told myself. But he was gorgeous.

As he settled in, we got more acquainted with small talk, asking innocuous questions: What is your name? Where are you from?

By the end of the week, we bonded more. This was easy because my new cellmate, Judas, and I were locked down 20 hours a day in medium custody. Unlike the raucous week of March Madness, the NCAA basketball tournament – that involved gambling and other foolishness by inmates – this particular day was fairly quiet on our cellblock. We guessed that most of the offenders were napping during this afternoon hour. The peacefulness gave us an opportunity to find out more about each other.

I had learned from Judas that he, too, was an ex-jock in his late 30s. He said he had gotten involved in illegal football gambling and racketeering while in college and was serving 10 years and had only done three. He hadn't shared yet exactly why he was placed in medium custody.

Another similarity: His criminal case had been turned over to the state of Texas by the feds via a plea deal. We shared our criminal pasts, and there were other similarities, particularly the large amounts of money involved.

The feds helped him get a lighter sentence, too.

Judas was 2 inches shorter, at 6 feet. His hazel eyes were unbelievably alluring. His youthful appearance was set off by his sandy-brown skin. He had a movie-star presence. His clean-shaven light-complexioned face was evenly toned and smooth, compared to my clear darker gleam, aided by the lotion I applied to my face and the striking beam of sunlight. I realized just how well our tones complimented each other.

He reminded me of former soap star Shemar Moore of The Young and the Restless, although Judas was a bit more buff.

His Louisiana traits were prominent, including his dialect. In the short time of getting to know him, he didn't seem to use profanity. And like my ex-cellie, he had attractive feet.

I then found myself comparing our bodies.

After about an hour of sharing our street stories and athletic accomplishments, he pulled out a photo album of images he had collected over the years while incarcerated. He then surprised me when he jumped down from his top bunk wearing only his white boxers and white socks and sat next to me on my bunk. I was dressed similarly.

As he nudged closer, I was confident in my appearance because my face was shaven and the waves in my hair were hittin'. I could still smell his powder fresh Speed Stick deodorant, and I was sure he got a good whiff of mine, too.

We flipped from page to page. And, then I was stopped dead in my tracks because an image caught my attention. At first I thought nothing of it. But then my curiosity got the best of me. He appeared next to Cajun Red in a photograph during what I learned was a visitation hour.

"How do you two know each other?" I asked.

His answer stunned me.

"Godwin and I are brothers," Judas answered.

•••••

Lazlo's emotions were everywhere that evening as he and Nathan prepared to have an honest, civil conversation in their Westside apartment.

At first Lazlo was going to start out inquiring about school and his classes, but he knew Nathan was doing fine in that area, despite his drinking that had affected their intimate relationship.

Lazlo had contemplated just throwing in the towel.

With dinner eaten, they geared up for some real soul-searching. Lazlo quieted the soft jazz and rested on the sofa next to Nate. Although it was good sitting next to his beau, it was a bit awkward for Lazlo due to his desire to touch and hold Nate while confronting him at the same time. But, at this moment, that was not what Lazlo really needed. He needed to unleash his pent-up anger. There could be no more avoidance of the issue, particularly with the concrete evidence he had.

After a gentle sigh, the talk ensued.

"You know, Nathan, growth starts in our heart," began Lazlo, who almost reached out to Nate. He refrained once more. "But something's not quite right."

"Huh?" asked Nathan, puzzled.

"Through every experience there has to be some sort of negotiation. A balance," Lazlo said, struggling to choose his words carefully.

"You're losing me, man," said Nathan, sipping wine and leaning forward to try to absorb the conversation.

"The truth about who we are is essential." Lazlo then stared at Nate, who was now looking toward the ceiling. "I've always been the type of person who analyzes things."

"An analyst. Hmmm," said Nathan, facetiously.

"Yes, you can say that," confirmed Lazlo, forcing a smile. "Some of us have a blind side that we can't see, but others can. A secret window, if you will. There are things we know about ourselves, yet we keep them from others."

Nathan then took his eyes from the ceiling and sat straight.

"Is there something wrong, Lazlo?"

Lazlo was taken aback by the question, given that the problem was with Nate, not himself.

"Yeah, Nathan. There is something wrong, but it isn't me."

"Well, then are you accusing me of something? Because if you are, I'm not feeling this gossip crap tonight from those funky-ass friends of yours."

Nate then finished his glass of white zinfandel, ready for a refill.

"This is no gossip, Nate. I'm going to come at you straight. And all I ask is that you be honest with me."

"Shoot. I'm all ears."

"Are you HIV-positive?"

There was a moment of quietness in the room, with exception to the jazz and the ticking wall clock in the mirrored bar area.

"What in the hell? ... What makes you think that?"

"Just answer the question, Nathan! Are you?"

"I don't believe you, you mother- ... "

"Stop! Don't even go there, man. It's real simple. Are you or are you not HIV-positive, Nathan?"

Nathan ejected himself from the sofa.

"I'm going to have a drink because you're talking nonsense, fool."

Lazlo then blocked his passage and got right in Nate's face.

"The hell you are! We're going to settle this issue right here and now. Drinking hour is over!" said Lazlo, grabbing him by the shirt collar.

The deception fired him up, and Lazlo began asserting himself more forcefully.

"Oh, now you want to fight, huh?" shouted Nathan, jerking loose from Lazlo's grip.

"Dammit, if that what it takes to beat the truth out of you, so be it, man. I trusted you to be honest with me, not to harm me."

"What have I lied to you about? Oh, is this about me drinking a little? Is that what this is about? What's the harm in that?"

They both stared each other down, each livid.

"This time it is not about your drinking but about your HIV status."

A stone-faced Nathan retreated, falling back to the sofa.

"Two years ago I was tested and found out I was positive. I shared this info with my people, my family, Lazlo!" He began to cry. "Don't you know they rejected me. They basically disowned me. They didn't understand the disease. I didn't want to experience that feeling ever again. So I hid my status from you because I was afraid you would reject me, too, just like my own blood did. There is no way I am ever going back to East St. Louis."

Lazlo sat next to Nathan, embraced him and said, "It's OK, man."

Deep down inside Lazlo was fuming. Even so, he tried to put a different, yet still serious, face on the discussion.

"You know, during pressure moments, everybody wears a mask. I've learned to look beyond the mask to see the real person, the real hurt," said Lazlo, who knew it was time to stop playing the role of the constant rescuer and allow individuals to fix their own problems. "So, when were you going to tell me?"

Lazlo released his embrace and stared Nathan in his eyes.

"I wasn't sure, man."

"You weren't sure, Nate? Does that mean you didn't intend to?"

"It means that I was waiting for the right moment."

"And what moment was that? When I got infected?"

"We protected ourselves," said Nathan, trying to remove any guilt associated with his sexual involvement with Lazlo. "I was waiting on the ... "

"That's a dangerous game to play, man," Lazlo interrupted. "In case you've forgotten, we've slipped a time a two. Didn't I share my negative status with you when we first got together? I did it out of love, care and concern?" fumed Lazlo, who then stood and paced the floor erratically. "You lied to me, man! You said you were tested, and the results were favorable. I should have asked how you defined favorable. But I didn't. And that's on me. But that still doesn't free you from telling the truth about your health."

"I'm sorry, man! What do you want me to do now that the truth is out?" said Nathan, planting his face in the palm of his hands.

"First of all, take your face out of your hands and be a man about who you are and be proud of what you have accomplished in life. Secondly, get some help and talk to someone about your drinking because alcohol isn't going to make matters any easier. It's only going to compromise your health. Then, embrace your HIV status, man. Trust me, I've been down this road before with Miguel and that taught me a lot, for the most part. I guess I should have learned, though, to be more inquisitive because then I might have found out the truth much sooner."

"Whuzzup, Diary?"

It's April, and only a few days have elapsed. This marks my first year of prison incarceration. Time is passing us by in here, and many inmates continue to be unaware of their fate. Most don't even know if they are going to make it out of here alive or healthy. Men in here are falling victim to their own lust, becoming swamped by the influence of things. Even I've fallen into that category. This place was like being at a buffet. I have a smorgasbord of men to choose from. Men of every skin tone and ethnicity engulfed me. I worshiped their bodies instead of my Creator. I was ISP'd for 30 days because I was out of place, out of mind and out of control.

Then there's the retrovirus issue. Many don't survive because they've adopted an attitude of idiocy that reaches far and wide like a fungus overtaking moist walls. It's hard sometimes not to be biased toward some people who don't care about life, family and personal enrichment, but I'm learning to improve. My former cellmate, Kiki, taught me how to stitch my life back together one thread at a time.

Just last evening Judas and I got deep into a conversation and, to my surprise, he shared with me that he knew why I was on medium custody: my 'busted rendezvous' with Sheldon, as he called it. But that wasn't the only revelation that caught me off guard. He revealed that he and Cajun Red are brothers. And this disturbed me somewhat. What are the odds that something like this would occur where you have two attractive biological brothers housed on the same unit. He then dropped another bombshell and shared with me, without hesitation, that he is HIV-positive. I respected that and shared my status, too. Subsequently, that action opened the discussion for more honest talk. It seems as if he and I have known each other for a long time, although it's just been a week. What I enjoy about him is that he's clean and respectable – much like his brother, Cajun Red, who has been giving me the cold shoulder ever since he discovered that Judas and I were cellmates. Besides him being so attractive, he's honest and smart. That goes a long way in my book. It appears we are going to be good cellmates.

It's rare for offenders to bunk with someone they feel compatible with, but Judas and I seem to be in sync. And I must admit, there is some chemistry between us. I'm not sure what to make of it, but I'm sure it's of a sexual nature. Damn! The struggle continues.

He and I have similar scars that are physical and emotional. And there is one thing that stands out even more: a disconnection with our fathers. Even though my dad wasn't absent from the home, he was absent from most of my activities during high school and college. For years, I blamed him for my problems because he was detached emotionally from me. With that, I still accept responsibility for my bad choices.

I still remember when he told me, "Men don't hug men. They shake hands."

Even though I knew he meant well, he left a crater in my heart. To this day, I can't remember running into the arms of my father. So, it would seem, I sought that affection from other men who didn't have my best interest at heart.

But I do remember him often taking Troy and me on long fishing trips after church on Sundays in his sky blue Buick Electra 225. I imagine it was an attempt to help me and Troy mend our hostility toward one another because we were highly competitive. He was kind but stern, too, when we got out of line. I have vivid memories of him disciplining me. He didn't spare the rod. Because of that, I never felt comfortable around him.

To tell you the truth, Diary, I'm not even sure if I ever loved him, in spite of his ways. Maybe I just liked him. After all these years, I recently decided to forgive him. While in ISP confinement, I decided to let go, and let God. (End: Tuesday, 1:45 a.m., Day 369)

Chapter 19
Inner Demons

As I have observed, those who plow evil and those who sow trouble reap it.

Job 4:8

An aggravated James Millner, the panty raider, dizzily plodded around the C-wing dayroom Saturday evening in a circle after returning from the unit's pill window. Before now, he had been free of psych medicine that was needed to keep him calm. A blowup, or mental meltdown, typically would result in violence and sexual aberration.

I sat near the hall window from the A-wing dayroom observing his erratic behavior.

Angry as hell, Millner screamed at the peak of his voice box.

"That bastard must take me for being weak!" he said as the television blared.

The medicine caused his muscles to twitch violently, with his head bobbing up and down, making him look like an African dancer at a tribal ritual.

We all knew he was in bad shape because he kept massaging his temple as if in pain.

"Leave me alone, I tell you. Leave me the hell alone!" he demanded to no one in particular, but he still circled the dayroom. He often did the same thing during chow time.

His constant babbling irritated us all, but no one confronted him because they knew he was unstable. He was also strong as an ox, so we just went on about our business. If it wasn't important enough for prison officials to intervene, then we reasoned that it certainly wasn't urgent enough for fellow offenders to jeopardize our health.

It would be 10 minutes later before the erratic Millner aroused the attention of the blonde female guard on duty. She cautiously moved toward the barred gate outside the dayroom area before trying to talk to him.

"Say you!" she yelled out, staring intensely at Millner. "Yeah, you!" she said pointing her finger in his direction. "You got a problem?"

The dayroom grew eerily silent, and this caught his attention. Millner then focused deeply on the guard's painted fingernails as her hands rested on the barred gate. With the pink nails arousing him, he approached her in a child-like manner.

"So, what seems to be the problem?" she asked, stepping slightly away from the bars with her small tanned arms folded. She wasn't sure of Millner's intentions, so she moved out of harm's way by putting some distance between the two of them.

As a beaming Millner got closer, she noticed the prison ID hanging from his thick neck.

"I'm just having a bad day. That's all. It's nothing I can't handle," he said, licking his full lips like a hungry wolf preparing to devour his prey.

"Are you sure everything is under control? If not, I ..."

"NO!" he shouted quickly. Then he instantly lowered his tone. "I mean no," he said, whispering. "There's no problem, Officer Evans," said Millner, gazing at her name tag that fell slightly below her full-size breasts. Evans was Millner's type because she was quite endowed and her bra gave her boobs a sensual lift. Millner was all aflutter, his sickness kicking in once more and, his yearning ever stronger.

On the first Thursday in April, the early morning started wickedly for Judas.

He was dreaming, sweating profusely and tossing in his bed. For several minutes, I stood and observed his behavior – feeling pain over his misery – though I had no clue to what was troubling him.

He seemed to be having horrible visions as if someone were fighting him.

"Don't slap me again," he murmured. "No. You're hurting my face," said Judas, holding his jawbone.

After a few moments of struggle, he freed himself. And he suddenly quieted down, unaware that I had witnessed his traumatic experience as he lie on the top bunk.

I decided against saying anything at the moment and went on about my business.

Later that same evening, I attended a rehabilitation meeting.

"Hi," I said, "My name is Miguel, and I'm just happy to be here."

I really wasn't that excited, but I pretended to be anyway. In all truthfulness, I was uneasy in the small circle of offenders who were attending voluntary drug therapy. This was my first session since incarceration. I figured this would look good for my next parole hearing.

This 12-step program was a song and dance I had endured before.

"Hi, I'm an addict," was a statement I'd uttered numerous times. I still couldn't quite understand why someone would continue to claim to be something that they say they've been delivered from. It seemed to me that if you continue to tell yourself you are a failure, you will remain a failure. My true philosophy is that you are what you speak.

Nevertheless, I didn't buck the system, given that the program has worked for massive numbers of people who consider themselves addicts.

As I prepared to get comfortably seated, the crowd responded to my greeting.

"Hi, Miguel," they said.

My cellmate, Judas, even chimed in for the welcome.

focused on the faces of those present and wondered about their drug of choice or addiction. I then told the crowd that I was feeling anxious and uneasy.

That was after I noticed Clear, the inmate who was beaten in the shower for sleeping with Sheldon. He cut his brown eyes toward my direction as if he had a chip on his shoulder. The funny thing this time around was his eyes weren't winking, and his ego not as large as before when I had walked upon him and Sheldon doing their thing.

After the robust group leader opened the floor for an hour discussion of sharing, he told me that anxiety was a part of recovery and to focus my mind on being cured.

"Does anyone else have something they want to share with the group?" the leader asked.

A hand raised.

"Yes, go ahead," the leader's husky voice encouraged.

"My name is Judas, and I'm still a dope fiend."

My heart skipped when Judas made that claim. I guess that was the one thing he hadn't shared with me the other night.

"But I suppose my problem today is sexual," he said courageously without hesitation. "It's a struggle to maintain and control a desire that constantly haunts you. It's worse than a drug, sex is, especially when it's on your mind day and night, even when you wake up in the morning." He slightly grinned my way, then continued. "I'm not even sure if I belong in this class or not. So that's where I am today," he said, scanning the room with his hazel eyes as if seeking validation.

I wanted to tell him that he wasn't alone, but the group leader beat me to the punch.

"Honesty is good. It's the beginning of the healing process," the leader said.

Instantly, upon hearing Judas and the leader, Clear sat up and began probing the room once again as if his number had been called. He was still somewhat cocky, and it seemed the beating in the shower only made him rougher around the edges.

I envied Judas for his courage in front of a group of closed-minded, dishonest inmates reluctant to open their minds and hearts about their secrets. I then hoped to follow Judas' lead one day and do the same. The interest was there, but I lacked bravery.

Later around 8 p.m., recreation was ongoing as medium and minimum custody offenders populated the rec yard lifting weights, playing basketball and just plain ol' shucking and jiving.

While I was on the basketball court doing my thing, Judas was back in the cell. Cajun Red was also on the court playing basketball but for some reason he wasn't defending me as usual. Matter of fact, he kept his distance from me and held some other dude that I knew he didn't like. It was obvious that he was agitated. His shooting was off all night, and he kept losing the ball because of lack of concentration.

Because of that I took advantage of his distractions.

"Two points," I said after flipping my wrist for a score.

I even got giggly and did a little dance.

That's when Red had had enough.

"Let me hold that fool!" he said harshly.

I laughed at his juvenile behavior. With that, he was all over me aggressively, but not like in the past. His body was stiff, his demeanor bitter.

There was no rubbing against each other like we used to do when we played against each other. His defensive moves were more of a push and shove. I sensed that his problem must be stemming from the fact I was his brother's cellmate. I sensed he was insanely jealous.

When the ball was in play again in my possession, I asked him to lighten up on the shoving. That's when he went off on me.

"What's your problem, man? This is street ball!"

He literally stopped the game to berate me.

I wanted to defend my ego, but I knew that Red was only overreacting and feeling bitter about his life.

I decided to play it cool because I did not want to end up in ISP for 30 days again. I was not going to let any of these foolish malcontents cause a setback for me by engaging in some dumb-ass fight.

Cajun Red was the one with the chip on his shoulder. And I was not going to knock it off.

Chapter 20
Low-Maintenance, High-Maintenance

Watch out for those dogs, those men who do evil, those mutilators of the flesh.

Philippians 3:2

Breaktime would expire shortly and then we would return to breaking our backs in the long dusty fields, pulling rows of vegetation like migrant farm workers. Yeah, my short moment of being out of work had ended, and I had been assigned to an area called Three Hoe. It was a medical squad, but to some officers that classification didn't mean diddly-squat.

Fortunately Judas, others and I were under the authority of a rather handsome young black field officer who seemed sensitive to our plight because he, too, had a brother confined to prison.

Judas and I worked the same row of carrots, enjoying the produce while also sharing conversation. Lieutenant RideOut eventually became part of the topic. Judas said he knew him from another unit and described RideOut as a rotten bastard.

He wasn't telling me anything new because I had already experienced that side of him. But there was one thing that Judas said that stuck in my mind the remainder of the day.

"Don't ever worry about that damn Lieut again while we are cellies. I got him by his balls," Judas claimed with total confidence.

I stared off into space at Officer Briggs, who sat on his horse staring into space too. It seemed he, too, was swept into deep thought. Something really, really heavy appeared to be on his mind.

I again dwelled on Lieutenant RideOut, wondering just how many boys he had a tight grip on. I began to wonder if Judas was in RideOut's circle, too.

And for that matter, what about Cajun Red?

Damn! What could Judas possibly have on that monster? Obviously, it must have been something few people knew about because he did not bother to reveal anything to me at this point. Of course, I was fine with that for now, because I figured I would eventually get an answer soon. That's the way things are in prison. Nothing stays a secret forever.

Cajun Red, occasionally glancing in our direction during our break, sat a few rows from us with a weed straw between his red lips. He never said anything because work squads aren't allowed to congregate. That was due to the fact that a security breach might occur and confuse the count.

At any rate, break time was over suddenly and the 12 squads regrouped to return to the fields, although dreading the labor.

Without notice, Cajun Red stood and began laughing aloud. I knew he was attempting to taunt me. That's when Judas said he would talk to him at his next opportunity.

Like a spoiled child, Red cut his fiery eyes toward me and began thrashing his row of beets with vengeance and then crushing them beneath his large booted feet as if he were sending a message of an impending plot against me. His behavior was so aggressive that I was surprised the field officer didn't catch him destroying and mutilating state property.

I merely glanced at Cajun Red in a cool, casual way, suggesting to him that I found his action silly and I was not in the least bit bothered by his crazy antics. I wanted him to know the excessive display was a waste of time, even if I believed that he had the potential to stage a senseless attack.

After "hat time" was announced, we all gathered our goods

and headed back to the unit. I was ready to hit the showers after another brutal day of labor.

While in the wet area, Judas and I, watching from across the full shower area as we do each day, glanced into each other's eyes in a way that seemed to suggest seduction. I knew that I should not even think of succumbing to my fantasies about my cellmate. It wasn't healthy for my spirit.

Even so, we ignored our feelings despite knowing the real deal. Our attraction for one another was quite obvious to Red, who would often watch me and his brother as if he were a lion lurking stealthily in a forest. Red wanted to see if he could catch us making sexual advances toward each other. For now, he was out of luck. He might have assumed we slept together but, again, he would be wrong.

He should realize that we didn't have to do anything in the open anyway. After all, Judas and I were cellmates. We didn't have to sneak around. We could easily do anything we wanted in our shared cell. I believe that this is what might have been eating up at Red – the fact that he couldn't watch our every movement. He was clearly at a disadvantage.

Anyway, after the shower, it was time for lunch. Judas lived up to his promise and met up with his brother, Cajun Red. They sat together to talk. I sat at a table with Druppy and Big Gee, who I hadn't seen in awhile. And word on this farm was that Big Gee was slinging cannabis like there was no tomorrow. Apparently, too, he was in conflict with some inmates because of their unpaid debts.

As Red and Judas talked, I looked their way from time to time. I tried to be careful to make sure that Red didn't see me peeping at them. I wished I knew what they were talking about. They seemed to be in a deep discussion.

I was glad that they were able to steal some time for a brother-to-brother talk without anyone around. Privacy in prison was a rare and precious commodity if you could find it.

Fact is, we were inside a clearinghouse of information, where men gossiped and dispensed other people's business like cackling hens. They talked about everything and everybody. Not even the chaplain was exempt from their assault.

Because I didn't engage with any of these other men, I felt like an alien in a strange land among vicious dogs. I believe that some of their behavior stemmed from the lack of having a positive relationship with anyone. Many had never been hugged in their lives by a male or female. And this alone is a tragedy that perhaps results in repeat offenses.

Some of these inmates seriously seek such a connection and when they can't find it, they become despondent. And I know that in desperate times, people do desperate things.

Later that morning, after returning back to my cell, Judas and I began to test each other's wit. Somehow the conversation went from Cajun Red to personality traits. First, he mentioned that Red was feeling a bit envious of us, but that Red had agreed to focus on his own issues from this point on. Still I wondered how they were dealing with their own relationship behind bars. For whatever reason, they seemed to have an enormous need to protect each other.

We talked nonstop, well into the afternoon, when most offenders on our wing were napping or in school studying for their GED. We had four hours left before the guards would roll our doors for dayroom time or recreation.

Judas remained comfortably on my bottom bunk in his boxers, and I wasn't complaining. This is when we began the discussion about personalities. I was vibing his intellect and his feel-good description of himself.

"I'm a low-maintenance person," he said, breaking down his traits. "I'm a person who minds his own business and likes to feel good about the things I do. A guilt trip comes on me every once in awhile but, generally, I manage to shake it off."

He continued, "I enjoy talking and sharing my feelings, and I am sensitive toward other people," he said, leaning back onto the wall and showcasing his beautiful legs. His large thighs were a clone of mine, just a different shade, and his athletic six-pack was to die for. When he spoke, all kinds of thoughts swam through my head as we were both half-dressed and feeling each other.

"I'm a good listener, cellie," he said, "and I have low tolerance for confrontations and arguments."

Finally, as I suspected, he admitted to a short temper.

"That would make you a person with a blue personality," I stated.

"How you figure?"

"Didn't you read your personality analysis from the last AA session?" I asked him. It matched his description.

And now, we were in each other's face. Matter of fact, we were so close that I could see the fine hairs on his plump chest that were illuminated by the invading sunlight.

He admitted that he had glanced at the chart a time or two.

"What do you consider to be a high-maintenance person?" I asked as I watched him explore my dark hairless body with his hypnotic hazel eyes. As he stared, I wondered what his thoughts were. I assumed, but I wasn't 100 percent certain.

Judas then cleared his throat and regained his focus.

"High-maintenance folks oftentimes cause a lot of trouble, always bringing drama in their lives as well as the lives of others."

I could tell he was hinting.

Even so, at that moment I wanted to touch him. I wanted to address my curiosity. But I resisted the temptation as we both played games with each other.

We were equally matched in so many areas, not to mention that we both had money on our books and wanted for little – other than our freedom. We didn't have to hustle like many men do in here.

After he admitted during an AA session that sex was one

of his strongholds, I was curious to know whether a sexual offense landed him in medium custody. With so many other similarities, I wouldn't doubt it.

We both seemed to be at a standstill, neither of us wanting to make the first move. So, instead, we just sat there suffering from lust while making sure that we kept our feelings locked inside.

On top of that, the reality was we were both HIV-positive and neither of us had condoms. At least I didn't.

Now, it was my time to spill my guts.

"In every game there is a winner and a loser. In this game, some of us are losing. We're in the penalty box and as far as I am concerned, real men don't play games in prison. They cope and deal with the here and now." I was hoping that he caught my drift.

"I'm feelin' you, cellie," said Judas, who seemed to catch on rather swiftly.

"We're considered to be high-maintenance by the administration no matter how you look at it. The way to beat the game is to stay penalty-free or not play it at all. For instance, if we walk down that hallway, we know there are signs that read, "No Loud Talking." If we cross over a line or even break that rule, punishment comes."

I watched as Judas nodded his head in agreement.

"You're a realist," said Judas, smiling at me. He then did exactly what I had expected him to do. He grabbed his crotch.

"So, what personality would that make me?" I asked, unable to hold my emotions a minute longer. My sex immediately began to rise as I lie there leaning against the wall anticipating the moment.

Judas confirmed my personality trait.

"I guess you would be considered an orange personality: spontaneous, good at shooting from the hip, full of energy and like taking risks."

Judas hit the nail on the head.

"And there's one thing I admire about you, cellie. When you fall down and get banged up by life you get up and try it again," Judas said.

After that analogy, I realized another thing. The issues I thought I had resolved in the past had now reappeared. And it was Judas. My same-sex lust was just as strong today as it was before I buried it. Now it seemed to have been exhumed.

Neither of us went out looking for anybody to sleep with by waging commissary. We didn't have to because our needs were well taken care of. Anyway, deep in our minds, we felt we had each other, even if we never openly communicated our feelings toward one another. But I knew that if the time ever presented itself, that we both would.

Since we both were sexually stimulated, I quoted my deceased grandmother: "Why buy the cow if the milk is free," I said, a reference to the idea that we should enjoy each other rather than looking for some fling that would cost us money or a headache. The solution to our desires was staring right at us: ourselves. And it wouldn't cost a dime.

At that moment, I felt Judas' warm, soft hands caressing my upper chest. I returned the favor by doing the same to him. It seemed obvious that he knew I was versatile. And I assumed he was, too. I was certain that he had heard rumors about me being referred to as the booty bandit. But that didn't seem to bother Judas.

We both stood and our lips met as we felt our hearts race from excitement. Our bodies were on fire. He put a peep mirror on the barred door then went to his locker. To my surprise, he revealed two condoms and a jar of lube, confirming his versatility. The lube had been disguised as hair gel, with the condoms tucked away in a potato chip bag.

I surrendered to my lust once more, thinking, "I'll just repent later."

Then it struck me that Lieutenant RideOut was on duty.

"What about the lieut? He's on duty," I said.

"What did I tell you earlier? He ain't gonna come barking our way ever. Mark my word, dude."

Judas pulled me in closer; I submitted.

"What makes you so sure?" I asked, pulling back for further certainty.

Judas smirked.

"I knew that fool from another unit, and he was in hot water then just as he is now as far as I am concerned. I'd witnessed his little scheme back then, and he knows that I know what he did and how it all went down. Ever since then, he's been dodging me, even transferring from unit to unit when he discovers that I'm on his tail. So don't trip, Moe. I got this. You feel me?" Judas was sure of himself.

"I feel you," I said. I then attacked his red lips, even though I felt a bit insecure about his non-detailed response concerning the secrets of RideOut.

"Let's keep quiet about us, Moe, OK?" he pleaded.

Chapter 21
STDs

All my enemies whisper together against me; they imagine the worst for me, saying, a vile disease has beset him; he will never get up from the place he lies.

Psalm 41:7-8

Donna had been patient with Lazlo for months but had now grown tired of the waiting game. She decided she needed to be more aggressive, so she picked up her cell phone to call him. A few seconds later his voice greeted her.

"Hello, Lazlo speaking."

He was out in the field at a westside doctor's office filling a pharmaceutical request. He looked at the number but wasn't sure who the caller was because it wasn't included in his call log.

"This is Donna, Lazlo. How about if we do lunch or dinner sometime today?" she asked. It sounded more like an order than a suggestion.

Lazlo chuckled a bit.

"What's your favorite cuisine?" he asked. Realizing they were both busy people, he wasted no time with small talk. Instead, he simply complied.

Now we're getting somewhere, she thought to herself.

"I trust your taste will suit me," she said, leaving the decision to him.

"Well ...," said Lazlo, pausing for effect. He wanted to make her sweat a little so as to enhance her anticipation for their date.

"I'm free for ... uhhh ... dinner. How does 7 o'clock fit into your schedule?" he asked.

"You're on," said Donna. She was delighted, feeling that she had finally accomplished her mission.

But Lazlo didn't stop there. He decided to take it a notch higher.

"Let's make an evening of it. Wear something very appropriate for dancing and dining."

Before gracefully ending the phone call, snazzy dresser Donna assured him that donning the proper attire was the least of her worries as her huge closets were chockfull of designer styles. Anyway, she'd already planned to sport something sexy that would accentuate her well-defined body that she worked hard to maintain with regular visits to the gym.

Lazlo always complimented her Fendi perfume. So, she figured if that by itself was a tease, he'd be blown away once she stepped out in one of her evening's finest that was guaranteed to be a showstopper.

But aside from her desire to share an intimate date, Donna's mission was two-fold. She also hoped that once she'd captured Lazlo's intimate interest the rest of her plan would be a cakewalk. She still needed him to get on board with Med Tech since she'd been given the green light to implement the company's security initiative. So far, she's had a difficult time persuading him to accept the security proposal. But now with the dinner date, her confidence had grown.

Women such as Donna are hard to resist, and she knew that she possessed that "it" factor. She'd already mapped out her preparations: sexy gloss for her full lips, a form-fitting spaghetti-strap dress and stilettos to click across the floor and highlight her sensual legs and fresh pedicure.

•••••

Darkness had already consumed the evening sky, and I was drowning under a cloud of gossip.

I wanted off the cellblock as word began spreading about inmates with HIV, and my relationship with Judas. We had been having sex every night and day since our first encounter. I had fallen deeply in love with him. I could not, or simply refused to, deny my lustful feelings for him. He and I were on the same page, and there was never an issue over role-playing.

For the first time, I began wondering if I could ever desire a woman the way I connected with Judas. I knew the answer would be no if I continued my current practices. But even before my current fling, I sensed that I had pulled away from the idea of heterosexual relationships.

Sure, I had often dreamed of being with a female, but that was all it was. Because I hadn't slept with a woman in years, there was a fear that I would become forever uninterested. That time may have arrived.

An example of my waffling about same-sex issues was illustrated in my desire for guys in prison to act more like men, not punks. But whenever I got involved with a male, I preferred someone who could express his emotions and passion. And based on those differences, I knew my life was still in need of serious reconstruction.

Well, with rumors and mess flying around the prison, I found an appropriate haven.

I sat alone at a long table in the unit's library, admiring a collection of hardback books.

Sometime during the course of my escape, the doors of the library swung open. Entering were Cajun Red and his brother, Judas. They didn't see me at first but later acknowledged me from a distance.

I began to wonder whether Judas mentioned our sexual encounters to Red. I didn't dwell on it much, though, because Judas had already requested that we keep our business secret. With that, I trusted he was holding up his end of the bargain.

After they went on with their business, I immersed myself in the poetry of Nikki Giovanni, whose works flowed with compassion, intellect and grace – some of which contained a level of complexity.

One such initial challenge for me was The Selected Poems of Nikki Giovanni, which I studied for further comprehension. I even indulged in her other works such as For an Intellectual Audience.

I came to appreciate her wordplay – hyperbole, simile and metaphors – and spent hours dissecting her introspection. She possessed a certain linguistic power.

I was particularly enthralled by Ever Want to Crawl. The poem leaped off its pages and into my psyche:

> "Ever want to crawl
> In someone's arm
> White out the world
> In someone's arms
> And feel the world
> Of someone's arms
> It's so hot in hell
> If I don't sweat
> I'll melt."

Need I say more?

•••••

White tablecloths, dimmed lights, chandeliers and fine china set the mood for an elegant evening at the Capital Grill near the ritzy Galleria area.

Lazlo, who hadn't been in the intimate company of a female for some time now, and Donna were all aglow in their first romantic outing. The excitement for Lazlo was clearly obvious as he flashed almost nonstop his white teeth that served as a megawatt source of power that illuminated their dim, candlelit reserved table.

"Why are you smiling so much tonight? I haven't seen this side of you before," asked Donna, gently dabbing her mouth with her cloth napkin as she finished her lobster.

Lazlo was taken by the sheer beauty of the buxom Donna, admiring her fire-red spaghetti-strap thigh-length dress that showed her Coca-Cola bottle curves without being raunchy and crass.

"I've never seen this side of you before, either. I guess I'm a bit baffled that I've been so blind for so long to not notice priceless art when it's directly in front of your face," he said.

Lazlo knew that being with Donna on this night was a reminder that he was entitled to better than the mess presently going on in his life with Nathan.

"You're not objectifying me, are you?" she asked, blushing. Although she wasn't being serious, she folded her arms for added effect.

He choked a little on his wine while laughing.

"Positive," he said. "True observations should always be taken as a compliment."

Donna liked his answer so much that she began to swoon, trying to figure out if it was the wine or the man sitting across from her. She was hoping that Lazlo was the real deal.

"Why do guys like you never make yourself known around the workplace? What's the catch?"

Lazlo pushed his plate to the side and summoned the waiter to clear the table. He asked for more wine to be delivered.

"There's no catch involved. Men like me are everywhere. We may not always be so outspoken in certain environments."

He left his comment there and ordered dessert.

"Hmmm. ... I see," said Donna, resting her hands in her lap. She wasn't really sold on that answer but decided against pursuing further explanation. She'd learned from past experiences not to rush things, just savor the moment. But, still,

Donna had a little suspicion. She'd always felt answers like those usually was a red flag.

Instead, she shifted gears for a more indirect probe into Lazlo's life.

"Just to get off the subject a bit, I was just wondering how your friend is doing – the one who was rather tipsy at my house party?"

She wanted to study Lazlo's body language for any type of uneasiness. At this juncture, she had no reason to suspect he was gay but still wondered about his relationship with Nathan.

Lazlo knew this game well enough that he kept his composure, staring her squarely in the eyes.

"We're trying to get him some help," he said, throwing Donna off a bit.

"I'm sorry, but who is we?"

"Friends and family," Lazlo said, stretching the truth a bit.

"Has his drinking become habit-forming, an addiction?" inquired Donna, expressing her sincere concern because she, too, had been down this road with friends and family struggling with chemical dependency.

"It appears so, but I'm not certain. I'm told he doesn't drink every day but when he does it is excessive – like that night at your party. I fear for him because he has so much to offer with his talent, and he is stuck in stupid mode."

Finally, the dessert arrived, as well as memories Lazlo had about me and my struggles. But he quickly erased thoughts of me and focused on his beautiful date.

"STD," whispered Donna.

"What was that?" asked Lazlo, his heart skipping a beat at what he thought he heard.

"STD. It's an old expression for `stupid thinking disorder.' My grandmother used to say it all the time when she caught us doing things we weren't supposed to be doing."

"Oh," said Lazlo, relieved after her explanation. "Things

like what?" he asked, digging into a bowl of strawberries and cream with Myers' Rum.

Suddenly, the shy side of Donna surfaced as she struggled to give an example before finally revealing her youthful wild side.

"Having sex with boys and skipping school when we weren't supposed to," she answered.

"You skipped school?" joked Lazlo, avoiding the more scintillating topic about sex. "Not Miss Corporate Exec, head of quality control."

•••••

It was now the last Sunday in April, and church services and lunch were over. Before Judas and I reached our cell, I paid close attention as Judas and Lieutenant RideOut passed each other in the hallway. They stared into each other's eyes with controlled glances and resentment.

I didn't say anything about this after we arrived in the cell. Instead, we discussed news issues and articles from Saturday's Houston Chronicle. Thanks to Lazlo, who gifted me a subscription, Judas and I spent time reading the daily paper during our 20-hour lockdown.

For a change, we kept our hands to ourselves and just combed through the newspaper. I wondered how long this would last, particularly since Judas proved to have a higher sex drive than me. He made me look like the pope because he was more aggressive and often initiated the contact, but I always complied.

"Listen to this, cellie," I said, reading the headlines from the metropolitan section: "Mom being held in child's death. ... Teen points to others in fatal gunfire. ... Partners' investment scam ends in 6-year prison term. ... Five officers convicted in case-fixing scheme." I had to pause on that note. "And check this one out: `City's air is condemned.' Is this what we're so anxious to get back to?"

"It's odd, huh?" Judas said. "The cycle continues. The very ones who point fingers are the ones who are doing the very crimes we have committed, and the crazy thing is they don't even realize that they are already guilty."

After Judas said that, I began to wonder again what his other offense was besides racketeering and gambling. Could he be a rapist, as sexual addiction is among his struggles? Or was he a pedophile? I looked up toward his bunk wondering if he was guilty of anything else that landed him in prison and in medium custody. I reasoned that my concerns probably were not valid.

I then put the paper down and gave my attention to Judas, who was babbling about the so-called establishment.

"They don't care about us. They could care less if we're handicapped, indigent or even illiterate. We're tucked away and left behind. It only matters to them when they get caught doing what we've done," Judas blabbed.

I agreed with him but chose not to get too caught up in the blame game because I know most of my emotional wounds were self-inflicted.

Our conversation then shifted to our neighbor on the floor beneath us. He's serving 99 years for murder and robbery, apparently shooting heroin at the time of his offense. The talk around prison is the media reported that his sister was visiting Houston from Alabama when she was fatally assaulted at a local mall while going there to purchase gifts for the family.

Her brother apparently followed her that warm summer day disguised as a robber. After she exited the car after parking, he leaped from behind a vehicle and attempted to snatch her purse that reportedly had more than $800.

They struggled; she screamed. After she grabbed his face mask revealing his identity, he panicked and struck her across the temple, killing her instantly.

He ran but was captured moments later after being injured in a hail of gunfire by mall authorities. He still had the purse in his hand. Six bullets lodged in his body, but he still survived, even with a shattered vertebrae. Now, he spends most of his time in his 6-foot, 9-foot cell with limited mobility and a colostomy pouch to excrete waste.

Judas used this extreme case to highlight his point about apathy toward inmates in general. He acknowledged that some people deserved to be ignored but that not everyone should be punished the same.

"Everyone is not a monster," Judas declared.

After our discussion about news events, we unwound with cappuccino and honest talk about ourselves. We still had a few hours remaining on lock, so it was now time for personal questions and answers.

With that being the case, Judas asked if I had shared my HIV status with my family.

I told him that my mom knew. I then asked whether he had done the same thing, but it seemed rather difficult for him to answer. So, I told him that I would withdraw my question.

"What happened after you told her?" he asked curiously with engaging yet sad eyes.

"She supported me, never belittled me and did not condemn my sexuality.

"Had your sexuality ever come into question before?" asked Judas, caressing my biceps. He loved touching my arms, legs and abs. And, likewise, I enjoyed touching him.

As he did that I leaned toward the bars to make sure no guard was coming down our row. I was still leery of the lieutenant.

I told Judas that my sexuality came into question only after I exposed my HIV status.

I then began touching him. I loved his skin and his masculinity.

"Had she ever questioned why you got married?" he

asked.

"I told her that I was bisexual and still desired women."

"You mean homosexual?"

I gave a peculiar glance at first, surprised by his line of questioning. It was a fair one so I answered, even though I was offended and hated the sound of "that" word. It was used by many inmates to disparage people.

"Well, if that's how you see it. But I admitted to her that I was attracted to the same sex even while married. I couldn't imagine what was going through her head when she heard for the first time that her middle son was gay."

"Do people realize that we were born this way – most of us anyway, whatever the circumstances?" asked Judas.

That response prompted my interest. What did he mean by "whatever the circumstances?" I wondered.

"I don't understand," I uttered, still baffled by his questions.

"Being gay is strange in a sense, but I feel that I was born this way, but I also believe I was programmed, too, when I was younger."

"Huh! I'm confused," I said.

"I love being masculine. Even though at times I feel attracted to the opposite sex, I can't resist the same sex. But there's a reason we are this way. There is a purpose for us somewhere out there, Moe. We just have to seek and find it. Still, I will always admire the male anatomy. It's in my nature no matter how hard I resist it. I will always like the touch of a masculine man."

I wanted to query him further on his thoughts about being programmed, but I resisted.

"You can't resist it or simply won't resist it?" I asked, amused by him yet understanding his pain.

Judas seemed amused by me, too. His eyes said so. He shared that resisting was futile for him as he continued to caress my body, arousing me.

"Maybe someday I'll get with a female, but for now that's not happening," he said.

"You ever wanted to quit?" I asked.

"Quit what?" he asked.

"Sleeping with men?"

He was silent for a moment then said yes.

"How did you start sleeping around with guys anyway?" I asked, shocking him with the question.

Judas released his grip and stood, pretending to need to stretch his legs and back. He suddenly became very uncomfortable.

"What's wrong?"

"Nothing. I'm going to get ready for dayroom. That's all."

His hazel eyes roamed everywhere in the cell except in my direction.

For a person who wanted to know so much about me, Judas wasn't willing to reciprocate. I reasoned that at some point in his life he must have had a terrible experience with someone. His abrupt withdrawal was very telling.

Whatever the situation, it was devouring him like some flesh-eating parasite.

Chapter 22
Confrontations

Do not make friends with a hot-tempered man; do not associate with one easily angered, or you may learn his ways and get yourself ensnared.
Proverbs 22:24-25

"Leave me alone," the voice of Judas could be heard pleading.

His recurring nightmare was haunting him. Once again he was tossing and turning and sweating. He also was breathing heavily. There were moments when it looked as if he were going to tumble out of bed. I was becoming more and more afraid for him. But I didn't know how to address this issue with him. I wanted to give him time to open up.

Throughout the night, Judas kept referring to the smell of alcohol and the threat against his life. He continued to make references about being attacked and bruised.

This time, he awoke out of his sleep, crying a bit with the innocence of an adolescent.

I didn't want to embarrass him, so I pretended to be asleep. But my heart was heavy. I wanted to jump up and embrace him, but I knew he wasn't ready – based on his refusal to share answers the other day to the very questions he asked of me. I figured that one day the conversation about his nightmares would arise.

•••••

By the time the middle of May arrived, the temperature

was already in the high 90s.

Around 8 p.m. on a Wednesday, Judas and I decided to go to recreation. Since most guys worked out in sleeveless T-shirts, Judas and I had purchased one for ourselves for five dollars in commissary from Clear. We managed to get our hands on a couple pair by sending an SSI to his wing for a small fee to retrieve the product. Yeah, Clear was still a hater, but when folks are desperate to negotiate a deal for commissary they temporarily abandon their rivalry to get what they want or need.

Sleeveless white tee's, tattoos and sagging white pants were the look on many prison yards. I embraced the tees but frowned on the sagging pants.

As minutes elapsed during our workout, Cajun Red surfaced suddenly. It was difficult to read his facial expression, but he seemed at ease.

He asked if he could have a word with me. And, of course, I obliged.

My workout was nearly over anyway, and Judas said his chest was burned out. I also sensed that Judas already knew about this planned conversation because he didn't seem bothered.

Well, Cajun Red and I went toward the left end of the yard, where we sat on the grass to chat. I removed my socks and Nike shoes to enjoy the coolness of the grass because it was one of those hot, muggy days. I then placed my focus squarely on him.

He wasn't sure exactly where to begin, so his first words were, "Beautiful night, huh?" He then stared into the heavens, studying how to break the tension between us.

"If you enjoy humidity, I suppose so," I joked.

Red, chuckling over my response, then jumped to the subject.

"I guess I was tripping, huh?"

"How so?"

"Don't make this hard for me, Moe," he said, staring into my brown eyes while occasionally glancing at Judas, who was holding a conversation with another offender.

"Why don't you tell me what's on your mind, Red?" I asked, watching him then take off his shoes and socks in much the same manner as I had done. Like his brother, his feet were quite attractive.

"When I was small I used to brush my feet and toes through the cool grass. It would always calm me," he said. "I'm just going to be straight up. I was jealous of you and my brother, Judas. When you screwed up and got caught doing "the do" with Sheldon, I knew that my opportunity to be with you was over. Then I found out that you were cellin' with my brother," Red paused. "I got angry at you, Moe. Not just behind the fact that you and Judas were now cellmates, but because ...," he paused, staring down.

"What, Red? What?" I asked.

"In prison there is a lot of stuff going around and a lot of lies, too," He continued, now staring into my eyes. "Scary stuff, Moe, like AIDS, hepatitis and herpes. I don't know if I've been infected or not, but it's always a possibility since the disease can lie dormant for years. But for now, I'm HIV-negative, and I know that the administration houses people who are medically compatible."

Red then caught me completely off guard.

"You feel I'm hiding something from you?" I asked, a bit uneasy. But then I suddenly thought about his little Latin friend, Angel, on C-wing. I wondered what was up with him and his health and his propensity to cut himself.

Red then got back to his point.

"Are you or were you tryin' to deceive me, Moe?"

"Of course not!" I said, putting stronger emphasis on not. "You know I'm positive, don't you?" I asked.

"Why couldn't you tell me, Moe? I've dated guys in prison who are positive. I know how to protect myself, man. I'm a big boy."

"It was my intent to tell you as soon as we came to an agreement concerning our relationship. I wasn't going to jeopardize your health, man." My sincerity showed in my eyes.

Red said that he believed me but that he still felt I was not as straightforward as I could have been.

After we were done sharing our thoughts, we gripped hands tightly and buried the animosity.

But I still wondered why Red mentioned only my health status and completely ignored a discussion about his brother's. Perhaps, he thought it was unnecessary and only wanted confirmation about mine.

•••••

On the unit, there always seemed to be some sort of ongoing chaos.

Druppy, the Anglo inmate from West Texas, and Big Gee could be heard arguing with another offender about Big Gee's taste in music. The dispute was over the comparison between Latino and black rappers. It occurred the night before when all wings, except those on A-unit, were up watching late-night television and music videos on Friday until 1 a.m. Medium custody for Judas and me meant we had to shut down by 10 p.m.

A black inmate criticized Latino-style rap as having no rhythm and flow. "That's something y'all don't have, fool," he was heard saying. He then laughed in Big Gee's face, who took offense at that comment. To make matters worse, he owed Big Gee money for two cannabis squares.

Big Gee pointed at him, warning that he'd better watch himself.

And since payback is a bitch, it didn't surprise anyone that this could mean trouble later on.

By 6 a.m. Saturday, showers were in progress on what

seemed to be a relatively quiet start to the weekend. That is until Druppy screamed, "Big Gee! Don't do it, man!"

This aroused the attention of Lieutenant RideOut, who was manning the showers. It seemed he was always present whenever trouble surfaced. He rushed into the shower area, but by the time he made it the damage had already been done.

Blood was everywhere as Big Gee, caught red-handed, was clutching a weapon in his right hand.

"Drop the shank, inmate!" commanded the lieutenant, pulling his mace and radioing for backup.

After reinforcements arrived, Big Gee obeyed. He was handcuffed and wrestled to the wet shower floor as the inmate who was stabbed sat in a corner in shock, hyperventilating.

Big Gee had overreacted to an incident that happened less than 24 hours ago.

"Who cut you, inmate?" an officer asked.

"No one," said the injured offender, still gasping for air.

His response was a reality of prison life in which a code of silence was generally the norm because snitching, even by the person targeted, could mean death.

•••••

Many people do break the chain of bondage from bad habits and addictions and begin applying healthy lifestyle choices.

Nathan put forth his strongest effort yet toward becoming sober, especially since finals were over and school was out. But he wasn't sure whether he was doing it for himself or Lazlo. Still, he kept his promise and his therapy appointment.

But at an Alcoholics Anonymous meeting in far west Houston, he felt disconnected – unable to relate or feel the pain of others in the room. Nathan thought he was so different from the rest of the people there. He never considered himself an alcoholic and wasn't about to let anyone convince him otherwise.

So, in the middle of the meeting, he left.

He was about to call Lazlo but changed his mind because he knew that Lazlo, who had given him an ultimatum, would be angry to know that he ditched the meeting. Go to an AA class or else, he was warned.

Meanwhile, Donna and Lazlo had been meeting on a regular basis for weeks. They'd recently abandoned the fancy restaurants and were now dining at her place, a fifth-floor condo at the Empire in the Uptown Galleria area. Judging from the looks, it must have been worth at least $300,000.

As they relaxed on his second visit to her home, Lazlo admired the windows, which were covered with fine Venetian blinds, and the hardwood floors were immaculate. He especially liked the granite tiles, too. Like her wardrobe, her furniture was designer-style.

As he sat on a burnt-red geometric-style sofa thumbing through a current issue of Paper City magazine, he absorbed the surround-sound music, with Toni Braxton setting the mood as he awaited Donna's return from the back room. He smiled as he recalled the soft touch of her lips just minutes earlier. He could still smell the gloss, some of which had transferred to his own lips. So, he slowly licked them as a reminder of what he'd been missing by not having a female companion for so long. He realized that the kiss was risky because it could lead to something more serious. And he wasn't certain that he was ready for that just yet.

But he was sure of one thing: He had become frustrated trying to find the right male partner. He'd grown tired of dealing with people with self-destructive behaviors. Because of this, he was more willing to embrace the company of a woman more than ever.

He reasoned that Donna was smart and refreshing, perhaps a bit too much for his comfort level. Even so, he delighted in the moment. She was a good listener, excellent cook and independently strong woman. For now, she appeared rather low-maintenance. As a self-sufficient woman, she could afford just about anything, or anyone, if she desired. But Lazlo was not up for sale. He was down for someone like her, but someone who could be submissive enough to allow him to spoil her and not have to engage in a battle of wits. He desired someone he could connect with totally, including spiritually and emotionally. He was absolutely tired of having to rescue pathetic men from their misery.

As he lifted his brown eyes from the pages of the magazine, Donna reappeared, standing near the doorway of the second hallway that led to her bedroom.

"A great magazine, huh?" she asked rhetorically.

Just as he had figured, Donna had changed into something more appropriate and fitting for the moment. Lazlo's heart raced from excitement at the sight of her but then he calmed himself before he was again ensnared by lust.

"Don't jump the gun," he murmured to himself. But he knew the race was now in progress, because his hormones were raging.

There was no doubt that Donna knew exactly what she was doing.

Seduction was an understatement as she sat next to Lazlo in her silky lingerie, smelling oh so delightful. Her skin shimmered in the soft light. Her touch made Lazlo shiver. She now believed she had Lazlo right where she wanted him – in a weak state of mind.

Lazlo didn't resist her approach. Instead, he welcomed her with open arms as his lips once again met hers. He then gently lowered her to the seat cushion of the sofa, where they caressed one another and explored each other's bodies, very much aware of what to do next.

Chapter 28
Childhood Trauma

There is a time for everything and a season for every activity under the heavens.

Ecclesiastes 3:1

From the hanging mirror over the stainless steel sink, my eyes met my image. I proceeded to brush the short waves in my hair on this early morning, trying not to awake Judas. I watched him tossing and turning during a nightmare. And I still couldn't figure out his problem, even as I wanted to comfort him during the 3 a.m. episode.

A short while later, he calmed down – perhaps from the breeze of the fan. After placing my brush back onto my makeshift shelf at the right of the sink and the adjacent wall that acted as a support for my shoebox, I turned and scanned Judas' uncovered body, looking at his attractive feet and hands, but especially taking note of his huge, genetically formed calves.

It was Sunday morning, and we had already planned on skipping our showers. Instead, I settled for a birdbath.

Even though I'd gotten over the struggle to resist my attraction to men, I began second-guessing my relationship with Judas. I wasn't sure that a long-term commitment was what I wanted, but I was certain that I wanted to stop what I was doing to embrace him. I withdrew from that thought because I didn't want to disturb him.

I then wanted to tune the radio to KTSU 90.9 for Sunday Gospel, but, again, I didn't want to disrupt Judas' rest. I just figured I could wait quietly three hours longer and then prepare for church services. With all that's been going on in prison, I felt a need for praise and worship. I also wanted to pray for Judas as I wondered how he got involved in same-gender relationships. Was it voluntary or forced? His bad dreams left me with many questions. I decided to simply wait for things to be revealed.

As the morning progressed, Judas decided to get his day started. He freshened up and we left together for church, and afterward we went to chow.

We actually had a rather productive day, being fed spiritually and secularly.

After returning to our cell, we began our usual moment of conversation. This time, however, the topic was different. We analyzed the day's sermon by a visiting minister from a Houston-area church.

The clergy's message weighed heavily on both of us because it dealt with homosexuality.

"Do not lie with a man as one lies with a woman; that is detestable," intoned the preacher, whose voice was still fresh in our minds and spirit. It wasn't a condemning message, just a biblical warning. He was speaking from the Old Testament of Leviticus, written by Moses that outlines forbidden sexual relationships.

"Sexual immorality has been around for centuries, especially this particular one," cited Judas, resting on his bunk.

I agreed with him while still affirming that the ancient behavior didn't give me the green light to practice it today.

"Why do you think we disavow the Word, Judas?" I asked, knowing very well the answer to my question.

"I suppose we want what we want and are unwilling to deny ourselves."

"So why do people act as if this gay issue is something new?"

I wanted to see where his thinking was at that moment.

"Most people don't have a clue what makes us gay and don't care to find out. They're consumed in their own little world."

His voice softened a bit. I even detected a sound of sorrow.

"Well, ..." I said, pausing. "For me, it was a choice. I was curious all my life about same-sex unions, and I began to explore."

Judas, peering into my eyes, laughed. "Ah, so you're an explorer?"

"Yeah. And I was instantly hooked, much like a drug, like cocaine," I said. "To some degree it was even worse than coke. I had become a booty bandit. I had to have a taste of it everyday. I knew that I was consumed by it."

"It wasn't that easy for me," Judas said sadly.

"What do you mean?" I asked, hoping that we were going to finally deal with his pain. For the most part, sharing had become a norm for us. This was mainly due to us being versatile and on the same page.

"Sex never came to me in the form of choice," assured Judas.

"What are you saying, cellie?"

"Can I come down to your bunk for a moment, man?" he asked.

I told him to stop trippin' and make his way down. I was happy this moment had arrived because most men live in fear of sharing their innermost secrets with another man, or a woman for that matter.

As he swung his legs over his bed, I was tempted to toy with him by grabbing his calves, but decided this was not an appropriate moment.

We kept our focus even though we were wearing only boxers.

"I know we've only known each other for a few months, but I feel that we've known each other much longer. We've shared a lot of our secrets, and I've come to trust you," said

Judas, looking into my eyes for validation.

I assured him that he could count on my loyalty.

"Among other things, what if I told you I was in here for murder, would you judge me?" asked Judas, looking me dead in the eyes.

One thing I'd learned from Kiki was to never let another man see the fear in your eyes.

"Who did you murder?" I asked.

"No one, Moe. I said 'what if?' It was only hypothetical."

His hazel eyes calmed me as I admired his beautiful white teeth.

"Why are you toying with me, man?" I asked.

"We're tested everyday, by something or someone. I was tested as a child, and I didn't understand and still don't," said Judas, sighing heavily. "I've been having these dreams. No, nightmares. They occur much too often, and I don't want to have to undergo psychological therapy like I'm some crazy person."

"What are the dreams about?"

"Nightmares, Moe. They're nightmares."

"Talk to me, cellie. Tell me what's up."

For the first time in a long while I felt I could be a comfort to somebody in need. I was so used to being the one in need that I almost forgot how it felt to be needed and trusted.

"It used to hurt so bad, man," he said, his voice lowered to a whisper. "Only Red and I talk about this, but I need help, man, from someone else other than him. I'm tired of talking about revenge and all that crap, considering there isn't much neither of us can do."

"Who hurt you, man?" I asked, knowing it was nearly impossible to get an offender to open up about his pain.

"I'm not sure how long it had been going on, but I remember back as far as when I was 10. It was after my birthday party in a back room of our house in New Orleans. He was always drinking and shit. Drunk like a skunk. I hated the smell of his breath even though he looked just like me. My mother loved his red ass! I, on the other hand, hated him for doing what he did to me, what he planted in my head. Programmed me like some damn lab animal."

I was pensive as I'd never heard Judas speak in this manner before.

"Who did it, Judas? Your uncle, a cousin?" I asked. I had heard stories of how some young boys were introduced to homosexuality by relatives.

"Hell no! It was my dad," he said harshly. "He would penetrate Godwin and me, and at other times force us to do each other as he watched and masturbated."

As Judas spoke, I could see the disgust on his face.

"After a period of time, Godwin and I found ourselves doing it on our own voluntarily. We were knowingly engaging in incest, and then one day we just stopped. By then we were teenagers."

As Judas recalled those moments, tears fell to his cheeks and bare chest. He vividly remembered being ordered by his dad to climb into bed with his brother. The two siblings, both naked, took turns penetrating each other as their sick, evil father watched.

Despite the gush of tears, Judas continued telling his story.

He said those events of yesteryear were so fresh and clear in his mind as if they'd happened today. He remembered the difficulty of breaking free his 100-pound body from the large hands and the 225-pound mass of his father, who issued him a stern and forceful warning: "If you ever say anything about this, you'll get more of the same."

Even now, his father's heavy voice haunts him, as well as the reek of alcohol from his dad's breath and the thick razor strap in his father's dominant hand that would strike at a moment's notice.

Judas recounted the unspeakable pain he felt was outweighed only by the heinous acts against his tender teenage body.

Eventually, throughout their school years, Cajun Red and Judas would soon embrace the opposite sex.

"When girls began to flirt with us, we became interested in them and sports. That seemed to keep us away from our dad a bit. And then one summer day our prayers were answered," said Judas, this time almost smiling. "Word got back to us that my Dad had thrown himself off the I-10 bridge into Lake Pontchartrain in southeast Louisiana. We were told that the fool put a large boulder and rope around his neck and jumped. Isn't there a scripture in the Bible that relates to that?" he asked.

"Yeah, it's in the book of Matthew, I think."

I reached for my Bible near my pillow and went into search mode.

"Here it is."

Judas leaned over and read the scripture from Chapter 18:6.

He began to read: "But if anyone causes one of these little ones to sin, it would be better for him to have a large millstone hung around his neck and be drowned in the depths of the sea."

"Jesus said that?" he asked, as if it was the first time he'd laid eyes on that particular scripture.

"Yep. He sure did," I responded.

"And people want to know why some of us are the way we are. It's the damn grown-ups who are causing a lot of us to do the things we do. And we are the ones who end up behind bars for crimes we commit. It's because we are wounded, Moe. Some of us didn't have a support system or a real family unit like you, Moe."

He waited for a response, but I didn't have one.

Despite his issues, one thing was for sure, Judas was certainly hurting and he needed a friend and a supportive parent.

His mom was still living yet in denial about Judas' and Red's dilemma. Cajun Red was his only close family member, and now I know why. They shared a horrible terror together. But now they were stuck in a place they didn't want to be.

•••••

With just 6½ months left in the year, everybody was talking about Y2K.

Fearing a technological collapse, corporate America was scrambling to upgrade its databases. Governments and media worldwide were speculating about possible massive disorder. There were warnings and even scare tactics across the lands by some segments such as religious fanatics foreshadowing Armageddon; the Second Coming of Jesus; and space aliens. Even correctional institutions across the globe planned lockdowns to prevent a breach in security.

Of course, all the talk about the end of the world and widespread destruction and death wasn't limited to the "free world."

Even inmates here and elsewhere around the state had their own opinions. The outspoken columnist for our prison newsletter, The Echo, called the commotion "rubbish."

I agreed with him. My thoughts were that it all boiled down to M-O-N-E-Y. For example, makers of software programs for database updates couldn't meet growing demands; food makers and water suppliers could not be happier as citizens stocked up on supplies, hoarding every product on the market. People were planning to flee to the mountains and go deep underground to escape the fallout of a nuclear attack. Bomb shelters were being constructed at a record pace and enormous amounts of money by the wealthy were being transferred from accounts to private storages.

I then placed the newsletter on my bunk, wondering where

my cellmate had disappeared. It was close to dinnertime, and the pill window was about to open in an hour.

Since our conversation about his father, Judas and I hadn't touched each other intimately for weeks, and I was definitely sexually frustrated. I so desperately wanted some of that sexual healing that Marvin Gaye was singing about on the radio. In reality, I knew that was the last thing I needed. To get my mind off sex and Judas, I pulled out my art supplies and began drawing.

•••••

Lazlo slowly strolled down the long hallway to Donna's office on the 15th floor as requested. He studied a series of sale reports from last quarter. The numbers were down a bit due to the Y2K issues, yet profits were not suffering. By the time he reached her door, he noticed a representative of a high-tech security firm heading in his direction.

They spoke when they crossed paths. As Lazlo reached for Donna's door, he turned to see where the fellow was headed. After he knocked, Donna invited him in.

Her office was just as immaculate as her Uptown condo. The tailor-made Prada outfit she wore was flawless, too.

She asked him to take a seat, offering him a drink. He declined.

Lazlo sat on her caramel leather sofa in the quiet, cool office.

They managed to separate their business and personal relationships. With surveillance cameras all over the place, it was best to maintain professional decorum.

As Lazlo got comfortable, Donna wasted no time and got right to the heart of the matter.

"It's been brought to my attention that you're still a bit apprehensive about the current security issue and its implementation," said Donna, with a serious expression that Lazlo wasn't used to seeing.

He almost wanted to laugh at her line of questioning, considering she wasn't his supervisor.

"You mean the skin implant issue?" he asked. "My decision has been made clear on that issue, Donna."

She leaned back in her leather chair, perplexed.

"And what decision would that be, if you don't mind me asking?"

Lazlo felt Donna was way out of bounds, despite being lovers.

"Donna," Lazlo sighed mildly, "implants are against my belief, my principles."

"This is the Information Age, Lazlo," Donna reminded him. She stood and walked from behind her desk, peering out the window and staring onto the downtown streets. "Terrorism is at an all-time high; computer viruses are unleashed every day; our company is at risk; Y2K is less than six months away," she said, defending the decision. She then abruptly turned toward Lazlo. "Are you interpreting any of this?"

"I understand it clearly, Donna. I also understand that this procedure is optional for management."

"It's also advantageous for those who desire to move up in the ranks within this company to embrace the security initiatives," said Donna, moving to Lazlo and taking a seat next to him. She was careful not to sit too close, but just enough to make her point.

"So, not getting the implant would stifle my growth in the company, huh?" Lazlo asked.

"You are very clever, love. Med Tech requires men like you to help shake things up in this business. Word has it that you are being considered to head one of the divisions in research and development. In order to do that, you can't rock the boat. I would like to consider you for that position."

"It's always been hard for me to kiss ass, Donna. I can't, and I won't," Lazlo said sternly as he stood.

As far as he was concerned, this conversation was over.

"It's about compliance, not sucking up, Lazlo. It's just a little implant. Besides Med Tech needs men like you," Donna reiterated as she caressed her right hand.

Lazlo noticed her spontaneous reaction as she concealed her hand. He grew concerned.

"I'm nobody's token. Besides, I love working in the field. My decision is final. I have work to do," said Lazlo, turning and walking toward the door. "Let's chat later. I have some further concerns, OK?"

Lazlo sensed that Donna had been prompted by superiors to persuade him to comply for him to be considered for the position.

But that was the least of his worries. He wondered if Donna already had accepted the implant. Based on her hand movements, he assumed she had.

If that were the case, it was not good. Not good at all.

Chapter 24
Double-Minded

I will not be with you anymore unless you destroy whatever among you is devoted to destruction.

Joshua 7:12

Venus was the brightest star shining from the West early on this Monday night. The moon was full and attitudes, aptly, were totally amiss. Among the people flying the coop was Angel, Cajun Red's little Latino friend. It appeared that Red's angel was anything but. Instead, he was more like a demonic figure. It seemed he, too, was suffering a mental meltdown, which led prison officials in riot gear to force him down from swinging on the main hallway fan. He was screaming from the top of his lungs about not wanting to move from C-wing, or else he would jump.

"Peligro! Peligro! I'll jump! I swear I'll jump if y'all try to move me!" he yelled.

Other inmates, unaware of what he was chanting, asked what he was saying.

I responded, "He's saying, 'Danger, danger.'"

Some fool in the crowd said, "He sounds like that damn robot from that old campy science-fiction television series Lost in Space that frequently used the expression "Danger! Danger! Will Robinson." The inmate even began mimicking movements of the robot, sending the dayroom into a cacophony of foolish laughter.

None of us on A-wing knew exactly what had occurred on C-wing that was forcing Angel's removal.

But there were plenty of people from other wings shouting and instructing Angel on how to handle this mess, most of which was bad advice as they dared him to jump. That's when Cajun Red intervened, asking the guards to let him talk to the lieutenant on duty.

I was surprised to see Cajun Red in the middle of the hallway during a security crisis because, in most cases, traffic in the hallways stops and wings are placed on high alert.

Somehow, Red was granted permission to try to calm Angel. One obvious issue was that Angel didn't want to be separated from Cajun Red.

I was unsure who had ordered his relocation so late in the evening.

As I turned to look at Judas, he seemed to show little sympathy for Angel. At one point, he appeared to be joyful over this event. I didn't understand what his reaction meant, but it raised questions in my mind, particularly his disapproval of Red's rescue efforts, which failed.

By now, Lieutenant RideOut had had enough of Angel's prank, too, and ordered Cajun Red to step aside and return to C-wing.

When other offenders continued to encourage Angel to jump, the lieut ordered a lockdown of the entire unit and maced Angel, forcing him to surrender. Now, instead of being moved to A-wing, Angel was placed under psychiatric care at a different facility.

•••••

It would not be long after the Angel incident before more disorder erupted.

With the lockdown only minutes old, a wicked spirit overcame Millner within that same hour.

It began as Millner, sitting on his cell bunk, was thumbing through a catalog from Victoria's Secret. He spotted a photo spread of black supermodel Tyra Banks. He was amused, but he preferred Caucasian models, or snow bunnies, as referred to in prison.

As he flipped the pages, his eyes were affixed on the pink lacy lingerie worn by a blonde model. He got especially excited and quickly stood and stared through the iron bars from his third-row cell, rambling incoherently.

The pink lingerie on the soft white skin of the buxom female was too hot for him to handle. He threw the magazine down and called out for the guard. Again, his demons had revisited. Millner was filled with sexual rage.

Some say his mind conjured up the titillating smell of worn panties. I imagined his nostrils widening like a predatory wolf as he inhaled the scent of the imaginary garment. He needed a fix, an orgasm. He was ready to rape again.

"No!" Millner cried out, massaging his temples as if experiencing a migraine. He tried to control his thoughts but his double-mindedness resulted from the many weeks of neglecting his medicine.

Again, he yelled for the guard and blamed doctors for his torment.

Someone finally responded.

"Where are you?" the female voice screamed out.

Millner was shocked but pleased that his estrogen counterpart had heard his cry and was coming to his aid. His heart beat rapidly from the excitement. He had even developed such a keen sense of smell that he could detect her approach as she climbed the stairs toward his cell.

"I'm here!" he said. "In cell 20, third row."

He pressed his face tightly against the bars to get a better view.

"Millner, is that you?" she yelled for confirmation.

She knew that she was walking into a situation that could expose her to sexual taunts and jabs by desperate inmates. It was not uncommon for exhibitionists to masturbate in the presence of female guards, so as she moved forward she instructed inmates to "put it up!" That meant no masturbation on her watch.

"If I catch anyone doing their thing while I'm on this row, consider yourself served with a major case."

Of course there's always a soldier in the crowd. One unidentified individual cowardly hollered from another floor, "You know what time it is, bitch!"

She retorted, "You damn coward, so do you if I catch your sorry ass!"

Millner then spoke.

"Officer Evans! Here, right here in cell 20." He was edgy and nervous.

After the guard finally approached Millner's cell, she folded her arms and leaned on the back rail and asked what his problem was. She was patient with Millner because she knew of his condition. And since she never personally had trouble with him, she cut for him, not out of pity but humane compassion. She knew he was sick and often wondered what drove him to such a low point.

"Hi, Officer Evans," said Millner, greeting her with boyish innocence.

"Hi, yourself. What seems to be the matter?" she asked. Her probing eyes could see he was disturbed. As she studied him, she also looked around to make sure no peep mirrors were present. Even so, she sensed that eyes were on her from every corner.

Millner noticed her blonde hair in a ball, displaying her distinctive female features.

"I'm having problems right now as you can see," said Millner, stepping back into a darker area of his cell, fearing that the lust in his eyes was too apparent.

"What can I help you with, Millner?"

He had filthy, lustful thoughts as he inhaled her scent.

"So what is it, James? Tongue tied?" she asked, calling him

by his first name. She smiled broadly while holding her black night stick with both hands, slightly stroking it with up-and-down motions.

He slowly approached the bars.

"What color are they?" he asked, inhaling.

"What color are what, James?" She placed the stick back into its sheath. Afterwards she moistened her lips with her tongue, further tempting him.

He hesitated at first but then decided he was in too deep now to be a coward. "What color are your panties?" he whispered with a raging heartbeat and perspiring palms.

The guard pretended to be offended at first. But the reality was that she liked Millner in an odd sort of way, despite his illness.

There had been rumors flying around that she was a freak and a control addict who loved to tease and would give cases to inmates whose masturbation in front of her was underwhelming.

"What if I told you I'm not wearing any? Would that make a difference?" she said, teasing. She really felt sorry for this poor pitiful fool.

"Please! Don't say that. Please have on panties, Miss Evans," a panicked Millner pleaded. "Please tell me you have on panties." He was becoming manic even through whispers.

Officer Evans looked around to assure that no other inmates was watching. When she thought it was clear, she answered.

"They're pink, Millner. I hear that's your favorite color. They match my gray uniform. My bra is pink, too."

"Uuh!" Millner swooned. "Can I do my thing?" he asked, reaching toward his crotch.

"Go ahead. But you know the consequence if I'm not satisfied."

She slowly revealed a hint of her pink garment underneath her pants. And just as she suspected, Millner was well-endowed and gentle with every stroke.

"I thought you needed to talk?" she asked, pretentiously, just to throw off folks who might have been trying to snoop on their conversations.

"Can I have your panties? I need your panties," demanded Millner, prematurely exploding into his palm. "Damn!" he cried out softly.

It was at this moment that other inmates caught on to their game.

"No. Not now, maybe later," she said. For now, the female guard had had enough. She turned and walked off.

"Where you going, Miss Evans? I need that! Come back. I need that! Come back. You hear me! I need those pan- ..." He stopped himself before completing the word. He was now more frustrated than before.

He convinced himself that this was not the end of the matter.

That's when images flashed in his head of his mother turning tricks for drugs and money. Because he hated her for doing that, he despised every woman thereafter.

Chapter 25
Mayhem

Do not gaze at wine when it is red, when it sparkles in the cup, when it goes down smoothly! In the end it bites like a snake and poisons like a viper.

Proverbs 23:31-32

Standing over him in a fit of rage, Lazlo confronted Nathan again in their Westside apartment. He was tired of a behavior that had become all too common.

"Your drinking is totally out of control. What happened with the AA classes, Nate? You stop going, huh?" asked Lazlo, wanting to slap the hell out his lover, with whom he had become distant. Nathan appeared to be calm even as he was being berated, but Lazlo knew it was all just a front. Nathan pretended not to be bothered, but, in reality, the conversation was eating up at him.

"Out of control! What are you talking about? I'm fine. I'm just fine. And I'm still in AA," said Nathan, lying as he sipped his vodka and cranberry juice while attempting to prepare dinner that evening over light music and dimmed lights.

But Lazlo wasn't feeling this façade. Sure, he was hungry, but the ambience had to go. He paused for a moment, sitting at the bar to gather his thoughts. He told himself that he was not stupid. Furthermore, if Nate was still going to those classes, why was he still drinking like a damn fish? He watched Nathan slice, dice and chop a sum of herbs and vegetables that would join the sautéed chicken breast browning in a light-cream sauce.

He often wished he could cook like Nathan, but tonight

food was secondary.

Lazlo had to be very tactful with Nathan, especially since he was still drinking. He knew that his friend's reasoning abilities were diminished by alcohol.

"It smells good," said Lazlo, offering a compliment to lighten the tension before continuing the subject.

His best friend Roland a few nights ago had urged him not to accuse Nathan harshly because of his denial over his addiction. Doing so could trigger chaos, he warned.

Lazlo then turned toward Nathan, asking, "You know what happened last time, right?"

"What last time?" asked Nathan, sipping his cocktail.

"The time I had to follow you home from Donna's party."

At that point, Lazlo wanted to slap the drink out of Nathan's hands.

"Oh, yeah! I wasn't feeling well that evening, remember," said Nathan sarcastically. He then placed the lid on the skillet and rested his buttocks onto the countertop near the stove, still drinking.

"The reason you weren't feeling well, Nathan, was because of your heavy drinking early in the day. Perhaps you were dehydrated," Lazlo said facetiously, knowing that was the furthest thing from the truth.

And this was just one of many episodes. Lazlo also recalled another incident during Kappa Fest, a weekend party on Galveston Island, south of Houston. He actually didn't want to go because the event attracted thugs and female strippers carrying on like Jezebels. Nathan, on the other hand, was lured by the rowdy behavior, sometimes even participating in the pandemonium. Still, out of love, he met up with Nathan anyway.

It was during this trip that Nathan had the gall to strip out of his white wife-beater and wag his tail out of Lazlo's convertible Mercedes as they tooled around the beach. And, of course, Nathan was toasted. He had had more than a few drinks. Lazlo ended up having to camp out with Nathan overnight in an island hotel, leaving Nathan's Jeep behind at Pier 2, near the Fisherman's Wharf, north of the Isle Strand where Mardi Gras is held annually in February.

Those events were basically an afterthought for Nathan, who continued to prepare dinner.

"Doctors say a little alcohol is good for the body. Haven't you heard?"

Not amused, Lazlo asked, "Have you not heard a word I've been saying? Your excessive drinking has to end."

Lazlo then ejected himself from the bar area, moving to the sofa.

Finally getting the message, Nathan finished his drink, placing the highball in the sink before joining Lazlo on the sofa.

"I've heard every word you've said, but I disagree. I'm not an addict and I'm under control. Addicts can't put their drug down for a minute, but I can. I don't need to drink, Lazlo. I choose to drink every now and then because it relaxes me. Can we just have a nice dinner tonight without arguing?"

Nathan then reached out to touch the left thigh of Lazlo, who flinched.

"What's wrong?"

"I don't want to go through this same drama I went through with Miguel."

"Miguel was a crackhead. I'm not," Nathan said.

"Who told you that?"

"Word gets around, Lazlo."

"You don't know him. Don't ever talk about him like that again! We all have problems, including you, Nathan."

An angry Lazlo exited the room, leaving Nathan on the sofa to simmer with the chicken on the stove.

Chapter 26
Lost in Transition

Those who devise wicked schemes are near.
Psalm 119:150

It was confirmed. Big Gee was now history. He was transferred last evening to Garza East in south Texas near the Mexican border. This resulted from the knife attack and refusing to cancel a debt. The warden assured him that he would send him to a unit where he could practice his art of fighting among some of the most violent Texas offenders.

The separation led Gee's best friend, Druppy, to take college courses. They were like night and day. With Gee gone, Druppy now had a purpose and a future to look forward to.

As for Angel Vasquez, he was now out of the "crapper" and back on C-wing with his beau, Cajun Red. Word was that he had convinced the unit doctor that he had a breakdown. Because of this, he was sent to the Jester unit for observation without garnering a case for his erratic behavior. The Jester facility handled the mentally ill, or those who pretended to be.

As for me and Judas, we were still kicking it somewhat by attending AA meetings, church, recreation and occasionally having sex. I could still sense a bit of tension in the air since the episodes two weeks ago with Angel and Red. Judas couldn't seem to get past the incident.

"These renegade punks in here are screwing up everything for everybody!" Judas complained. His disdain for many of the inmates had grown more intense. "Angel ain't no good for Red. That shit gotta stop! He's a cutter, man, and a nut case: practicing voodoo and crap with that doll of his. My brother's sprung and can't see that he's going down a one-way road. He's all caught up into this vato who ain't nothin' more than a piece of game!" Judas was riled up and testy. "You believe in hexes, cellie?"

"No, and neither should you," I said firmly.

Then Judas got quiet all of a sudden, and with him being from Louisiana, I wondered if he, too, believed in voodoo.

I wanted to offer an opinion, but I declined. One thing I'd learned in the streets and in the pen was to stay out of people's family business.

On Wednesday, the following day, lunch was being served in the chow hall. It was fried chicken day. The chow area was chaotic because "bird day" was an opportunity for indigent offenders to traffic the popular fowl back to their cells and then sell it for commissary items such as stamps, canned goods, pastries and toothpaste. Indeed, the commerce system thrived in the Texas penitentiary. Fried chicken was prepared only on Wednesdays, but this day was tantamount to owning stock and then selling it to the highest bidder.

But even on this popular day, Judas was conspicuously absent.

His "missing in action" was made more memorable for me because it was also the day the unit doctor had been fired and escorted off the facility in handcuffs by Lieutenant RideOut and several other officers.

Psych patient Millner was more than happy about the developments, shouting, "Doctor Death was fired! Doctor Death was fired!"

The sad part is that "Doctor Death" had gone the route of many other offenders, officers and civilian workers caught with their hands in the cookie jar. His firing resulted from stealing Prozac and anti-retroviral drugs and selling them on the black market.

"Whuzzup, Diary?"

It's been a minute. We've gone through the month, and things around here are getting very crazy. Not because of the Y2K thing but because of the relationship between Red and Judas. Something is strange about those two, and I can't quite put my finger on it

Judas has been somewhat distant lately and non-responsive. He's been staying away from the cell more often. He's practically gone all day, and he's not in school or at work. So what is he doing during lockdown? It's anybody's guess.

Well, I got a letter from Lazlo yesterday, and he said things between him and Nathan have soured; he is dating a woman. He says he likes her, but she is very ambitious and aggressive, not to mention the head of her department at work.

He tells me that Nathan continues to drink heavily again.

I remember those days of drug addiction all too well, and my past denial. Now that I have been redeemed from chemical dependency and overcome the fear of my sexuality being exposed, I can breathe again.

I discovered that most people could give a hoot about another person's sexuality anyway. Even so, it took me a long time to realize that fact. Unfortunately, I had to learn this in prison.

I'm now looking forward to one day dealing with deeper issues upon my release from this chaotic place. Education, employment and housing will be my new challenges when I'm set free. (Day 428; Thursday: 9:15 pm.)

Chapter 27
Same Script, Different Cast

We all stumble in many ways. If anyone is never at fault in what he says, he is a perfect man able to keep his whole body in check.

James 3:2

"I'm convinced that she may have already received the implant," expressed Lazlo, sharing his thoughts via cell phone with his best friend, Roland, as he ambled through the aisles of Whole Foods Market on Kirby Drive.

"What gives you that indication?" asked Roland, with a bit of concern.

"She keeps grasping her right hand as if there's some discomfort. She rubs it all the time, caressing and nursing it like a pet."

Roland laughed.

"The rubbing and all may be just a bad habit, Lazlo. You have no proof that she's accepted the implant. Furthermore, she's not confirmed it, and if she has the implant, then that's totally up to her," he said.

"Yeah, maybe so. But I'm still dating her, and I'm not comfortable being with someone who's willing to sacrifice her body for the sake of technology. Granted, we all stumble at times, but that is just a tad bit too ominous for me!" exclaimed Lazlo, gathering the last of his groceries and strolling toward the checkout.

As long as Roland didn't bring up the conversation about Nathan's drinking, Lazlo didn't mind talking about his relationship with Donna.

"Well, since you seem to be cool with her decision, I hope you're not telling me you're on that Y2K bandwagon, too?" Lazlo asked.

"Hell, no! I'm not feeding into all that bull. Most of it is all about money anyway. The idea is to create a little panic so people will lose the little sense they possess."

"You got that right. Anyway, don't tell me you're getting cold feet after you've gotten this woman all hot and bothered."

"She's passed the hot and bothered stage, my brother. I cooled her off long ago," Lazlo said confidently.

"So, you've earned bragging rights, now? You got it like that, huh?" laughed Roland.

"I'm not bragging."

"Don't get all bawled up in a knot; it was just a joke, bro."

"I'm cool," Lazlo assured. "Tell you what. Let's pick up this conversation up later on, OK?"

"That's a bet. Call me later. I have a hungry brotha I'm supposed to feed right about now. This dinner date is my newest prospect I've been working on and anticipating for some time now."

"Let's hope he doesn't come with any baggage," Lazlo joked.

•••••

Like a mad man, Millner gritted his teeth, bugged his eyes and tightened his huge fist.

"Shut up! Go away!" Millner chanted to an imaginary character.

Some offenders observing him began to stare. Others simply ignored him because they were familiar with his out-of-control behavior.

After a few minutes of mania, Millner calmed down just as the guard on duty was being relieved. He might have been acting out because he didn't care much for the officer.

When the shift change brought on a new guard, we were granted an "in and out," which basically meant "coming and going" — a period administered each hour for inmates to use the toilets, get commissary items, etc.

Millner was the first to blast toward the dayroom. He skidded to a halt upon seeing Officer Evans, the blonde officer who often allowed inmates to ejaculate in front of her while she performed an inmate head count from floor to floor.

Millner calmly wiped the sweat from his face and lips, applying the moisture to his white pants legs.

Officer Evans remained silent. She didn't even acknowledge Millner, not even as much as a stare.

Millner then re-entered his cell as usual, the doors closing slowly behind him. He placed his face between the bars and watched Officer Evans from a distance. He waited for her to do something, anything. But there was nothing at that moment, only the usual loneliness and abusive language, common to prison.

Minutes later he paced his cell floor. With teeth gnashing, he mumbled, "I won't be ignored. I won't be ignored."

"Do it, Millner," an inner voice instructed him. "Do it now."

"Shut upppppp!" It seemed his demons were back. He began beating his large chest like King Kong.

Soon after, Officer Evans, hearing the shouts, ordered everyone to stand clear as the doors rolled open again.

"Do it now, Millner," the voice rang out, only this time much calmer.

Millner exited his third-level cell, preparing to head downstairs. But suddenly he stopped in his tracks, making a 45-degree turn, just enough to make his move.

"Millner, no!" an observant inmate shouted. He saw tears flowing from Millner's cheeks, the desperation in his eyes. "Don't do it, man!" he pleaded again.

Officer Evans, oblivious to the commotion at first, moved in to investigate. In seconds, she swooped in to try to rectify the problem.

"Stop!" her frantic screams demanded. Her voice ripped through the air with the pitch of a whistle we could hear throughout the wing and corridor. "Millner! Please, don't do it!" She quickly shifted from panic mode to crisis intervention. She peacefully instructed him to settle down.

Then, Officer Evans ordered everyone to return to their cells. Most did, but Druppy quickly ran toward the area to intervene.

"Calm down, Millner," he requested.

"He's gonna jump!" a panicked Officer Evans alerted her fellow guards. "Help, help! help! Officer needs assistance!"

James Millner stood on the handrails from the third level with both hands elevated toward the ceiling. One wrong move would send him plunging to the waxed floor below.

"Millner, please get down, man," Druppy pleaded again.

Then a bitter, hurt, dejected Millner spoke: "Officer Evans, I love you." He spread his arms wide like that of the pterodactyl, a large prehistoric flying reptile, and began a fatal free fall.

His expressions of love for the female officer were his last words before his suicidal decent.

"Damn!" was the only response from all the witnesses of the tragic end for a disturbed prisoner who could never find the peace he desperately sought and needed.

Once again, the entire Ramsey unit was placed under a state of emergency. For two days, the Huntsville office wanted some answers because of a previous suicide attempt in the same month.

The incident triggered an investigation into conditions and treatment of inmates.

The final report, however, exonerated Officer Evans, barely.

Lieutenant RideOut made sure that she was not implicated in any accusations made by inmates. He had a goon squad to cover her back. And, of course, they all were inmates who would do just about anything for a favor from prison officials. Many summoned to testify in an investigation on behalf of the guards benefited by being allowed to hoard ice or keep contraband without fear of reprisals. Some even received illegal cell phone privileges, and others were given the right to commit certain sexual offenses.

After the probe ended, Judas and I decided to play Scrabble since we couldn't put our hands on each other due to the constant security checks every 15 minutes. Even with the tension between the two of us, we decided to remain cellmates because of our sexual past. We couldn't fool ourselves. Our attraction for each other was still strong and deep.

Even now, Judas and I were in violation because board games were not allowed in cells at any time. But somehow Judas was able to work out a deal with the SSI and the guard on duty.

I wasn't sure how this came about, but I wondered about the kind of pull Judas had. Was he a snitch for the officers? I had to eventually tell myself not to be accusatory. After all, I had finally met someone in prison I could connect with. It seemed everybody wanted a guy like Judas and I. We weren't thuggish, but we were both masculine and sexually versatile. Not to mention, we were both intelligent.

There were plenty of thugs in prison, and many sought companionship from brothers but were too afraid to drop their hard-core image.

After convincing myself there was no way my cellie was a snitch, I still wanted to find out what was going on between him, Cajun Red and Lieutenant RideOut.

There was a history there that I could not quite figure out.

Chapter 28
Parting Ways

Better what the eye sees than the roving of the appetite.
Ecclesiastes 6:9

The entire matter with Lazlo and Nathan was becoming redundant and pointless. To say Lazlo was frustrated was an understatement.

"Your anti-retroviral medication isn't going to be effective, Nathan, if you continue to carry on like this."

"Says who?" Nathan asked arrogantly.

"Look!" said Lazlo, walking in his boxers down the hallway, determined to settle this issue now and forever. "I've already gotten over the fact that you'd been hiding your HIV status. But this drinking and staying out late at night won't fly anymore, man! You've got to make a choice."

"Like you've done already, I guess, huh?" Nate asked.

"What are you talking about? Don't try to shift blame here."

Nathan, walking into the kitchen in the early morning hours before dawn, poured another drink.

The gall of him, an appalled Lazlo thought. This had become too much for Lazlo to deal with because he didn't drink much nor did he frequent bars like so many other gay men.

"So, how's the little girlfriend I've been hearing about?"

It was clear that Nathan was jealous. He turned and stared Lazlo in the eyes, searching for the truth. With the exception of the thunder from the evening storm, the apartment was quiet.

"Donna. You mean, Donna," said Lazlo, adamant about his answer.

"Donna? The executive? Well, does she know you're dating men, too? So who's the real cheater in the house, my brotha? Yeah, I might go out to the clubs, but I don't sleep around. You're cheating on me with her and pointing your fingers at me? I don't cheat! Surely your spies can tell you that," he said, slurring his speech.

"Don't get cocky, fool! You're drunk," said Lazlo. "You have two choices."

"What do you mean two choices?"

"Getting help for your alcoholism or moving out." Lazlo had become physically and mentally exhausted from lack of sleep and worrying about Nathan. "I'm not going through this again like I did with Miguel. If you want to kill yourself, I'm not going to be a part of it, Nathan. And look at the time. It's 3:15 on Sunday morning."

"You of all people shouldn't be giving me an ultimatum with your cheating ass! You screw yourself! I expect you to be supportive, and don't you ever compare me to Miguel again. I've asked you not to on several occasions. Why do you do that?" Nathan was not only pissed, but drunk and still drinking. He stormed out of the apartment and slammed the door behind him.

Lazlo knew that he was in the relationship too deeply to just let Nathan go like that. So, he dressed and grabbed his keys and cell phone to try to stop him. He thought that perhaps he'd been a bit too harsh on his beau. And the last thing he needed on his conscience was for the second man he's been in love with to end up incarcerated.

Lazlo hopped into his car racing down Richmond Avenue like a wild horse galloping in sprawling country. He spotted Nathan's red Jeep. Because the streets were wet and still crowded with bar patrons, he had to be especially careful traveling at such a high rate of speed. Even the sidewalks were full of pedestrians waiting to enter restaurants and after-hour nightspots.

Continuing his pursuit, Lazlo was stunned to see Nathan zip through a red traffic light. The chase continued as Nathan floored his Jeep like a bat out of hell down a stretch of avenues where cops were known to patrol.

"Damn, boy! Slow down!" Lazlo cried out, trying to avoid the excessive speed race. He tried calling Nathan on his cell phone a sixth time, but there was still no answer. That's when Lazlo hit the gas and barreled down the thoroughfare. At this point, he didn't care about getting a speeding ticket. He knew that he needed to stop Nathan because innocent lives were at stake.

Blasting through another red light, Nathan could be seen darting in and out of lanes.

A traffic light held up Lazlo. He struggled to see where Nathan was heading. He lost visual contact but not his hearing. There was an enormous crash that seemed to reverberate throughout the area.

Lazlo panicked and quickly made his way toward the site. He forced his way past a parade of red taillights from stopped vehicles.

Lazlo was in total disbelief.

"Oh, man! Nathan! Damn!" cried Lazlo, bolting out of his Mercedes toward the accident scene. He arrived to see the red Jeep demolished after hitting a heavy metal street pole that was uprooted from its foundation by the impact.

The Jeep was totaled and had flipped over with smoke billowing from the engine. Nathan wasn't in it. Where was he? Lazlo looked around furiously and headed toward a crowd of people gathered around Nathan's bloody, broken and lifeless body that had been thrown from the vehicle 40 yards away.

"Ohmigod! Someone call an ambulance, please!" a terrified pedestrian cried out.

By the time Lazlo made his way through the crowd, he was too late. Nathan died on the spot.

●●●●●

Lazlo never thought he'd be placed in a position where he'd be identifying a dead body in a morgue.

The pressure in his head intensified as his eyes filled with tears as he approached Nathan's remains in the refrigeration unit. The room reeked of formaldehyde, almost causing him to puke. He knew he had to be strong because next he would be left with the arduous task of notifying Nathan's next of kin about the tragic news.

Warning Lazlo that the battered body had experienced severe trauma, the morgue technician slowly pulled back the white covering to reveal the face.

At first glance, his heart skipped a beat. His throat tightened.

"Yes, it's my roommate."

Chapter 29
Lost in Translation

Woe to those who go to great depths to hide their plans, and do their work in darkness.

Isaiah 29:15

In the wake of Millner's suicide, Internal Affairs concluded no wrongdoing or misconduct by officers at the Ramsey unit.

What a surprise, huh? I thought.

Judas concurred and then began delving more into his family's background.

"Men in the Forté family have always been screw-ups," claimed Judas, sitting on his bunk on a Saturday in August waiting on the mail.

Judas continued, saying, "My granddad was a bootlegger and a drunk like my dad. My great-grandfather was a horse thief. Now, look at me and Godwin. We're both locked up in a prison system that's spinning out of control. So the Forté name don't mean nothing to me anymore, Moe."

"So, who breaks the cycle – the feeling of being worthless?" I asked, determined not to ever adopt that sort of thinking. I was further surprised that Judas thought that way.

"I don't feel worthless," he was quick to point out. "I just feel that the Forté surname is worthless. We're dysfunctional in a way."

"You've been redeemed from that past, haven't you?" I was sure hopeful that he had been, but I didn't let him know that my suspicion had set in. "What's up with all the AA classes we attend together? Aren't we supposed to be getting to the root of our problems that we've been in denial about, huh?" I touched his left cheek with a firm hand.

"You're playing psychologist now?" he said, returning the affection by caressing my full lips with his fingertips as if to say I was getting too deep.

"I'm just in search for some right answers. Aren't you also, man?"

"Yeah," he said in a child-like manner.

"So, how can you claim that your family name is worthless? You can repair it. You can break the cycle and set yourself free, so don't get on that self-pity wagon."

"We all have those days, man. So, I guess this is mine," Judas said.

I almost wanted to agree, but I frowned at that claim, realizing that Judas was holding onto deep emotional scars. He allowed his nightmares and other troubles to snowball into a pattern of negative thinking.

Finally, the mail arrived and I received a letter from Lazlo marked "urgent." I put the conversation between Judas and me on hold and tore open the letter. It began with a dreadful message: "Nathan was killed in a car accident last week."

The words tore through my heart. My throat knotted, and my spirit grieved.

I was in total dismay, feeling powerless again and wanting to be free to comfort my best friend. I became emotional and withdrawn because I knew Lazlo was in pain, and there was nothing I could do. I was angry for being unavailable in his hour of need. I was frightened that this loss could crush Lazlo. I got on my knees to pray, citing Deuteronomy yet again: "Do not be afraid or discouraged."

•••••

An inmate and Clear clasped their hands during recreation, greeting one another as if they were longtime friends. In a quick instant a note was passed.

Once again, it seemed Clear was up to no good, back to his old ways. He opened the "kite" smiling and agreeing to its contents.

It read: "That vato, Angel, is a snake. Find out what's the deal with him, and that hex crap I've been hearing about. If it's true, you got a job to do. Payment is no object, homeboy. Get with me when you know the deal. Holla!'"

Clear wasted no time.

The following early morning a C-wing SSI passed a note to Angel, who had been officially labeled mentally disabled. The message, courtesy of Clear, indicated a threat to his life. Angel was warned to get transferred or suffer the consequences.

"You better find a way to get your ass shipped off this unit and fast," the kite read.

With that information, Jose "Angel" Vasquez knew what he needed do to protect himself. He began devising a strategy, but he didn't want to hurt Cajun Red in the process. With his life at stake, he figured no amount of affection was worth the risk.

•••••

As she sat on her desk, Donna was becoming more convinced that her suspicions about Lazlo were correct. She always suspected that there was more to his relationship with Nathan than she was led to believe.

Her girlfriend, Irene, had always warned her to keep her eyes open for any suspicious behavior from Lazlo. She had her philosophy about men who kept secrets. But at the time, Irene told her to enjoy Lazlo's company and "get it while the getting is good." Irene didn't mince words and advised Donna to test Lazlo's love by "giving him something he can feel."

Donna could do nothing but laugh at her friend's offbeat

but sage advice. Still she waited patiently for her thoughts to be confirmed. As she did that, she stared at her right hand. She wanted to convince herself that she had made the right decision by complying with the new security protocol adopted by her company, Med Tech.

With all that was going on, she began to accept the fact that maybe her relationship with Lazlo was merely temporary because of his resistance to agree with her work philosophy and his avoidance of a serious relationship commitment.

As she examined her life closely, she realized that she didn't really want to commit either. But she would be flattered by the idea of someone desiring her in that way. But for now, she would be content with just a little affection from a man.

Chapter 30
Justifiable Cause

So then, banish anxiety from your heart and cast off the troubles of your body.
Ecclesiastes 11:10

He was more bull-headed than a Texas longhorn. But now, he needed to prove that he was also clever. Angel was contemplating his next course of action early Friday morning as he watched from his cell the prison field force going out on a short day's labor.

The morning was warm and cloudy. The heavy air held a strong odor from nearby livestock grazing on moist grass and weeds that were covered by dew.

Angel continued watching them until the field trailers carrying the offenders disappeared from his sight. Minutes later an "in and out" was called, and he vacated his cell and strolled down the stairway toward the captain's office for an unplanned meeting. But to get close to the captain, he first had to convince the guard on the wing that he had an appointment.

Fortunately for Angel, this was easy. The guards knew about his temperament and preferred to wrestle with a cobra than to deal with a nut case like him.

The scene was set and ready. Would his plan for a transfer work, particularly since it meant life or death for him?

Angel set out to exaggerate the bruises on his body. He knew that the best time to make this work was while the field force was out to work. This would eliminate an immediate challenge to his scheme and the courage to betray Cajun Red, who was away with the field crew.

To begin, he moved lockstep with offenders on their way to 8 o'clock court call for alleged infractions to determine their fate. A guilty verdict would mean immediate ISP.

Angel, though, deviated from the crowd and made his way toward the captain's office. He knew he had to be convincing if he wanted his plan to work. This absolutely needed to be the best acting performance ever for a prisoner whose life was hanging in the balance.

•••••

Well, the crap finally hit the fan as Cajun Red went ballistic. He felt as if he'd been pummeled by a massive blow to the abdomen similar to punches that had been wielded so many times in the boxing ring by power blaster Mike Tyson.

"I did what?" exclaimed Red. "Captain, you know that ain't true!"

"Well, Angel Vasquez said you attacked him, Forté," using Red's last name. "You know I have to act on this matter. The boy had bruises all over his body even between his thighs, man!"

He provided photos of Angel Vasquez as proof.

"Hell, he could have gotten into a fight for all you know, Captain! I didn't put them there. Not me."

The photos revealed marks on Angel's lower back, inner thighs and buttocks.

"He said you did, Forté."

"He's lying, Captain! I didn't touch that dude."

Cajun Red leaped from his chair.

"Sit down, Godwin!" instructed the captain, reaching behind his back to retrieve a pair of handcuffs. "I have to subdue you," he said. He then asked Red to kneel.

As the cold cuffs clasped tightly around Cajun Red's wrists, the captain used his strong grip to hoist Red from his knees.

"So what are you going to do? Lock me up?"

"Yes, for now. Angel is in safekeeping until we get to the bottom of this. This is a justifiable cause. Have you eaten?" asked the captain, hearing Red's stomach growl.

Cajun Red ignored the question; instead he continued to vent.

"Justifiable my ass! I didn't touch that ho'. He's lying, Captain!"

The captain reiterated that he would investigate the matter with "care and concern." But everybody in the pen knew that statement meant "you'll be locked up until further notice."

It didn't take long for word to spread that Red was in investigative segregation for the alleged sexual assault of Angel.

But what puzzled me most was how Judas was able to remain calm over the charges against his brother. When I pressed further about his thoughts, his response was similar to that given by the administration.

"They said it was a justifiable cause."

He then rustled through his locker and gathered a heap of his commissary and dumped them into a white bag.

Not once did he look me in the eyes. His nonchalance would lead one to believe he had significant involvement in this matter. But why?

And why was he gathering his commissary? What was really going on here? Could Judas be part of a gang? After all, I had seen him occasionally fraternize with some of those scoundrels. But, still, joining a group was far out of character for him, given that he sported no tattoos or scars.

There was, however, one commonality that he shared with those miscreants: a killer instinct, although Judas seemed to have acquired this trait more recently. Or did it always exist? This current matter further raises the question in my mind whether he murdered his father, a point that he has denied. Did his father commit suicide? The issue surrounding Red and Angel makes me question his veracity.

Chapter 31
Personal Rediscovery

The acts of the sinful nature are obvious; sexual immorality, impurity, debauchery, idolatry, witchcraft, hatred, discord, jealousy, fits of rage, selfish ambitions, dissensions, factions, envy, drunkenness, orgies and the like.

Galatians 5:19-21

Gloom hovered over the morning as Lazlo escorted the remains of Nathan back to East St. Louis on a Continental Airlines jet. The cool air at 30,000 feet left him chilled, so he closed the tiny vent above his head and, subsequently, stood to retrieve a small blue blanket from the overhead compartment.

His teeth began to chatter, and he wasn't sure whether he was coming down with a cold or his body was experiencing a case of bad nerves. This entire experience had been rather traumatic for him.

He seemed to be the only one shivering, which made him wonder if everyone else on board were Eskimos.

Lazlo's typical calm demeanor seemed to be overshadowed by his grief and rage. He mourned deeply for Nathan, but it seemed his anger was even greater, not because Nathan lost his life to a preventable death but due to the foul, unsympathetic attitude of his only sibling over the demise of her brother.

Nathan's parents had been deceased many years now. Lazlo never knew the exact nature of their passing because of Nathan's inability, or refusal, to entirely express his emotions about his family.

Lazlo learned that Nathan's sister hadn't forgiven him

because of his sexual preference. She told me that he had embarrassed the family name, which is why she was refusing to accompany his body home. Furthermore, she claimed she had important matters to take care of at her job and couldn't break away, saying his death was "too untimely" for her hectic schedule. The gall of her, said Lazlo, incensed by her ludicrous excuse.

That's when he lost it, angrily asking her, "Well, when is it a fine time to die?" He pre-empted a response by telling her not to bother to try to answer.

He realized that some females had high expectations for their brothers.

Lazlo didn't see the need to try to convince the sister that despite his sexuality, Nathan was the same person who once threw for 200-plus yards in a game during his high school years. He had a rebel's nature. He was also that same brother who saved her ass from getting pregnant from her abusive boyfriend years ago, and he was that same brother who introduced her to the love of God after the death of their parents, even when she blamed God for their deaths.

Those were just a few of the things Nathan had shared with Lazlo during their relationship.

Then came the real reason Lazlo knew he should simply dismiss Nathan's family. The straw that broke the camel's back was when the sister asked harshly and selfishly, "Why can't we let the state of Illinois bury him since there's no insurance?"

He didn't use the B-word, but he came close. He told her that he would take care of the arrangements himself, including the burial costs. He only requested that she simply handle flight costs.

Because of her uncaring attitude, Lazlo didn't bother to share that Nathan owned a $50,000 life insurance policy, and Lazlo months ago was named the beneficiary.

It was unfortunate that she wanted to erase Nathan, her only brother, from her memory. Their rivalry was deep and the relationship forever fractured – even in death.

During his flight, Lazlo tried to put all of that madness aside. He knew he had another hurdle in the name of Donna Dangerfield.

He also knew this pretense had to end, particularly after strong evidence that she had received the security implant.

He found out by "pimping" a young ambitious white manager for information about the procedure, such as the time frame for healing and side effects. The gentleman confirmed that he'd taken the implant, as well as everyone in Donna's department – including her.

•••••

Eight days had passed since the investigation into Angel Vasquez's claim against Godwin "Cajun Red" Forté.

It was good for him that Angel was in "safe-keeping," because word was out that a small contract was out on his life.

How fitting that it was Friday night, commonly referred on the streets and in prison as Devil's Night, a period – according to urban legend – when all hell breaks loose. It shared this distinction much like some cults on Halloween.

Then there were rumors floating that Judas had something to do with all of this mayhem.

Meanwhile, in safe-keeping, Angel had been feeling sick to the stomach after finishing his dinner. He attributed it to nerves. So he decided to lie down for a spell, wishing he had his hex contraband to heal his ailments, specifically a chicken bone and string. He wanted to conjure up a remedy.

He stood to shake off his painful cramps but got no relief, so he returned to bed and curled into a fetal position. He wanted to call out for help, but he just gritted his teeth and tightened his face, begging to be relieved of his agony.

After he coughed up blood that also spewed from his nostrils, that's when it hit him. He realized he'd seen this condition before. He'd been poisoned by "homegrown" bacteria.

Here's how it works: Some inmates, known as wannabe chemists, would smear the inside of a water bottle with bacteria, or fecal matter, from a toilet rim. Then, they would allow it to grow for several days in the corner of a hot, dark locker. And, presto! They have successfully begun a germ warfare against enemies, who become infected after drinking water from the tainted bottle or ingesting laced food.

Angel Vasquez began to lose hope as he felt he would never see the free world again, because he was serving 70 years for murder. With so few options, he decided to take matters into his own hands.

He set out to accomplish this with a razor that he had smuggled into confinement. He then methodically carved into his wrist, where a gradual flow of blood poured from his vein. And since no one would be checking on him regularly, he slowly lost consciousness. He made the ultimate decision that allowed him to slip away from his physical and mental pain, incarceration and even Cajun Red.

And just like that, "Angel" expired – his life snuffed away. The question now is, "Will the man known as Angel be able to earn his wings beyond this world?"

Chapter 32
Blind Ambition

There is only cursing, lying and murder, stealing and adultery. They break all bounds, and bloodshed follows bloodshed.

Hosea 4:2

With all the talk about Angel Vasquez's suicide, I didn't sleep a wink Friday night. And when I got up early Saturday morning, I noticed that it was business as usual for Judas. I watched as he placed his face towel back onto the peg after washing his face. He brushed his teeth, combed his hair and even made coffee. He seemed to be in a rare, giddy mood even as the unit remained on lockdown – again. He wasn't the least bit bothered that breakfast and showers had been postponed.

I, on the other hand, was sick of all this lockdown crap. But what could I do about it? Absolutely nothing. And since I was powerless over the situation, I just went along with the flow.

I wasn't, however, limited in my ability to play the role of detective. So, I decided to engage Judas in conversation.

"Did you hear some talk about a suicide last night?" I asked as I listened to the rainfall striking against the windows.

Judas jumped to his bunk as if angered by my inquiry.

"Maybe I did; maybe I didn't. I try to block out crap like that. Besides, that Mexican probably deserved everything that came his way."

"Who? Who are you talking about, cellie?"

"Angel," he answered, looking down on me with distressed eyes.

"I didn't mention anything about Angel."

"You said that he was attacked," Judas said.

"No. I said there was talk about what had caused the lockdown. A suicide. I try to keep my ears open, but I didn't mention a name," I declared.

I was now totally convinced Judas was involved. It was clear that a hit was ordered on Angel, and Judas hinted on several occasions that he wanted that "renegade punk" dealt with.

I also discovered that Judas had, indeed, been meeting secretly with and passing notes to Clear in the gym despite us being on medium custody. Somehow he managed to do all this when we were supposed to be locked down for 20 hours. Besides being a Crip, Clear was perhaps a murderer, too.

With Judas showing defiance toward my questions, I retreated from the conversation.

He seemed pleased with that decision and was more than willing to change the subject.

"So, when are you moving?" asked Judas, attempting to pre-empt my announcement and cast the dark cloud over me that had already completely covered him. Perhaps he wanted to embarrass me by letting me know he was aware that I wanted to separate from him.

Yet, I was still surprised that he'd heard about me wanting to move. I assumed it was a slip of the tongue by Druppy, with whom I had shared that I was contemplating a relocation request from the administration.

"Do you ask because I can't get out of your sight fast enough?"

"I was just curious," Judas said.

I then stood and put on my flip-flops, approaching the sink to wash my face. The coffee that Judas had made earlier was still hot, so I offered him a cup. He accepted the cappuccino, thanking me with his eyes instead of his mouth.

"Judas, I'm just curious, too, brotha," I said, placing the pot back to the corner of the sink area. I then retrieved my toothbrush before confronting him again. "Whoever it was really wanted Angel out of the way."

Judas sipped his coffee then responded. "That's not my business." His facial expression was stiff.

I then returned to sit on my bunk for a mild interrogation.

"Well, is it true?" I asked, trying to get to the heart of the discussion.

"Is what true?"

"The rumors about you putting a hit out on Angel?"

"Why is that important to you, Moe? Matter of fact, why is any of this stuff important to you?" he said, becoming louder as he had become noticeably irritated.

I wasn't about to be punked, so I stood again, just in case this fool wanted to get "froggy." Lovers or not, I knew not to fully trust these hardheads in this pen. I've witnessed what happens when men start dating these insensitive, egotistical men who lose ground and self-esteem. The result is always tragic.

"Why are you trying to be so damn hard?" I said, leaning on the wall and staring him squarely in the eyes.

"You think you know me, don't you?" he said, laughing and then sipping his coffee. Then suddenly the tone of his voice shifted again, becoming mellow.

I couldn't deny that he had a valid point. I really didn't know Judas at all. I knew that he was good in bed and from Louisiana. I assumed that he was truthful about his nightmares and that he and Cajun Red are biological brothers.

"Come on, Moe. You haven't heard?" he whispered.

"Heard what?" I asked, wanting to touch his shirtless upper body.

"Angel was infected with hepatitis C and had been practicing voodoo on Red, putting chicken bones and other shit in front of his cell and burning those damn candles like some fool-ass witch doctor. Red's my blood, Moe. I won't allow no punk ever again to come between us," he said, confirming rumors that had been circulating about Angel. I had to sit down after that.

I wondered who Judas was referring to when he said he would not let anyone else ever come between him and Red again.

"So, Judas, why did Angel accuse Red of rape?" I asked.

"He was ordered to, Moe. It was a sure way to get his ass locked in safe-keeping and away from my brother. If Red had found out that Angel had falsified his medical records by concealing his hepatitis status, he'd have a murder case on his hands right now. That wasn't about to happen to my brother. Red has this blind ambition about things and people. It's my job to protect him. Why do you think I'm here? It's not by accident, Moe."

This was another rare occasion when Judas volunteered to get a bit deeper about his family history. I accept the fact that blood is thicker than water, but I still couldn't understand why he needed to go this route and concoct a story because of his brother's weaknesses. Well, I decided to explore the subject deeper.

"So, tell me. Why did Angel commit suicide?"

Judas laughed again.

"He was weak, man. Besides, he was one sick puppy in the mind. He was a cutter, man, with a killer's instinct. But he was weak, nonetheless. I didn't think he would kill himself," said Judas, swallowing hard. "I gave orders for Clear to rough him up a little, you see," he bragged. "But that fool Clear went in Angel's house and got him some of that boy's kitty cat," laughed Judas.

At this point I had had just about enough of the conversation, but I continued anyway.

"So, Red had to go through all this bull just to ..."

"Just to learn a lesson, Moe," said Judas, interrupting me. "If you can't survive prison, you ain't gonna survive on those streets out there when it's time to be released."

Chapter 33
What Shall I Do?

Rid yourself of all the offenses you have committed, and get a new heart and a new spirit.

Ezekiel 18:31

Lazlo was back to work in Houston after the trip to East St. Louis to deal with the funeral and burial of Nathan. Now, he had to shift gears to deal with Donna and the Med Tech offer. He knew exactly what he needed to do.

After sharing the news to Donna about Nathan's accident, he felt the time was ripe for cutting ties with her – at least their sexual relationship.

When the lunch hour arrived, the two trotted throughout the downtown tunnel to Birraporetti's, an Italian restaurant in the heart of the Theater District.

Once there they were seated at a table near a window on street level. They ordered drinks and calamari as an appetizer, then their lunch entree.

Lazlo was really digging the atmosphere, and the jazz broadcasting throughout the restaurant.

As had become routine, Donna began slightly digging her nails into the back of her right hand.

"What's wrong? Something eating at you?" asked Lazlo, taunting as he leaned back into his chair wondering why she sacrificed her body to the science of technology. Was her career advancement all that important?

Not wanting to give the impression that she'd been a fool, Donna lied and said that everything was fine.

"So, Donna, why couldn't you tell me the truth?" Lazlo asked.

Even as Lazlo posed this question, he was on guard just in case she tried to turn the tables and ask him about his past with Nathan. He knew that this could be a time for her to attempt to get messy and nosy.

But much to his surprise, she decided to forgo that route, perhaps due to the fact the man was just recently laid to rest.

"The truth about what, Lazlo?"

"The implant," he said specifically, wanting to avoid any doubt about what was on his mind.

"Oh, that. I never said whether or not I'd taken the implant."

"But you led me to believe that you had not."

"I did no such thing," an exasperated Donna exclaimed.

Lazlo just smiled.

"Well, it's water under the bridge. How does it feel?"

"How does what feel?" said Donna, being evasive.

"The device."

"Oh, that thing. It's nothing," she said, smiling uncomfortably. "I just don't know why some black folks are so apprehensive about today's technology? It's such a simple procedure. No different than a tracking device scientist implant into whales and dolphins."

Donna felt the need to defend her right to choose.

"The belief in superstitions and all that other stuff is so outdated, Lazlo."

"Maybe for some," Lazlo said, "but we aren't sea mammals, Donna."

"You believe in all that Revelation talk, don't you?" asked Donna, suggesting she was not down with religion and spirituality.

"I consider it to be from the inspired Word."

"That's only if you are part of that mix," she responded.

Lazlo was now further offended, but he kept his cool.

•••••

"Donna, we can't see each other anymore as far as dating is concerned."

She was aghast at his statement but tried not to show her surprise.

At that moment, the squid arrived, but before she began preparing to eat she said, "I understand." She didn't bother to challenge him. And Lazlo wasn't sure what to make of her initial reaction.

She then chomped down onto the calamari before expressing further thoughts.

"We had our fun, didn't we?" she asked. "No harm done. Well, I have another candidate who has taken me up on the position that you're passing up."

She almost sounded condescending.

As a parting gift, Lazlo let her get away with that because breaking things off with her proved relatively easy. Painless even. At first, he wasn't sure how she was going to react, but expected tears or an attempt by her to change his mind and push harder on the Med Tech offer. Still, he wanted confirmation about her feelings.

"So, you're fine with my decision, right?" he asked, sipping iced tea. Lazlo then began wondering about her non-secular life. Did she ever believe in God? If so, when did she stop and why? Had she become so self-sufficient that there was no need to embrace a higher power anymore?

"We're consenting adults, right? When one thing fails, we move on to other opportunities," she said.

Although she might have speculated about other aspects of Lazlo's life, she didn't see the need to dwell on that. One thing for certain that was never in question: She knew that Lazlo was totally against the implant for him, her or anyone else.

Donna decided to accept that reasoning for why their relationship fizzled. She was convinced it had nothing to do with Lazlo being under her supervision had he accepted her offer.

In the middle of their lunch, Lazlo leaned in closer at the table, extending his right hand.

"Friends," he said.

"Friends," she agreed. "Now help me devour the rest of this calamari."

"Whuzzup, Diary?"

It's December 31, 1999. The unit is on lockdown due to issues swirling around the Y2K issue. Everybody is talking about rolling blackouts, airplane crashes, shipwrecks and criminals on the loose going wild. No one knows what tomorrow will bring, except the Creator himself. If anything were to happen, I'm not scared of death because He said he would never leave me or forsake me – even when I'm at my worst.

Aside from that, I'm quite content with my peace as I listen to the radio and legendary gospel great James Cleveland belt out one of his popular releases, What Shall I Do. I often asked myself that question even when I knew the answer to dealing with internal demons and selfish ambitions: Confront them and move on. It took me almost 40 years to realize that I had the power to do just that.

Well, Druppy made parole last month and is now out the door. I sense he'll be all right because he graduated from college while on lockdown.

Lazlo and Mom came to visit me together one Sunday, and it was a big surprise. She was healing fine from cancer surgery and even hinted that she knew Lazlo and I had had a sexual past but that she came to grips with that and embraced us, regardless. The week prior, siblings Troy and Adrea visited. All four of them are anticipating my release. And right now I don't have a clear picture when that'll happen.

It has now been two weeks since Judas and I separated as

cellmates, and it was strange how it went down. We both agreed it was time to depart, so Judas cooked up a scheme and presented it to Lieutenant RideOut. Judas was confident it would work because he'd been saying all along that he had the lieut eating out of his hands. I rolled right along with the phony plan, which suggested Judas and I were in conflict and on the verge of having a physical altercation. We relied on our high-credibility profile and prison officials' usual efforts to accommodate warring cellmates. So, weeks later, we met up with the lieutenant in the hallway after chow and jacked him up about our bogus "ordeal." Not to my total surprise, RideOut was all too willing to meet our request. But his acquiescence was still sort of spooky. Nonetheless, his actions and demeanor didn't seem to bother the calm, cool, collected Judas one iota.

But the real stunner happened a week later. That's when I found out the true connection between Red, Judas and that damn Lieutenant RideOut. And this information came from the mouth of my newest cellmate, who's now resting peacefully on his top bunk as quiet as a field yard country mouse.

I discovered that the Forté brothers' mother and Lieutenant RideOut are sister and brother, making RideOut their uncle. The lieutenant, who was well aware of the boys' sexual abuse many years ago, was responsible for the death of Judas' and Red's father. The lieut knew that his sister was in denial over the boys' molestation by her husband, but he wasn't. So he took the law into his own hands and did the unthinkable by first subduing his oft-intoxicated brother-in-law and then strapping the body of the boys' unconscious father to a huge boulder. Then he watched the man submerge into the murky Lake Pontchartrain after throwing him off the causeway in southern Louisiana.

And since there is no statute of limitations on murder, the brothers know that the lieutenant can still be prosecuted for the death. This explains why RideOut tries to avoid any conflicts with them, fearing exposure and the possibility of one day trading his gray officer uniform for similar prison garb that the three of us are forced to currently wear.

I spoke to Cajun Red earlier in the week, and he is back on the slab doing his usual thing. I'm still cool with him, as well as with Judas. But there's a bit of tension between Judas and me because of my new cellmate – which proved to be a hater move orchestrated by Lieutenant RideOut, who thought he was being as slick as motor oil. But his plan appears to be backfiring.

Y2K, which is even closer now (just minutes away), will not just mark a new year and a new century, but it will also mark my second year of prison incarceration as my term slowly creeps along.

For some odd reason, the lights keep flickering here as I make my final diary entries for 1999.

Oh, crap! Now, the lights just went out over the entire unit, and I'm struggling to pen my thoughts, relying only on light from the full moon slicing through broken glass windows.

There are shouts from the guards ordering us to "stand clear" of the cell doors, which automatically swing open when the emergency system trigger its default settings. To avoid further disorder, the guards are demanding that we remain in our cells.

Officers and inmates are now cussin' up a storm. I don't know what caused the blackout.

My cellmate has now jumped from his top bunk. So, I will take that as my cue to end my writing for now. (Dec. 31, 1999; 11:59 p.m.)

•••••

When the lights came back on, shouts ceased and calm was restored. The doors rolled back shut again, and all appeared well on the Ramsey Unit.

The voice of Lieutenant RideOut sounded off like a cannon, ordering everyone to get back on their bunks for a head count to ensure there had not been a breach in security. I glanced at my watch.

It was now 12:01 a.m. on Jan. 1, 2000. Y2K had arrived.

At that point, I didn't know if the advent of the new century had anything to do with the prison blackout. Whatever the circumstances, I simply decided to finish my diary entries.

"Whuzzup, Diary?" (Continued)

Before calm was restored after the blackout, my cellmate and I frantically tried to figure out what led to the chaos. During the ensuing jostling, I mistakenly backed into his groin area. My cellmate responded, in the darkened room, by gently grabbing my waist and asking if I were OK. I told him I was good. During that short moment, I felt his heavy breathing on my neck. Much like me, my cellmate is dark chocolate. But he's a force to be reckoned with. Not because he's violent, but because he's Clear, the inmate who previously had been the bane of my existence. Oddly, though, Clear is strikingly different from our early association, when he was more complicated and difficult. Now, as my cellmate, he is as gentle as a bear in hibernation.

Ol' Lieutenant RideOut thought he was being a smart-ass by housing me with Clear when Judas and I separated. I've since come to discover that Clear is a 'daddy boy' in disguise. I had noticed that pink side of him a week ago. From time to time, he would intentionally brush up against me with his irresistible big black buns whenever the two of us were fiddling around at the same time in our tiny cell.

Typically, offenders – before leaving their bunk – would yield to the other person already on the floor because of the small space. But there have been times when Clear would intentionally jump from his bunk when I would be grooming or removing commissary items from my locker. This allowed him to casually brush up against me. Truth is, I knew he was hustling me for commissary. This was his way of getting my attention. Yet, most of the times, I simply ignored his advances.

One thing I can say is that Clear, athletically, is all of that and then some, particularly in the fatback area. And he knows it. But I know that all that gang-banging crap from his past, and perhaps still ongoing, doesn't mean a thing when a man is desperate – and a natural hustler. Indeed, Clear was both.

Anyway, I often took pleasure in seeing him sweat a little. I felt he needed to break away from his pretentious wild side. I was sure that I had the right potion for luring him. And it was tucked away in my metal locker box beneath my bunk: commissary.

Granted, I had no intention of trying to rescue anyone in this hellhole, but only to meet a need. I knew how to manipulate Clear, but I preferred to interpret any potential fling with him as consensual because he already knew the prison game all too well. And, besides that, I knew that with Clear there was no raping of the willing. And he already was at the point of doing just about anything to meet his desires, even if that meant exposing his real sexual identity for the sake of a few delicacies.

I noticed that during our lockdowns he's had very little to eat, aside from those damn cold bologna sandwiches. I, on the other hand, had a locker full of canned goods and knickknacks. If he played his cards right, he just might crack the code to my heart tonight. My raging hormones notwithstanding, I've come to recognize and witness the differences between 'chicken soup' attitudes and 'chicken crap' confusion. And I consider Clear to be associated with the latter. I'm not judging him, but only stating an observation because only God knows the heart. And right now my heart is out of bounds.

All the crap I went through, even before my incarceration, was due to my selfish desires. And that attitude took me to places I shouldn't have gone. As a result, my wayward decisions opened Pandora's box. *(Jan. 1, 2000; 12:15 a.m.)*

●●●●●

Considering that I had developed a strong dislike for Clear over the Sheldon matter, the past tension that existed whenever I was in his presence had begun to gradually fade in the two weeks that we've been cellmates. We respected each other and even engaged in small talk. And not to mention the sexual sparks firing between us. I had become a bit more yielding and decided to supplement his meager meals with a few commissary items from time to time. He showed great appreciation for my efforts to look out for him. I felt that it was my duty as a God-loving man to be unselfish. I had to remember that were it not for my mom, and especially friends such as Lazlo, I would not be as fortunate to have plenty of money on my books, daily newspapers, monthly magazines, art supplies and other amenities. In comparison to indigent inmates, I lived a stately, royal life.

There was a bit of satisfaction knowing that I was helping someone in need. This was an act that was demonstrated to me repeatedly by Lazlo.

While it seemed that I had found common ground with a former nemesis, there was still Lieutenant RideOut – the unrelenting barracuda – who kept nipping at my butt everywhere I turned.

He was bent on trying to make my life miserable. Now that I was not Judas' cellie anymore, he found every reason to harass me: "Morris, keep your pants zipped," "Keep your eyes on yourself in the shower, Morris," "Don't get caught with your pants down, Morris," "You take your meds today, Morris?" "Don't screw up, Morris," "How you like the cellmate I picked for you, Morris?"

RideOut took joy in trying to ridicule me every chance he got.

But on a recent day as he approached, he caught me in one of my sour moods. And before he could torment me further, I launched a pre-emptive strike.

"So, RideOut," I said, without even using his rank in front

of his name, "When was the last time you visited Lake Pontchartrain? I hear it's a great place to take a leak, uh, I mean, leap," I said cynically.

At the sound of those words, RideOut was paralyzed. It was one of the few times he'd been silenced. He was in such shock that his mouth was left wide open, but words didn't or couldn't flow out. If I had been an otolaryngologist, aka ENT doctor, I could have given him a full throat exam. I could actually see beyond the back of his tongue as he remained speechless.

His non-responsiveness suggested that he knew I had become aware of his misdeed — the murder of his brother-in-law by his hands. Ol' Lieut began sweating, and it didn't help that the entire Ramsey site was having problems with its air-conditioning system during a rare unseasonably warm winter day. One minute it would work fine, the next it would simply conk out. It was probably because the unit had not been serviced yet for warm weather since it was still officially winter. Even the administrative offices were "hotter than hell in July."

RideOut did an "about-face" but not before giving me a poisonous stare. I knew then that I had rattled him and stirred his venom.

It was just as well, I thought. Maybe now he'd lay off with his barrage of attacks and insults. His acid tongue needed to be ripped out anyway.

As days passed, we were still coping with warmer days and evenings more than usual. Oddly, I had not run into Lieutenant RideOut. He was missing in action. And, man, was I glad. I was feeling like a bad mofo now, thinking I'd been a major reason for his absence. Even other prisoners seemed less tense without him around.

Hours after dinner I was summoned by a ranking officer to help distribute extra face towels to inmates because of the warmer conditions amid the problems with the air conditioner. Hell, this was strange because I wasn't even on the "laundry squad." So why was I designated for this miserable task in such stifling conditions?

At the laundry facility, there was no one there in the hot room with industrial-size dryers operating with linens and towels inside.

After a few minutes of waiting, I heard a series of footsteps approaching, although rather quietly. I gazed toward the entrance and saw the resurrected image of Lieutenant RideOut. He had finally returned to work. But following him were his nephews, Cajun Red and Judas. I figured this was odd since they were rarely seen together – and certainly not all three at the same time.

They looked at me, said nothing. Got closer, said nothing. Within a few feet of me, the trio stopped.

Then the lieutenant spoke.

"So, smartass. We face each other again," he said.

"What's your beef this time, Lieutenant? I asked.

"Don't give me that bullshit, Morris. It's time that I teach your black ass a lesson."

"Yeah, Moe," blurted Cajun Red, "blood is thicker than water, punk."

Unlike his left hand, I noticed Red's tightened right hand gripping a barely visible shiny object. A shank, perhaps. I carefully took a few steps backward while trying to avoid showing signs of fear. I then asked the reason for the posse. And that's when RideOut spoke again.

"I don't like you, Morris," he said.

"Well, that's something you're going to just have to deal with, Lieutenant. I haven't done anything to you."

"Wrong, Morris," he said. "You're trying to threaten me over some family matter that's none of your business. If you think you gonna try to expose something about me or my family, then you just gonna have to pay up."

"Look, Lieutenant. You have been riding my ass since Day

One. And I have had enough of that BS. So yeah, I was angry. Every day you found something to pick at me about."

"Well, after tonight you won't have to worry about it anymore. I thought about transferring your ass to a maximum facility, but I decided I would handle this on my own."

"On your own, huh? So, why have you deputized Red and Judas?" I asked, wondering if the two felt indebted to RideOut for rescuing them from their juvenile years of molestation.

Judas stared pensively while maintaining his silence. It was as if he were in a zone. At that moment, I recalled the origin of his name, which is the same as that of the disciple who suffered a harsh death after betraying Jesus. At Ramsey II, this Forté brother epitomized treachery and deceitfulness.

"Because we are family. And family knows when to come together, Morris," said RideOut, explaining why he didn't come to the laundry alone.

At that very moment, another blackout, reminiscent of the last minutes of New Year's Eve, occurred suddenly.

"What the ...!" said Lieutenant RideOut, suddenly caught off guard in the pitch blackness.

The sporadic failing of the air-conditioning unit over the past days might have been a precursor to the current blackout, which left me standing blindly with three men with a score to settle.

I could no longer see them, and they couldn't see me. But we immediately heard a fifth voice not far away scream, "Oh, hell, who turned out the lights?"

I bent my ear toward the direction of the voice, which sounded rather familiar. I distinguished it as being that of Clear, who had been known to sneak off to smoke a blunt from time to time.

It seemed he'd been listening to the confab between RideOut, his ad hoc gang and me.

Clear panicked because he knew he could get busted and given a major case for harboring and using contraband. Under the cloak of darkness, he bolted blindly from behind one of the huge dryers, with feet trotting vigorously toward us and the exit. Because he couldn't see where he was going, he plowed into us like the force of a bowling ball gunning for a strike. With the hot air in the laundry room moistening the floor and making for slippery conditions, Clear collided with me, causing a domino effect that pushed me into Judas, and RideOut into Cajun Red. I heard the sound of a piece of metal strike the floor right before we all tumbled atop one another. It's possible that it could have been the shiny shank I thought I saw in Red's right hand.

A struggle ensued as we all tried to free ourselves from the darkened pileup, not knowing who was friend, foe or family.

Once I rolled free of some of the stacked bodies, I began sweeping the floor with my leg as I lay there, hoping that I could kick away the possible weapon, once held by Red, under one of the dryers or at least out of reach.

My legs were working like a furious machine with extraordinary horsepower in an attempt to rid any threat against my life. In the process, I kicked and squirmed, knocking at knees and ribs, and any other body parts of those who crashed onto the floor with me. I was so relentless that I struck the legs of someone who had managed to stand once again on the slippery floor, only to have him later topple on me with what "seemed" to be a sharp knee to the chest.

The strike to my upper area stung and left me breathless. As the scramble continued, I dragged my weary body across the floor and gripped a nearby table leg. It was even hotter now in the laundry, and I was sweating like a hog. My clothes were drenched, and while I could not see in the darkness, I felt fluid on my clothes that seemed to have been thicker than just moisture from sweat. With all the tussling, I tired out. I gripped and took refuge under the table that was used for folding linens and towels.

I could hear more voices moving in closer that sounded like

other prison guards investigating the blackout and rounding up people for count.

I was so exhausted from the blackout battle that I kept falling in and out of consciousness.

Muffled pleas from faint voices from the floor called for help as flashlights shining upon us helped to lift the fog of darkness.

I was totally dazed and physically drained. All the action surrounding me seemed now to move at a slow-motion pace. With my eyelids tightly shut, while holding onto the table for dear life in a mostly pitch-black environment, I faded out completely as my shirt gathered more and more fluid.

•••••

Editor's Note: Please join us for the final installment of the trilogy, An About-Face, slated to come your way soon. It looks at the remaining years of Miguel's incarceration and what happens when he's freed. This soon-to-be released novel was preceded by For What I Hate I Do (www.forwhatihateido.com) and Internal Chaos (www.mwmoore.com).

Character Profiles
(Alphabetical order)

("pg." indicates the start of the page where each character is introduced)

(Protagonist: **Miguel Morris** – Former athlete and crack-cocaine addict serving time in prison for a series of Texas bank robberies in the Houston area)

1. **Agent Pat McClure** – Lead FBI agent who displays a merciful side (pg. 10)
2. **Angel** (Jose Vasquez) – Latino inmate with a death wish; practices voodoo on his romantic interest (pg. 122)
3. **Big Gee** (Alberto Gomez) – Latino former gang member who hasn't completely given up violence; best friend to fellow inmate Druppy (pg. 146)
4. **Cajun Red** (Godwin Forté) – Sensual rec yard basketball player looking for passion, hooks up with Angel; has biological brother – Judas – in prison (pg. 147)
5. **Clear** – Crips gang member who suffers wrath of ranking prison officer for ignoring the code of respect when sleeping around (pg. 190)
6. **Donna Dangerfield** – Company executive with eyes for Lazlo; they clash over ethics (pg. 24)
7. **Druppy** (Shawn Grimes) – Hip-hop Anglo inmate who helps shatter stereotypes of East Texans; best friend of Big Gee (pg. 141)
8. **Judas** – Miguel's cellmate who ultimately becomes his secret lover; battles traumatic recurring nightmares; Cajun Red's biological brother (pg. 230)
9. **Kiki** (Barry Williams) – Miguel's first cellmate who had adopted a subservient, flamboyant role after being raped; teaches him about prison jargon and behavior (pg. 92)

10. **Lazlo Veasey** – Miguel's best friend and former lover in the free world; pharmaceutical sales rep struggles to balance a straight (Donna) and gay relationship (Nathan) simultaneously (pg. 17)
11. **Lieutenant RideOut** – Mean-spirited, tight pants-wearing ranking prison officer with HNIC attitude; has grudge against Miguel (pg. 113)
12. **Lil' D** (Arthur Bishop) – Young hot-tempered former gang member cooled by prison; Kiki's lover (pg. 149)
13. **Mattie Morris** – Miguel's mother; determined to remain positive in spite of son's incarceration; battles breast cancer (pg. 19)
14. **Millner** (James) – Inactive Marine known as the Panty Bandit; has derision for women; suffers mental breakdown (pg. 130)
15. **Nathan** – Relocates to Houston from East St. Louis to partner with Lazlo; relationship and life threatened by alcoholism (pg. 130)
16. **Officer Evans** – Female prison guard who sexually teases inmates (pg. 239)
17. **Roland** – Lazlo's best friend, frat brother and pharmaceutical sales rep colleague who tries to calm him during bouts of drama (pg. 34)
18. **Sheldon** – Quiet, attractive, vulnerable indigent inmate who sexually hooks up with anyone willing to provide commissary; Miguel's first prison fling (pg. 162)
19. **Troy** – Miguel's youngest brother who agrees to put the past behind them and to accept one another (pg. 9)